# Elderkin Chronicles Volume II

I0615828

# Broken Oaths & Boundaries

## Elyse M Grasso

Superior Magpie Press

Ebook ISBN: 978-1-966887-02-7
Paper ISBN: 978-1-966887-03-4

Superior Magpie Press
300 Center Drive #G 399
Superior CO 80027
info@superiormagpiepress.com
https://superiormagpiepress.com

# Table of Contents

Broken Oaths & Boundaries

## Dedication

To all who have suffered losses

and life changes due to

Plagues, disasters, and governmental malice

Broken Oaths & Boundaries

# A Warning to Readers

If very early Covid hit your community hard, maybe give this book a miss.

In our world, the late 17th century on the Continent was not a gentle time or place. There were wars – civil and sectarian and otherwise – and plagues and famines.

Legal penalties were ferocious and often involved removing portions of the anatomy. So did medical care. Composers created great musical works assuming that castrato soloists would be available.

Slavery was legal everywhere but mostly found in cities and government installations.

Outside the cities, many jurisdictions still assumed that non-Nobles were serfs, bound to the land.

Women of all ranks and in most jurisdictions had even less control of their own persons and property than their male kin.

Most men of Noble rank found much of this – except, possibly, for the wars and famines and plagues – quite proper and convenient and satisfactory.

The world of the Chronicles is not as different as one might hope.

Hazards in this volumes include:

Plague. Pre-modern medicine. Pre-industrial infrastructure. Governmental incompetence. Bureaucratic malice. Sectarian malice. Covert homicide. Implied/reported harm to children. Death, often off-screen.

Deaths of children. Deaths of parents. Walking dead. Transformed dead. Mention of Blood sacrifice. Deaths of animals. Deaths of birds. (No guarantees about reptiles, fish, frogs or insects. )

Broken Oaths & Boundaries

## Fairy Gold

The old stories warn that the Elderkin are very careful about observing the exact terms of contracts and agreements, enforcing them strictly even after the payment is made. Those who give false value in a bargain with the Elderkin may find that the treasure they received in payment has been transformed into trash.

# CHAPTER I: Turn of the Seasons

## *Wherein the Traventine Household Is Introduced and There Is Much Restlessness*

Winter in the imperial city of Karnburg was long and damp and dark. As the coldest season approached, the early snows turned to muddy slush where the streets were cobbled, and slushy mud elsewhere, and the snow on the rooftops was stained by the smokes of cook-fires and forge-fires and fires for heating long before it had time to melt and drip smudgy water all over everything. There was little to attract three children peeking out through frost-fogged windows.

The children's home did not have a door that led directly to the outdoors – at least not one meant for the use of respectable people. Their home was a set of apartments at the north end of a long building that formed one wing of Karnburg Palace. To go outside properly, you opened the entryway door, stepped across the Threshold, walked out into the North Gallery, and continued all the way to the far end. Then you passed through an archway into the Grand Entry and went down a huge, slippery, ornately carved stone staircase to the East Door, where the doorwards might be nice or might be mean, depending on which ones were on duty. The doorwards opened the big doors, and finally you stepped out into the weather, whatever it might be.

There were fireplaces and candles in the North Gallery and a huge chandelier in the Grand Entry, but the chamberlains in charge of the common areas of the Palace placed a high value on frugality. The elegantly stacked logs in the fireplaces rarely needed replacing, and the candlewicks carried dust more often than flame. Like the winter, the North Gallery was generally long and dark and damp, despite having windows that looked east over the Palace gardens.

It was not much more cheerful in the rooms that had been the Residence during his lifetime of Prince Leon-Alexander von Falkenburg but were now formally designated the Wolfsberg Residence, after one of his estates. They were more commonly spoken of as the Traventine Residence after the homeland of the Prince's widow. Officially, the Residence was the home of Leon-Alexander's widow, Childe Silvia of Traventi, and their three children, not their prison, but sometimes it was hard to tell the difference. During Leon-Alexander's lifetime, Childe Silvia had referred to the Residence as 'home' as often as not, but now that she was widowed it was always just 'here' or 'the Residence': 'home' was the House on the Rock in Traventi, which she had not seen since before her wedding.

If a chamberlain or someone who answered to them was in the North Gallery when the children passed through, there were almost always complaints about the noise they made. Even when they walked very quietly. Even though there was hardly anyone to be disturbed, since there were only three residences that opened into the North Gallery. The Residence Next Door had been locked and empty for as long as any of the children could remember, and Residence nearest the stairs was the home of a widowed Countess, the Graefinwitwe von Steinach, and several companions who were lesser Noble widows. They sent their servants out with treats when they noticed the children at all.

Walking through the North Gallery to reach the world outside the East Door was almost not worth the bother. The grounds inside the Palace Wall surrounding the imperial residence of His Excellency Friedrich-Augustus included gardens that were impressive mainly because they were nearly as large as all of the small churchyards and tiny kitchen gardens sprinkled through the walled city, combined. The Palace gardens were arranged more for being looked at – preferably from some window or other, or by people in fancy clothes who stayed strictly on the paved paths – than for doing things in.

The Karnburg Palace Gardens were especially not arranged to provide a space for children's games. Most people who lived or worked in the Palace did not consider that a problem.

Even though Her Excellency Aurelia was His Excellency's second wife, His Excellency Friedrich-Augustus von Falkenburg was so old that all of his children with Her Excellency had grown up long ago, and so had most of the grandchildren in his first family with Her Late Excellency Theodora. The Latest Heir of the Falkenburg Line was still a child, but Friedrich-Karl, the grandson of His Excellency's eldest son and Direct Heir, lived with his parents in a smallish palace with its own gardens in the less crowded suburbs outside the City Wall. The only children who lived inside the Karnburg Palace – other than servant children who had work to do – were the three small children of His Excellency's recently deceased younger son, products of an alliance that was not greatly favored at court.: Philip-Augustus, Franz-Karl and Sophie-Alexa.

The three children were carefully watched by the various Court factions, but a suggestion that their own children should play with Leon-Alexander's family would have horrified most of the Noble members of those factions. The imperial authorities had arranged Leon-Alexander's marriage to Childe Silvia of Traventi to acquire a territorial claim to the independent Duchy, but Childe Silvia and Prince Leon-Alexander were among the few who were happy about the marriage. The people of Traventi were Elderkin: part-human descendants of eldritch beings. They were feared by many in the Empire, and viewed as properly less than livestock by the religious doctrines of an influential minority.

Even during the Prince's lifetime, the imperial authorities had been much quicker to claim the benefits promised to the Empire by the Traventine Marriage Contract than to acknowledge the responsibilities to Silvia and to Traventi that they had formally accepted. Now that Prince Leon-Alexander was dead, many who served and worked in the Palace chose to view those responsibilities and agreements – however carefully written down in the Marriage Contract – as optional.

The Prince's eight year old heir, Philip-Augustus, had been announced as the new Count of Wolfsberg, but the estates and wealth that should have accompanied the title were buried in disputes over trusteeship and management. Unlike the customs in her own land, where she was a government official as well as Heir, Childe Silvia – being a woman, a foreigner and an Elderkin – had no standing within Imperial law to serve as trustee for her son's inheritance.

The Falkenburg Privy Council was supposed to approve a proper trustee who could accompany her and provide the needed formal authority, but they kept finding reasons to delay their choice of that protector. This also complicated the financial affairs of the Residence and was annoying enough that the children saw sparks start dripping from the end of her braids whenever Childe Silvia needed to deal with practical matters. Besides being a Widowed Countess – a Graefinwitwe – in the Falkenburg Domains, Silvia was the Childe of Traventi, Heir in her own right to the rule of her homeland, the Sovereign Duchy of Traventi of the Elderkin, where her mother was Duke and ruled with the Council just as a male Duke would.

While the Privy Council felt free to ignore the requirements of law, custom and the Marriage Contract, the Elderkin were bound more tightly by exchanged words, written or spoken, than fleshier creatures. They had no such luxury of interpretation, though Elderkin words also bound Worldfolk tighter than the Worldfolk preferred to acknowledge. Being Count of Wolfsberg officially – but not usefully – did nothing improve either Philip-Augustus' temper, or his health. He lacked the support of a Notary's oaths and was more openly impatient than his mother.

Childe Silvia's daughter Sophie-Alexa – half the age of her eldest brother – had spent most of her short life in the rooms of the Residence. She was as quiet and unpredictable as if she was being raised in some isolated farmstead instead of an Imperial Palace. Her chief attendant, Nurse Rosa, was a Karnburger woman who had begun to learn Elderic partly in an effort to encourage the little girl to speak more in any language at all, Allemanic or Elderic. The world famously went strange around silent Elderkin.

The middle child of the household, Franz-Karl, was the considered the oddest of the three by nearly everyone in the Palace outside the Residence. The other children shared their Falkenburg father's fair coloring and blond hair and wore proper black Court mourning, and while their Elderkin eyes had the wide, oblong pupils of goats, at least they were a proper blue. Franz-Karl shared the family features, but had his mother's golden-tan skin and brown hair streaked with green. And his eyes... his eyes showed very little white around pools of brown so dark there were few who could confidently say what the shape of the pupils was: round, oblong, or vertical like a cat's. Instead of wearing the black of Allemanic mourning, he followed Traventine mourning customs and wore very plain, undecorated garments in a dull, muddy hue they called color-of-sorrow, with plain buttons of bone or ivory.

Leon-Alexander's funeral had been marred by a burst of Elderkin activity that centered on his younger son, so the boy had been sent away to his Traventine kin to be gotten under control. He had returned a fully sworn Notary... and equally fully qualified to permanently stand as his mother's heir in the line for the Duchy.

If and when Philip-Augustus became a Notary and was added to the formal line of succession, he would be his brother's heir, not his mother's, so the inheritance of Traventi was most likely severed from the County of Wolfsberg. Philip-Augustus was not pleased with that outcome. At all. He had heard a great deal about the Allemanic rules about male inheritance and primogeniture from his tutors and was quite fond of them, even though they seldom applied in Traventi, and only applied erratically in the Karnburg district of the Eastlands, which surrounded the Palace.

The imperial officials who had instigated Leon-Alexander's marriage primarily to give the Empire a claim on Traventi were even less pleased. Their chagrin was increased because Franz-Karl's new status derived from strictly following the terms of the Marriage Contract, and if they complained too loudly the results might be even worse. Further, on his return, Franz-Karl – well-coached in his role as a Traventine Notary – had pointed out, emphatically, that the Contract had been breached, repeatedly, by the Imperial side. Notaries who were also minors were barred from exchanging oaths – even the oaths of hospitality – across a broken contract, so Franz-Karl's position in the Palace was not clearly defined. He said himself that he was neither a guest nor a resident, but merely present.

Philip-Augustus knew better than to try to bully a Notary, and Franz-Karl stood between him and their little sister, but that did not improve anyone's temper. The world went strange when Elderkin were crowded together, and it was worse when they were unhappy. With its residents unhappy, the Residence was not a large enough space for the

Elderkin it held, even though they were far fewer than the number the Marriage Contract specified. It was not a comfortable situation

Walking through the North Gallery was not comfortable, either, but it led toward the open air outside the walls of the West Palace. It helped that Franz-Karl had his own staff outside the authority of the Palace, so there was always a grownup available to go places with them.

Franz-Karl's legal and diplomatic status in Karnburg and within the Palace Walls remained a tangled mess. He was a child and a Falkenburg, officially something like eighth or ninth in line for His Excellency's crown as Archduke of the Eastlands. No one could dispute that, much though some might have preferred to. But he was far too Elderkin. Some people called him 'the Changeling'.

Then the shock of his father's sudden death had awakened the powers of an Elderkin Binder in Childe Silvia's second child and younger son, and he had returned from a hasty trip to her eldritch homeland of Traventi confirmed both as Her Royal Grace's direct heir in line for the Sovereign Duchy, and as a sworn Notary. Being a Notary provided some protection against sorcerous accidents and also made him an official of the Traventine government. By the laws and customs of the Allemans and Falkenburgs, Franz-Karl was a minor child in his mother's household due to his youth. But Traventine law held that anyone who tried to command or speak for a Binder with the Manifest weight and control to qualify as a fully-sworn Notary was likely to deserve what would happen to them.

As a full Notary, Franz-Karl could speak for Traventi – more as an envoy than as a judicial advocate – though the Palace officials usually ignored him. And as a Traventine official he was provided with a small – very small – staff. And his grownup Elderkin attendants answered only to him – not to his Mother, and certainly not to his older brother as the patrilineal head of their Household – whatever the Imperial and Palace officials might think.

Franz-Karl's Notarial staff did not particularly mistrust Childe Silvia or the direct members of her household, who were mostly Elderkin, or from Traventi, or both. But many of the tasks required for life in the Residence were performed by Palace servants and overseen by Palace officials, and the Palace swarmed with factions. Even men and women who were not themselves partisans of factions that were opposed to Traventi or covetous of it, might be commanded or suborned by those who were. At the end of their journey from Traventi, Franz-Karl and his attendants had settled into the Wolfsberg Residence in much the way an embassage might settle into a public inn while traveling: anything private or precious or personal was kept under lock and key, or careful observation, or both, and packing for a visit elsewhere consisted largely of tightening the straps on the luggage.

Franz-Karl's personal and Notarial household included just two attendants, neither of them female despite possible ritual complications due to that absence. He had refused to bring any decent Traventine woman out into a land where she would have no right to govern her own person and property. Franz-Karl did not understand the problems faced by his mother and her ladies in attendance before he visited Traventi, where things were different, but he had heard too much weeping and seen enough that the idea of taking an Elderkin woman to Karnburg gave him bad dreams several nights in a row.

Friedrich Boukolyos, called Fritzel, was a Traventine from a Notarial family, but he carried less Manifest weight than a Notary: the world bent around him less. His formal rank was Tiarna, which still officially counted as Noble. Fritzel's official job was to serve as Franz-Karl's aide and look after his books and papers and education, and his unofficial job was to look after Franz-Karl's safety.

Like most Elderkin with moderate amounts of Manifest ancestry Fritzel could not quite pass for a Worldfolk human, even when fully clothed. Fritzel was a very young man – he had not yet legally been an adult for a full year – but he was very tall and very wide and very strong. The bones and muscles of his head and neck and shoulders expected bull's horns, and when he let his voice drop into his chest it rumbled like thunder. But he was young enough that he had not yet sprouted the bull's horns that marked most of the adult men in his family: his least human features when clothed were eyes as dark and lacking in whites as any bull's. He was a champion in an antique, ritualistic style of wrestling, and a favored pastime when he was off-duty was attending lectures at the University.

Franz-Karl's other attendant, who looked after the Notary's clothing and personal and household possessions, was known as Tam. Tam was a narrow Elderkin with a puff of oddly textured crimson hair and gold eyes with vertical slits for pupils. Tam used male language references in the Allemanic and Remoran languages used in Karnburg –

where women's legal status was impaired – and indeterminate ones in the Elderic spoken in Traventi. The title for Tam's job in Traventi would have been Tirewoman, regardless of the shape of the person filling the position, but in Karnburg, they used Valet, which was foreign enough to annoy almost everyone but gave Palace Officials fewer excuses for being rude. Some people were made nervous by glimpses of teeth when Tam laughed.

When the Residence started feeling tiny, unless the weather was being especially unfriendly, Fritzel escorted the children and Sophie-Alexa's Nurse Rosa through the public spaces of the West Palace and out into the Palace Gardens. Usually that was not a problem. The servants taking care of the Palace were fine, especially if the children avoided doing stupid things that made the servants' jobs harder. The doorwards were usually fine, especially after that one time when Fritzel turned one upside down and dunked him in a water trough 'to cool his hot head'.

The Graefinwitwe von Steinach and her ladies were better than fine: when they were visible at all they generally offered the children sweet drinks and little jam-filled pastries that needed to be eaten up before they went stale: they were not quite the ritual offerings of Traventine Hospitality, but they were near enough that it felt like having proper neighbors. Once, the ladies brought out a shuttlecock and some rackets that had been found stored in the bottom of some old chest and gave them to the children as a gift.

When there was trouble in the North Gallery, it was usually because of minor Palace officials: bored junior Chamberlains who were inspecting things that were fine, or nervous supervisors who were watching the servants doing work that the supervisors did not really understand, so they made a fuss to show that they were Nobles in charge of things, not servants, themselves, and certainly not Elderkin.

One of the most annoying was Ritter Philemon von und zu Ostwald, who was the junior Chamberlain in charge of the North Gallery and the adjoining Residences. He was a member of the Pristinist sect, so he believed that women were unimportant and Elderkin were less important than that. Being in charge of some Residences full of women and Elderkin annoyed him, and he went out of his way to annoy everyone back.

One day in late Autumn when the children were on their way back in from the Garden, von und zu Ostwald blocked them from walking into the North Gallery after they reached the top of the Grand Staircase. He pretended that he was part of the doorway and was too busy to notice them, but whichever way they turned to try to go around him, he just happened to move in a way that blocked them.

He should not have done that. Nurse Rosa was a commoner, and Philip-Augustus's tutor was a commoner, and Fritzel's rank of Tiarna was about the same as Ritter, so blocking them was merely rude. But the children were two Princes and a Princess of the Imperial House of Falkenburg, and Franz-Karl was a foreign Prince and an ambassador – sort of – so the chamberlain should have stepped aside to let them pass. Even if he was a rude person. Even if he had been a lot higher in rank than a Ritter and assistant chamberlain. And he should have bowed while doing it, as well.

After the third time von und zu Ostwald stepped into his path, Philip-Augustus made a sort of huffing, snorting sound and said firmly, in very clear Palace Allemanic, "Kindly step aside, sir." His tone was not even very sarcastic.

The chamberlain whirled to face them and raised a hand for a backhand blow. He was holding something that might have been a measuring stick. It was not sturdy enough to be much of a weapon, except that they were gathered at the top of a long flight of slippery stones stairs with lots of knobby stone decorations along the balusters. Nurse Rosa gathered Sophie-Alexa into her arms. Philip-Augustus's tutor flushed and looked worried, but he moved to stand between Philip-Augustus's back and the staircase.

Franz-Karl's attendant Fritzel – Tiarna Friedrich Boukolyos – stepped forward to grasp the Chamberlain's wrist gently using one thumb and forefinger. For a long moment Fritzel held the Ritter's arm as immobile as if it had been nailed to a tree, then he released him and the chamberlain stumbled back. Fritzel was always very tall and very wide and very strong, and he somehow looked even larger and stronger during that long pause. He let his voice drop from his usual baritone speaking range to its natural deep rumble, and said in pure, unaccented Diplomatic Remoran, "By Heaven and all the Saints, I promise that if you ever lay a weapon or a violent hand on any of these children, I'll toss you down these stairs." Then he repeated the warning in slightly accented Court Allemanic – it was still less accented than anything the

Chamberlain spoke – in a voice that was so deep it was heard with the bones, not the ears.

The Chamberlain stepped aside, trying to pretend that he was not hurrying. He still did not bow.

The other chamberlains and supervisors must have heard about what happened. They were less annoying after that, standing at a distance and speaking more politely to the children when they passed through the Gallery. When he was present at all, von und zu Ostwald himself always seemed to be busy in the area of the Gallery that was farthest from where the children and their attendants were standing or walking.

## CHAPTER II: Winter Festival

*Wherein Our Hero Is Barred from a Celebration*

As the year darkened, people began to look toward the great Midwinter festival season and the holy day of Dies Natalis Solis Invicti, when the days began to lengthen and everyone celebrated the Sun's victory over the darkness. The Traventine Residence began to sprout decorations, and the family and their attendants and servants made plans for the long cycle of feasts, celebrations, and church services.

The decorations in the North Gallery were rather sad. The doorway of the Residence was decorated thoroughly, and so was the doorway of Graefinwitwe von Steinach's Residence. The decorations in the rest of the Gallery were as sparse as the authorities could manage and still claim that they had decorated at all.

The Master of Protocol for the Palace was a minor Baron who went by the name of his estate, Hornberg, rather than his family's name, which was von Schmidt. He was part of a faction that was very annoyed about the disruption of the plan to annex Traventi for the empire, so they hated Franz-Karl's existence. As the great Midwinter festival approached von Hornberg announced that Franz-Karl's uncertain status in the Palace barred him from all but the most deeply religious of the Midwinter observances: Franz-Karl should go to the church services if he wished to be considered a decent person, but he would not be admitted to the feasts and other celebrations in the main Palace.

Master of Protocol von Hornberg did not even come to the Wolfsberg Residence to announce the ruling in person. Instead he sent one of the chamberlains – who naturally turned out to be the Ritter von und zu Ostwald – to make the announcement. Franz-Karl kept a mental list of candidates for being turned into newts once he was grown up and the protective Bindings that limited his actions dissolved: the Master of Protocol was high on the list.

Chamberlain von und zu Ostwald was only a little lower on the newt list, and always seemed eager to climb higher. When he arrived at the Residence, he set his foot on the Threshold instead of stepping across it, and he pushed past Roland the majordomo without pausing for any formalities of greeting. He strutted over to Franz-Karl, standing too close and looming over him while he announced the news. He gloated openly while he named and described the wonders of the festivities that Franz-Karl must expect to miss, peering down at him. Franz-Karl was sure the Chamberlain was disappointed that he did not cry.

Franz-Karl looked the Chamberlain in the eye as well as he could. Ostwald was a fibber, while Franz-Karl had a Truth-seeing Gift, so to his Elderkin eyes the man showed the marks of fibs crawling on his face like caterpillars or maggots and his edges rested uncertainly in the World. He waited until the Chamberlain fidgeted and looked away before he said, calmly, "Very well. 'Elderkin lords do not thrust themselves in where they are not welcomed, unless they come arrayed for war.' I shall find other entertainments." He held out one hand, but the Chamberlain just stared at him, shifting his weight from one foot to the other: that quotation had been worrying enough that he had flinched. Franz-Karl rolled his eyes, though the lack of whites may have made that hard to see. "I assume that this important Palace policy has been written down, and signed and sealed by the correct officials. I will naturally need an attested copy to share with the Duke and Council of Traventi. Perhaps it should be two official copies."

Von und zu Ostwald clearly found the request as uncomfortable as the quotation. He sputtered something incoherent, but his bow before he hurried away was actually the proper one from a Chamberlain to the Heir of a foreign monarch. When he was feeling confident, he skimped on the courtesies.

A single copy of the signed document from Master of Protocol von Hornberg arrived within the hour. It was delivered by one of von und zu Ostwald's assistants. Franz-Karl and his Mama, Childe Silvia, both examined it carefully.

Childe Silvia had been seated nearby during the discussion, but von und zu Ostwald had shied away rather than greet or acknowledge her. Different groups and sects among the Allemans had different sets of rules for the actions of a widow in her own home, and Childe Silvia did not follow any of them.

Allemanic or Traventine, all the rules agreed that the Chamberlain should at least have bowed.

Childe Silvia had raised an eyebrow at Franz-Karl's quotation, but said nothing. The oaths that made Childe Silvia and Franz-Karl Notaries also made them each responsible for their actions under Traventine law. Pressing a Notary who was already quoting from ancient declarations of war was more likely to cause trouble than to avoid it. Franz-Karl was a fully sworn Notary, but living in Karnburg, away from the examples and customs of their own people, had left him in some ways nearer to being a feral sorcerer: he frequently startled his Mama. Sometimes he even startled himself.

Sophie-Alexa cried angry tears because Franz-Karl would miss the parties, though she did not show them until the Chamberlain had left them. She did not quiet until Franz-Karl hugged her and whispered that it was all right... that he had plans for Midwinter. He admitted to Fritzel that he had better make those plans quickly.

Philip-Augustus did not, quite, gloat openly that he would attend parties that his brother would miss, though his comments had a slightly triumphant tone. His current tutor was clearly pleased that his charge would appear at court events unaccompanied by the younger brother some called 'the changeling', but was more careful in his phrasing. Franz-Karl just looked at his brother calmly until Philip-Augustus blushed and looked away.

Unlike the rest of the Palace, the Residence followed Traventine customs, and maintained fully consecrated Thresholds. When Franz-Karl had returned as a Notary he had sworn proper Guest Oaths of peace and alliance with the Household before crossing them. But the Residence belonged to Philip-Augustus by Allemanic custom, and Philip-Augustus was equally bound by the Host side of the oaths of Hospitality. Not challenging an insult offered to a Guest by an outsider under his roof was ... highly questionable, at best. If von und zu Ostwald was considered an official attached to Philip-Augustus's household, it made things even worse, especially since by Traventine rules Franz-Karl – as a fully sworn Notary and Recognized Heir to the Ducal line – currently outranked his older brother.

Philip-Augustus did not apologize for falling short of the requirements of proper Hospitality and fealty, but he avoided his brother during the preparations for the festival, which was possibly more useful. It made it easier for Franz-Karl and his staff to make their preparations away from the attention of the tutor.

On the Eve of Dies Natalis Solis Invicti, Franz-Karl attended the sunset rites at the cathedral with the rest of the family and their various attendants. Then, while his Mama and his siblings and their nearest attendants continued to the main Palace to join the Imperial household's festivities, he returned to the Residence with the rest of the Traventine party to change back into his color-of-sorrow mourning clothes.

Then Franz-Karl put on a warm hooded cloak over the rest of his clothes, and left the Palace, accompanied by both his attendant Fritzel, and his valet, Tam. He was sure that as long as they were with him, he would be as safe outside the Palace as in it. Possibly safer.

The three Elderkin did not go out through the main Palace Gate. Instead they used the western Servants' Gate, which was nearer their Residence in any case. Franz-Karl did not need more than a touch of his nameless "do not notice me' Gift to pass unchallenged. The guards and others watching looked at two tall Elderkin and a small Elderkin boy in very plain clothing walking between the gateway torches, but what they noticed was not a foreign Noble Lord and his attendants: they just saw two Elderkin servants and a page. Since Franz-Karl was not officially a guest or resident of the Palace – and no one had dared to suggest to their Excellencies that their grandson should be treated as a prisoner – he saw no great need to inform the various Palace functionaries about his comings and goings.

The trio began by visiting the Bright Market – or one of them: the city of Karnburg was more than large enough to support several festival markets, both inside and outside its defensive walls. The Market they visited did not have a bonfire, to leave more space for booths and for dancing, but there were plenty of lamps and torches, and braziers for warming cold hands as well as food. The Elderkin from the Palace drank hot spiced cider and nibbled on roasted chestnuts and sweetmeats while they listened to the musicians and strolled among the booths and open shops. Fritzel and Tam even joined a few of the dances, before they began to shop in earnest. Franz-Karl watched from the sidelines: his legs were still too short to match the strides of grownup dancers.

Tam was a wonderful dancer, quick and precise, and familiar and friendly with the people in the market. Fritzel and Franz-Karl stood at one stall selling hot spiced cider while Tam danced with the stall-keeper, Netka. She was small and jolly and reminded Franz-Karl of Guildsmaster Mathilda, back in Traventi, except that Netka lacked horns and had human eyes, and Mathilda was as wrinkled as an apple-headed doll.

While Tam and Netka danced, Fritzel joked with the customers and tended the brazier and ladled the drinks from the large simmering vat, and Franz-Karl took the payments and made change. Most Palace officials and Nobles would have thought it was disgraceful for a pair of Nobles to work at a market booth, but Franz-Karl thought it was fun. Those stuffy officials and Nobles would have missed some fine jokes and truly excellent spiced cider.

When the dance ended and the trio turned their attention to shopping, Fritzel and Tam handled Franz-Karl's money as well as their own, because they were grownups and people expected it. But the money that paid for the items Franz-Karl selected was his. He had earned it in Traventi months earlier as fair payments for tasks that required a Notary.

All three of them bought gifts for people in the Residence, and some people in the rest of the Palace – Franz-Karl's purchases included some toy soldiers for his brother and some furniture that was the right size for his sister's favorite doll. They also bought gifts and treats for the officials and servants at the outer Traventine embassy, because when their arms were full of bundles and they left the Market, they walked to a House in Greenoak Square whose gate was flanked by stone torches that shone with eerie green light, and knocked.

The gate opened and people with not-quite-human eyes and hair and features welcomed them properly in the Traventine fashion, taking away their burdens and offering them the holy tokens of Hospitality: fire and water and wine, meat and cheese and bread and salt. They were greeted with various formulas of welcome for members of the Household returning home to it: there was no need for oaths of peace before crossing this Threshold. And everyone – every person in the Household at Greenoak Square – was speaking Elderic the whole time, not Allemanic, not even the Remoran that was used for religion and diplomacy.

The household ate a proper feast in the Traventine style. The gate-guards ate in shifts, coming and going from their duties, but everyone else in the house – including the cooks who prepared the meal – sat down together to share the good food and drink, and everyone from Franz-Karl to the newest stableboy joined in the distribution and exchange of small gifts afterward.

As midnight approached, the trio from the palace gathered up the remainder of their purchases, and added a number of parcels from the embassy storerooms: items that they had brought all the way from Traventi to Karnburg during their journey in the autumn. There were so many parcels that some of the men from the House helped carry them as far as the Palace Servants' Gate, where they called on some of the Palace servants to help carry things to the Traventine and Wolfsberg Residence.

The guards at the gate were not pleased to have a Noble Elderkin re-entering the Palace when they had no record of him leaving, but most of them had become resigned to such things over the preceding months. It was often said that too much fussing about minor Elderkin mischief was asking for worse trouble, and most of the guards acted as though they believed that.

Once in the Residence, Franz-Karl hastily changed out of the color-of-sorrow, and back into colors permitted for the Festival rites. Medium gray was nearly as boring as color-of-sorrow, but it was not officially a mourning color, so it was not rude or unlucky to wear it in church during the festival.

Fritzel escorted him out the main Palace Gate and down the road to the cathedral, while Tam stayed behind to sort parcels and prepare for the morning and help Childe Silvia's attendants watch after affairs at the Residence.

Fritzel and Franz-Karl arrived half-running and breathless at the cathedral vestibule, but they were not the only ones arriving so late, and they arrived in time for Franz-Karl to join his family for the parts of the midnight rites that were open to non-initiates. Fritzel joined Childe Silvia and her attendant Itron Gwenlian during the Cathedral rites that were restricted to Initiates, while the children waited with Nurse Rosa and listened to the great organ and the choirs. Childe Silvia was summoned to the main Palace afterward, and Roland and Itron Gwenlian went with her.

Fritzel and Nurse Rosa took the three children home to their beds, then stayed at the Residence keeping watch while Tam joined the Household's other attendants and servants at the late night rites for Initiated servants in the Palace chapel.

The dawn rites came far too soon for everyone, even though they ended a long midwinter night: the whole Household attended those except for the most junior pair of Childe Silvia's attendants, who stayed behind to tend the fires and lamps in the Residence: putting out fires on the Festival day brought bad luck, but leaving flames unattended would be foolish.

After the dawn rites were done, Franz-Karl changed from his gray clothes back into color-of-sorrow clothes for the final time for the festival – there were no more rites that banned mourning clothes – and helped his little sister return to her own black mourning garments. Nurse Rosa was busy dealing with a problem with Philip-Augustus' waistcoat.

The previous year they had not needed to change: the three children and both of their parents had gone from the cathedral to the main Palace building and breakfasted with Their Excellencies and various aunts and uncles and cousins and other nobles of the court. This year, the household mourned, but the Residence was bright with beeswax candles and fresh with the scent of evergreen garlands, and the main reception room was heaped with carefully sorted parcels.

The family had not finished their morning meal before messengers began to arrive bringing gifts from Their Excellencies, and the various aunts and uncles and other relatives. The messengers went away more heavily burdened than they had arrived because they were carrying gifts from the Bright Market and the Traventine gifts from the storerooms at Greenoak Square as well as the ones Childe Silvia had prepared to send in return.

Months earlier, when Franz-Karl had first returned to Karnburg from Traventi, he had given gifts to Their Excellencies, and to his Mama and siblings and others in their Household, and to a few others of his relatives at court: his Uncle and resident Aunts. But he had not given out the gifts he had brought for his cousins or more distant relatives. The breakage of the Marriage Contract terms and being formally neither a guest nor a resident of the Palace made official gift-giving complicated, so he had left most of what he had brought across the long days and miles from Traventi safely stored.

Midwinter gifts – addressed only to his kin, viewed broadly, since he was not attending any of the usual gift-giving events – followed different rules. They were less likely to cause unwanted entanglements than gifts at less generous times.

When Franz-Karl looked at the piles of small parcels he had gathered, he also thought about other gifts that he had arranged. He hoped that his cousins and other friends and relatives far away in Traventi liked the presents he had left behind for the Duke his Grandmother to give them. Winter travel was so slow that it might be weeks or months before he heard from them. He could only hope that he had guessed right in his choices.

He was relieved that the gifts he gave in Karnburg were well-received, though he had not been greatly worried about those: they were Traventine wares. The goods sold in the markets of Traventi were precious, but not because they were fashioned of such common stuff as gold or silver or jewels or silks or exotic woods or resins. They were precious because they were fashioned by Elderkin artisans who could use Bindings and Gifts to perform wonders and create impossibilities. And sometimes, of course, the artisans also began with materials that were considered precious in themselves.

Being precious and amazing did not – at all – prevent some Traventine wares from also being dangerous. Or sometimes just extremely creepy: there were some things that just should not exist in the Living World, but that did not always stop the Elderkin artisans from creating them. Franz-Karl had avoided the creepiest creations: aside from being very unpleasant to travel with, he suspected that perceiving the full effect required more Manifest ancestry than most Allemanic nobles would admit to possessing.

The trinket that Franz-Karl, Heir to the Duchy of Traventi, sent to his Aunt the Grand Duchess Erminia at that Midwinter Fest might have ransomed a king if it had come to auction among the mightiest and wealthiest lords of the nations. It did not surpass all of the other gifts given in Karnburg that season only because the gifts that Franz-Karl sent to relatives he actually liked were even finer. The gifts were all small, since they had needed to travel a long distance by mule train and river barge, but they were all amazing. And because they were intended for people Franz-Karl knew, and he had advised those who made or selected them, they were... apt. Frighteningly so, in a few cases, where that had seemed appropriate.

Many of the the gifts Franz-Karl gave to the Imperial Court at Karnburg had been discussed and approved for export by the Duke and Council of Traventi. They were meant as a reminder that Traventi was more than a tiny discolored splotch on the map of the continent. There were reasons the Empire was trying to gather Traventi into its control. And reasons the Duchy had long remained independent despite being very small and full of precious things. Not all of the dangerous gifts had been eliminated from the Council's list, and a few of the ... worrying... sort had been added as well, that Franz-Karl would not have thought of on his own.

Franz-Karl's gifts from Traventi for the grownups in the Residence – other than his Mama, and his own small staff – were almost all Elderkin-made tools and utensils to replace the duller, mundane ones supplied by the Palace.

The gifts Franz-Karl received were largely overshadowed by the ones he gave, but some were wonderful. Philip-Augustus, who usually kept a tight grasp on any of their father's possessions that he could reach, gave Franz-Karl a compass and book of maps that had belonged to Leon-Alexander. Their Excellencies his Grandparents sent an inkstand that was beautiful and well-made, but clearly intended to be a working tool for a Notary, not just an ornament. His Royal Grace the acting Archduke Uncle Helm-Friedrich had sent a case – well matched to the inkstand – that held a moneyer's balance and set of weights, precise as any in the tax office. Her Royal Highness Aunt Queen Gertrude and her companion sent accessories for Franz-Karl's toy horse, Harvest Prince, and a beautifully embroidered version of Franz-Karl's personal banner: the banner of Traventi with the addition of a compass star.

Her Royal Grace Grand Duchess Aunt Erminia sent nothing to Franz-Karl, despite the fine gift he sent her, but she sent formal tokens of the season – too old for uninitiated children – to Philip-Augustus and Sophie-Alexa.

Because Franz-Karl could not attend the Palace's official imperial dinner, the Residence Household held their own dinner. They invited their neighbors, the Graefinwitwe von Steinach and her ladies, but they had been summoned to the Court dinner, so the households just exchanged holiday treats. They were joined for their meal by Franz-Karl's aunt Gertrude, Her Royal Highness the Dowager Queen of the Szekelys, and her companion, who arrived together with as much pomp and ceremony as if they were arriving at Their Excellencies' table and swore the Guest Oaths with as much solemnity as if they had arrived at Duke Adriana's door in Traventi.

Their party was received with full Traventine Hospitality. The Hussars and ladies' maids in the Szekely party were surprised to be seated at the same table as Her Royal Highness and the other Falkenburgs, but Childe Silvia followed her own people's customs within her own Thresholds: all of the household and guests ate together.

Franz-Karl had seen the companion of Her Royal Highness Aunt Queen Gertrude at court on various occasions, but he had not been introduced to her, or really heard her proper name. The Masters of Protocol at the Court and the people who announced arriving guests did their best to ignore her existence. Ladies of the court who were less pretty than she was – which was most of them – generally snubbed the companion unless they were especially friendly with Her Royal Highness, or wanted something from her.

Her name was Helena. Franz-Karl hoped that his surprise was not too rude: being a beauty named Helena probably led to a lot of bad jokes and worse poetry. He was relieved when she laughed and said that she went by Lenke for daily use.

# INTERLUDE I: The White Hall

## *Wherein the Pristinists Celebrate the Holiday*

Master of Protocol Baron von Hornberg and the chamberlain Ritter von und zu Ostwald did not attend the holy rites at the cathedral. Like many others from the Northern provinces, they were followers of the teachings of Pristinus de Millau, who a few generations ago had summoned his students to set the order of the World aright.

The gathering places of the Echelon of the Pristinists were each, always, called 'The White Hall' not because of any external color but because of the decoration – or lack of it – of the main gathering chamber. The White Hall in Karnburg was composed of a former ballroom and some adjoining chambers in the city house of the Margraff-Elector of Ansbach, the highest ranked Pristinist lord in the city. This was unusual: in most places inhabited by Pristinists, the White Hall was a separate building, and only the clergy and their families and servants lived there. But if anyone in the Echelon would have preferred to regularize things in Karnburg, they did not mention it loudly.

There had been other White Halls in Karnburg, but that had been during the upheavals of the Sectarian Wars. The local population in Karnburg were largely Ecclesialist, and Pristinists prided themselves on being plainspoken, so each of the free-standing White Halls had lasted about a year before they were burned or desecrated past repair... while leaving their neighbors remarkably unharmed. The Margraff-Elector's White Hall in Karnburg was older than the current Margraff-Elector, and had been unmarred through all that time.

There were no decorations in the White Hall at Midwinter, and the Echelon that gathered there included neither women nor children. Men of the lowest orders – both the fully enslaved, and the indentured sons of serfs – were only present to be useful to their betters: furnishings in the White Hall did not include racks for cloaks or shelves for other possessions, so human hands tended the belongings of those higher in the Echelon.

There was no music in the White Hall, and no material offerings were made, not even of fire or incense. The evening gathering began and ended with spoken recitations of 'purged' versions of ancient hymns and texts. In between, the Echelon heard readings by the Teacher from the writings of Pristinus de Millau and his nearest colleagues alternating with sermons: 'discourses', by the Preacher. The predawn session was much the same, but preceded by a shortened ceremony of public Purgation, and the holy day was marked by opening one east-facing window shutter and allowing the rays of the rising Sun to reach into the Hall, briefly, before the shutter was closed again.

The Preacher on this festival night was a recent arrival in Karnburg, replacing a colleague who had left unexpectedly. He was a small man, and quiet in private discussions, but most of the Echelon approved of his vigorous sermons. He went by the name Dieter Weiss, though Weiss was not his family's name: Preachers had begun to use aliases during the harshest years of the Wars, and the custom remained fashionable among graduates of the oldest Pristinist schools.

There was no midnight gathering announced to the Echelon, nor recorded in the White Hall's journals, but Preacher Weiss and the Teacher and the Margraff-Elector and a few others among the highest reaches of the Echelon gathered in the smaller Inner Hall adjacent to the White Hall to discuss certain matters. These included plans for the steps that were being taken to purge the Palace, and eventually the Empire, of the corrupting influences of artists and musicians and idolaters and the beast-born. There were also plans to win favor with the Court and some of the non-Pristinist courtiers by the distribution of gifts drawn from the riches of the North. Gifts that went beyond the limits of what might be accounted as attempted bribery if the gifts were secret or occurred on any other day.

## CHAPTER III: Beyond the Palace Gate

### *Wherein Our Hero and His Family Venture Out*

For some weeks after the long Midwinter holiday season ended, life in and around the Palace continued quietly. The Falkenburg Privy Council and the Privy Council of the Kingdom of the Allemans both met regularly in the Palace, but Winter was not a season for war or for trade, so the lower levels of government were not very busy. Officials worked short hours even when measured against the brief northern days, and in the long winter evenings the Highborn entertained each other with music or dances or gambling, or all three.

The family from the Traventine Residence did not join the entertainments, not even when the brief gaiety of Carnevale erupted through the city. Naturally, a household that remained in deep mourning would not be invited to take part in such events, even if its members had been considered fully human by all of the revelers.

Aunt Queen Gertrude and Lady Lenke dined at the Traventine residence a few times as the seasons turned: Philip-Augustus spent as much time as he could manage speaking to any of Her Highness' attendant Hussar officers who had enough Allemanic to answer his questions.

On other occasions, acting Archduke Uncle Helm-Friedrich invited both the Wolfsberg household and the Szekelys to dinners at his Residence when his children and grandson were visiting.

Master of Protocol von Hornberg made a fuss about not inviting a family in full mourning to the most formal imperial events, but their Excellencies included them in the less public gatherings. After all, Their Excellencies were also in mourning for Prince Leon-Alexander, their son.

It was hard to imagine that the quiet emptiness of the Palace could become worse. But after Carnevale passed, it did. It was customary in the court at Karnburg for courtiers who had country estates that could be reached from the city to retreat to them between Carnevale and the festival of Reawakening. In theory they would spend the quiet weeks of the Withdrawal supervising the beginnings of the new agricultural season. Their wives and children traveled with them, if they were not already residing at the country estates.

Franz-Karl's Mama, Childe Silvia of Traventi, Heir to the Duke of the Elderkin and Widowed Countess of Wolfsberg, did not plan to leave the city at first. Despite all of her titles, and her authority in her homeland, by local custom she did not have the authority to supervise her young son's holdings because she was a woman. The Falkenburg Privy Council had been instructed months ago to approve a proper trustee who could accompany her and provide the needed formal authority, but they kept finding reasons to delay their choice of a protector for Philip-Augustus and his property. His Excellency had full authority, but was reluctant to use it to enforce his directive – he was not supposed to need to ask twice – while acting Archduke uncle Helm-Friedrich was loaded with responsibilities but provided with only limited authority within the overlapping jurisdictions of His Excellency's various holdings. So nothing got done.

Childe Silvia was not much inclined to travel in any case: Traventi was as least as traditional in its Ecclesialist religious practices as anywhere in the Falkenburg domains – people were not entirely joking when they said that Traventines were even more Ecclesialist than the Remoran Pontiffs – but travel during the Withdrawal season was not a custom they shared with the Eastlanders. Traventi was mountainous and prone to deep winter snows and boisterous spring floods: so Traventines who found themselves safe and dry and warm at Carnevale were unlikely to stir far before the Reawakening.

Without even the activity of private dinners and less formal Court gatherings, the Palace became quiet and empty as the days passed after Carnevale and Spring and the Reawakening came nearer. The weather did not encourage trips outdoors, and the children were restless within the familiar rooms. Childe Silvia developed a habit of pacing through the rooms of the Residence late at night, and stopped reading books written in Elderic.

Philip-Augustus, Count of Wolfsberg argued at every meal that his estates were being neglected to an embarrassing degree, which had the advantage of being mostly true. His claims that it was embarrassing to seem to be disregarding the Withdrawal were far more debatable, and Childe Silvia's hair began to drip sparks more often.

When his arguments to his Mother failed, the young Count stomped into the nursery, scattered the toys his younger brother and sister were playing with, and tried to order them to play a different game by new rules which would make him paramount. That did not go well. It went less well since Philip-Augustus was far too important to be a resident of the nursery, himself. He was an intruder, not a resident. Sophie-Alexa kicked him in the shins without speaking to him before firmly turning her back to check her dolls for damage.

Franz-Karl answered his brother in Allemanic and began by using Philip-Augustus' full personal and lineage names and his titles: all of them, from the County of Wolfsberg, through the various Baronies, down to the lordship of that half-ruined watchtower on the border that was supposed to be haunted. When he reached the end of the list, Franz-Karl formally inquired – as a sworn Guest – what aid his Host was requesting. It was exquisitely polite, and all the more infuriating because they both knew on the one hand, that Philip-Augustus' demand had been improper, and on the other that all of the Falkenburg ranks and titles were empty as long as the Privy Council dithered, while Franz-Karl's own Traventine titles of 'Notary' and 'Heir' carried real authority, besides being backed by the potential wreakings of an Elderkin Binder.

Philip-Augustus scowled and his face turned red. Franz-Karl faced him calmly. Sophie-Alexa laughed, and said in Elderic, "Ooh. Do that again!"

Philip-Augustus deflated, looked at her blankly, and asked in Allemanic, "Do what?"

Sophie-Alexa did not turn to face him full on, but watched him out of the sides of her wide-spread Elderkin eyes with their wide oblong pupils: she was still turned to face Franz-Karl. Her answer was more Elderic. "I was not speaking to you, Lord Count of Wolfsberg. Franz-Karl's shadow went strange. It was pretty."

Philip-Augustus turned to look toward the shadow – which was now perfectly shadowish and had stopped doing anything at all strange – then hastily looked away. He retreated from the nursery, but he did not apologize for scattering the younger children's toys.

Elderkin children were blocked from major mischief using Gifts or Bindings, even when they were enraged – perhaps especially when they were enraged – but their Manifest ancestry was heavy in the children of the Ducal line, and with three bored and unhappy Elderkin children crowded within it, the luck of the Residence was becoming thoroughly curdled. Nothing – and no one – caught fire and nothing precious or irreplaceable was destroyed – not completely – but the household suffered an excessive and increasing number of spills and breakages and other minor accidents. People stopped expecting candles and fire-starters to burn steadily when they were first lit.

The hair of Philip-Augustus began to produce an occasional spark much like their Mother's: but where her sparks fell from the ends of her braids, his tended to drip from the front of his hair onto his nose. Franz-Karl's hair did not spark, but sections of it insisted on pulling out of the hair tie at the nape of his neck and twisting into tendrils of green and witch-locks of russet-brown... and his shadow was definitely up to something, but never when it fell in front of him where he could see it. Sophie-Alexa was so young that she was still deeply enfolded in the protective Child Blessings, but the way her hair escaped from its careful arrangements was not always entirely natural.

Almost as much curdled luck spread from Sophie-Alexa as from Philip-Augustus, but very few of the problems trailed after Franz-Karl. That was part of the usefulness of being a sworn Notary instead of a free or feral Binder: Bindings happened – and, generally, Gifts worked – when a Notary chose, not in response to random promptings and the tides of the Living World. Having one child of the three living by different, quieter rules was a slight relief to the adults in the Residence, but Itron Gwenlian and Roland made plans for the day when he would no longer find his expeditions to Greenoak Square a sufficient defiance in the face of Palace rudeness. The results of pushing a Notary too far tended to be memorable.

Franz-Karl was trying not to make things more difficult for his Mama: she usually showed a calm face to the world but he had heard her weeping too many times early in the mornings. It was said that two were needed to make a peace, but only one was needed to start a fight, and he tried to avoid being that one. But he could not speak falsehoods, and he would not give Philip-Augustus authority over his Notarial staff, no matter what Allemanic tutors said was proper. Franz-Karl would also not leave his sister to be bullied as if she was some Allemanic female, so moving to Greenoak Square would not solve things, though the thought of it was sometimes very tempting.

One morning Franz-Karl woke even earlier than usual, after a night troubled by turbulent dreams. Tam helped him dress and arranged his hair, then, yawning, returned to bed until it was nearer breakfast time. Fritzel had spent the night outside the Palace and would not re-enter the gates before sunrise. Franz-Karl slipped out of the nursery and was walking toward the study, with its filled bookshelves, when he heard his Mama's voice.

Childe Silvia was sitting in the Household Shrine, speaking to her husband in Diplomatic Remoran as she had when he was alive. Her voice did not sound like she was weeping, but it sounded like she had been weeping earlier.

She said that she was lonely, and reaching the end of her patience, and worried for their children. She said the marriage had been acceptable because it included him, and the terms of the Contract were nearly tolerable provided she remembered the unwritten clause about not having a war, and provided the Empire lived up to their side of things. She said that she was beginning to doubt the unwritten clause was worthwhile, when so many of the written ones had been broken by the imperial authorities: that was Notarial phrasing, when Franz-Karl translated it into Elderic in his head.

When Franz-Karl reached the study, he did not go to the shelf holding the book of old tales that he had planned to read. He got out both copies of the Marriage Contract – the one in Elderic and the one in Remoran – and read them carefully. Then he looked through his Mama's law books until he found one that talked about contract breaches ... and repudiations. The Curse of Rano ensured that Traventine contracts could not be changed unless all of the signers were alive to agree, unless the contract included sections that the Marriage Contract lacked. The more he read and thought about it, the uglier things looked. He wished there was another Notary available to talk to, besides his Mama.

When a day arrived that provided a distant promise of spring and a more immediate promise of sunshine, Childe Silvia gathered her three children into the family coach for an expedition to the nearest Wolfsberg estate, despite the lack of a trustee to manage things. Philip-Augustus, Franz-Karl and Sophie-Alexa were well-behaved children for the most part, despite their occasional squabbles – even the curdled luck was generally not the result of any deliberate actions or malice toward others in the household – but the prospect of a change from leaden skies and the too-familiar walls of their apartments within the Palace had them nearly fizzing with exuberance and relief.

The various attendants who would accompany the party caught the mood. Philip-Augustus's most recent tutor, Meister Seidl, who had joined the Household just after Midwinter, packed the chessboard and some other games along with his school-books. Sophie-Alexa's Nurse Rosa made sure that all three children would travel with clothing suitable for outdoor play. Even Childe Silvia's serious aide, the Itron Gwenlian, was seen to smile close-lipped, and the majordomo and footmen who would be left behind to watch after the Wolfsberg Residence within the Palace made various quiet plans.

Franz-Karl's attendants were nearly as cheerful as the larger household around them, which they were still not formally part of. Fritzel whistled a dance tune as the traveling party settled themselves in the coach, then took a small book out of a pocket. Tam put on a broad-brimmed hat, tied it on with a scarf so the wind could not steal it, and settled into one of the exterior seats on the carriage roof, keeping a watchful eye on the sealed trunks strapped to the roof farther forward. Franz-Karl had books in two of his pockets, but he was also carrying his wooden horse, Harvest Prince, in his own arms for safety's sake, and he was engaged in a quiet four-way conversation between himself and Harvest Prince and his little sister Sophie-Alexa and Sophie-Alexa's favorite doll, Mina, while they waited for the carriage doors to be closed.

Sophie-Alexa was almost too excited to talk as the carriage rolled toward the main Palace Gate. The doll Mina, being an elegant lady, was more composed, even though Sophie-Alexa was speaking for her. Harvest

Prince made sarcastic comments about one of the horses pulling the carriage, but at least he did it quietly. Philip-Augustus, Count of Wolfsberg, rolled his eyes, turned his back as well as he could, and began a conversation with his tutor that ignored the 'babies' and their toys.

When the coach arrived at the Palace Gate, the guards there refused to let them out. They were not very polite about it, either. Franz-Karl wondered whether keeping people in was even properly part of their job at the Palace Gates... was there a crime that was the opposite of dereliction of duty?... but he stayed silent. People did not notice him if he stayed quiet and did not look them in the eye, which could be a very useful way to learn things. Or to avoid trouble. Or to make trouble.

Sophie-Alexa clung to Nurse Rosa and looked ready to cry. Philip-Augustus, current Count of Wolfsberg and a Grand Duke of the Falkenburg Domains, settled in to sulk – he was a champion sulk-er, and at nearly nine years old as the Allemans counted age his Elderkin Gifts were beginning to flare enough to be dangerous. A few small sparks even leaked from his hair, but the material of the coach ignored them. Philip-Augustus was still some distance from either fully Manifest sorcerous Gifts or Notarial self-control, but Franz-Karl kept a wary eye on his brother and saw that their Mama was doing the same. Comprehensively curdled luck was worrying: it had a tendency to splash in unexpected directions.

Even though Franz-Karl was two years younger than Philip-Augustus, he had been what the Elderkin called "born old and open-eyed", part of why his Gifts had awakened so emphatically the previous year after their father was killed. Hastily becoming a sworn Elderkin Notary had set protections around his Elderkin powers, but had also provided some training and independent authority, though the Palace officials tried hard to ignore them.

Franz-Karl stopped being unnoticeable, met the Chief Guard's eyes, and called out loudly, "Oh? Is there a war or insurrection? There has not been a death among the Falkenburgs..."

The guard wearing the fanciest suit jumped. He paused in his gloating apology for stopping them to look befuddled, stare at the side of the carriage where Franz-Karl was sitting, and say, "What?"

"Well, we are all von Falkenburgs ourselves – Grand Dukes and Grand Duchesses: Their Excellencies' grandchildren and daughter-in-law

– so if someone in the family had died, we would have been informed," Franz-Karl explained reasonably.

"What does that matter?" the guard grated. Two of the three other guards were being careful to smirk only when their leader's back was toward them. The third and scruffiest just looked angry at everything in general: he was leaning on the barrier, and would probably be the one doing the work of moving it, if and when the time came.

Franz-Karl recited in his best, most formal, least accented Palace Allemanic, "The Marriage Contract between Childe Silvia, Heiress of Traventi and Imperial Prince Leon-Alexander von Falkenburg qualifies as one of the governing laws of the Falkenburg domains because it was signed with their own hands by His Excellency Friedrich-Augustus and Her Excellency Aurelia – and by His Royal Grace the acting Archduke Helm-Friedrich besides – so breaking it counts as at least minor treason in the Falkenburg Domains, certainly punishable by maiming, thought possibly not by death. Unless His Excellency chooses to be very annoyed." He paused, then added confidentially in a less formal dialect, "It might be punished by anything up to being turned into newts under the laws of Traventi: the details are unclear, and it might depend on the mood of Her Royal Grace Childe Silvia." He bowed to his Mama, who bowed gravely in reply, carefully not smiling. He returned to his recitation: "The Marriage Contract specifies that Traventine nobility housed in Falkenburg holdings in association with Her Royal Grace's household will be allowed to come and go freely – not 'may be allowed': the exact words are 'will be allowed' in both the Elderic and Remoran versions – unless there is a current local state of war or insurrection, or an important member of the line of Falkenburg has died within the previous week... so... for the second time of asking: is there a state of war or insurrection in the Falkenburg domains?"

The mouth of the guard who had confronted Her Grace dropped open. The two guards who had been smirking moved hastily to help their companion open the light barrier that was blocking the carriage's passage. Even people who had mostly ignored the stories their Grannies told them knew that when Elderkin started talking about 'times of asking' things were getting dangerously eldritch. And flirting with something that was being described as open treason was not something anyone sensible wanted to risk without direct orders from someone with rank and authority.

The carriage rolled forward.

"Do you have the whole Marriage Contract memorized?" Philip-Augustus asked somewhat indignantly, once they were away from the guards' hearing.

"Of course. Don't you?" Franz-Karl was annoyed enough to tweak his brother. "It is not very long if you ignore the huge lists of signatures. The people who composed the Elderic version provided a lot of practical examples of really... interesting... verb forms. And I think that someone working on the Remoran version was being sneaky in a few places."

Philip-Augustus groaned theatrically, while his tutor smiled: irregular verbs – in any language – were a favorite topic of Meister Seidl. Though in all honesty, all of the previous tutors had also been fond of them. Philip-Augustus was even less fond of Elderic than he was of Remoran, so he was not as fluent in Elderic as Franz-Karl had been even before visiting Traventi the previous summer. And he honestly loathed irregular verbs in any language.

Their Mama began to smile a little. "Newts?" she prompted.

Franz-Karl shrugged, the one-sided Traventine shrug he had learned from Fritzel, "Newts are traditional. People never forget that we are Elderkin, but they like to forget that Elderkin are dangerous..." He looked at the cross-street they were approaching. "Should we go somewhere inside the city walls instead of going out to the estate? Reciting the Marriage Contract may not work on real soldiers at the City Gates without serious fuss or actual newts involved. Damian says that they are still annoyed about the Wild Hunt last summer."

"And we are not packed to travel all the way to Traventi without stopping after we pass the Karnburg Gate," Itron Gwenlian agreed with an approving nod. "The estate might not be far enough for safety." She was not smiling. She rarely smiled, especially not in ways that would show her teeth.

Sophie-Alexa had grown more cheerful once they passed through the Palace gate and out into the busy city streets. So had Philip-Augustus, but now he seemed to be preparing to sulk again: the Wolfsberg estates outside the city walls were officially his property, and he was quite proud of them even though he had seldom visited most of them, and had never seen some of them at all, and the deeds and charters remained tangled in some official mess that seemed to get worse with time, not better.

Their Mama considered. "Well, we have not visited the Menagerie since before the cold weather arrived. Shall we see whether there are any new baby animals?"

All three children agreed eagerly, so the carriage continued north from the Palace, toward the great Daonas river, but avoided the road to the River Gate.

# CHAPTER IV: The Altturm

## *Wherein the Family Surveys an Outpost of Karnburger History*

The Imperial Menagerie held His Excellency's collection of exotic beasts that had been gifts from foreign monarchs. It was contained in the Altturm, an ancient citadel built on a rare stone outcropping in the Daonas River's flood plain that made it nearly impossible to undermine. The tower was nearly as far from the Palace as it was possible to get while remaining inside the City Walls. Centuries earlier, it had been a major part of the city's defenses, until the river channel had moved decidedly away from the tower's base. The stone outcropping and defensive Bindings added during the original building made reuse of the site for other purposes inconvenient, so the built stone walls of the tower itself had not been quarried for their worked stones, but the old tower was not connected to the current city walls and no longer directly part of the general city defenses. The bulk of its surrounding fortress had been removed during the passing centuries, quarried for its convenient stone, but there was still a wall around the tower itself, nearly as tall as the Palace Wall.

A long series of lords and dynasties had used the Old Tower's thick walls at various times to protect its contents from the city, or the city from its contents. In the decade since the last great siege, only the Menagerie with its fascinating animals had been occasionally opened to outsiders, but there were rumors that the Old Tower still contained – in addition to the animals and their supplies – a powder magazine and munition store, prison cells of varying degrees of unpleasantness, an assortment of spooks and haunts of various sorts, and parts of the Allemanic treasury or the Falkenburg treasury, or both. Prince Otto von Leonstein of Karnburg had claimed publicly that the tower stored part of Karnburg City's armory and none of its treasury – and he was known to have too much Elderkin blood to lie safely or successfully – but he had not said anything about what else the tower might contain. Nor, if you considered the words carefully, anything about any property of his Falkenburg overlords or the overlapping Allemanic Kingdom.

There were fewer guards at the Menagerie Gates than there were at the Palace, but there were still gates, and guards. The Menagerie guards had better weapons than the Palace gate-guards according to Philip-Augustus: he approved of the weapons and thought the fortifications were adequate for a place inside a city. Open countryside would be another matter, of course.

Unlike the Palace, the gates opened promptly when a carriage bearing the Falkenburg device arrived. The guards were surprised when Her Grace and her aide Itron Gwenlian formally announced their names and stated that they and the children and servants came with peaceful intent before they moved to cross the Threshold of the fortress. They were even more surprised when Franz-Karl and his aide, Fritzel, made a similar, but more non-committal declaration. Someone went running to find the Chief Keeper and the rule book that contained the proper formula for the responses to the various declarations of alliance and peace, but people seemed pleased rather than annoyed that the Menagerie's history as an enchanted fortress was being taken seriously.

Some of the guards smiled when Franz-Karl stopped at the Threshold and repeated, "I am Franz-Karl of the lines of Falkenburg and Leonstein and Armorius and Capradaventi, a fully sworn Notary of the Elderkin in the line of succession for the Duchy of Traventi. I come with peaceful intent toward any that will deal peacefully and in good faith, and my attendants with me."

For a moment he thought he might have to explain that no one else could swear on behalf of a full Notary, but the Chief Keeper bowed gravely and read out a Remoran version of the proper response: he used the right one even though it was a little different from the response used for Childe Silvia and the rest of the party. The Chief Keeper even offered the tokens of formal greeting and hospitality in the full Traventine style: fire and water and wine, salt and meat and cheese and bread, even though it involved a bit of a scramble. Many non-Traventines allowing Elderkin across their Thresholds were careless about the rites of hospitality and ignored such details.

The carriage stopped in a rare sunny spot within the walls. Most of the passengers alighted, but Tam stretched out across the trunks and parcels on the coach's roof, took a deep breath, and relaxed to take a nap in the sun.

Fritzel looked up at the valet, and said in country Elderic, "That canna be easeful, surely."

Tam took another deep breath and settled deeper across the lumpy surface in a way no human with an unbroken spine could match. "I'll do well enough here..." The valet already sounded half asleep.

Fritzel reached up to pat a booted foot that was near the edge of the carriage roof. "Fair enough. I'll see you dinna miss the meal." He turned to join the others.

The Menagerie was not a disappointment. There were no baby animals – the keepers recommended returning in a month, as it was early in the season yet – but even without babies, there were some new animals in the collection. The children's favorites were some clever creatures with ringed tails and masked faces that had recently arrived with an ambassador from West-over-Sea. The keepers called them wash-bears because they liked to wash their food before eating it, but they were much smaller than proper bears: nearer badger size.

Franz-Karl wondered whether there were Elderkin in the western lands who showed signs of being wash-bear kin: there seemed to be Elderkin showing traits of most kinds of clever creatures in the world. And, to be honest, more than a few stupid ones as well: the whims of the Manifest did not always make sense to mortals. He and his Mama leaned toward being goat aspected, though their ancestry was diverse and complicated and the green parts of their parti-colored hair came from nowhere Franz-Karl had ever heard of. His valet Tam and Itron Gwenlian were... whatever they were: generally not mentioned in either case... and Fritzel, of course, was of the line of the Lord of the Labyrinth and strongly bull aspected, though he had no horns, at least not yet.

Philip-Augustus and Sophie-Alexa looked like proper Allemanic children of the Falkenburgs, except for their eyes and the areas around them – at least when they were fully clothed. That was surprising: a notable weight of Manifest heritage was usually visible in those that carried it. But his Mama was a more experienced Notary than most, and little happened by pure chance when there were Notaries in the vicinity. Dice were more likely to stand up on one corner and spin like a top than to display sensible values when Notaries were involved.

After a morning spent admiring the animals and birds, and offering treats to any that would accept them, the food that had been packed to be eaten on the road to the country estate was served up in the Tower's dining hall. All of the Tower's people – guards and keepers and servants, along with those in authority – were invited to join the meal. Traventines followed strict rules about sharing food, and Franz-Karl and his Mama followed the Traventine rules of hospitality as well as they could, even though customs were different in Karnburg. The Tower folk brought out excellent bread from their own bakery as their share of the feast, and wine and beer and cider from a remarkably well-stocked cellar.

Fritzel bowed to the Chief Keeper and said that the wine-cellar was clearly the Old Tower's famous treasure, and everyone laughed, but things were less stiff after that. Fritzel was not the leader of their party, but he was male, and a grownup, and not too worryingly weird in his appearance, so he made an acceptable spokesman. It probably helped that Fritzel was very large and his voice was very deep. People in Karnburg outside the Palace were not as silly about women speaking and acting in public as folk from some other parts of the Kingdom and Domains, but that was not a difficult measure to surpass.

Toward the end of the meal, when most of the food was done and the wares from the wine-cellar were still being shared out, people began telling old stories about the ancient citadel... including some stories that very carefully did not admit that there was real treasure stored somewhere in the tower, but would not really make sense without it. The storytellers mentioned at least three ghosts – one accidental death and two executions – and something occasionally present in one of the cellars that might not have ever been human.

Being von Falkenburg Grand Dukes and Grand Duchesses was not entirely useless. After the last remains of the meal were cleared away, the Chief Keeper offered to show the guests some of the parts of the Tower other than the sections of the Menagerie that were commonly opened to visitors. He opened offices and storerooms, one after the other, and showed them many curious things that were quite respectably old for being this far north of the Mothersea, and talked about their stories and histories. Karnburg had started as a Legion outpost about the time Remora was becoming an Empire instead of a Republic, and the Tower foundations were very likely begun by the Legions, so it had a lot of history piled up in it.

Philip-Augustus asked many questions about some of the weapons on display. Most were trophies and memorials of antique battles, but some were as recent as the Great Siege by the Sultan's forces little more than a decade earlier. Their Mama looked sad at some of those. Her marriage into the Falkenburgs had been arranged just after the Sultans forces were driven back, when the Kingdom and Domains were feeling vigorous and expansive, and someone decided that the spot on the map that was independent Traventi was an unsightly blemish in the swath of territory that answered to His Excellency.

Franz-Karl expected that he himself would have little use for weapons made of steel or the sorts of battles that used them. Being a manifest Binder and a full Notary before he had even lost his baby teeth meant that he had other means of dealing with problems. He paid attention to the stories – he always paid attention to stories – but he did not much care about the weapons themselves.

Some of the Tower's other possessions were more interesting to a Notary training to be an advocate. There were shelves of volumes of old Karnburg laws and chests full of ancient diplomatic documents. Franz-Karl pleased the Chief Keeper greatly by taking special notice of one ancient charter that was more than a thousand years old, carefully framed and proudly displayed. He did not explain that the Antonia Adrasteia who was one of the signers was presently Count of the South Valley in Traventi and still a member of the ruling Council of the Duchy. He took out his wax tablet and scratched a note to ask her about the charter the next time he wrote to her. He thought that there was something odd in the phrasing, but that might just be the age of the Remoran used, not someone being sneaky about formulating the contract. Of course, it could also be a bit of both.

When the Chief Keeper offered to take the party into some of the below-ground areas of the Tower, or else up to the top of the Tower to see the view, Franz-Karl sighed. "Is there gunpowder stored below? Even in smallish amounts?"

"There is, Your Honor," the Chief Keeper answered, eyeing him a little uncertainly.

"Then I fear I must stay above," Franz-Karl said. "It's an Elderkin thing," he added apologetically, when the man looked surprised. "I have been warned that I should avoid powder stores for safety's sake until I am older and more... settled in the way of things. So it must be the Tower for me."

The man's eyes widened and he bowed, "Of course, your Honor." He assigned a junior officer to serve as Franz-Karl's guide and ordered him to command anyone they might encounter carrying a powder-horn to keep a safe distance.

"I want to see the lower levels," Philip-Augustus said firmly. He always insisted that he did not dislike high places, exactly, but he certainly did not seek them out as Franz-Karl sometimes did.

Their Mama decided that she and Sophie-Alexa would join Philip-Augustus in the lower levels, which promised fewer stairs to deal with than the tightly spiraling staircases that climbed the upper tower. In the end it was only Franz-Karl and his aide Fritzel who made the long climb to the top of the tower: higher than anything in the city except the top of the cathedral's bell tower, or the Lamps that topped the spires of the very tallest parish churches.

There were small squads of men on duty up at the top of the tower at all hours. They had spyglasses and signal flags, and a horrible, loud tuneless bell, and watched the river and the surrounding countryside as well as the city itself. They could see a great distance in good weather. At night they watched for uncontrolled fires in the city, and unexpected fires beyond the walls that might be signs of a camp of brigands, or enemy scouts trying to approach. By day, they watched for anything that seemed unusual, and they were part of the reason the Daonas river near Karnburg was considered pleasantly free of river-pirates.

The days were still short, so early in the season, and the sun remained well south. When Franz-Karl and his companion and their guide reached the top of the tower, the sun was well above the horizon, but it was already settling low enough that the walls and buildings of the city were beginning to cast the streets into shadow, even though the great, many-channeled river and the suburbs and farmlands beyond the walls to the north were still well lit. The Tower's own shadow made a dark streak across the city roofs near the river channel, a heavy mark among the narrower streaks of shadows of the tall cathedral and various lesser church towers. The Palace was almost invisible at this distance, shadowed by the southern arc of the great city walls and separated by its own walls from the city streets to its north.

Fritzel looked out beyond the huge city walls and the earthen mounds that were meant to protect them from cannon fire. "The buildings yonder seem a bit patchy," he said quietly in Elderic.

Franz-Karl answered in Allemanic, as a courtesy to their guide, "The Sultan's army cleared a lot of space beyond the walls for their camps and artillery and maneuvering, but I think they left some of the nicest buildings for their officers to live in. Papa said the rebuilding is uneven because building is expensive, and also there are a lot of lawsuits about missing wills and boundary markers that people think were moved or lost."

"Sounds as bad as spring floods." Fritzel's Allemanic was as fluent as one could ask, and pure Palace when he wanted, but usually carried a slight local Karnburger accent.

"Worse, probably. The floods don't move things on purpose..."

When they turned to look inside the great Walls, the top of the great oak at Greenoak Square was a few blocks south and west of the Tower, sticking up above the buildings that surrounded it and looking very odd and ragged in the afternoon light. Despite the name, the tree was not truly evergreen, and now that spring was arriving it was beginning to drop the clumps of last season's leaves that it had clutched all winter to make room for the new leaves that were budding. The shadow it cast across the roofs east of the square looked like a stretched, screaming face because of the gaps not yet filled by new leaves.

Franz-Karl and Fritzel followed the parapet walk all the way around the Tower, looking out in every direction at the city's streets and buildings and the lands beyond the great walls.

Fritzel said in Elderic, "I had thought the kitchen garden at Greenoak Square was tiny, but it seems I should have been surprised by its breadth. There is little green in this city outside the Palace grounds."

Franz-Karl shrugged, "Part of that is the early season, I think. It will show more green in a month or two." He remembered more of the stories his Papa had told. "When you were about my sister's age, these city walls held out the Sultan's army long enough to matter, despite all their cannons. Long enough that by the time help arrived from the North and the West and from the Szekelys, the people inside the walls were running out of dogs and rats to eat, and the horses were long gone, and the plants were eaten down to sticks and inedible roots. But it is true there is little room inside these mighty walls for anything but people. The food comes in from the fields outside the walls and elsewhere to be stored and the great armies muster and drill outside the walls for lack of space."

Fritzel leaned on the stonework beside them. "Not sure the Palace's formal gardens are what I'd plant, then..."

"The Palace gardens are partly a defiance and a boast, but also not as useless as they seem at first."

"They do lean hard toward fruit trees," Fritzel allowed.

Franz-Karl glanced at their guide, who was standing a polite distance away, not really out of earshot but with the glazed look of someone hearing a discussion he could not follow. He said very quietly, still in Elderic, "Not just the trees. Not all pretty flowers from exotic places are just table decorations in their homelands. Though some fruits and some roots need very careful preparation to be served safely."

"Is that the way of it, then?" Fritzel smiled the kind of Elderkin smile that 'made friends happy and enemies nervous'. Though he generally carried the aspect of a bull, his teeth were not only for eating grass. Sometimes that was more noticeable than others.

"The folk West-Over-Sea seem to have a lot of lumpy but nourishing roots, besides the bits that grow above ground. Perhaps it's no wonder those little wash-bears dunk their food."

When they saw the first Lantern lit, on a steeple of one of the city's parish churches that was shaded by the City Wall, Franz-Karl and Fritzel began the long climb down to meet the rest of their party in the Tower's courtyard. It was easier going down than climbing up, but the ancient stairways had been worn down by centuries of traffic, so they went carefully and avoided the hollowed centers of the steps.

# CHAPTER V: Greenoak Square

## *Wherein the family visit an enclave of Elderkin*

The best road back to the Palace from the Menagerie went past the entrance to Greenoak Square, where a mansion belonging to Childe Silvia's father was being used as as the formal home of Traventi's representatives in Karnburg. It provided a place where Traventine merchants and other travelers could readily find assistance in dealing with Falkenburg and Karnburger officials without needing to pass through the Palace Gates. Her Royal Grace Childe Silvia, who was the highest ranking representative of Traventi in the city, resided within the Palace, not the Square, but the Palace guards – despite their responsibilities as defined in a number of treaties and contracts – were annoyingly reluctant to let unfamiliar Elderkin into the Palace to speak to their Duke's Heir, no matter what the treaties and regulations said. The officials at the Square dealt with minor matters and prepared reports for Her Royal Grace regarding matters that needed her attention.

It had been some time since Childe Silvia had visited Greenoak Square personally: annoying and uncooperative though they were, the Palace authorities generally made it easier for those stationed there to come to her than for her to leave the Palace, though they were not usually as heavy-handed as they had been that morning. She decided that since she was outside the Palace walls she should pause at Greenoak Square before she returned to the Palace. Tending the Household Shrine was not a task she could properly delegate to someone outside the family. Franz-Karl's occasional expeditions outside the Palace could assure her that the Household and its staff were well taken care of, but children did not tend the offerings to the Ancestral Guardians if there was any alternative.

The time for the evening meal was approaching. Philip-Augustus, Count of Wolfsberg, was not much involved in Traventine matters, and he was still annoyed at missing the visit to his own estates, so he was inclined to complain about the delay in their return to the Imperial Palace to visit a Traventine estate.

But Her Royal Grace had duties both as Heir of Traventi and as a child of the Armorius line that owned the house, and she was not the only person in the carriage with business at Greenoak Square. The carriage turned in to the Square and drove around the great Tree at its center to the mansion's Gate and Threshold.

Franz-Karl and his personal household were thoroughly entangled with the Greenoak Square House. He had awakened the Household Shrine after his return from Traventi – despite being far too young for the task – and felt responsible for the ancestral guardians it honored. His status in the Palace was complicated enough that many of his personal possessions were kept stored at the House in the Square. His valet Tam would welcome the chance to retrieve some of those items and leave behind some that were presently enclosed in the locked trunks strapped to the carriage roof.

Franz-Karl's companion Fritzel was formally Deputy Steward for the property in addition to his other duties, since Karnburg law did not allow a woman to do the job and Fritzel was a Tiarna and counted as minor Nobility. He had papers to sign involving the household's supplies and city taxes, though they were not urgent: he visited Greenoak Square at least weekly, and often spent the night there after attending evening sessions or entertainments at the University.

Besides his more official duties, Franz-Karl himself had spent weeks traveling from Traventi in the company of some of the people now living at Greenoak Square. He would be glad to see them again, and just to be in a place where Elderkin were in charge and where he was not existing in a weird space outside the proper rules of hospitality.

Philip-Augustus and Sophie-Alexa said 'Ooh' and 'Aah' when they saw the gates of the Greenoak Square House. The two carved stone torches flanking the gate had begun to glow an unnatural green when Franz-Karl awakened the Armorius Household Shrine and the glow had not ceased during the succeeding months. The torches glowed brighter after Childe Silvia of the lines of Armorius and Capradaventi stepped down from her carriage to knock on the gate and formally announce her arrival at her father's gate.

Following Her Royal Grace the Childe Silvia, each of the travelers – from the family to the coachman – announced themselves at the Gate Threshold using the formulas of the full Rites of Hospitality. They used the complete Elderic forms that no one had bothered with during their visit to the Menagerie, since the keepers of the Altturm had no Elderic. Neither Allemanic nor Remoran could really support a full translation. Each person recited their names and lineages, and claimed household membership or kinship, or offered or renewed oaths of peaceful intent toward the household they were entering. They were greeted with equally full formality and all of the tokens of Welcome: fire and water and wine, salt and meat and cheese and bread, made up into the delicacies called aogreamana by a proper Traventine Cook.

Philip-Augustus and Sophie-Alexa had never visited Greenoak Square before – despite being children of the Armorius line that owned it and living not far away – so they were welcomed with the special forms for newly arrived kinsmen. Philip-Augustus stumbled a bit over the formal Elderic phrasing and his choice of a formula to announce himself was a little hesitant. Sophie-Alexa had used the Elderic Rites and formulas many times when narrating the adventures her doll Mina shared with her and Franz-Karl and the toy horse Harvest Prince, so she neither stumbled nor hesitated.

And then the whole party moved from the Threshold of the House's Gate to the front door of the House itself, and performed another full set of ceremonies at the Threshold of the House using somewhat different formulas. "Again? Do we really need to?" Philip-Augustus complained.

Franz-Karl sighed, then thought of the view from the Tower parapet: walls upon walls of defenses, pierced by fortified gates. "Houses in Traventi have Thresholds and gateways, but not even material gates, unless they need to keep the livestock in, or out. They are defended by oaths and Bindings and the laws of Hospitality, not stone walls, because stone is no great defense against Gifts and Binders, and there are a lot of Binders and Binding powers and Gifts in Traventi. You'll be a full Binder yourself soon enough, so it's important to weave you into the house's defenses here... Worldfolk use layers of walls and gates: we use layers of Oaths."

Philip-Augustus sighed and started to turn back to the rites, then spun back around, eyes wide and reflecting the green light. "Wait! You! You are already a full Binder... even a fully sworn Notary... but you haven't sworn any oaths to the Palace! You've been refusing!"

Franz-Karl kept his face as still and his tone as bland as he could manage. "No one has greeted me properly except at Mama's doors, which have the only well-maintained Thresholds in the Palace. In any case, scholars and jurists write that it is a great folly to exchange oaths with someone when broken contracts already stand between you, and the state of the Marriage Contract remains a tangled mess. His Excellency Our Grandfather and acting Arch-Duke Uncle Helm-Friedrich don't seem to think the matter urgent enough to bar me from the Palace. If they change their minds, I can live here."

Philip-Augustus looked at him for a long moment, his indignant expression gradually turning thoughtful. "Perhaps they hope you'll turn some of the most annoying and disobedient officials into newts." Then he turned back to the Rites of Hospitality with a muttered comment that made Sophie-Alexa giggle. But he was more careful with his responses than he had been at the outer gate.

Once they were across the inner Threshold, Philip-Augustus found more reasons for discontent. He and Sophie-Alexa were welcomed warmly as children of the line of Armorius. But Franz-Karl was a Notary of the line of Armorius: a Manifest Binder who had taken responsibility for his own actions before Heaven and the Living World and the Council of Traventi, and might be advised but not controlled or commanded, despite the years that must pass before he was Initiated or reached the age of majority within the Empire. The Elderkin of the household did not make a fuss about it, but they treated Franz-Karl as a person of authority, not as a child. Philip-Augustus, who was the eldest son and eldest child in their family and would hold all authority within the household by Alemannic custom, was treated as a child because he was as yet neither an Initiate nor a Notary nor of age.

Franz-Karl was included in the discussions between their Mother and Fritzel and Itron Gwenlian and Damian – who had charge of the House when Fritzel and her Royal Grace were both absent – with a closed door between them and 'the children'. A few others in the household were called in briefly to speak about specific problems, but Franz-Karl was present for the entire meeting. He did not speak much, but listened carefully to the discussion of the relations between Traventi and the Falkenburgs and other factions at court, and the problems some Traventine merchants and traders were having with city officials. In the end, everyone agreed that the guards behavior that morning was worrying, but conditions had not really changed since before Childe Silvia's wedding: the Empire was not likely to risk open conquest, and Traventi was too small to be much of an actor in the world, despite its many Binders.

Franz-Karl agreed, reluctantly, to return to the Palace with the rest of the family even though at the moment all of his possessions were safely at Greenoak Square and he was not formally, legally, a resident of the Palace at all. In the end, Fritzel took a knee so that he could face Franz-Karl nearly on a level, looked him in the eyes, and asked seriously, "Are you sure of this choice, Your Honor?"

Franz-Karl sighed and rubbed the hard spots at his hairline where horns might someday grow. "If the factions are willing to break agreements by His Excellency and the acting Archduke even within the Palace, there's no telling what they will get up to in the countryside between here and Traventi if we give them anything they can claim as an excuse. This –", he waved vaguely to indicate the building that enclosed them, "is a more comfortable trap than the Palace, but a less useful one. WE cannot do anything from here."

"And should not do anything in the Palace," his Mother warned firmly.

Franz-Karl did not say a word to agree or disagree with that as Damian walked over to open the door of the study where they had been talking. But he thought, "I can listen. And watch what happens. And bear Witness as a Notary." There were people in the Palace who were accustomed to saying or doing one thing, then calmly insisting they had said or done something quite different. Being Witnessed by a Notary made that sort of fibbing less easy.

Franz-Karl and the other children were nowhere near the age of Initiation, so they had no important roles in the rites in the Household Shrine, or elsewhere in the House. Other than bowing before the tokens of their kin and ancestors and lighting some candles and incense, they were expected to politely ignore the grownup matters going on around them. Franz-Karl found that harder than his brother and sister: he had read too many old stories, and since becoming a Notary and awakening the shrine he had one foot across too many thresholds.

The furniture in the major public rooms was mostly draped in dust covers, which made it all a bit spooky, but after they had paid their respects to the shrine, the children found that the partly unused mansion was a glorious place to play hide and seek. Since they had brought Mina, and Harvest Prince with them from the Palace, both toys joined the game. This made Philip-Augustus grumpy – again – since he had brought games in his luggage, but not a toy that could have adventures. When Sophie-Alexa asked where his toy soldiers were, he got even grumpier, and did not answer.

Philip-Augustus said, in Allemanic, "Franz-Karl! Give me one of the toys from among your possessions." He did not say 'please'. Or 'lend'. Or ask in Elderic or Diplomatic Remoran, which were both in more common use in their Mama's household than the Allemanic that gave so many privileges to eldest sons.

Franz-Karl considered the language and phrasing and answered, in Elderic, "No, I think not," using a verb form that was not so much emphatic as... decided. It was a form used more in contracts and Notarial witnessing than in ordinary conversation.

Sophie-Alexa hastily suggested, in Elderic, "Why don't you use one of your chessmen to speak in the game, Brother? Size doesn't matter for adventures: Mina and Harvest Prince don't match for size. Not properly."

Philip-Augustus huffed, then stomped off to order his tutor to unpack the chess set. He handled several of the pieces, including both wizards, before he settled on the black king, who was not carved sitting on a throne, but on a horse, waving a sword.

The game proceeded smoothly after that. Mostly. Philip-Augustus and his King were both inclined to be bossy, and Harvest Prince did not entirely refrain from sarcasm. But they found one of the written clues that Sophie-Alexa and Franz-Karl were used to encountering during their quests in the Residence – a tricky rhyming riddle in Elderic, written in an antique style of letters – and by the time they had chased the mystery through three additional clues to find a plate of treats fresh from the ovens, they were all laughing together. Even Philip-Augustus was speaking Elderic more often than not.

When they prepared to leave the Square, most of the party from Palace settled into the carriage, while four Initiated Elderkin women carried pitchers out into the Square to the roots of the Tree. It was not the sort of thing uninitiated children were supposed to notice, so Franz-Karl did not look straight at them. But the broad, horizontal oblong pupils of his Elderkin eyes gave him a fair view in his side vision as his Mama, and the Laundress of the House, and the Cook, and Itron Gwenlian fed the Tree with wine and water and milk and something that counted as the blood of sacrifice.

His Mama and Itron Gwenlian did not return to the house when they were done, they just handed their pitchers to the other ladies and climbed into the carriage, which was waiting outside the Gate Threshold.

Broken Oaths & Boundaries

# CHAPTER VI: Return to The Palace

## *Wherein the Travelers Return to Share a Family Dinner*

The roads were growing very dark by the time the carriage finally left Greenoak Square, so they returned to the Palace through its West Gate: the one Franz-Karl and his companions had used at Midwinter. The West Gate was generally used more for deliveries of supplies than the entry of Palace guests and noble residents, but it opened directly into the road that passed Greenoak Square, unlike the Main Gate they had used to leave the Palace that morning. The streets that went around the Palace from the West Gate to the Main Gate were neither well lit nor well repaired, so traveling them after sunset was a hazard for the horses and carriage.

The guards at the West Gate were very flustered when the carriage arrived and asked for entry: the Palace Gates were supposed to exchange information about the people passing through them – the guards were supposed to do the work of keeping track not the Nobles who went in and out –but apparently that had not happened. No one at the Gate asked for oaths of peaceful intent from the grownup Elderkin, or from Franz-Karl, or offered any oaths either, even though the structure and markings on the gateway clearly showed that it had originally been constructed with a properly consecrated Threshold. Despite omitting the proper rites, the guards dithered until a senior guard – not the one the family had encountered in the morning – arrived from the Main Gate with a squad of other armed men.

The Guard officer ignored the servants riding on the outside of the coach. But he insisted on bringing the 'Graefinwitwe' and her children and attendants immediately to the hall where Their Excellencies were dining, without allowing them time to wash or change into proper attire.

That was most improper with or without oaths or the rites of Hospitality. It would all be plain clothing, and either black or the color-of-sorrow in any case, since they were still in full mourning for the children's Papa and Childe Silvia's husband, but people did not approach their Excellencies wearing clothes that had spent a day feeding treats to birds and animals and exploring seldom used sections of an ancient fortress. And chivying nobles as if they were prisoners when they had not been accused of a crime – much less convicted of anything – was completely contrary to both courtesy and protocol.

Tam and the coachman assured Her Royal Grace Childe Silvia firmly that they would keep watch on the luggage lashed to the carriage's roof. The Guard officer looked annoyed, but could not quite argue: they had not spoken to him, and neither did Her Royal Grace, not directly. Tam's eyes caught the torchlight at odd moments in a way that the guards were trying not to notice.

Just as with the Gate Threshold, the Guard Officer and his men rushed the party across the neglected Threshold of the main Palace building without any pause for oaths of peace or rites of greeting. They did not quite dare to shove, but they tried to crowd close on the heels of those they were supposedly escorting. Fritzel and Itron Gwenlian walked at the back of the group and kept the guards from crowding as close as they would have preferred.

Her Royal Grace Childe Silvia gave no sign that she noticed anything wrong, except that there was a golden spark clinging to the end of each of her braids, ready to drop. At first she held one of Sophie-Alexa's hands while Nurse Rosa held the other, but since the guards kept trying to rush them, Nurse Rosa picked up Sophie-Alexa to carry her. Philip-Augustus walked steadily, but the heels of his shoes sounded too loud on the Palace floors.

Franz-Karl, walking silently beside his brother, had begun to think about a number of feats in old stories that he had never promised not to re-enact within the Palace. Signing the Marriage Contract blocked his Mama from some of them, but he himself had not been born until years later, so he could not in any way be claimed as a signatory, and he had not spoken nor signed any other oaths, either to the masters of the Palace or to those who managed it from day to day. Curdled luck was the least of what might be arranged if the Living World was willing to do him a small favor... and the Living World being willing to do small favors was what made someone a Binder.

The guards took the Traventine party on a winding and indirect route through the Palace. They passed several groups of minor nobles and functionaries who seemed entertained by their disheveled state. Itron Gwenlian, Her Grace's aide, pressed her lips tightly together for a moment, but she kept walking steadily to give the soldiers no shadow of an excuse to shove her. She said something softly and gestured with both hands. Franz-Karl felt his shirt and other linens ... twitch ... and then they arranged themselves so that they were as neat and tidy and freshly starched as when he had put them on that morning. At the same time, every smudge and bit of dust vanished from his coat and waistcoat and breeches and boots, and presumably from his hat as well. Sophie-Alexa, in Nurse Rosa's arms, giggled as though she was being tickled. Philip-Augustus' eyes went wide and he squirmed a little.

Franz-Karl heard Fritzel, walking behind him, say "Ah." Franz-Karl tried to keep a serious face, but inside he was snickering a little. Fritzel had needed Itron Gwenlian's aid least, for he never, ever looked scruffy. When he wore clothes, they were somehow always tidy: Franz-Karl was still trying to figure out whether there was an actual Gift like Gwenlian's defending his aide from smudges. There were some Gifts Elderkin did not ask about unless the Gift holder spoke first. Franz-Karl's own knack for walking unnoticed was among them.

Part of his aide's tidiness was not a Gift in the full sense. The black hair on Fritzel's head and face grew seasonally like a bull's pelt, not continually like human hair, so he almost never showed a shadow in the shaved places on his face despite having very black hair and very fair skin. Things were likely to be amusing when Fritzel shed out his winter coat, but that was not going to happen this evening, and until then Fritzel was going to make even freshly-shaved Worldfolk men look scruffy by comparison, at nearly any hour of the day or night. The tutor walking behind Philip-Augustus did not have the same advantage, but he was a pale blond from somewhere near the north coast, so the long day's stubble did not show much.

When they arrived in the banquet hall, the Guard officer led them between the lower tables all the way to the head table and bowed deeply to their Excellencies. He began a speech that seemed to want to refer to the Franz-Karl's Mama and her companions as culprits or malefactors, but Her Excellency Franz-Karl's Grandma Aurelia interrupted him. She beckoned sharply to the Hall Steward and instructed him to have places laid for her daughter-in-law and grandchildren at the high table immediately, and to find places for their attendants at the lower tables. Then she turned to Franz-Karl's Mama and said pleasantly, "I'm glad to see you, Silvia, my dear, but a bit surprised. Hadn't you planned to withdraw to one of the Wolfsberg estates for the rest of the Quiet Weeks?"

Franz-Karl's Mama bowed gracefully to her mother-in-law. "We had that intention, Your Excellency," she said calmly, "but there were ... complications... at the Palace Gate. We spent the day at the Menagerie instead, with a brief stop to tend my family's Household Shrine at Greenoak Square during our return to our residence here in the Palace."

His Excellency said, "I do apologize for the inconvenience, Childe of Traventi. I am certain those complications will not occur again." He looked hard at the Guard Officer and added, "Will they, Corporal?"

The Guard turned very pale and Philip-Augustus coughed twice, so Franz-Karl was quite sure that the man had not been a Corporal before His Excellency spoke. He did not know what the man's rank had been, though Philip-Augustus would almost certainly know.

Franz-Karl thought that it would be very helpful if the officers in different units of His Excellency's forces agreed to use similar insignia for similar ranks. But that was not likely to happen in Franz-Karl's lifetime unless he lived as long as Count Adrasteia, who measured her life in centuries the way others measured in years. Soldiers seemed generally stodgy and traditionalist, and not very sensible: there were a lot of different military units within the areas of the Allemanic Kingdom and the Falkenburg holdings, and many of them seemed to dislike their allied military units nearly as much as they disliked the enemy. So people who cared – or needed to deal with soldiers frequently – needed to learn whole catalogs of ranks and insignia to know who they were talking to. Those dealing with senior officers needed to learn names and faces besides: most common soldiers wore uniforms, more or less, but Noble-born officers often did not.

The Guard Officer who had brought them to the dinner managed a deep though flustered bow and a feeble "Of course, Your Excellency," before the group of guards left the dining hall. Franz-Karl thought that a different man seemed to be commanding the squad of guards during their exit. The man who was now a corporal was so busy looking at the nobles sitting at the lower table nearest the dais that he nearly tripped over his own feet, and the new commander hissed something at him that turned his face red.

There was a pause while the Hall Steward and the Master of Protocol fussed about who should sit where. Even though it was a Quiet Weeks' dinner, not a formal banquet where the strictest rules of precedence would apply, the absences of those who had retreated to the countryside had disrupted the seating arrangements even before an additional handful of senior Falkenburgs suddenly needed to be inserted.

Looking around, even without turning his head much – Elderkin eyes were so handy for that – Franz-Karl could see some of the problems. Acting Archduke Uncle Helm-Friedrich and Princess Aunt Denise Amalie were absent – that was probably why the guards had been so stupid: they had been given stupid orders, and there was no one to give sensible ones instead – and Prince Otto of Karnburg and his Princess were also absent. And while the men and women were loosely balanced among the nobles gathered at the dining tables, it was the wrong women and the wrong men.

Too many of the women at the tables were widows with no more control over their own property than Franz-Karl's Mama had under Allemanic inheritance laws. Even those who observed Ecclesialist practices and might have wished to follow the Karnburg custom of Withdrawal, had nowhere to go, or no way to go there safely.

Too many of the men were from districts ruled by His Excellency that were far to the north or west or both. Most of their estates were too far away to visit briefly: even farther away than Traventi in some cases. Besides the distance, most of the Northerners were not Ecclesialists and had different religious practices. Most of the men at the lower dinner tables were either Harfnerans or Pristinists, and both groups were reluctant to converse with the widows, who were women outside their own households.

The Harfnerans had broken from the Ecclesialists some generations ago, but still shared many of the same festivals. They recognized the Withdrawal but did not observe it, particularly, nor hold a festival at Carnevale, so they did not find it inconvenient to remain at court, or keep their families in Karnburg. Their celebrations of the Reawakening were said to be subdued compared to the exuberant Ecclesialist traditions.

Franz-Karl was not sure what the Pristinist religious practices were like. He knew that they hated decorations – especially in churches and cathedrals – and the public festivals in the Ecclesialist traditions: they made a lot of fuss about that. And he knew that they held their women in servitude and mostly out of sight, and considered Elderkin to be abominations who should be treated worse than livestock: they made a lot of fuss about those things, too. But he had never seen a list of Pristinist festivals nor a description of how they honored the Gods. Even really extreme Ecclesialists were not that strict about barring non-Initiates: they usually at least told outsiders what their holy days were, so that people would not be surprised when the shops were closed or the public squares and country groves were full of revelers.

Aside from the usual rules of court protocol, the Pristinists were a problem for Master of Protocol von Hornberg and the Hall Steward – who acted like an ally of the Pristinist faction at court, even though he did not usually dress like them. Adding any of the Traventine Elderkin into any table where Pristinists were already seated would cause trouble, and lead to pointed questions from Her Excellency and possibly even from His Excellency Friedrich-Augustus.

No one wanted His Excellency asking pointed questions: instant demotion to Corporal was very far from the worst thing that could happen.

In the end, the tutor and Nurse Rosa – the members of their party who were not Elderkin – were placed at the lowest table in the hierarchy, which was mostly filled with Harfnerans, but included a couple of Pristinists who proceeded to be very rude to Nurse Rosa. Fritzel and Gwenlian ended up at a table full of Ecclesialists and Harfnerans that was higher than their ranks of Tiarna and Itron warranted, but no one in the Karnburg court really understood Traventine titles, and His Excellency's annoyance counted for quite a lot. Fritzel ended up sitting beside their neighbor, Graefinwitwe von Steinach – whose personal named turned out to be Wiborada – while Itron Gwenlian sat between two of her ladies.

Her Royal Grace Childe Silvia and the three children were squeezed in at the high table, which was fortunately a bit sparse in the absence of those Falkenburgs who had withdrawn to their country estates.

Franz-Karl's place was finally set between Her Excellency His Grandmother Aurelia, and his aunt, Her Royal Highness Dowager Queen Gertrude of the Szekelys. They were comfortable people to be with, and comfortable with each other: they were both clever. Gertrude was only a few years younger than her father's second wife. Listening to their gossip was likely to be very instructive.

While Franz-Karl waited to receive his share of the dishes that had already been served to others at the table, Her Royal Highness Aunt Queen Gertrude, asked, "Your Honor, did you really quote the Marriage Contract to the gate guards?"

On Franz-Karl's other side, Her Excellency said something that sounded like, "Oh, dear Heaven," very quietly.

Franz-Karl took a deep breath, then spoke carefully. He knew that His Excellency, seated beyond his grandmother, would be able to hear, if he chose to acknowledge it. "Since I left these Gates nearly a year ago and was bid farewell, His Excellency has not formally acknowledged my return as a Falkenburg kinsman, nor as a Guest, nor as a Traventine official. I am sometimes addressed and referred to by the Falkenburg courtesy title that was assigned to me at my father's funeral, but that has no official force. My lawful standing inside these gates is as a product of that Marriage Contract. What else should I quote?"

Her Royal Highness Aunt Queen Gertrude looked surprised, then thoughtful. "Product, not party?"

"The Marriage Contract was written and signed some years before my conception. It is impossible for me to be counted as a party to the Contract. Or as a Witness either."

Her Royal Highness made a noise that might have been described as a snort if she was not a Queen. "I was present at your birthing, and should remember, but Your Honor always seems older than I expect."

"They say that happens with Elderkin sometimes, that the heritage of the Manifest complicates childhood. We call it 'born old and open-eyed' –" he translated the phrase from Elderic to Allemanic, adding, "sometimes it is useful to look small and young. But often, not."

"Would it be helpful to arrange proper standing as a Guest?" One of the nice things about Her Excellency his Grandmother was that despite her rank she asked about things before deciding to do them.

"There are proverbs about the foolishness of exchanging oaths with someone whose existing contracts stand in breach." Franz-Karl turned to look directly up at Her Excellency. "There are also rules about oaths for Traventine children, and fully sworn Notaries, and Heirs of the Line, and they all pull in different directions, complicated by the tangle around my arrival and presence in Karnburg. The usual Guesting oaths might be neither safe nor sufficient, and there is no one here to ask. When people gossip you can say that, without mentioning the breaches in the contract." He prevented the efficient removal of the main course plate that had just been placed in front of him and hastily took a bite.

On his other side, Aunt Queen Gertrude commented, "You are fond of that word: 'breach'."

Franz-Karl swallowed and explained "The term 'breach' has a broader, more hopeful prospect than some alternatives." He took another bite of his dinner, which was truly excellent. Lunch at the Old Tower seemed a long time ago.

"Does a word have a prospect?" Her Royal Highness asked.

Franz-Karl swallowed again. "As Maestro Petros in Traventi explained it, the word 'forsworn' has a narrow prospect. If you tell someone that they are forsworn, especially if you do it before witnesses, the main prospect is for blood on the tiles, sharpish, and likely ankle deep before things are finished." He quickly took another bite of food and chewed and swallowed it before continuing. Grownup courtiers probably had a trick for eating and discussing things at the same time, but he had not learned it yet. "According to Maestro Petros, saying 'the contract is irreparably breached' provides a broad prospect – even though it means much the same thing as 'forsworn' – because it allows for discussions of things like culpability and indemnification, and thus supports the possibility of negotiation and a variety of choices into the future. The injured party may yet decide that blood on the tiles would be prettier or more useful than any of the other alternatives on offer, but that is less of a certainty. Though of course there will be limits on the expected forbearance of the parties: excessive delays can be viewed as evidence of lack of good faith, or become an additional breach in themselves, requiring additional redress." He ate another bite, then took a sip from his cup. "Have you noticed? It is nearly the end of the year since my father's death. Soon I will be able to set aside my mourning clothes. And no doubt other changes may be expected as well." He took another sip. "Naming a proper trustee for Count von Wolfsberg's properties will no doubt be among them. Mama and Philip-Augustus are both upset about the current state of things, and it is one of the breaches of the Contract."

Her Excellency His Grandmother said hastily, "There is no need to recite the Contract here."

"Of course not," Franz-Karl agreed cheerfully, between bites of his dinner. "In any case, if I was going to recite part of the Marriage Contract at this table, that would not be the section I would choose."

Her Royal Highness Aunt Queen Gertrude coughed once, then looked at him thoughtfully.

Franz-Karl turned his attention to the next course of his meal. After a while he remarked to no one in particular, "I cannot exchange oaths with Contract signers while the Contract is in breach, so if His Excellency is minded to become ... observant ... about requiring Guest oaths from Elderkin Binders in the Palace, I will need to move to Greenoak Square. Or possibly somewhere farther."

Her Excellency his Grandmother said, "Oh, dear Heaven," also to no one in particular.

Her Royal Highness said quietly, "There are stories about foolish people who try to force oaths from Traventine Notaries."

"Lots of stories," Franz-Karl agreed cheerfully. "Lots and lots and lots. People should pay attention when the old tales are told." He ate a spoonful of food from the next course of the meal.

# INTERLUDE II: The Inner Hall

## *Wherein the Pristinists Seek Paths Forward*

Most of the Pristinists who gathered in the Margraff-Elector's White Hall never passed through the door into the Inner Hall. Only the Preacher, the Teacher and some of the Select gathered there, attended by a few servants so low in the Echelon that their deaths or disappearances would go unnoticed if one of their superiors decided to take precautions against gossip and rumors.

The men who were neither Select nor disposable listened to readings and sermons in the White Hall, and lingered afterward to discuss the state of the world, and the city. Many of them had never set foot through the Palace Gates, nor ever would, so most of their discussions were based on rumors, Imperial pronouncements, announcements by the Select, and gossip from their companions who held Imperial positions within the Palace Gates.

The talk in the White Hall was properly dismissive of the gifts from Traventi that had filled the gossip of the City and Palace since Midwinter. But they did not stop talking about them even when interest had largely faded among the other factions and sects in Karnburg. The gifts from Traventi were like a sore tooth that the Pristinists could not stop poking.

The writings of Pristinus himself assured them that the gifts of the beast-born would prove to be manufactured from trash and trickery. And even beyond their source, gifts at holiday times and birthdays were denounced as an affront to Heaven by both the sermons of the living Preachers and the writings of the dead ones. So the men of the Echelon anticipated the dismay of those who had rejoiced at receiving false treasures.

But days had turned to nights, dark was ended by dawns, new moons and full moons rose and set, and the short days of winter lengthened toward spring, and there were no reports of the gifts from Traventi failing. Nor did their owners cease to display them in public. The Teacher and Preacher assured their congregation that the eventual collapse would be all the greater for the delay.

The few who gathered in the Inner Hall did not concern themselves with such displays of Traventine fripperies. They were more concerned with maintaining the network of authority that had been constructed to divert the authority and wealth of the Palace and the Falkenburgs into their own, more righteous hands.

The temporary escape of the Falkenburg beast-born into the city beyond the Palace walls was a dire hazard. The Ecclesialists showed no signs of comprehending the hazards that accompanied beast-born that were not strictly confined and controlled by righteous, properly human, Men. And if the beast-born could leave the enclosure of the Palace walls at will, there was no telling where they might end up, or what they might do when they arrived.

But if the movements of the beast-born were a hazard, the unexpected demotion of a moderately high member of the Echelon – during the reasonable exercise of the authority and attention to his duties besides – had been a blow, not just a warning. Keys and purse-strings that had been safely in Pristinist hands were now held by a Harfneran standing outside the Echelon. The Select assured each other that things could have been worse: surely it would be better to deal with a Harfneran than an outright Ecclesialist. But not enough better. Not soon enough to avoid disruption to their plans.

There were plans, already active, that had been devised with the certainty that Pristinists were making the choices in particular positions within the defenses of the Palace and around the imperial family. Now there was a gap in their network of influence that threatened to spread like a hole in a knit stocking as that first unexpected demotion was followed by a spreading ripple of promotions and reassignments. And the expected schedule for various events – events that affected people and places far beyond the Palace, or even the city of Karnburg – could no longer be relied on.

Trying to directly repair the gap in the palace Guards would carry too much risk: His Excellency and the acting Archduke were clearly so bewitched by the beast-born that they were willing to listen to the pernicious creatures, and protect them as if they were truly Falkenburg kin. The Pristinists could not rely on decisions from their overlords regarding the beast-born that they would consider sensible, but they also could not hope their own actions would be overlooked. Friedrich-Augustus and Helm-Friedrich were neither of them stupid, and after this current upheaval they would be paying attention to the Guards for this next while.

To avoid having parts of their plans failing publicly, the Pristinists would need to establish new lines of authority and of funding – especially funding – and quickly, but Pristinists were quite rare in the offices of the Treasury and the taxation authorities of the Falkenburg Domains. They were only slightly more common in the Treasury and tax offices of the Holy Remoran Empire and Kingdom of the Allemans, which in any case handled a smaller flow of funds.

There were four of the Select in the Inner Hall during the discussion when they reached their conclusion: the Margraff-Elector of Ansbach, and the Prince-Elector of Bremerhaven in their chairs of state, the Preacher leaning on his lectern, and the General of the Army of the Empire.

The General's pacing took him near both the door that barred access from the White Hall, and the hidden door that was used by the slaves who tended the candles and cleaned the Inner Hall when it was unoccupied. He paused twice during the discussion to jerk open the servants' door. Once he revealed a passing servant carrying linens bound for some other destination within the Margraff-Elector's establishment. The second time he revealed only the empty passage. He closed the door panel and stood glaring at it for a moment before he resumed his pacing.

The discussion was much like the General's pacing: it covered the same ground over and over without reaching a destination.

The Prince-Elector was most concerned with the schedule of their plans to reduce Ecclesialist power outside the Palace and Karnburg. Plans which might work if they struck without warning in several places, but would likely fail if any one strike happened earlier than the others, allowing time for the alarm to spread. Pigeons were faster than express riders, and not slowed by muddy roads, though vulnerable to weather and hawks, which worked both for and against them. Time was growing short if they needed to make changes in their plans because of the changes in Karnburg and then warn the distant Echelons of any new schedule.

The new Preacher was less pliant than his immediate predecessor, and his sermons mentioned heroes who had been martyred for denouncing corrupt rulers in the marketplace on occasions other than the days when the martyrs were traditionally remembered. He agreed with the laudable goal of freeing Friedrich-Augustus, King of the Allemans and Elected Emperor of Remora, from the pernicious influences of the Ecclesialists and beast-born and the empty words of females. He accepted assurances that their plans were not, in fact, treasonous, and that they did not contravene the Electors' solemn oaths to their overlord. But he had not been in Karnburg during the long months of planning, and he tended to press for details about their plans that the other Select increasingly preferred not to share. There had been no public announcement of a reason for the previous Preacher's exit, and the new Preacher had never mentioned any of the events around that time, so it was unclear what he might know, and less clear what he thought.

The Margraff-Elector rarely spoke of matters outside the walls of Karnburg, except when he spoke of the accursed, beast-born-ridden realm of Traventi, and the beast-born who were falsely considered members of the Falkenburg family rather than their possessions. He was emphatic about the urgent need – for safety's sake – for all beast-born to be properly subjugated and kenneled, including the entire populace of Traventi, and most especially the Falkenburg whelps currently residing in the Palace. But he was willing to wait for an opportune moment.

The General pointed out – in each circuit of the discussion – that his regiments were stationed outside the walls of Karnburg, and well out of reach of the Palace and any other offices unless summoned in case of open insurrection or invasion, so their aid could not be relied on.

The discussion made another circuit. The Electors agreed that there was no time left for excessive subtlety. They would need to be more direct in their methods, while still taking some care to escape notice.

"What do you want from me?" the General asked.

The Margraff-Elector tapped his gloved fingers rapidly on the arm of his chair, then stopped the jittery movement. "Only to be ready in case of surprises, I think," he said slowly. "There are ... tokens ... available that await their lawful occasion to influence those who might otherwise be reluctant to assist us. Perhaps it is time that some of them were put to use."

"Oh? I had not heard that you had replaced your kennel-master," the Prince-Elector said, "or that ... clerk? who managed your texts, either."

The Preacher kept his face expressionless. "Is Your Royal Grace certain that these tokens will suffice to suborn the servants of the Falkenburgs?" The others all flinched at the word 'suborn'.

The Margraff-Elector glared, but answered them both. "The tokens I speak of were ... acquired... in my father's time. They have not been used often, but they have never failed when used."

The General sighed. "That may well work, but best choose your targets carefully, and as narrowly as seems safe. Too much meddling may be more readily noticed, but we need to influence both those with access to the privy purses and authority to distribute their funds, and those who might notice diversions." He sighed again. "I will make what preparations I can." He bowed to the others and took his leave.

The Preacher took a step as if to follow him, but stopped and returned to his lectern. The Inner Hall was formally his, even though it was under the Margraff-Elector's roof. It was against custom to leave the other Select there in his absence.

The two Electors began a long discussion of possible targets of persuasion. Most of the names they mentioned were men who served the Falkenburg Eastlands and the greater Falkenburg Domains, not officials of the Holy Remoran Empire and Kingdom of the Allemans that they themselves were sworn to.

Preacher Weiss listened to their discussion, but did not comment.

# CHAPTER VII: The Falkenburg Privy Council

## *Wherein Childe Silvia and Our Hero Are Ensnared in Politics*

The day after the visit to the Menagerie, it rained. Or slushed, to be more accurate. The family decided to postpone their visit to the estate outside the city – as promised by His Excellency himself – until the next bit of good weather. Philip-Augustus was so very annoyed that Franz-Karl was glad to be sharing the nursery with his little sister instead of sleeping in the room he had shared with his brother before his visit to Traventi.

The three children made excited plans about what they would do when they finally reached the estate. Outdoor games and pony rides were mentioned. Franz-Karl sighed at the pony rides: after the long journey to Traventi and back, he was a fair rider, but the flippy little goat's tail hidden within his clothes made time in the saddle less amusing than it might have been.

But their expedition needed to be postponed further: when the skies began to clear on the following day, Her Royal Grace the Grand Duchess and Graefinwitwe of Wolfsberg, Childe Silvia of Traventi was summoned to attend the Falkenburg Privy Council discussions about what to do about the breaches of the Marriage Contract.

Franz-Karl did not understand why the discussions were still going on after all these months, and it worried him. The general problem was quite simple: the contract was a set of promises that had been made, sworn to, and Witnessed with the full weight of thousands of Elderkin witnesses to make them a permanent part of the World. For most purposes, the Living World itself should be counted as one of the witnesses and could be expected to help enforce the promises in the Contract. And then some of the promises had been broken. Nearly half. And a few of the ones that were not broken were pretty much things that could not be broken, so they did not really count in the balance any more than if you put a clause about the Sun rising in the east in a contract: you couldn't really take credit for partial fulfillment of the contract when the Sun did rise in the east.

The solution to the problems seemed equally simple to Franz-Karl: people absolutely needed to stop breaking the sworn promises and prevent them from being broken again in the future. And then they needed to undo as many of the things that previously had been done wrong as possible. Preferably before the Living World got too cranky about the situation, which it had been known to do in the past. The recent winter had been described as unusually unpleasant by a some of the oldest people around the court, and while there were no records of strong earthquakes ever happening in Karnburg, there was always a first time for everything.

One slight complication was the Curse of Rano. Some of the Allemanic and Falkenburg Court officials were probably expecting that the Contract would be adjusted to be more to their liking if they held out long enough. But unless special measures for making changes were defined within a contract itself – and there were none in the Marriage Contract between Prince Leon-Alexander von Falkenburg and Childe Silvia of Armorius and Capradaventi – no contract in Traventi or involving Traventi could be changed after any of the parties or witnesses died. If people tried, the World would get very, very unhappy.

Maximianus Rano – Maximianus the Frog – was an ancient Traventine Sorcerer and General who had been understandably annoyed at being knifed during the peace negotiations after his great victory. He had managed to use his own death and all of the battlefield dead as blood sacrifices to seal the curse and make extremely certain that the Treaty he had fought and died for could not be revoked or modified after any signer or Witness had died. He had also arranged to die dramatically in his wife's arms immediately after signing the Treaty himself. The Death of Rano was the most common image in Traventine art except some images of the Gods and Saints, even if you did not count the occasional coinage that showed it on the reverse.

Franz-Karl was sure that attempts to change the Marriage Contract were not going to work and were likely to fail badly, even without living Traventine people and Binders helping things along, which they had no great reason not to do. It was clear from the numbers of the plebiscite that had ratified the Contract that the populace of Traventi had been resigned to the Marriage rather than happy about it. They would not be pleased to be offered even worse terms after the bad ones had already been broken so badly. The large number who had not agreed to the contract – at all – would be even more annoyed.

There had been some small improvements in matters involving the Marriage Contract over the past months. Some of the least broken promises had been fixed, so that the promises that remained broken were about one quarter of the full number instead of nearly one half. But all of those things had been fixed months ago, when Franz-Karl first returned to Karnburg as a full Notary from Traventi, carrying annoyed messages from the Duke and Council of Traventi. Since then nothing had changed except that people seemed to be trying to break some of the repaired promises again, or find new ways to break the promises that had not been broken before.

Franz-Karl should not have needed to recite part of the Marriage Contract to a Palace Guard, and the guard officer should probably be glad that the year had not yet turned around to thunderstorm season. The Living World was famously cranky when the Curse of Rano got involved.

Franz-Karl's Mama was one of the primary parties for the Marriage Contract and as Heir to the Duchy she could speak for the interests of Traventi, so summoning her to the Privy Council sessions made sense. Her presence in the discussions should help get things moving again. Unfortunately, after attending two sessions, she did not seem pleased or relieved. She seemed annoyed. Her hair had started to drip sparks from the ends of her braids even when she was safely at home behind the consecrated Thresholds of her own Residence. The drips were slow, but they did not stop.

Franz-Karl had a horrible thought, so he and Fritzel slipped out of the Residence and went to the place in the Palace where the Falkenburg copies of the Marriage Contract were supposed to be kept. They compared the copies there to the official copies of the contract they had carried all the way from Traventi. The Palace copies all looked correct: no one had replaced them with fake contracts that were tricking people into doing the wrong things. People were being stupid all on their own.

Franz-Karl was not sure whether that was better or worse than people being tricked.

The day after they compared the copies, the Privy Council sent a supposedly official message to Her Royal Grace the Dowager Grand Duchess of Wolfsberg and Heir of Traventi saying that she should bring the Imperial Grand Duke Franz-Karl – her reported Heir for the Duchy – to the Privy Council meeting with her. Reported was not quite the right word for what Franz-Karl was, but the message came in Allemanic, not in Elderic nor the formal Remoran that was supposed to be used for diplomatic matters. The message was insulting in several ways even before you got to the Grand Duke part. Or 'reported'.

Franz-Karl's Mama was very upset about the message, especially because it was not in either of the official languages of the contract: someone was being sloppy or deliberately rude. Or both. She said that Franz-Karl would need to come to the session, at least once. She warned that he would need to stay still and quiet even though he would probably be very bored.

"They will not notice me unless I wish it," Franz-Karl assured her cheerfully. He thought that he should probably have used the 'don't notice me' Gift when he and Fritzel went to look at the Contract, but it was too late to change that choice. And getting at the documents without the keepers noticing would have been very tricky.

"Not that quiet!" his Mama said hastily. "If they don't see you, some of them will make trouble about it."

Franz-Karl rolled his eyes and took a deep breath and let it out. He showed her that he had a set of five waxed tablets for taking notes, strung together like the pages of a book, and two spare styluses in case the first one broke. "I am a fully sworn Notary , and I sat in the May-tide and Harvest-tide sessions of the Traventi Council as an Observer," he reminded her. "Perhaps I will write a letter to Reverend Count Great

Aunt Adrasteia and Her Grace the Duke my Grandmother about the differences between the councils. Not on matters where I am sworn to confidentiality, of course: I mean the different customs and ceremonies and things."

"Of course," she agreed seriously, but her eyes were laughing and the dripping of the sparks from her braids slowed.

When they arrived at the council session, Franz-Karl was welcomed by His Royal Grace acting Archduke Uncle Helm-Friedrich, who had been summoned back from his country estate to keep the imperial court in order even though it was still the time of Withdrawal. His Royal Grace formally presented and introduced Franz-Karl to the Councilors, but using his courtesy title, not any of his real ranks.

Franz-Karl thought about going back to the Residence, because calling people the wrong thing was on the list of signs that people were dealing in bad faith. Maestro Petros, one of the grownup Notaries in Traventi, had said that signs of bad faith happening very early meant that nothing useful would happen in a discussion. But he had promised his Mama to stay with her, and he did not want to leave her alone with a bunch of mean people when acting Archduke Uncle Helm-Friedrich was too busy to take proper care of her.

Half of the people at the conference table did not even look at Franz-Karl. A few others sort of peeked sideways at him. And he was not asked to promise to keep the things he heard confidential. He was not asked to promise anything at all. Reverend Count Great Aunt Adrasteia – who had been Spymaster of Traventi for more than a thousand years in between various other pastimes – was going to receive a very thorough report using the very best of the codes and ciphers that she had taught Franz-Karl. And he would write it with the special secret inks, in the colors few but Elderkin could see, colors that did not even have names in Allemanic and Remoran.

Since the council members were not properly presented to Franz-Karl, he was never quite sure who a few of the quieter people around the table were. Some others were such awful fibbers that if he saw portraits of them, he would not recognize them without all of the marks of fibs, so it did not matter. He already knew some of the rest, and others became clear during the course of the discussion.

He was given a chair to sit in that was carefully not near his Mama, and too large for him to sit in properly. His tail did not like it.

Two men at the council table that Franz-Karl recognized were the Margraff-Elector of Ansbach and the Prince-Elector of Bremerhaven, who were very important people at Court, and loud about it. They were both Pristinists, and dressed in what should have been plain, un-patterned cloth, but the Margraff-Elector's clothes were always marked with scribbled drawings and words in colors that Elderkin had words for and other folk did not. Someone in his household must dislike him. A lot. Franz-Karl looked mostly toward the Prince-Elector because looking at the Margraff-Elector too long made him want to giggle. Some of the words and drawings on his clothes were funny as well as very rude.

The Electors were both important Nobles in the Allemanic Kingdom, but their lands were near the Northern Coast, outside the parts of the Kingdom that were in the Falkenburg Domains. They had been in Karnburg all winter, and in the Palace as often as not.

That was not surprising. If the Northern Lords were in Karnburg at the beginning of winter they were not likely to leave until better weather returned. Their lands were even farther from Karnburg than Traventi was, and traveling to or from Traventi took weeks even in good weather. Looking at maps and at the books explaining how governing was supposed to work in the Allemanic Kingdom, it seemed that there should be whole swaths of the year when one or the other or both of the Margraff-Elector and the Prince-Elector were absent from the Palace at Karnburg, away in the North governing their territories. That was the way it worked with the other Northern Lords, but not those two. They were just always in the Palace, as long as he could remember, and Franz-Karl did not know why.

He did not think asking why would be useful. It would probably need an audience with His Excellency to get any kind of answer at all, not even a good answer.

Franz-Karl also did not understand what two lords from outside the borders of the Falkenburg Domains were doing sitting at the table in a meeting that was supposed to be the Falkenburg Privy Council. He was fairly certain that asking why that was happening would not be useful either.

And after living in the Palace all his life except that one summer in Traventi, Franz-Karl knew better than to ask why the two North Allemanic Lords were able to divert the council's discussion onto a matter of tariffs that had nothing to do with the Marriage Contract between Traventi and the Falkenburgs, which was the official topic of the meeting: Electors were important. The Margraff-Elector of Ansbach raised the first question, and more questions every time the discussion seemed to be moving back toward the Marriage Contract, and the Prince-Elector tossed answers and more questions back to him. In the end, the discussion came to no conclusion, but it went a long way around on the way to nowhere.

Franz-Karl took notes of the bits Count Great Aunt Adrasteia might find interesting and spent time doodling during the most useless arguments. He also spent part of the time watching the sparks that occasionally dripped from his Mama's hair.

Some of the men in the meeting were sitting in the wrong places to see the sparks, while a few of the others clearly could not see the sparks at all. The Margraff-Elector seemed to notice some of the sparks, even though he did not notice the marks on his own clothes – he sort of flinched, sometimes, when a spark dripped –but the sparks were a sort of greenish gold, like the weird torches at Greenoak Square, not any of the special Elderkin colors.

When they paused for refreshments, the Prince-Elector of Bremerhaven walked over to stand looming over Franz-Karl and demanded to know what Franz-Karl had been scribbling.

Franz-Karl smiled up at the man. He had a grownup tooth coming in, now, and an empty space where a tooth would come soon. "Pictures of newts," he answered, showing him the top tablet in his stack, not one of the ones with useful notes on it. The Prince-Elector, who was already pale and frowning, turned even paler, and frowned even harder. Elderkin talking about newts made Pristinists very unhappy. Franz-Karl wondered whether their holy writings included some mean stories about Elderkin and newts and people being rude. Probably not: they would be more polite.

Acting Archduke Uncle Helm-Friedrich coughed, and asked, "Spotted or striped?"

"Spotted." Franz-Karl answered, as seriously as he could manage. "I don't believe that I have ever seen a living striped newt..." He considered, then added, "Or a dead one either."

The Prince-Elector took a step back.

When the Council session resumed, the councilors finally turned their attention to the Marriage Contract, but for all of the progress they made, they might as well have continued the discussion of tariffs, which the Margraff-Elector kept trying to go back to. Some of them seemed unwilling to agree about which sections of the contract had been breached, or how. A few of them seemed reluctant to admit that the Marriage Contract existed at all.

The sparks began falling faster from Franz-Karl's Mama's hair, but they were still not very fast. Her braids were wrapped around her head so that each ended near an ear, and the drops looked like earrings or hair ornaments and grew much like the water dripping from an icicle. They began as tiny specks shining against her dark brown, green-streaked hair, and grew slowly until they fell free, not quite at the same time. The process was taking about ten seconds from start to finish. Each pair fell silently, but Franz-Karl thought they really should make a sound, something like "Bi-dip!" when they fell.

That evening, Franz-Karl wrote a letter about his lessons in Grammar, Logic and Rhetoric to Reverend Count Great Aunt Adrasteia using ordinary oak-gall ink. Then he turned the paper a quarter turn and wrote a report about tariffs and the Council session, using the best codes and ciphers she had taught him and ink in a color Worldfolk did not see – though the Margraff-Elector's tailor seemed very fond of it. He carefully explained that the session was supposed to be about the Marriage Contract but the councilors were insisting on discussing many other matters in his presence. No one could accuse him of spying... well, the Pristinists probably would, if they thought of it, but they had no valid cause for complaint: Franz-Karl had not even asked to attend the session, they had summoned him. And no one had said anything about keeping the things he heard secret.

He added the letter to the pile for the next special fast courier to Traventi. Unless there was a special emergency the couriers only rode once a month from before midwinter until after the Spring thaw, so the messages piled up. Everyone at both ends of the journey put dates and sequence numbers on their letters, and mentioned which ones they had received. It was not often that a whole package went astray, but sometimes the piles got jumbled. Smaller messages about very urgent things were carried by pigeons, but they did not do well in the cold weather either. Hawks got hungry in the winter.

The second Privy Council session that Franz-Karl attended, a day later, was much like the first, but instead of the Margraff-Elector of

Ansbach complaining about tariffs, the matter that took precedence over the planned agenda was the Prince-Elector of Bremerhaven complaining about some fool beyond the western borders of the Allemanic Kingdom trying to instigate a war with the Kingdom of Borgonne, where Franz-Karl's Papa's full sister Valeria was Queen and his cousin Odo was heir to the throne.

Franz-Karl was not sure that the Falkenburg Privy Council had any business discussing diplomatic matters that did not involve Marriage Contracts: the rules about which business belonged to which Council seemed to be a mess... And there were not any Falkenburgs or other parties in the Borgonne matter who were of an age where a Marriage Contract might be considered, except the ones who were already married. The discussion of the existing Marriage Contract that was supposed to be the topic of the Privy Council session seemed to be moving away rather than making progress toward solving any problems.

The sparks in his Mama's hair were taking nearer five seconds than ten to grow and fall, and they were getting bigger and brighter before they fell.

Franz-Karl considered drawing striped newts, but he realized that he did not know whether the stripes should run crosswise or lengthwise, so he made a note to find out about striped newts, and continued to draw spotted ones. That evening he wrote to Reverend Count Great Aunt Adrasteia about the threat of war in Borgonne – even though no one seemed to be taking it very seriously – and added that letter to the pile waiting for the courier.

The next morning a pigeon arrived from Reverend Count Great Aunt Adrasteia. According to the codes on the strip of message, the roads to Traventi were beginning to open after the snow and flood seasons, and they hoped that merchants and messengers would be arriving soon. The piles of messages were carefully counted and packed up, and Franz-Karl's Mama sent the first fast couriers of the new season.

The third time Franz-Karl attended a Falkenburg Privy Council session with his Mama, he brought Fritzel with him. He stepped away from his mother as they entered the Council Chamber at the beginning of the session, and bowed to His Royal Grace the acting Archduke Uncle Helm-Friedrich.

His uncle nodded to him politely. "Your Honor?" Which was at least the correct style of address for a Notary.

Franz-Karl took a deep breath, let it out slowly, and spoke as clearly as he could, in his best, most proper Palace Allemanic. He had written out his speech and memorized it carefully, practicing with Fritzel as if it was one of his school lessons in Rhetoric. "Your Royal Grace, I have sat here these past sessions watching members of this council have great difficulty in recognizing the meaning of the plain text in front of them. I have wondered whether the discussion in Allemanic of a document that properly exists in carefully defined versions in Remoran and Elderic may be contributing to these difficulties." He gestured to Fritzel, who held out a sheaf of papers, but did not set them on the council table. "It happens that I have prepared a translation of the Marriage Contract of Silvia and Leon-Alexander into Palace Allemanic as a school exercise. Of course, this text is, and must remain, completely unofficial, since it is not in one of the official languages of the contract and no one has signed anything in this language, but it seems possible that some of these gentlemen might find it helpful as a reference."

Justice von Trebice of the courts of the Falkenburg domains held out a hand and said, "May I...?" and Fritzel handed the papers to him with a slight bow. The Justice read through the text carefully before he looked up. "This is very well done and quite accurate, I think. There are a few places where I would prefer to use specific terms that we use in legal documents instead of the more common phrases. May I have one of my clerks make the adjustments before we make copies for the council?"

"Certainly," Franz-Karl bowed slightly toward the Justice. "We have special legal phrases in Elderic as well, but I have not learned any of the Allemanic ones yet. My training as a Notary has been largely in Elderic, and a little in Remoran. Does your Honor's office also have someone who can provide a Northern Allemanic variation?"

"Northern Allemanic?" His Royal Grace acting Archduke Helm-Friedrich asked. He sounded honestly startled.

"Well, the gentlemen from the northern provinces seem to be having the greatest difficulty with the text," Franz-Karl explained in the gentlest, most matter-of-fact tone he could manage. He had expected this: almost hoped for it. "Anyone who listens can hear that the Northern dialect is much farther from Palace Allemanic than the local Karnburger or nearby Eastlands provincial dialects. And having severed ties with the Holy See some time ago, the gentlemen from the North may well have less use for Remoran than the rest of us. So these proceedings are asking them to discuss documents in two foreign languages – Elderic and Remoran – using a third language that is also foreign to them: Palace Allemanic. That seems... rude."

Someone made a choking sound at the other end of the table, but Franz-Karl was only looking at the Justice, who kept a straight face, though his eyes crinkled with laughter at the corners. The Justice had a cheerful face that showed very few marks of fibbing: the laugh lines were at home in it.

Justice von Trebice bowed toward the acting Archduke. "An excellent point, Your Royal Grace, and one I myself had not considered. I believe I do have a clerk who can provide the version suggested by His Honor."

Acting Archduke Helm-Friedrich said, "Since His Honor Grand Duke Franz-Karl has kindly provided us with the means to smooth the path forward, I will adjourn this Council session until suitable reference materials have been created and provided to the councilors." He stood up, so everyone else had to stand as well, so that they could bow as he left the room. Franz-Karl had never sat down, which was convenient: he did not need to scramble down from a chair made for a grownup before he could bow.

The Margraff-Elector and Prince-Elector scowled at Franz-Karl and walked the long way around the edges of the room, to avoid coming near him or his Mama and their attendants.

Justice von Trebice lagged behind as the room cleared out, and finally bowed to Franz-Karl and said, "May I ask, is it correct that your Honor is a full Notary and Advocate before the courts in Traventi?" He was not the Chief Justice of the Falkenburg Eastlands: that gentleman was also a Duke in the Falkenburg lands east of the Allemanic border, and had gone home for the Withdrawal. Justice von Trebice was the chief Justice of the Falkenburg courts that were held in Karnburg, which was not quite the same thing. It was also different from being the Chief Justice of Karnburg... either the city or the province. And it had nothing at all to do with the Chief Justice of the Kingdom of the Allemans.

Franz-Karl returned an appropriate bow... he hoped. "More accurately, I am a full Notary and something of an apprentice Advocate."

"That seems a bit ... backwards."

Franz-Karl held out a hand and turned it over. "I am enough of an Elderkin that I cannot speak an outright falsehood without harming myself. I have a Gift for noticing when things are not quite what they seem. And I am enough of a Binder that what I bear Witness to will be true, sometimes regardless of whether it was entirely true when it started. The oaths and Bindings that make me a Notary rather than just a Binder are meant to guard against that sort of thing happening, at least not by accident. So I can Bear Witness as a Notary and Bind a Contract as well as anyone else who is fully sworn. But an Advocate needs to know things about laws and contracts and negotiations that take time to learn." He considered for a moment. "Being already a Notary may speed the process of learning to be a proper Advocate. I have no basis to compare."

"Of course." Justice von Trebice bowed again, very politely – a bow to a colleague – and took his leave.

As they followed Franz-Karl's Mama back to the Residence in the West Palace building, Fritzel commented quietly in Elderic, "I think you made no friends this day."

"That is not so," Franz-Karl answered in the same language. "Justice von Trebice approved... I believe he thought it was funny that I was making it harder for some of them to be deliberately stupid. And the Northern Electors have been enemies of the Elderkin and the Marriage Contract since before I was born, and I think nothing I can do will shift that in either direction. For the rest?" He shrugged, the one-shouldered Traventine shrug used when work was being discussed. "If they did not want the truth spoken, they should not have summoned an Elderkin Notary to attend their council."

"Her Honor your Lady Mother is also a Notary," Fritzel suggested.

Franz-Karl held out a level hand, then wobbled it. "Both of those Northern Electors are Pristinists, assured by their founder's doctrine that the words of women are of no more account than the squawking of parrots. You have seen how they interrupted her whenever she spoke?"

Fritzel made a disgusted noise.

"Most of the council would not go that far... but any woman speaking to the Council, even as a witness, is contrary to custom: my Papa used to attend in Mama's place, before – " He took a deep breath. "The whole Northern faction will back the speakers and Councilors completely about being rude to Mama. I'm ignored because I'm small and young, but it's a different kind of ignoring. And reminding them that I'm a Notary makes the others less confident. I hope."

# CHAPTER VIII: A Visit to the Library

## *Wherein Our Hero and His Companion Travel Unseen*

Franz-Karl did not know what to do with his time after he followed his Mama out of the Council Chamber and back to their Residence. It was another nearly sunny day: a relief after the long, wet winter. It would have been nice to play outdoors with his brother and sister and some other children – there were not many games that were good for only three – but that was unlikely to happen. Children whose families were high enough in rank to associate with the Emperor's grandchildren were scarce inside the Palace walls – especially during these weeks of the Withdrawal – and Noble children whose parents would let them play with Elderkin children were even scarcer. And even if there was someone to play with, the Palace Gardens were not exactly arranged for convenient play, not even for grownup games like lawn bowling or wickets. Besides all of that, the household had expected him to be trapped in the Privy Council again for much of the day, so Philip-Augustus was busy with his tutor, and Sophie-Alexa was busy with Nurse Rosa.

As for visiting anywhere outside the Palace, that had not gone well or ended well last time. It was not likely to end well in the future unless the Privy Council did its job, which it showed so little sign of doing. Fritzel was able to go in and out of the Palace Gates without much difficulty because he was known to be the Deputy Steward at the Greenoak Square estate – and he was huge – but most of the other members of the Traventine household had difficulties at times, even the grownups. Franz-Karl was sure that he could go out with Fritzel, as he had at Midwinter – he was an Elderkin Notary, after all, and had Gifts, besides – but he was less certain about returning without causing a fuss. The gate guards were nervous, since the Traventine visit to the Menagerie a few days earlier.

It was not quite time for causing another fuss. Yet.

But looking out the window at the Palace gardens was not enough. Franz-Karl felt like he wanted to kick something. Hard. Or butt it with the horns he did not yet have. He rubbed at the two hard places in the skin above his forehead, but that did not help much.

He looked at the work table where he wrote his lessons.

If he could not get out under the sun to do anything useful or amusing, Franz-Karl could at least get out of the Residence. Franz-Karl considered...

Almost everyone who lived there called their section of the West Palace the Traventine Residence, and quite a lot of the Palace servants did, but most of the Palace authorities referred to it officially as the Wolfsberg Residence, especially in anything written, and very often Philip-Augustus did as well. The name mattered. It was stupid that it mattered, but that did not stop it from mattering. But it mattered differently to different people.

The Count of Wolfsberg was a vassal of his Excellency who resided at the Palace in Karnburg as part of his duty, but the Duke of Traventi was an independent monarch who maintained an ambassadorial presence at the Palace in an area that had ritually consecrated Thresholds to mark its boundaries. The rules were different for an official of Traventi representing the Duke, than for a vassal of his Excellency, and even more different and complicated for an official of Traventi who was also close kin to his Excellency. Even one who was just present in the Palace, and not properly either a resident or a guest.

They had expected to be stuck in the Privy Council session for most of the day, so Fritzel was neither busy being the Deputy Steward of the Greenoak Square estate, nor lurking at the back of some lecture hall at the university. Franz-Karl collected his aide and a satchel of books and set out on an errand that had been delayed by his attendance at the Privy Council sessions during the past few days, and was likely to be interrupted again by the Privy Council in the future.

They did not leave the Residence by the main door out to the North Gallery of the West Palace. The footmen at the outer doors of the West Palace had no right to ask where Franz-Karl was going within the Palace grounds, but that would not stop them from doing it. He had spent too much time, the past few days, dealing with fools who were ignoring contracts and protocols.

The newer parts of the Palace had not yet wholeheartedly adopted the modern fashion that the less decorative sorts of servants should pretend to be ghosts – or perhaps rats in the walls – and be occasionally heard but rarely seen. But there were unobtrusive doors and staircases that allowed things like firewood and water to be brought in and ashes and slops and dirty laundry to be taken out without defacing the ornamented halls and fine stone staircases frequented by the Nobility in their finery.

Franz-Karl did not use the servants' door nearest the Nursery he shared with his little sister Sophie-Alexa. That door stuck and popped in all but the driest weather, and he did not wish to disturb his Mama. The door in their dining room was better tended, and led to plenty of places besides the kitchens. Eventually.

The kitchens at the bottom of the staircase were not a bad place to start their travels. Fritzel was recently just over six feet tall – no longer just under. He was still looking a bit thin after recent growing, and was always ready to eat. Franz-Karl himself was growing enough on a smaller scale that he did not quite trust the fit of his clothes from one week to the next: his valet Tam and Itron Gwenlian seemed to be constantly adjusting the seam allowances of his coats and waistcoats and trousers. The cooks in the kitchen nearest the Residence were all Old Palace Servants or local Karnburger folk, so they were usually friendly to the Elderkin from the Traventine Residence who ate the food they prepared – or at least they were polite. Frieda, one of the senior cooks, gave Fritzel some freshly baked tartlets because he moved a heavy pot full of water for her, and Marna the baker made sure that Franz-Karl ate some tartlets, too, because she thought he looked too thin. Noble children were supposed to be plump and well-fed-looking.

At the back of one pantry there was a wall that wasn't: it had a latch and a pivot balanced so lightly that even Franz-Karl could open the panel himself, though it was hard to reach the latch... Well, it had been hard to reach the latch the last time he came through the kitchen: it was easier now.

There were three steep steps down, and the opening was narrow enough that Fritzel had to turn partly sideways to fit his shoulders through, but the space was a little wider at the bottom of the steps. Once the wall closed behind them, it should have been totally dark but it never was, not any time Franz-Karl had passed through the wall. They followed a crooked tunnel toward the dim light until they reached a small, surprisingly tidy room with lumpy stone shapes in the walls on one side, a small pool of water with carvings along its rim on the floor below the shapes, and a small, lit oil lamp hung on the opposite wall.

Franz-Karl and his brother Philip-Augustus had paced out the distances on the surface, once, with their Papa. They had guessed from the location that the lumpy shapes had something to do with the great fountain in the Palace garden. The boys had no idea who kept the room swept or filled the lamp, and a very good idea of the trouble they might get into for asking anyone but their Papa about it...

Their Papa had promised to tell them more about it later. At the time, it was more fun to leave it a mystery, and know about part of a secret. And now their Papa would never keep his promise.

On the far side of the small room there was another crooked tunnel that wandered around the foundations of various outbuildings or garden structures until it reached the main building of the Palace. The false wall on that end opened into what seemed to be a forgotten storeroom – except that the floor was always too well swept to show footprints. The objects stored there had dust in various nooks and crannies, but had been wiped down occasionally to clear their major surfaces. Moving through the room did not raise a cloud, nor leave smudges on clothing.

Franz-Karl and Fritzel opened the storeroom's door a crack, listened for footsteps on the tiles of the corridor outside, then slipped through, closing the door behind them. They turned away from the kitchens that served the great, formal feasts in the main Palace.

Franz-Karl began to pay more attention to not being noticed. One rule for using his don't-notice-me gift was not looking people straight in the eyes, and with Fritzel's eyes being above most people's sight-lines, and Franz-Karl's being below them, they could usually get past even alert guards if they were careful of where their shadows fell. Lately, Fritzel's size was the only thing that made staying unnoticed even a little bit of a challenge: Franz-Karl's Gift was getting stronger as he exercised it, or grew older, or both.

There were rarely guards cluttering the servants' stairs and passages except in the passages quite near whichever room of state His Excellency was actually in, so they were able to get quite close to their goal without much difficulty. They stepped through a panel used by the poor footman who had to tend the many candles in the sconces along the public corridor, strolled a short distance, and slipped through the door of the room they wanted.

The windows of his Excellency's library had heavy drapes that were kept closed when the room was not in use to protect the leather bindings from sun damage. The remaining light was too dim for even most Elderkin eyes to read text comfortably, but adequate for selecting volumes from the shelves and checking that the contents matched the claims of the bindings: not something that was guaranteed, especially for some of the older, hand-copied volumes.

Franz-Karl suspected that some of his ancestors had been more than a bit strange. Not just the Elderkin kind of strange, though there might have been Elderkin, too: he had not found books in this library written or printed in Elderic but there were marginal notes in some of the books written in odd colors. Some of the titles of the books in His Excellency's library were... odd. Some of the contents were odder.

Fritzel was good at reaching the upper shelves and they were both very good at remembering the original locations of things. They began by returning the volumes contained in the satchel to their proper homes, then poked about looking for different volumes to refill it with.

Fritzel had a written list of books that would be discussed at university lectures during the next months. Because he was Elderkin and held a position at Court, he was not quite a formal student at the University, though the Duchy was paying full student fees. When Palace collections included the books he needed, it was less complicated to use those than to contend with more official students for the use of the copies in the University libraries.

Franz-Karl was looking for books that discussed newts, and beyond that, for books that told him they wanted him to read them, or perhaps that he needed to read them. He was not entirely sure how that worked: being Elderkin with a heavy load of Manifest heritage could be confusing.

He was not surprised that his new stack included discussions of the more annoying bits of the history of the past couple of centuries. Sometimes he felt like he was drowning in history. He was relieved that it also included a few books that looked like fun. There were also two volumes – both manuscripts, not printed books – that might go either way: one was a Palace history from when the Allemanic kings mostly resided in a different city entirely – it was not even about the city immediately before Karnburg – and the other was very old and either had never had a title on its spine, or the title had worn away. When Franz-Karl flipped through it, the nameless book seemed to be a collection of shorter texts all bound together. Perhaps the binder had not been able to decide what to call it.

He found two books that mentioned newts. One was too large to take away with him, but it contained a few engravings of newts including two showing long-ways stripes. The other had no pictures, but he added it to the satchel anyway.

Franz-Karl was trying to decide whether to find one more book to add to the satchel, when the door of the library was opened with such force that the inner handle bounced off the wall. Fritzel and Franz-Karl quickly moved into the back corner of an alcove behind where a tall bookshelf stuck out into the room. Franz-Karl sat on the floor and Fritzel stood between him and the main part of the library, and they both kept very still and breathed shallowly. With Franz-Karl paying attention to his Gift, they might not be noticed even when the people entering opened the drapes: most of the books in the alcove were things like old treasury accounts that had not been touched in a hundred years and would probably not be touched in the next five hundred, and there were no windows there. There was no reason for anyone else to come into the alcove unless they were also looking for a hiding place.

There was a note in the satchel, written in his Excellency's own hand and sealed with the Imperial seal, saying that Franz-Karl had free use of all of the books and libraries in the Palace. With people causing his Excellency to be forsworn on every side, Franz-Karl thought the note would just become flame and ash – or a small shower of torn scraps – if he showed it to people in any of several of the Palace factions. And then they would try to do something awful to Fritzel, and possibly to Franz-Karl himself, and soon after that the people in the Palace would remember to be afraid of Elderkin Binders who were not sworn guests. And who knew what might happen after that?

Newts? Newts would be the least of it. The old tales were full of scary things. Franz-Karl was supposed to be too young and too small to manage most of them, even though he was a Notary. But he would try, if things got bad.

The three men who entered the library did not open the drapes, which was good. And they moved into the center of the room instead of any of the alcoves, which was better. If they had stayed nearer the door, their voices would have been harder to hear.

There was a man who stepped lightly and spoke Allemanic with a strong Northern accent and boasted in a slimy sort of voice of carrying more than one blade and knowing more than one way to use them. There was one who spoke Northern as if he had a mouth full of something and would likely have counted as a large man in any room that did not contain Fritzel: his footsteps thudded heavily even where there was a mat on the floor.

The third man stumbled as though he had been tripped or shoved. He spoke Eastlander Allemanic, but not quite Karnburger: he might have been from even farther east: in the lands that were Falkenburg Domains but outside the Allemanic Kingdom, or perhaps from the western region of the Eastlands near the Wald. It was hard to judge: he seemed to be mostly gagged or muffled after the first few sentences.

The conversation was not really a discussion or negotiation. The big, mush-mouthed Northerner put the Falkenburger in some kind of hold that left him unable to struggle effectively or cry out. His companion reminded him that it was important to leave no marks that would be visible while their 'friend' was clothed.

Then the blade-man informed their victim that 'high and righteous authorities' had decided that it was inappropriate for the wealth of the Holy Remoran Empire to be wasted in the support of abominations like childless female households, and households of accursed ancestry, and servants of the corrupt hierarchy that passed as the Holy See. Their victim was being given the privilege of assisting in the purification of the Palace and the Empire instead of being culled immediately along with his family. He should remember that while he might be useful to his betters, his family were less so.

There was a thud – perhaps a boot-heel against a table-leg. The captive must have tried to struggle or protest: the blades-man said, "Hold him, curse you!" There was no sound of a blow, but the captive made a horrible, stifled, wordless sound of pain. Part of Franz-Karl noticed that the man with the blades sounded quite happy that their victim was resisting, despite the curse.

Another part of him was wondering a little manically why it was always the ones who hated the Pontiffs in Remora the most who insisted that the Allemanic Kingdom should be called the Holy Remoran Empire. Did they not see the contradiction? Were they confusing the Holy Remoran Empire with the original Remoran Empire? 'High and Righteous Authorities' would be Pristinists – most likely – who gave their own meanings to words as often as not. Though his Papa had said once that even the Pristinists had factions: some were more extreme than others, and some people called themselves Pristinists out of convenience, not philosophy.

Or perhaps these were from one of the other Northern factions who talked about the Holy Remoran Empire and hated the Holy See: the Margraff-Elector and Prince-Elector were noisy, and very rude in the Falkenburg Privy Council, but that did not mean they were the only troublemakers in the Palace or in Karnburg. He knew a bit less about the Harfnerans because their factions were not currently being openly annoying, and they were usually a little more polite to Elderkin. There were too many factions to pay attention to them all equally.

Franz-Karl used the ribbon around his neck to pull his signet out from inside his shirt. Working as a Notary did not really need tools, not even pens and ink, or wax and signets, but it was nice to have something to use as an anchor. So much of being a Notary was aimed at preventing accidental Bindings from happening that most of the formulas deliberately made it difficult to work with neither his voice nor a pen. But he could not risk writing or speaking aloud, here and now. He would need to be sneaky.

The blades-man began to open the layers of the captive's clothing to reach bare skin, while speaking in slow and loving detail of how the man would betray his office and ruin his own kin to serve their masters' convenience. He did not undo the buttons of the layers of the coat and the waistcoat, he just cut the button threads with what he assured his companions was his smallest – but not sharpest – knife, so that the buttons fell to the floor with small clatters and skittered away.

Franz-Karl pushed his own right cuff back to reveal the string of thirteen prayer beads wrapped around his wrist, and let the pendant at the end hang free. Sometimes he thought the faint carvings on the strawberry-shaped lump of ivory made it look like a bunch of grapes or the tree of life, or a burning bush. Today it looked more like a heart. Not the symbol that was called a heart: more the sort of heart you might see in a butcher shop or on a dissection table. Or at a sacrifice.

The fine cloth of the bullied man's shirt was slit from neckband to crotch with a long tearing sound. The man with the blade praised the fine quality of the fabric.

Mush-mouth mumbled something about blood stains, and his partner said "Pfft... just a scratch. Won't bleed enough to matter. Might help wake the talisman."

Franz-Karl made a gesture that formally offered a blood sacrifice: children who were not yet Initiated were not supposed to know the gesture, but there were vesets – people in frescoes and paintings – making the gesture on the walls of a dozen of the most important rooms in the palace. And it was no great secret what stories they were acting out. He hoped that if the gesture would work for a minor child, his own Manifest weight would outweigh anything the Northerners tried to do with the blood. He was glad to suddenly feel a heavy weight of distant attention from... somewhere.

Franz-Karl quickly tapped the pendant with his signet four times: Notary Bindings went by fours, except for some very old ones that went by threes. He was relieved to feel the weight of distant attention turning more toward him even though he was still leaning hard on the 'don't notice us' Gift. He had shaped his right hand into the gesture that rhetoric classes recommended for the formal rejection of falsehood – another gesture that was popular for the vesets – and was holding the signet with his left hand.

The blades-man made an elaborate business of unpacking a thing he referred to as 'the talisman'. The package had several layers. Two sounded sort of crackly, and opening the innermost layer filled the library with a dank, musty stench.

Franz-Karl tried to hold his breath, or at least breathe shallowly to avoid coughing or choking. He saw that Fritzel was doing the same, but the men in the center of the room did not seem to notice the smell at all.

"This will stop you from inconveniencing the Select," the blades-man assured his victim. "And leave you bearing a mark that will proper get you drowned as a witch if you show it in any righteous place north of the Mothersea."

Franz-Karl used his signet to tap the prayer bead nearest the pendant, which was properly the last in the series. Then he worked his way quickly back along the strand from last to first, undoing the pattern, still making the sign against falsehood. He tapping each of the thirteen beads and paused to trace the sigils carved on three of them: the knife, the key and the wheel. After the last – or first – bead was traced: the table or altar, he tapped the pendant again.

There was a sound like a drop of water hitting very hot metal, and the stench was replaced by the scent of rain after drought. The captive made a small noise that might have been surprise or pain.

"It dint mek a mark," mush-mouth protested.

"Takes a bit to show, sometimes." The blades-man assured him cheerfully. "Easy enough to test it... " He hissed something in the captive's ear.

Whatever the test was – it sounded like a scuffle – at least it was quick. Afterward, Mush-mouth released the captive with a shove that left him crumpled on the floor, and both Northerners strolled out of the room. They moved casually, but were careful to check the corridor before they went out. They closed the door soundlessly behind them, despite the noisy way that they had opened it a short time earlier.

The injured man lay still for a few moments, then dragged himself to his feet and tried to pull his garments in to some semblance of normality, scrabbling for the fallen buttons and muttering at the damage the blades had done to seams and fastenings. Clothing was expensive and hard to replace: a minor official might have only a few outer garments fit for official business. And now these were damaged and the good linen shirt beneath was most likely ruined.

After a careful pause listening at the door, the man followed his tormentors out of the room. He moved furtively as he opened the door, at least partly because he would have needed at least three hands to hold his clothes in decent order and manage the door latch besides. The door latch closed behind him with a small click.

Franz-Karl and Fritzel remained motionless until they were quite sure none of the men were returning, and then for a little longer. Finally, Fritzel said softly in Elderic, "Well, that was a vile thing, and no mistake." He added firmly, "Your Honor, you do not want to know what they did to him, there at the end."

"I know one thing they did not do to him," Franz-Karl answered quietly, "and that's chain him to their desires as they intended."

Fritzel raised an eyebrow.

"Notaries can Bind things by bearing witness, but we can also block Bindings that we know to be false. *That* was false and contrary to the poor man's will." Franz-Karl considered. "I suspect I've wrecked their talisman for good and all besides."

"From way over here?"

"Such Talismans are made by using trapped bogles, generally – or sometimes whole herds of wisps – to provide the Manifest weight for Binding the particular pattern that's meant to be imprinted. The traps are not... durable... especially after a talisman is used a few times. And a failed use does them no good at all: failing at a Binding task outright will have cracked the Binding holding the bogle as well. If the creature is not free at this moment, it will be the next time they try to use their little toy."

Fritzel eyed him worriedly. "Exactly how is it you know so much about talismans, Your Honor?"

"Her Reverence Count Great Aunt Adrasteia recommended a book with a section about Talismans. And I read the original 'Silver Chain' grimoire in Remoran with Her Reverend Grace the Duke my Grandmother after we tangled with it last summer. She did not want to risk my reading a usable grimoire unsupervised."

"Heaven and the saints be praised for that!" Fritzel muttered.

Franz-Karl politely ignored the comment: prayer and swearing were both private matters where Notaries should not meddle. He continued, "Her Grace wanted me to be able to recognize the shapes of workings from that grimoire, since we knew someone here had a copy. So I did not need to guess at the weak spots of their Bindings."

He stooped, on their way to the door, and picked up a very elegant button that had eluded its owner. When they reached their apartments, he carefully put the button safely away in the box with a

Bound lock that only he and Fritzel could open that he used for the prayer-beads when he was not wearing them. It seemed like a bad idea to leave something lying around that had been tangled in a matter with wicked Bindings and trapped bogles and who knew what other vileness.

That evening Franz-Karl wrote a very long, boring letter about the Palace and Karnburg to Her Reverence Count Great Aunt Adrasteia, then added the encoded and ciphered account of the events in the library in ink that most people could not see, with a Binding to make them less likely to look. He left the letter unsealed, as if it was unimportant, and added it to the pile of documents waiting for the next fast courier to Traventi.

Franz-Karl spent the rest of the evening reading the worst-written history book. He was in the mood for something dull rather than exciting. It did not seem to help him sleep.

# INTERLUDE III: The Study

## *Wherein a Package Returns Home*

The Margraff-Elector's study remained as bare and clean as ever, with everything of interest locked securely away in various cupboards bolted to the walls. The cupboard in the far corner showed no external marks of the autumn fire. It remained empty except for the tokens that Bound the twelve remaining beast-born residents of the kennels to the service of the von Neumark family.

The grimoire and other documents it had contained before the fire had yet not been replaced, partly because there was no hedge-wizard to bear the taint of reading them and no kennel-master to ... induce ... the creatures held in the kennels to craft the required materials. Such texts were also harder to come by in these peaceful times than they had been a generation earlier during the chaos at the end of the Sectarian Wars.

A trusted servant – though not so trusted that he had ever seen the inside of that damaged cupboard – knelt in the study doorway until his master noticed him, then offered a lumpy, multiply wrapped package with both hands, head bowed, keeping the bundle as far from his face and body as he could manage.

The Margraff-Elector pointed to one corner of his desk where a rough earthenware tile rested. The servant rose into a hunched bow, scuttled to the desk, carefully placed the package on the tile, and hurried away as quickly as he could without earning a reprimand.

The Margraff-Elector unlocked a cupboard on the far side of the study from the damaged one. He stood for a long moment surveying its contents, frowning, then picked up a pair of silver tongs from the lowest shelf, and a slender, pointed rod of polished wood, and placed them on the desk. They were followed by a carefully wrapped stick of sealing wax and four different seals.

When he tried to use the pick and tongs to tease open the outer layers of the wrappings, they resisted at first, then spread wide, releasing a puff of rusty soot into the air that settled on everything within arm's reach of the package. Horst-Konrad held his breath until the dust had fully settled, then took a deep breath and let it out in a sigh. He did not try to examine the contents of the opened parcel.

The Margraff-Elector returned the pick, tongs, wax and seals to the cupboard, carefully wiping them clean with a silk rag which he left draped over the tile and its burden. He counted the contents of the cupboard carefully, twice, then removed a small sealed package, which he placed in one of his pockets. He closed and locked the cupboard and returned to the seat behind his desk before he summoned a slave to remove the trash from his study and arrange the scrubbing of the dirtied surfaces.

The wretch who answered the summons removed the tile along with the draped parcel resting on it, and managed to do it without looking at the burden or too directly at his master. As the slave reached the doorway, the Margraff-Elector said abruptly, "Can you read?"

"Regrettably not, Your Worship," the wretch answered, turning very pale. The Noble waved him away with an abrupt, annoyed flick of a hand. The man did not sigh with relief until he was safely past the doorway and out of his master's sight.

After a long pause, the Margraff-Elector retrieved one of his code books and some strips of the thin paper used for messages that would be carried by pigeons. He composed a message to the steward tending his provincial palace in Ansbach. Three specific books from his father's library should be carefully wrapped and sealed and sent to him in Karnburg, as soon as the state of the roads would allow. At the same time, the most reliable of the kennel-masters that controlled beast-born captives in the kennels of the province should also be sent, accompanied by trusty guards in case of escape attempts, or brigands or other road-hazards. Any rumors of an alchemist or hedge-wizard seeking a patron in the North should be pursued with due caution.

He wrote out the message four times, and sealed the message capsules carefully. The usual rule was to send three pigeons with any important messages, but since it was so early in the season, the order the Margraff-Elector sent to the dovecote authorized use of an extra bird.

# Broken Oaths & Boundaries

## CHAPTER IX: Bindings and Oaths

### *Wherein Our Hero Loses His Temper*

The next day Franz-Karl and his Mama were summoned to the Falkenburg Privy Council again, and Franz-Karl took Fritzel with them. As they approached the door to the Council Chamber, Franz-Karl saw the Margraff-Elector of Ansbach standing in the corridor a little beyond the doorway, with his entourage gathered around him. The Northern lord was talking to two men – one largish, one smaller – wearing clothes that were not nearly fancy enough for a Council session, even for minions who would merely fetch and carry: the cloth was wrong, the cut was wrong. Even the buttons were wrong. The two men looked familiar in a distant way, as if Franz-Karl had seen them before, but taken no notice.

The Margraff-Elector handed something small to the men, but instead of receiving it smoothly, they flinched away and it nearly fell to the floor. All three men turned pale even for Northern men, though the rest of Margraff-Elector's retinue seemed not to notice.

The two men hurried away. The taller, heavier one had a jaw that was oddly shaped, and a slave's iron collar showing at his throat inside the rough fabric of his shirt. The shorter man looked tough and wiry, and moved with his weight on the balls of his feet.

Franz-Karl was certain that he knew the sounds of both of those men's voices: he had to stop walking for a moment and breathe, to let some of the anger at the vileness done under his Grandfather's roof drain out of him. He was glad the two men were not following the Margraff-Elector into the council chamber. He was not sure what he might do, knowing that they were so near him again.

The morning seemed to improve after Franz-Karl entered the Council chamber and greeted the acting Archduke his Uncle. The Falkenburg Justice's clerks had two piles of documents prepared. Documents from one pile were handed out to the Northerners seated at the table, while everyone else received the others. His Royal Grace acting Archduke Uncle Helm-Friedrich made a speech thanking Franz-Karl for suggesting the 'memory aids' and Franz-Karl scrambled down from the chair he had been given to bow a proper acknowledgment.

Before Franz-Karl could climb back up into his seat, the Prince-Elector of Bremerhaven asked, in a very nasty tone, what the current state of the Contract was supposed to be. It was against the Council rules to ask a question while someone was standing unless you were asking the standing person, so Franz-Karl could pretend to assume that the question was aimed at him. He stopped trying to climb into the chair, politely turned to face the questioner, bowed very slightly – as a Notary to a client – and answered.

He answered very, very thoroughly, with proper citations of the pages and sections of the contract for the listeners to refer to even though his copies of the Contract, in all three languages, were laying on the table out of his easy reach. He included a detailed list of every breach he was aware of – including little fiddly ones no one usually bothered mentioning – and whether or not each breach was fully healed, partially healed, was not healable, or remained unaddressed. He had compiled and memorized the list after his first visit to the Council session and reviewed it each evening and morning. Grownup Worldfolk might be sloppy and unprepared: they would find that a full Notary of Traventi was not.

Finally, he paused, took a deep breath, and let it out slowly. But he did not turn to climb back into his chair. He was fairly certain that as long as he was standing, no one at the table could properly speak to anyone other than himself or His Royal Grace acting Archduke Uncle Helm-Friedrich, who was presiding at the meeting. Certainly, no one could properly change the topic of discussion unless he allowed it. If

Franz-Karl standing there until midnight was what it took to get the Contract discussed, well, that horrible business in the library had left him angry enough to do it. Drawing newts was not going to be sufficient, not today, especially not after seeing those two men in the corridor.

The Margraff-Elector turned to one of the other men at the table and asked a question that had nothing to do with the Marriage Contract.

Franz-Karl took a deep breath and let it out. His vision went strange in a way that was different from the strange things his eyes usually did, and he remembered Maestro Petros telling a story by the Victoria fountain in Traventi. He turned to His Royal Grace acting Archduke Uncle Helm-Friedrich, bowed, and asked loudly, "Your Royal Grace, are there written rules of order – protocols for who speaks when – for these Falkenburg Privy Council sessions?"

The Margraff-Elector started to protest, but His Royal Grace spoke over him and said flatly, "There are, Your Honor."

"May I see them?"

"Of course." A clerk was sent to fetch a copy of the rules.

Franz-Karl could see the Margraff-Elector and some of his supporters smirking. They expected him to complain that they were not following the rules, and then they would ignore him to show how much power they had and how little he had... But that was not how events in this session were going to go. The power that they thought they had was not the only kind of power in the room. He felt his hair pull out of its tie, and the ribbon fell to the floor. He thought someone might have said 'eek'.

When the pamphlet was brought, Franz-Karl read it carefully to make sure that it included a method for updating the rules, and did not include any stupid clauses that people had been politely ignoring for a few generations. Then he turned to set it on the seat of the chair behind him. He turned back to face the table, raised his hands over his head, snapped his fingers four times, and began to sing in Elderic.

It was a simple formula, though the tune was in an antique mode and a bit tricky: just six lines of a verse in very old Elderic, but only the first two lines and the last two were ever written in the chronicles or repeated in old stories. He had learned different variations of the middle lines from Maestro Petros and Chief Justice Laurentina in Traventi, and from her Reverence Count Great Aunt Adrasteia, and had no doubts about which version to use now. Any contract could be Bound by the presence of a Notary, and most official documents could be considered contracts if you looked at them properly – or possibly a little sideways. And sometimes a Witnessing that did not use paper and wax and signatures was harder to evade.

Franz-Karl could see under the table that Justice von Trebice was counting the repetitions on his fingers. All four repetitions. When he finished the last repetition, he bowed to His Royal Grace acting Archduke Uncle Helm-Friedrich, picked up the pamphlet, handed it back to the clerk, and finally scrambled up into his chair. He was careful not to meet the eyes of either his Mama or Fritzel, who had understood exactly what he was singing. He was afraid that he would start laughing, or they would.

There was a long pause. Franz-Karl used the flat end of his stylus to smooth out one of the tablets that was filled with his wax sketches of newts and began to fill the smoothed wax with a sketch of the traditional graffito that stood for the Death of Rano. He was fairly certain that since he was in line to be Duke of Traventi, the Binding he had just created would be sealed by the Curse of Rano as soon as anyone now present in the room died. Until then, the Binding might be breakable by someone with a large amount of Manifest weight. Reverend Count Great Aunt Adrasteia might carry enough weight. Or she might need Count Valens to help. He had used a very emphatic version of the Binding.

Finally, His Royal Grace acting Archduke Uncle Helm-Friedrich said, "Your Serene Grace, Grand Duke Franz-Karl, may I ask what you just did."

Franz-Karl looked up and met the acting Archduke's eyes. His uncle flinched slightly, and he wondered if his eyes were doing something strange, or possibly his shadow was.

He could tell that his hair was being strange: it had completely abandoned the ribbon that tied it back at the nape of his neck. But that was not unusual for him. He could see some of the tendrils wavering slightly in the edges of his vision, which was far less usual.

Franz-Karl said, very calmly, in crystal clear Diplomatic Remoran, "The Rules of Order of the Privy Council of the Falkenburg Eastlands have been Witnessed by a Notary of Traventi and inscribed on the walls of the Living World. People attending meetings of the Falkenburg Privy Council under the auspices of Your Royal Grace or any of your successors are now fully Bound to observe the current Rules of

Order, along with any future modifications that may be formally adopted."

Franz-Karl shifted in his chair, which was not intended for a person his size. Standing had truly been more comfortable. His Uncle was still silent, so he added helpfully, still in Remoran, "The Binding attaches to the Council defined in the document, not to the specific Councilors and Observers present today. I do not believe that the Binding will kill anyone, even if they break the rules... It might cause them to lose their voices if they insist on speaking out of turn: how permanently is their choice, not mine."

"Your Honor, may I ask: could you choose to kill them?" Justice von Trebice asked, after His Royal Grace waved him to speak. His Remoran was even less accented than his Allemanic. The Justice always used Franz-Karl's proper titles and style.

"Well, not for rudeness, of course." Franz-Karl smiled, more or less, and his fingers moved... not quite as if he was counting. Two of the Ecclesialists in the Council signed themselves. He said very clearly, "During my minority I am barred from using immediately deadly Bindings unless I am attacked or someone is attacked in my presence. And as a sworn Notary I have pledged to try to exercise due proportion in my responses to attacks. Accidents are always possible, but the precision of Elderic makes them less likely than they would be in a squishier language like Allemanic or Remoran."

"I am sure we all appreciate your Grace's restraint," His Royal Grace acting Archduke Uncle Helm-Friedrich said dryly in Allemanic.

Franz-Karl shrugged with both shoulders: people in this place might not recognize the one-sided Traventine shrug. "'It is good to be useful, meritorious to encourage courtesy'." he quoted, still in Remoran. "If there are any other committees that might benefit by being Bound more closely to proper civility, I shall of course be glad to assist Your Royal Grace."

His Royal Grace acting Archduke Uncle Helm-Friedrich looked at Franz-Karl for a long moment, then turned back to the rest of the table. By the time he was looking down the length of the table at the Councilors, he was smiling. Franz-Karl was glad he was not the one being smiled at by that smile. He doubted that his own shadow was doing anything that scary.

His Royal Grace flicked a hand at one specific clerk, who stepped forward to place a silver tray on the table. On the tray was a note written entirely in His Excellency's own hand and sealed with the Falkenburg seal. When the clerk read it aloud, it reminded the members of the Falkenburg Privy Council and any others in His Excellency's service that because His Excellency had personally sworn to uphold the Marriage Contract of Leon-Alexander von Falkenburg and Silvia di Armorius, any deliberate interference with the provisions of the Contract was ignoring an imperial edict and should be counted as treasonous anywhere within the borders of the Falkenburg Domains.

It seemed that Franz-Karl was not the only one who had reached the limits of his temper.

The decorum enforced by Franz-Karl's Binding prevented the uproar that might otherwise have occurred after His Excellency's note was read. It seemed to him that most of the officials present had never previously considered the Marriage Contract as a decree from His Excellency's hand, despite the signatures. Some of the men, mostly the Ecclesialist Falkenburg vassals that were proper members of the Falkenburg Privy Council, were clearly surprised, but seemed relieved to be told in so many words to treat the Marriage Contract as an edict from His Excellency. It provided a quick way to end some arguments.

The Harfnerans in the room were divided in their reactions, but the division did not follow the line between vassals of the Falkenburg Domains and vassals from other parts of the Allemanic Kingdom. Or at least, Franz-Karl did not think so. There were only a few Harfnerans present, and he did not know how many estates they had on various sides of which borders.

The Margraff-Elector of Ansbach and the Prince-Elector of Bremerhaven did not at all like His Excellency's letter, and the other members of their faction and allied factions – mostly Pristinists or vassals from the Allemanic North or both – followed their lead. Despite the unhappiness of the Northern Lords, His Royal Grace the acting Archduke did not call on anyone from outside the Falkenburg territories. They were not invited to comment about His Excellency's Note, and they were prevented from yelling by Franz-Karl's Binding. The two members of the College of Electors looked like puppets, with their mouths opening and closing and no sound being heard. Eventually, the Northern lords decided that opening and closing their mouths with no sound coming out was undignified, and they subsided into quiet seething.

Neither the Binding nor His Excellency's 'reminder' note prevented arguments, but together they ensured that the arguments that occurred were related to the official topics and agenda for the Council session, which was the problems of the Marriage Contract. Acting Archduke Uncle Helm-Friedrich stopped calling on anyone who did not speak to the point, so the discussion was able to move forward. Slowly.

The note and Binding did not prevent stupidity, either. After one senior official failed to answer a plain question three times, His Royal Grace summoned guards to remove the man to safe storage. He also sent senior auditors to examine the fellow's offices and accounts, referring to him by name, not by title or office. Two of the other officials present turned pale and began sweating at that. His Royal Grace did not bother arresting them: unlike some others at the table, they were not important enough to have small armies awaiting their call, or to employ entire companies of bodyguards. He just sent more messengers to seal their offices and added them to the list for the auditors' attentions.

Finally, His Royal Grace acting Archduke Uncle Helm-Friedrich turned back to Franz-Karl, speaking formally in Diplomatic Remoran. "Your Honor? Given the Marriage Contract as it stands, in the view of the Notaries of Traventi, is there anything at all that can be usefully done about the breach of the twenty-fifth section of the Marriage Contract?"

Franz-Karl climbed down out of his chair again. Several people flinched, including both of the Northern Electors who were present: they had stopped trying to interrupt after the first bit of silent mouth flapping, but they were both scowling. The Prince-Elector of Bremerhaven was leaning back in his chair with his arms crossed – which was not proper, but at least he was not trying to make a fuss. The Margraff-Elector of Ansbach was sitting rigidly, with his gloved hands on the arms of his chair and his lips pressed together so tightly that Franz-Karl wondered whether they were going numb.

Franz-Karl bowed to His Royal Grace, then stood in the formal pose for recitation of school lessons and such. He spoke in Diplomatic Remoran, not Allemanic: the question had been in Remoran, and it was about Traventi, which used Elderic and Remoran, but not Allemanic. "It is written that in order for a breach to occur, an element of intention or negligence must be involved. If one party to an agreement has not received a benefit that they were promised, but the counter-party claims that failure was contrary to their intention and efforts, the situation must be investigated." He swallowed. "The commentators say: Name the culprit. Name the penalty. Then negotiations can begin in the full knowledge that the one side has been injured and the other has been demonstrated to be untrustworthy."

"Hypothetically, Your Honor, what if there was external meddling?" Justice von Trebice asked. He and his clerk had both written down a number of notes during Franz-Karl's recitation.

"I am not a trained advocate, not by some years of study," Franz-Karl said carefully, "but I have been told that – hypothetically and given the absolute wording in the contract – the claim might be made that the Falkenburgs negligently failed their obligation to prevent the external meddling."

The Justice nodded and added to his notes. His Royal Grace winced.

There were two other Justices in the room, invited – unlike the Northern Lords – to help unravel the existing legal mess. One of them asked, with the permission of His Royal Grace, "Is there precedence in Traventi for disregarding unexpected factors?"

"There is precedence in Traventi that if someone swears that a thing will be done, being dead without heirs is no reason the oath should not be fulfilled... but that is rare even among Elderkin," Franz-Karl said seriously. "As a less extreme case...according to the chronicles there was a man who swore absolutely that certain property would be handed over at the midpoint of a bridge, but the bridge was swept away in a flood before the appointed day. He paid for the building of a barge that was towed to the place where the bridge had been, and anchored there with great effort just before the appointed hour so that he would have a place to keep his appointment. Afterward, of course, he gave the barge to be built into the new bridge." Franz-Karl paused for a beat. "That story is taught among Traventine Notaries and Advocates as a warning against the kind of absolute phrasing we see in the twenty-fifth section of the Marriage Contract. It is told among other folk to explain why the construction of the Oath Bridge is so odd. I have walked across that bridge and spoken to descendants from both sides of that bargain."

One of the justices said, "Dear Heaven."

The other asked, "Do your chronicles mention any attempts to break this Rano's Curse that you have mentioned?"

Franz-Karl rolled his eyes, and hoped that they could see him do it, despite his eyes lacking whites. He said as patiently as he could manage, "The scholars of Traventi say that the varieties of Bindings include three kinds of death curses: the kind that kill people outright, the kind that are triggered by the death of the caster, and the kind that are driven by deaths as mills are driven by wind or water. Rano's Curse was triggered by his death and is driven by the many deaths on the Battlefield of the Desolation. It is not generally counted as a curse of the sort that are deadly outright, but people who plan to poke at it tend to die... mmm ... memorably? ... before they make their attempt." Franz-Karl used the one-shouldered Traventine shrug. "If someone wants to break the curse, then as a traditional matter of policy the Council of Traventi cordially invites them to try." He counted on his fingers. "Maximianus Rano died 27 years before the Ecclesial gathering in Alexandria that defined the boundaries and structure of the Holy Church. Rano's curse has remained Bound since then, and most likely strengthened over time."

"Fourteen centuries..." someone murmured. It sounded like Justice von Trebice's accent.

"Nearly," Franz-Karl agreed cheerfully. "I have not seen any records of attempts as recent as the past five centuries, but I have not looked for them. Some of the deaths mentioned in the older chronicles were extremely memorable. People in Traventi tend to point and laugh at the tombs of those who tried and failed... provided that there was enough left to bury. Sometimes there are merely changes of terrain."

Chief Justice von Trebice said, "I assume the deaths of the failures are added to the battlefield dead?"

"Decent people do not discuss such things in front of small children... which is sometimes annoying. But the chronicles are less reserved: I suspect that Your Honor is correct, but the matter is presently outside my scope as a Notary."

His Royal Grace the acting Archduke Uncle Helm-Friedrich suffered a small coughing fit. When he had recovered himself, he looked around the table, considered for a long moment, then ended the Council session for the day.

The Lords Elector left the room immediately after His Royal Grace, which might not be entirely correct in what was formally a

Falkenburg gathering, but no one was inclined to argue the matter. The Margraff-Elector was looking very stiff and even paler than usual, and getting in the way of his retinue seemed unwise.

Justice von Trebice offered Franz-Karl's Mama his arm, which confused a couple of Lords who wanted to cut in front of her. The two men paused and bowed politely and waited their turn to walk through the doors eyeing the Elderkin warily. Franz-Karl and Fritzel followed the Justice and Franz-Karl's Mama, and two of the Justice's clerks trailed behind.

They walked down to the ground level in the main Palace and out into the Palace grounds away from ears before Justice von Trebice asked, "Your Honor, may I ask... was that planned ahead?"

"Planned ahead?" Franz-Karl was confused for a moment, then said, "Oh... No... I did not conspire with His Royal Grace acting Archduke Uncle Helm-Friedrich. Before the session started I saw some of the Northern Lords talking to some evil men... planning more evil under the roof of his Excellency my Grandfather! Then I could see those Electors sitting at the table planning to turn the courtesy of honest men into a weapon against them, as they have done every session. I got angry. And I remembered a story I heard in Traventi. So I stopped them from being rude."

"I thought there were rules about things like that," the Justice said. "Making people change."

"There are." Franz-Karl's Mama did not sound angry or worried , she sounded like she was trying not to laugh.

"I did not make them polite! I don't think Heaven and all of the saints could make those awful people be polite: not without dunking them in a couple of hells and a rebirth as something pitiful... and in any case, I'm not allowed to change people until I am grown up. I just asked the Living World to enforce the official protocols for the council session. Those people are as rude as ever in their hearts, and they can be as rude as they want outside the council sessions. They can even be rude in the council sessions if the presiding official lets them... but only if he lets them." Franz-Karl was still annoyed at the way acting Archduke Uncle Helm-Friedrich had been letting a bunch of observers trample over the rules and bully the council. He did not really expect things would improve much in the future.

Justice von Trebice stopped walking and turned to look at Franz-Karl. "Your Honor... asked the Living World?"

Franz-Karl looked up at him. "The protocols were like... like a labyrinth laid out with ropes on the ground. Polite people walked in the marked paths, but rude people trompled wherever they wanted to, and shoved people out of their way. Now the labyrinth is like tall stone walls instead of just ropes." He took a step back so that he could look the Justice in the eyes more easily. "They should be glad I did not ask for something like walls of thorns or stinging nettles: I think the Living World offered that." He bowed very slightly, Notary to client, and turned to continue along the path to the West Palace without waiting to see whether his Mama and the Justice were ready to continue walking.

Fritzel, at his shoulder, asked quietly in Elderic, "The World's getting tetchy, is it?"

Franz-Karl sighed. "I don't know... ask me when I'm twelve, maybe." Twelve seemed very far away. And Initiation and his majority were nearly twice as far. He felt tired just thinking about all of that time. Fritzel gripped his shoulder briefly, not long enough that anyone who noticed could make a fuss.

# INTERLUDE IV: The Pristinist Echelon

## *Wherein a Purgation Begins*

The Electoral Princes did not ... quite ... flee from the room where the Falkenburg Privy Council sessions took place, but they did not hesitate even a little once they were released. The few attendants permitted withing the Council chamber stayed close. The members of their retinues waiting outside the Council chamber had to move with unseemly haste to join their superiors.

The Margraff-Elector was just outside the Palace Gate when his stomach rebelled, though it did not produce much since he had not eaten recently. His retinue shielded him from view but kept a safe distance to avoid being spattered.

When he straightened he saw a proclamation by His Excellency posted by the gate on a board that was commonly used for announcements of executions. It was a formal announcement that the Marriage Contract and two other unrelated treaties had full force as Imperial Edicts.

His stomach tried to empty itself again, but there was nothing left to purge.

The Margraff-Elector reached his home and rinsed the taste of bile from his mouth with a glass of sweet wine before he proceeded to the

White Hall. He did not eat anything before stepping through the entrance of the White Hall after the Council session, though his servants offered his customary light meal.

The Prince-Elector of Bremerhaven, paused to eat a little bread and cheese before he followed his colleague into the gathering of the Pristinist Echelon. He drank beer, not wine.

The Margraff-Elector was already in his seat, but the Prince-Elector paused long enough to inform the Preacher and the Teacher, "We will need a full rite of Purgation for those that have suffered the influence of the beast-born," before he sat in his own chair of state. His voice was little more than a whisper.

The various retinue members who had been inside the Council chamber remained standing, gathered around their lords, since there was nowhere for them to sit. Even the General of the Army of the Empire, who had not attended the council session and had arrived shortly after the other Select, would need to stand through the rite.

"They dared..." the Margraff-Elector said, in a voice that was a harsh whisper shaking with emotion. "The Falkenburgs dared to use beast-born vileness to constrain us..." He swallowed hard. Twice.

The Teacher began paging through the volumes of Writings and Commentaries, placing markers by the passages he would read aloud during the Purgation rite.

The Margraff-Elector glared at Preacher Weiss. "This corruption among the Falkenburgs should be denounced. Publicly," he forced out.

"The Writings assure us that beast-born are capable of nothing but mindless violence and chaos unless they are aimed and directed by a human master," the Preacher said calmly, looking up from his own books. "Who directed the beast-born at the council session?"

"Acting Archduke Helm-Friedrich," the Prince-Elector answered promptly, but very softly. "He had an order from his Excellency ready as well... a very emphatic one." He shook his head ruefully. "The Binding was made to enforce the Rules of Order for the Council session: it was impressively subtle work."

"Then a public protest would be both inappropriate and unwise," the Preacher said calmly.

The Margraff-Elector straightened in his chair, then leaned toward the Preacher. "WHAT?" It would have been a shriek if his vocal chords were working.

The Preacher stepped back, but only half a step. "Pristinus de Millau himself wrote that use of the beast-born by those who own them is lawful and even meritorious on certain occasions. And the First Lawful Occasion for making use of the beast-born is to chastise insolent or disobedient subordinates. A Binding that enforces respectful behavior by subordinates is the purest example of the First Lawful Occasion that I have heard of."

The Teacher began to move some of his markers in the Writings.

The Margraff-Elector huffed, "Our actions are entirely aimed at the protection and prosperity of the Holy Remoran Empire."

The Teacher winced. The Preacher answered calmly, "The definition of the First Lawful Occasion says nothing about goals: it mentions only demeanor and obedience ... or the lack of it. His Excellency and the acting Archduke seem to disagree with your judgment of the matter, as is their prerogative as overlords."

The General said, almost dreamily and to no one in particular, "When a subordinate is chastised, it is the superior who decides on the necessity and amount of discipline." He looked around. "I see plenty of witnesses for the Purgation... and I have duties to attend to. I'll take my leave, for the moment."

As he turned toward the entrance, the Margraff-Elector suddenly stood, took a few quick steps – shoving the General aside – and went to one knee with his head outside the purified space of the White Hall. After another bout of retching, he stood and continued out into the main part of the house. The General shook his head and followed, stepping around the tiny puddle of wine and bile that was already being attended to by a slave. A few other members of the Echelon who had not been at the Council session followed him, but others stayed to serve as witnesses.

The Teacher sighed and moved a few more markers in his texts. On the one hand, the teachings of Pristinus de Millau excused a sick man from Purgation until he recovered unless the matter was so dire that a risk of death was acceptable. On the other, the rite could not end properly with the highest ranked member of the local Echelon left abandoned among the Defiled. Ending the rite at all became complicated if the delay was extended: there were specific texts that applied in that case.

The Preacher began the other preparations for the Purgation for the Prince-Elector and the other men who been affected by the Council Binding. The lowest ranked free man of the Echelon who required

Purgation stripped to his shirt and breeches – removing hat, gloves, shoes, stockings, coat and waistcoat – before kneeling before the pair of lecterns.

The rest of the free men present settled and braced themselves. A thorough Purgation required stamina, and a recently-arrived Preacher, tasked with Purging a community whose Select had just been chastised by a sworn overlord, was more likely to be thorough than hasty.

The first beneficiary of the Purgation had not been present at the Council meeting. Heinrich Bauer was a ferociously righteous man who had never set foot inside the Palace gates. But he stood at the bottom of the Echelon because he had been born a serf, bound to the land, though he had been freed when young by some whim or need of his lord. Whenever the Echelon in Karnburg performed a Purgation, it began with Heinrich Bauer doing penance for abandoning his proper status in the world.

Some years earlier, when the Old Teacher who died in the siege still presided in Karnburg, the penances required of Bauer had often been perfunctory. Now, the presiding Teacher was Bauer's son, and the other men at the bottom of the Echelon made very sure that Heinrich Bauer received the full benefit of the rites of purification every time there was a Purgation.

The results of the rite for Bauer were never really satisfactory, and could not be. Even in the Northern provinces, once the bond tying a man to the land was broken, it was difficult to repair the gap in the world's order. At the very least, repair would require the cooperation of the freedman's former lord. Matters in Karnburg were even worse: the city had laws that could free a serf – far too easily in Pristinist views – or even free a slave, but no laws that would bind a free man to the soil and few that would enslave one. So Bauer performed his penance over and over, but the damage to the order of the world was not affected. His answers to the formal Questions that ended the rite could not change.

Once Bauer's penance was done and the witnesses were helping him to rise and dress, the Teacher and Preacher turned their attention to one of the Margraff-Elector's retinue, the lowest ranked man that had been present in the Council session when the beast-born's Binding had been placed on those present.

The process began with a detailed recitation of what the man had seen and heard and experienced when the Binding was applied, repeated and expanded through the Questions until the witnesses and Preacher were satisfied that it was complete. The Penance exacted was harsh and lengthy, since some of his early answers were deemed unsatisfactory, and the readings during both the recitation and penance included quite a lot of quotations about unfaithful servants. In the end, the results of the Purgation were nearly as unsatisfactory to the Echelon as Bauer's purification: the effects of the Binding could be fenced and limited so that it would not affect other aspects of the man's life, but would retain full force in matters related to the Council, so the taint of contact with the beast-born remained.

The Prince-Elector's lowest attendant was next, with a similar process and result, followed by a body-guard for each Elector. None of the four men had struggled against the Binding, but that did not weaken its hold on them.

Two clerks serving as secretaries – one for each Elector – had been left silenced and fumbling by the Binding. The Purgation returned their voices – eventually – and the skill to their hands, but the Teacher and the Preacher cautioned them very strongly toward care and obedience during Council sessions and urged caution in other matters.

The night had passed its midpoint and was lengthening toward dawn before it was time for the Purgation of the Prince-Elector of Bremerhaven. His recitation was factual: it needed to match the descriptions by the six men who had gone before him or his answers would be rejected. His answers to the Questions were prompt and careful and nearly satisfactory. But he did not mention any plans or intentions that he or his colleague might have had, nor any events that might have happened outside the chamber where the Council met. When the rite was over, his voice remained somewhat hoarse, and his hands still suffered a slight tremor. His attendants dealt with the buttons on his garments. He left the White Hall with as much dignity as he could manage.

# CHAPTER X: News from Traventi

## *Wherein Rumors of Sickness Arrive*

The morning after the council session when Franz-Karl set the Binding, he expected that they would spend much of the day in another Council session, but pigeons from Traventi arrived before breakfast: three of them, each bearing the same message in the simplest merchant code, a code that was used for reasons of space, not secrecy. There were just nine symbols: combinations of letters and numbers that identified the entries in the code book. The message read: "Greater Plague Law Decreed in Traventi. Something new. From the South. From the Sea. Stock for Siege. Water. Wood. Beware Fire. Look East."

Franz-Karl's Mama picked up one copy of the decoded message, read it again, and said, "I must report this to the proper officials here in Karnburg and the Palace." She looked at her children and added, "This may be nothing – there are often alarms about sickness in the first merchant parties that arrive after the months of no news." As an Elderkin and a Notary she could not make false statements, but that did not prevent words that came from hope rather than certain knowledge, and these sounded... blurred... to Franz-Karl.

He picked up one of the message copies to look at it for himself, and did not like what he saw: 'stock for siege', from Count Great Aunt Adrasteia or Count Valens was not likely to be nothing. He held up the slip of paper. "Damian at Greenoak Square needs to see this, in case their pigeons were taken by hawks or storms. It's a long flight from Traventi... but I need Fritzel with me."

His valet, Tam, stood immediately. "I'll take it, Your Honor. If I reach the West Gate before the watch change I'll have no trouble getting out. Coming back... "

"If you need to wait for the return of the night guards, do so," Franz-Karl said firmly, handing him the message slip. "It is now acknowledged Falkenburg law that Elderkin must reach my mother promptly, but the common soldiers may not have heard, or listened, and executing some treasonous fool will not undo whatever harm you may take... Fritzel?" He picked up another copy of the message.

"Coming, Your Honor." Franz-Karl's aide stuffed the last half of a roll into his mouth and finished chewing it while Franz-Karl changed into his very finest color-of-sorrow waistcoat and coat. "I don't carry a blade for this?"

"Not where we're going first," Franz-Karl agreed.

They hurried down to the tunnel below the Palace grounds and across to the main Palace building, avoiding the guards and door-wardens at ground level in both Palace buildings. Franz-Karl did not know exactly where to find his quarry, but that did not matter. He simply kept moving toward whichever guard he could see that was dressed the most ornately, while being careful not to let the guards notice him or Fritzel. When they were past the last guard in the series, he tapped politely on the door, but did not wait for a summons before he opened it and they slipped inside.

Fritzel leaned against the door while Franz-Karl advanced into the room.

Their Excellencies Franz-Karl's Grandparents were seated at a small table wearing dressing gowns, finishing the last bits of their breakfast before they dressed for the day. They were attended only by His Excellency's valet and Her Excellency's chief Maid of Honor. His Excellency looked toward the door with annoyance at the interruption, saying, "Who?" but immediately smiled when he saw who it was. "Franz-Karl, dear boy. Come join us."

Franz-Karl took the small paper bearing the message out of his pocket. "I regret, Your Excellency..." He bowed formally. "We have received a message from Traventi. My Mama is informing the proper officials, but I thought your Excellencies should be informed more directly. Despite the laws about blocking messages, some new still flows like treacle in midwinter."

Her Excellency Franz-Karl's Grandmother went pale and pressed her hands to her dressing gown below her breasts. "Has Her Grace come to harm?"

His Excellency signed himself.

"We don't know... can't know," Franz-Karl felt tired thinking about the time that would pass before settled news arrived. "The borders are closed to all but the pigeons, and no others had arrived before I came here. The message holds nine codes: Greater Plague Law Decreed in Traventi. Something new. From the South. From the Sea. Stock for Siege. Water. Wood. Beware Fire. Look East."

"Look east?" his Excellency said thoughtfully.

"The Daonas flows east, but ocean ships and river boats are much faster than mule trains. Troubles that reaches Traventi by walking north from the ports on the Mothersea are more likely to come here to Karnburg by sailing around the coasts and then coming upriver," Franz-Karl suggested.

"Ships also carry more than mules," his Excellency agreed wearily. A small clock on the mantelpiece chimed, and he glared at it. "I will be conferring with the acting Archduke ... very shortly. I will ensure that he knows of this news."

Franz-Karl bowed , then looked directly at Her Excellency His Grandmother. "His Highness Prince Otto of Karnburg should, perhaps, also be warned. The Traventine Embassy unfortunately has no formal contacts with the city government."

Her Excellency smiled a little at that: Prince Otto was her twin brother. "I shall suggest that he should remedy that," she agreed.

Franz-Karl bowed to her, then looked at his aide. There were sounds beginning to come from beyond a door opposite the one they had used to enter. Fritzel listened at their door and held up a hand, folding down one finger after another. On five, they slipped out of the room.

Moving out into the more public areas of the Palace was easier than moving toward Their Excellencies, since the guards were not watching for people moving away from the fount of authority. That was not a reason to be sloppy, of course: guards could be mean.

When they were back in a quiet part of the servants' passages, Fritzel said "Back to our apartments?"

"Not yet... perhaps... I hope this will work..."

Franz-Karl followed the stairway all the way down to a secondary kitchen. It was not the fancy kitchen where the important foreign chefs presided and produced banquets for Their Excellencies, but a kitchen that fed the main Palace's workers and lesser residents. The chief cook in this kitchen was a stout woman with the look of the Old Palace Servants. He bowed to her politely. "Rathvin." The Servants did not exactly have their own language – at least not one that they used in public – but they mixed a lot of special words with the Palace Allemanic that they spoke. Franz-Karl was almost certain that this word was a title of respect, and a bit less sure that he had pronounced it properly.

She eyed him. "Your Honor." In moderately accented Elderic, no less. This was very encouraging.

"If the Faithful Ones look to elders or leaders not appointed by the Chamberlains, I believe it would be a useful thing for me to confer with such a person." A polite register of Palace Allemanic, not quite equals, but not Noble to servant, either.

She shooed a boy who was peeling turnips away from a small table, settled Franz-Karl and Fritzel in chairs beside it, and wordlessly provided all of the items that would have constituted a proper Elderkin guest-welcome if they had been accompanied by the formal spoken formulas. When they had eaten and sipped, she said quietly, "If Your Honor will kindly wait a bit?" The title was Elderic, the rest, Allemanic.

"Of course."

The kitchens were not quite basements: seen from inside, there were strips of windows along the tops of the walls that were only obscured by the deepest winter snows. But the room that Franz-Karl and Fritzel were eventually brought to was definitely an attic room, at the top of long, narrow flights of shabby stairs that most Nobles ignored. There were only a few tiny, nearly opaque, windows, and use of candles by servants was strictly regulated by the Palace authorities, so the room was very dim. Though it was perhaps less dim to Elderkin eyes than to the servants that were housed there.

They were faced by five Servants, including the cook: two men, two women, and an ancient person swathed in shawls who might be either.

After the message was repeated, one of the men, whose face showed pockmarks, said warily, "New is bad? I don't understand these warnings."

"Do you yourself greatly fear the return of the smallpox?" Franz-Karl replied. The man shook his head slowly, but still seemed mystified. The one good thing that could be said for that affliction was that almost no one suffered it more than once. Franz-Karl sighed. "Karnburg and the Palace together hold plenty of fuel for a plague's burning, but beside them? Traventi is three handfuls of straw on bare rock: plagues that strike once burn out quickly for lack of fuel... and ten days by mule train to the nearest settled places provides a fair quarantine. When measles or smallpox return only one year in fifty, they return to a fallow field, new each time, so we know the habits of new plagues well, in Traventi."

Fritzel had survived a measles onslaught when he was small, so he could speak as a witness. "When measles comes to a new place it sickens nine in ten that encounter it, all at once, so the sick are left to tend the sick. One in ten passed by is not enough when they may also be too young or too old, or ailing from some other cause, and so are unable to sustain the needs of life. One or two of the nine will die, eventually, of the measles itself. How many others will die with them, of mischance or lack of care?" He shrugged and held out his hands. "Hunger will not improve their hope of survival, but measles and small pox burn fast enough that the sick are not likely to starve outright, not that season. But sick or well, people must have water and they must have warmth, with water that is heavy and firewood that is bulky, and flame that is unchancy when those that tend it are weakened and shaking, or mazed by fever."

The Servants looked at each other and nodded. One made a 'go on' gesture.

Franz-Karl took a deep breath and straightened his shoulders. "Is it permitted to draw water from the well in the tunnels? Or light a taper from the flame? Fire can be a problem for being lost as much as for spreading unwanted."

"You expect that much trouble?" The other woman – not the cook – not doubting: still honestly questioning.

"When ancient sorcerers offer advice freely, only a fool ignores it. Besides, I have heard it said..." he quoted the blades-man's speech about denying support to abominations, mimicking the man's Northern accent, then added, "Better to prepare what we can, and have no need of it than to trust in promises that often have been unreliable and find ourselves wanting."

The old person said quietly, "The flame and the waters are no mortal's to offer or deny. But take care not to foul the water or quench the flame. An offering of a fresh or hard-boiled egg left by the well will not go amiss."

Franz-Karl performed his deepest, most formal bow: the one for in church, not even for His Excellency.

Fritzel asked, "Is there a place to contribute oil for the flame? Damian made a good bargain last month for a shipment from the south, so we have plenty at Greenoak Square, both early pressing and late."

The man with the pock-marks looked surprised, then bowed politely, and explained in detail where the oil store was, and how to check and refill the reservoir for the lamp.

Returning to the West Palace through the tunnel, they paused to make sure they had understood the instructions about the oil correctly. Franz-Karl checked the level of the oil in the lamp, to begin the habit of always doing it.

He tried not to mind not knowing the names of their new allies: many people avoided telling their names to Elderkin. It was almost a sign of respect. Or at least, belief.

# CHAPTER XI: Rest at Home

## *Wherein They Begin to Stock for a Siege*

Once Franz-Karl and his aide had returned to the apartments, Fritzel left on an errand elsewhere and Franz-Karl looked for his Mama. She had left, accompanied by a pair of footmen, to present a report about the message from Traventi to the Chancellor's office, and had not yet returned. He told his Mama's aide, Itron Gwenlian, about his conversations with their Excellencies and the Old Palace Servants so that his Mama would hear about them as soon as possible.

With that task completed, he returned to the Nursery he shared with Sophie-Alexa to change out of his 'audience with the Emperor' coat and waistcoat. The color-of-sorrow garments were dull – and very boring after all these months – but the fabric was some of the finest available, and he would really prefer to avoid tearing or staining his finest court clothes before he either out-grew them or was finally able to set formal mourning aside and wear ordinary colors again.

Good buttons were as expensive as good cloth, if you counted the work of attaching them and creating the elegant buttonholes, and they did not technically count at decoration so they were not prohibited during mourning the way embroidery and braid would have been. The best court clothes of Franz-Karl von Falkenburg, grandson of the Emperor and King of the Allemans, Recognized Heir in the line of Succession of the Sovereign Duchy of Traventi and fully sworn Notary, had about twice as many buttons as might be expected even with all of those titles. Even though not all of the buttons were functional, it still took a while to button or unbutton them: the fabric around the buttonholes was stiffened so that they would lie flat, and did not cooperate with small seven-year old fingers. Some of the buttons that needed to be unfastened were also hard to reach: no one expected nobles to be able to dress and undress themselves... wearing clothes that you could not manage yourself proved that you were important enough not to need to.

Nurse Rosa was busy with Sophie-Alexa and both Fritzel and Tam were attending to important matters, so Franz-Karl carefully worked his way down the front of his coat until he could take it off and set it carefully aside. The sleeve cuffs were open enough that those buttons did not need to be undone. Tam would undo them when he put the coat away so that the buttonholes did not stretch in storage.

The buttons on the waistcoat were smaller and nearly as numerous, and the fabric was less sturdy. The sleeve cuffs were tight enough that they should be unbuttoned and loose enough that it was very tempting not to, especially after doing all of the other buttons, so it was safer to do them first. Franz-Karl was working on the cuff buttons on his off hand when a messenger from the Falkenburg Privy Council was announced.

Franz-Karl had him shown in: it would take too long to get dressed enough to be seen outside his own room. He managed the last cuff button and continued unbuttoning the front of his waistcoat. Messengers saw a lot of partly undressed nobles, because otherwise nothing would ever get delivered with any timeliness. He looked up as the man entered and gave him a bow that was little more than a nod.

The man was clearly surprised to be shown into a children's nursery, but he delivered his message: a summons to the Privy Council session.

Franz-Karl thought about the situation as he continued unbuttoning: even if he went to the Privy Council session, it would not be in this waistcoat. The summons said nothing about his Mama, and he did not know what announcements were planned, or when. His

Excellency and Franz-Karl's Mama were the ones who should decide when the news from Traventi should be announced generally – Franz-Karl had already gone a bit past what was strictly proper in his dealings with the Servants, but instructing servants to make preparations was not quite the same as mentioning things out of turn to the people who officially mattered.

He was quite sure that he could not sit in that room full of men busily tearing the Marriage Contract and their own oaths into tiny sharp splinters to affront the Living World, and know that there was Plague in Traventi, and say nothing.

He said, "No" now, then carefully set aside the waistcoat, and sat down to remove his boots. That messenger should feel honored: it was very rare for Elderkin outside of Traventi to remove their shoes or boots in front of strangers. If it caused a fuss, Franz-Karl would move to Greenoak Square, or possibly farther...

He took his brightly painted carved wooden horse down from the shelf where it usually lived, climbed up onto his bed, and pulled a blanket up to his waist.

The messenger said, "Your Grace, you are needed at the Council session." He sounded tired.

"Those stupid grownups don't need me to help them find new ways to break their oaths!" Franz-Karl hugged his horse, Harvest Prince, and rolled onto his side so that his back was to the man. He closed his eyes.

He expected more argument, but the messenger tugged the blanket into a tidier arrangement, patted Franz-Karl on the shoulder, and went away.

Itron Gwenlian came into the room, closed the drapes at his end of the nursery, felt his forehead, and quietly went away again. Franz-Karl kept his eyes closed and petted Harvest Prince's nose.

"Hsst. Hsst." Someone poked Franz-Karl. He knew it was Philip-Augustus: he recognized the hiss, and his brother always poked him in the same spot. Franz-Karl was not sure whether he made a special effort, or it just happened that way.

Franz-Karl opened his eyes. The sunlight in Sophie-Alexa's end of the nursery had moved while his eyes were closed, and his little sister was laying on top of his blanket, fully dressed and curled against him like a cat. Philip-Augustus was standing beside his bed, preparing to poke him again. Franz-Karl moved the wooden horse in the way.

Philip-Augustus said, "Wake up! There are things happening!"

Tam appeared from the little room where he took care of the clothes and helped Franz-Karl into a respectable waistcoat and coat, and gave him a pair of house-shoes to wear instead of boots. Palace nobles did not hug their valets – not without being gossiped about, anyway – but Elderkin children hugged those who cared for them. Franz-Karl glad that Tam had returned safely well before evening, so he hugged Tam, and was hugged back, before his hair was attacked by a few token strokes of a comb.

There was a joke in the household that either Franz-Karl's hair had eaten at least two combs or the combs had run away in shame at their own failures. Where Fritzel's short pelt always looked tidy, Franz-Karl's locks clumped into tendrils that resisted combing and actively pulled themselves out of hair ties, so his hair was almost never properly styled. The green streaks were getting more assertive, too.

Philip-Augustus had been jittering from one foot to the other while Franz-Karl got ready to leave the nursery. He led the way to the end of the Residence where most of the attendants had their rooms, and where some rooms had been emptied as less attention was paid to the requirements of the Marriage Contract.

One of the ways the Marriage Contract was broken was that it said that Franz-Karl's Mama should have five Elderkin Ladies in Waiting, but they had been treated so badly in the Palace that they had all been driven away except the Itron Gwenlian. The room that had been used by a lady named Juliana until shortly after Sophie-Alexa's birth now had its door open. The bed had been taken out and there was firewood stacked against one wall – not big logs for heating, but the smaller pieces that allowed adjustments to a cooking fire. The fireplace in the room, which had a flue that worked quite well – as flues in the Palace went – had been equipped for basic cooking, with a pot and kettle and griddle and the cranes and spiders to support them over the fire, and a ladle and spoons.

"Why?" Sophie-Alexa asked in Elderic.

"Stock for a siege, water, wood, and fire," Franz-Karl quoted in Elderic, then translated to Alemannic for their brother. "I wonder what they will do about the water."

He was answered by the arrival of servants carrying a pair of trestles or racks, followed by others carrying two empty beer barrels each equipped with a spigot on one end, a large funnel for filling them through their bungholes, and three lidded buckets of the sort used to carry water through the Palace without spilling or splashing it where it was not wanted. They set up the barrels, and went away.

The last man to leave was the pock-marked man Franz-Karl had spoken with that morning. He closed the room's door behind him, smiled at the children, and gave them a nod that was almost a bow. "It would be wise to keep that door closed and locked when Outsiders are about."

Franz-Karl bowed to an ally. "Of course," he said. "This is all very helpful."

"We serve the lawful owners of the Palace. That's been the Falkenburgs, recently... and there are rumors from the river wharves."

"I am not sure what we here –' Franz-Karl's wave indicated the children, and the Traventine apartments -- "can do to assist you..."

The man looked surprised: he was still thinking of himself as a servant, not an ally. He eyed Franz-Karl uncertainly. "Is it true Your Honor can see when food has gone off?"

"Very commonly. Though I'm not entirely reliable about very old cheeses and such..."

The man chuckled. "That's fair. Well, if Your Honor should have occasion to visit the pantries and storerooms, there are a few items where a word of advice might be of use."

They exchanged bows and the man went away after his colleagues.

Philip-Augustus was staring at Franz-Karl. "Is that what it was like in Traventi last year?" he asked in Allemanic.

"In Traventi? No," Franz-Karl groped for words. "In Traventi there were lots of useful grownups, so I was able to learn by watching them and listening to them. Here, if things need doing, I keep needing to do them myself, or trying and failing."

"And no shame to you that's so," Itron Gwenlian opened the door looked in, and closed it firmly. "Was that all Your Honor's idea?" All in Elderic of course. Philip-Augustus was looking confused, so Sophie-Alexa began translating for him.

"No. We told them 'stock for a siege, water and wood and beware fire' and explained why. And I told them what I heard a man say." He repeated the Northerner's comment again, adding, "and then all this just happened." He waved toward the door of Juliana's Room.

Itron Gwenlian hissed: not a sound a human voice might make. "Was that one of those councilors?"

"We did not see his face, when he spoke. But we saw a man talking to the Margraff-Elector that seems likely... Fritzel agreed on that. The man had a companion that makes it almost certain."

"His Highness Prince Otto is dining with us the day with his lady, and Her Highness Dowager Queen Gertrude and some of her people. Will Your Honor tell me that all 'just happened' as well?"

"Her Highness is a surprise entire." Franz-Karl assured her. "But I ... may have mentioned to her Excellency my Grandmother that I knew no way to contact the authorities at the Prince's House quickly, and believed Prince Otto should hear the warning sooner than later."

Itron Gwenlian nodded and smiled her close-lipped smile. "That's well thought..."

Franz-Karl spent the rest of time before dinner reading old chronicles and commentaries that did nothing to improve his mood. Plagues came rarely to Traventi, and faded quickly, but while they were present they hit hard. Plagues in the Lowlands, where there were so many people that a plague could spread and spread and spread, were often far worse.

Franz-Karl hoped that Reverend Count Great Aunt Adrasteia was just being careful, but he did not truly believe that. Adrasteia had witnessed the Death of Rano, all of those centuries ago. In more recent centuries she had adopted the form of a winged sphinx, and even though she was no bulkier than most people – and notably smaller than someone Fritzel's size – the Living World trembled at her footsteps. Doubt her judgment? No. The Gift that came with being 'born old and open-eyed' usually clouded his view of fibs and fibbers, but when he looked at the message the pigeons had brought, the warning was as clear as the clearest Sunrise. Reverend Count Great Aunt Adrasteia knew that the danger was real.

And so did he.

"Something new. From the South. From the Sea. Stock for Siege. Water. Wood. Beware Fire. Look East."

# CHAPTER XII: A Family Dinner

## *Wherein There Are Useful Discussions*

His Royal Highness Prince Otto arrived at the Traventine Residence with Her Royal Highness Princess Emilia on his arm and a secretary ready to write notes or messages trailing behind them. All three of them were very well dressed – only a notch or two below full court finery, which for a Prince of a city and his wife was very impressive – but they faded away compared to the other arrivals.

Her Royal Highness Aunt Queen Gertrude was wearing full court finery or better. She had her companion Lady Lenke on her arm, the Captain of her Szekely Hussars at her shoulder, her own secretary in attendance – a woman named Margaret: such a scandal! almost worse than the companion according to the Palace gossips – and two other Hussars she said were guards for the dangerous journey across the Palace gardens from the East Palace to the West Palace.

Franz-Karl was not entirely sure whether that last bit was sarcastic. Her Royal Highness Aunt Queen Gertrude was clearly in a mood to make other people see the error of their ways, and he thought that if she carried another mark or two of Manifest heritage her elaborate hairstyle might be dripping sparks like his Mama's hair when she was annoyed.

The Hussars wore bright, dramatic clothes with such panache that they could not really be called uniforms, despite general similarities in colors and cut. The colors they wore were neither Falkenburg colors nor the colors of the Szekely lands where Her Highness was Dowager Queen. Franz-Karl did not know whether they were anyone's historic colors, or just ones that Her Highness liked. The captain doffed his hat and made elaborate gestures with it when he bowed to Franz-Karl's Mama, and also to Sophie-Alexa, which made her giggle. His bow to Philip-Augustus, Count of Wolfsberg was elegant and formal.

The Captain's bow to Franz-Karl was respectful and antique, and included an old gesture of acknowledgment and respect to Binders and the Manifest. Followed by a wink.

The secretary wore clothes that were... sleeker... than the usual fashion for ladies. She went by a title and her family name, like a male commoner: Meisterin Wallner. People like Chamberlain von und zu Ostwald just referred to her as Margaret, as seldom as possible.

The entire Szekely party renewed their Guest oaths and oaths of alliance with the Traventine Household with full formality. Then everyone ate together, in the Traventine style.

"Has there been more news from the Duchy?" Prince Otto asked finally, when the main part of the meal was done.

Franz-Karl's Mama looked sad and shook her head.

Franz-Karl shifted in his chair. Prince Otto looked at him and said politely, "Your Honor?"

He had been reckoning the times, even in his sleep earlier. "They won't send riders during Plague Law: it would be rude to send riders who might carry the sickness along with the messages. And once pigeons fly home, they need to be taken out again in carts, which also can't be done during Plague Law, so the available pigeons cannot be used lightly."

The Hussar Captain – his name was Istvan Som – nodded, "Of course. Our eagerness for news is outrunning our sense. May I ask when would Your Honor expect news?"

"For the pigeons? Not sooner than... Fritzel? Five days, do you think?"

"That sounds about right, Your Honor." His aide answered.

Franz-Karl added sadly, "Riders will depend on the course of the sickness. If the Counts are right that this is new? There is no way to judge. If Heaven is very merciful, it is something that progresses quickly and only strikes each person once."

Her Royal Highness Aunt Queen Gertrude asked, "If the Counts are right? Are we sure there is something there at all? Or new?"

"There are codes for thirty-five kinds of sickness in the list." Franz-Karl's Mama said. "If the pigeon message said 'something new' it is unlikely to be one of those."

"Provided the signs are recognized," Prince Otto said.

"Reverend Count Valens is about a thousand years old and more than half Manifest, and Reverend Count Adrasteia is more than three quarters Manifest in her ancestry and nearly fifteen hundred years old." Franz-Karl said. "They have both seen a lot of plagues, and they have good memories. That is why the plague laws in the Duchy are so thorough, and not ignored when there seems to be reason to worry."

"If the Counts are so mighty, why aren't either of them the Duke instead of Her Grace our Grandmother?" Philip-Augustus demanded.

"Read the histories," Franz-Karl retorted. "They've each been regents, at different times and more than once each. So has Reverend Count Severin, who is centuries younger than Valens, but still much older than Worldfolk live to be. Reverend Count Adrasteia told me that human form got boring after the first thousand years. After sitting in sessions of both the Traventi Council and the Falkenburg Privy Council, I think ruling a bunch of mortals probably gets boring after a while for people that different, and probably even quicker than wearing a human form."

Her Highness Aunt Queen Gertrude snorted. "His Excellency seems to agree, though he merely counts his age in decades, not centuries. My Revered Father is very good at getting other people to preside at Council sessions in his place."

"What shape has the Reverend Count Adrasteia adopted, after she wearied of human form?" Princess Emilia asked. Her eyes were wide.

"Reverend Count Adrasteia usually appears as a winged sphinx... with leopard spots. Reverend Count Valens is ... sort of twisty and dragonish?" Franz-Karl shook his head. "I do not believe either of them is likely to raise a false alarm."

Prince Otto said, "After Her Excellency Aurelia passed the warning to me, I directed the city officials in the Riverside district to listen carefully for rumors of sickness, upriver or down. I was answered more quickly than I would have preferred. There are no clear reports of sickness in the Riverside district here yet, and nothing unusual from upriver. Downriver – eastward – would not seem suspicious if we had not been warned. There may be something there: exactly what is not yet clear."

Franz-Karl's Mama pressed her fingertips against her forehead, just at the hairline, where Franz-Karl had the buds of his horns. "The chronicles say... new cases of measles or pestilence take days to show, cholera can be faster, smallpox can take a week or a month. There may be people already in Karnburg who are sickening but not sick. Until the sickness... ripens... there is no way to tell."

"I don't think there's ever been an outbreak of cholera in the Duchy." Itron Gwenlian did not sound certain.

"The chronicles also talk about events in more crowded places. Traventi is ten days by mule train from anywhere large enough to support a really brisk pestilence. Merchants sick with anything that strikes as quickly as cholera are likely either dead or recovered before they reach us," Franz-Karl felt tired just thinking about trying to travel while sick, even if it wasn't a deadly plague. "The journey provides a partial quarantine."

"Can Traventi itself support a brisk pestilence?," Princess Emilia asked. She patted Franz-Karl's hand.

Childe Silvia shook her head. "The writers say that pestilence burns lives the way fire burns fuel. A city with a hundred thousand people can be a bonfire, and hundreds of miles of riverbank where it's hard to be more than a full day's walk from the next village will... smolder, but," she sighed. "Traventi is twenty-five thousand people, thinly scattered. And since the mountain passes are not considered reliable after Saint Denis' day in the fall or before Saint Willem's day in the spring – that's next week – it may better be said that Traventi is five and five and fifteen thousands. If the Plague Laws closed the bridges in time, it may even be five and five and nine and six, or eight and seven... starve the pestilence of victims while tending the sick and keeping the healthy safe and fed and you can wear out even a pestilence that afflicts the same person more than once."

"And if closing the bridges fails?" Prince Otto asked.

Fritzel answered him, "These past four centuries, closing the bridges has spared Over the Water about one time in four or five. The Plague Laws plan accordingly."

"I'm sorry for that," Franz-Karl said.

Fritzel shrugged. "The House on the Rock is where foreigners come first, so it is always hit hard when something arrives with them, but even so, even the Home Quarter will not be afflicted entirely. There is no good time for a pestilence, but a week before Saint Willem's Day is not the worst time for it."

"Heaven and all the saints grant we still think that three months from now," Franz-Karl said. Everyone signed themselves, though the Hussars and Lady Lenke used a different gesture from the others.

The conversation turned to matters of the Court and the city of Karnburg. Franz-Karl listened with some interest: since he had begun attending the Privy Council sessions, some of the names mentioned were turning into people, not just faceless grownups somewhere outside the Traventine Residence.

He also liked and agreed with Prince Otto's plans for improvements to the city of Karnburg outside the Palace. The roads inside the city walls were terrible, and the Prince was planning to do something about it. It would be foolish to stop making plans just because a plague might come: there was always a plague that might come, whether it was known or not. Or a drought and famine, or floods or some other disaster. And even if the plague came – when the plague came – it might not be bad enough to stop everyone from working. Workmen would need pay to feed themselves: it would be good if the plague left them time and scope to consider such matters.

# INTERLUDE V: Purgation

## *Wherein the Echelon Reaches Toward Purity*

Pristinus de Millau and his followers had reviled altars and offerings as barriers rather than bridges between Heaven and the world's people. In Pristinist practice, the proper location for the transmission of offerings was the community, and the only proper offering was the Echelon of Righteous Manhood itself, purified and fashioned into a flawless instrument of the Will of Heaven for the purpose of purifying the material world of its corruption and iniquities. Many of the writings spoke of the Echelon as the tip of a spear or blade of an ax, with the parts of community that were ineligible to join the Echelon properly serving as the shaft or haft. The rest of the material world had not even that much hope of righteousness, and existed only to be useful or convenient for the Righteous.

The activity that folded eligible men into the Echelon, justified the presence of the Echelon's existing members, and cleansed those that might be contaminated by corrupting worldly influences was called Purgation. It had been refined by de Millau and his followers from various rites of purification used by the Clergy and Initiates of older traditions before they approached the Altars and Sanctuaries of Heaven and the Gods.

The rite of Purgation properly ended with the purification of any Select at the head of the Echelon who might be clouded by the world. And it was vital that the rite of Purgation should not be left incomplete, leaving the entire Echelon possibly open to untoward influences due to a weakness at its peak. All of the members of the Echelon in Karnburg spent a long day of uneasiness because it was known that one of their Select, the Margraff-Elector of Ansbach, had been entangled by the wiles of the beast-born, and the foul influence of that Binding was not yet Purged.

Some of the Echelon's unease was because only one man, the highest-born in the Karnburg Echelon, remained to be purified. Purgation was never private, and normally Purgation was never applied to a single man, but always to groups of members of the Echelon. The witnesses included those awaiting Purging and those who had already been purged, as well as those who had no present need of Purgation.

But now there was only one man remaining to be purified of the effects of the Changeling Brat's Binding... when he was ready. And he had not heard the testimony of his companions. Purgation expected consistency among those reporting a common event, and penalized differences.

Horst-Konrad von Neumark, Margraff-Elector of Ansbach stood outside the White Hall and took a few deep breaths. He was not well, but he had not properly slept nor kept anything in his belly since the Changeling's Binding, so waiting would not improve matters. The longer he delayed, the more... unsettled... the Echelon would be and the more thorough the Purgation would need to be to reassure them of the community's righteousness. He stepped through the door into the White Hall, and paused.

Preacher Weiss gestured toward the place where a man being Purged would kneel. When Horst-Konrad glanced toward the man Bauer, the Preacher said firmly, "The Purgation begun after the session of the Privy Council has not finished. Let us complete it now."

The witnesses, including all of the men previously purged, from Bauer to the Prince-Elector, settled themselves while Horst-Konrad removed his coat and waistcoat, shoes and stockings, and then, finally, reluctantly, removed his gloves to reveal hands that had been scrubbed raw, almost to the point of being bloody. No one had seen him ungloved since the summer.

He knelt alone before the lecterns with his hands at his sides, with the witnesses of the community of the Echelon some distance away on each side. Behind him, unseen, were the questioners, a small sandglass too small to time the cooking of an egg, and the wielder of the Rod.

The Rod was made of green willow. It was thin enough to flex, too thick to bite deep, debarked and polished smooth so that it would not cut or snag. Creating it properly took skill, wielding it took more.

The core of Purgation was called the Litany of Purity by scholars, but more often referred to as the Forty-eight Questions by ordinary Pristinists. Each un-Purged man in the Echelon knelt, partly or fully stripped, before the witnesses, and answered questions until his answers to forty-eight questions posed by a small group of examiners were acceptable to the community. If he gave an answer that was unacceptable or did not answer within the time measured by the sand glass, he was usually struck with the Rod and an alternative question was posed. Sometimes the questioners or witnesses demanded details, which might still lead to the Rod.

The questions took the pattern "have you done this thing" or "have you not done this thing", and in either case the approved answer might be either "I have done this thing" or "I have not done this thing", so the man being questioned needed to stay alert. The distraction of trying to keep count of the questions asked might lead to delays or confusion. It was considered safest to simply answer, and wait for the next question or the Rod, while trying to avoid the touch of the Rod too often. There were less than one hundred possible questions, and no one spoke about what happened if the questioners during a Purgation ran out of questions. If the questions ran out, so the man was judged past correction, he would be cast out of the Echelon, which usually resulted in his enslavement. Ejection from the Echelon was rare, but not so rare for commoners that anyone could doubt that it was a real danger, though vastly unlikely for one of the Select. If he knew too much about private matters, ejection might result in a common man's death. There were occasional whispered rumors of purported members of the Select being cast out, after their falsehoods were revealed, but there were never names attached to those rumors.

Besides demanding elaboration of answers, the Witnesses could challenge the man being examined to strip farther to prove that he carried no witch-marks or signs of non-human ancestry.

Despite being weary and ill, Horst-Konrad answered the first several questions posed promptly and clearly. His answers generally matched those given by the men Purged earlier, even though he had not been present during their Purgation, so the questioners and witnesses found little reason to press a sick man more closely. Carefully phrased answers were to be expected when he had been chastised by his overlord's representative. Too much similarity in his accounts, especially when he had not heard the other reports, would have been viewed with more suspicion than minor variations.

Then a questioner asked about the history of the damage to his hands. Horst-Konrad swayed where he knelt, and delayed the start of his answer too long, considering secrets, so the words of his answer were cut off by the Rod striking his back. He fell forward under the blow, caught himself with his hands, and straightened back up. The blow broke his concentration, and things went badly after that.

When the count had reached twenty-one and twelve, a second question about his hands produced a garbled answer, and Horst-Konrad did not rise after receiving the blow of the Rod. They woke him with a ladle-full of icy water, and required him to remove his shirt and use it to mop up the mess from the White Hall's floor. When he returned to kneel in his place, shirtless and showing the fresh welts against pale skin, he was ordered to hold out his hands, palms up, and the Rod landed across them with full force, twice, before the questions resumed.

His answers were quicker and less carefully phrased after the break in the questions, and the Prince-Elector of Bremerhaven occasionally nodded thoughtfully as he listened.

Finally the Teacher read a passage from one of his books, removed the final marker, and closed it. Then the Preacher did the same. The final count of the questions of the Purgation of Horst-Konrad von Neumark was forty-eight and twenty and two, and for the last twenty-five questions he had supported himself with his hands as well as his knees. Some of the Echelon members murmured relieved thanks that things were no worse: having one of the highest of the Select fall and be proven false was a thing to be dreaded. There were dire warnings in the writings about the rot that could spread from a man who was falsely acclaimed as Select.

Some of the witnesses put his stocking and shoes onto the Purged man, and then hauled him to his feet and buttoned him into his well-tailored waistcoat and great-coat. Any other man would have walked home through the streets thus shirtless, but since the White Hall was located on his estate, the Margraff-Elector was spared that much.

His steps were almost steady as he walked to his bedchamber, but he collapsed face down onto the bed once he reached it. His slaves removed his shoes, but did not dare to touch him otherwise, so he slept in his clothes for some hours. When he awakened, his hands and back were too swollen and painful to move much, and his clothes felt tight, as if he was wearing a corset instead of a waistcoat.

He shouted for his servants, and they got him upright, but neither his limbs nor his clothing were useful or cooperative. Before he was successfully undressed, his tailor had cut loose many of the buttons holding the coat and waistcoat closed, and used a small sharp blade to slice the stitching of many of the seams. The garments were taken away to be sewn back together.

The Margraff-Elector spent the next several days wearing garments that were soft and loose and unfit for public appearances.

# CHAPTER XIII: A Useless Council

*Wherein Only Our Hero Cares About the Contract*

The next day began quietly. Franz-Karl was summoned to the Privy Council along with his Mama, and could not think of a reason not to go. It would be better than fidgeting all day. And he hoped that if they managed to repair some of the broken places in the Marriage Contract the fierceness of the plague would be lessened. He was dreadfully afraid that the cracks in the World caused by oath-breaking were part of why the sickness was coming now.

The mood in the Palace was strained. There had been no official announcement about sickness in Traventi or along the river, or anywhere else, but people seemed to know that there was something to worry about. They were treading softly and speaking in voices that were slightly hushed, as if outside a sickroom, or else too loud, as if to deny worry.

Despite the fog of worry elsewhere in the Palace, the Privy Council seemed no more ready to do anything useful about the Marriage Contract than they had been during the previous sessions. Though perhaps it might be more accurate to say that the Northern lords were no more inclined to let the Council do anything useful. The Prince-Elector looked exhausted and hollow-eyed, the Margraff-Elector was not present at all, their various allies and followers looked tired, and they were all cranky. Franz-Karl's Binding had improved things a little, but not enough. The Northern faction could not pull the discussion off into the wilderness: not without the consent of His Royal Grace the acting Archduke. But none of them would agree to any useful measures despite the time spent discussing them.

Franz-Karl still did not understand why the Allemanic lords from outside the Falkenburg territories were allowed to speak in the council at all, much less trample all over its proper tasks. Had these grownups never looked at a map?

After a while, Franz-Karl decided that sitting in the council meeting was worse than sitting in the Residence would have been. He felt twitchy and sort of stretched – the wrong size and shape for his skin – and he had to sit quietly while a lot or grownups who were supposed to be in charge of things ignored both the approaching sickness and their other proper business.

Considering the Marriage Contract, Franz-Karl thought that there were several major areas that were still problems, and the council was mostly agreeing that they were problems, they just did not want to solve them.

First, by Traventine custom, the irreparably broken twenty-fifth section of the Marriage Contract needed to be acknowledged and renegotiated, some memorable compensation for the past breach needed to be paid, and some really emphatic guarantees, with penalties, needed to be established for the future. The council flinched away from discussing that at all.

Second, the properties attached to the title of Count of Wolfsberg had still not been fully transferred to Philip-Augustus. The Contract negotiators had used language that was absolute about that transfer, ignoring the possibility that the inheritance might need to pass to a minor. That did not make the delay any less of a breach of the terms. Naming trustees – even horrible trustees – would be better than the nothing that the council had agreed to so far. They made a list of names, and changed the list occasionally, but went no further.

Third, there needed to be penalties defined for people who caused breaches by doing things that were contrary to the expressed will of his Excellency, like the rule that Traventines could go in and out of the Palace. Executing people for being stupid would be unfair. Probably. But the council refused to treat open disobedience as treason, and also refused to treat it as anything less. So people were safe if they disobeyed, even though the Council spent time talking about how terrible and insolent it was.

Franz-Karl personally thought that there needed to also be penalties for people who gave orders contrary to both the expressed will of his Excellency and the promises made in the Contract, without actually doing things, but he had sat in the council long enough to recognize that punishing people in charge was unlikely to be agreed to if the lower ranks were not being punished. Some of the people sitting at the table were also giving the orders that were in need of punishment. If they would not even stop giving the orders, they would not agree to punish themselves.

Fourth was the whole tangled mess around the several sections of the Contract that discussed the establishment and support of his Mama's household. There needed to be Elderkin ladies in waiting attending to her, living in her household without being harassed and abused by other people in the Palace. There needed to be proper food provided as a matter of course, without constant arguments and people trying to sneak horrible stuff into the dishes served to the Traventines. Servants supplied by the Palace needed to take proper care of the rooms of the Traventine Residence, or his Mama should be allowed to move out of the Palace. And her children needed to be assured of proper teachers and attendants who were fluent in diplomatic Remoran and Elderic, and, for that matter, proper Court Allemanic: not some dialect that was foreign to the lands of the Falkenburgs. Franz-Karl was planning to make that particular complaint at the first opportunity: it might as least make it a little harder for the Northern Lords' partisans to get at them, if they could not insert their own people into the Traventine Residence at will.

Before the plague started running around through the lands and the borders closed, Franz-Karl had sometimes thought they should try announcing that his Mama and her children would return to Traventi as soon as the roads were passable if the worst breaches were not addressed. It would not have been allowed, just as his Mama had not really had a choice about the wedding, but if they leaned on that lever hard enough, they might manage a move into Greenoak Square and away from some of the nastier people who were in positions of authority inside the Palace.

Franz-Karl was suspecting more and more that he was unlikely to reach his majority without turning someone into a newt or doing something equally horrible: the Northerners kept pushing him and pushing him trying to get him to prove he was the inhuman monster they predicted. His little tail was not really public knowledge, but there were rumors about something physically odd, beyond the eyes and hair and the basic fact that he was Elderkin, and it was likely that someone would try to use the oddness as an excuse for something. If the Northern factions poked at him long enough and hard enough, they were likely to get their wish: ten more years was a long time. Moving away from the Palace, even a little way, would make it harder for them to keep poking at him. Maybe then he would stop being so angry.

And beyond all of those matters that were properly part of the Marriage Contract there remained some of the odd things like the trade agreement that had been wedged into the contract, and sworn to by all of the parties to the Marriage, and then ignored as thoroughly as all of the rest.

And all of these things were sometimes being discussed in the current council session, but the discussions never went anywhere except in circles. It was almost more annoying than when they were simply refusing to allow discussions of the problems.

And now they had started discussing a separate problem, maybe out of habit.

Franz-Karl would not have minded at all if the councilors were discussing possible ways to prepare for the avalanche of sickness that was coming toward them, if not already in the city. That was an urgent matter of great concern.

He would not have minded, much, if they were discussing Prince Otto's projects to see to the maintenance of the city's walls and roads. Those matters were not exactly urgent – except possibly that one sinkhole that was rumored to have eaten an entire cart and the ox-hitch pulling it – but at least they were problems within the Falkenburg domains, affected the people there, and were the sort of things that the Falkenburg Privy Council was supposed to care about. And they were things the Council might usefully do something about.

But no, what the council spent part of the morning talking about – after briefly mentioning the Marriage Contract problems – was some dynastic squabble in the northern Isles. The Isles were not part of the Falkenburg domains. They were not part of the Northern Allemanic territories outside the Falkenburg Domains that answered to His Excellency as King of the Allemans, either. You could not even see the

Isles on a clear day from anywhere that answered to his Excellency, so His Excellency's servants and vassals had no authority in the Isles to do anything about any dynastic squabble there.

There were not even any Falkenburg Princesses married into the Isles... which was a little surprising, actually. If you included some of the more distant cousins, there were Falkenburg Princesses married into half the Courts within a thousand miles from Karnburg.

The Councilors were not even talking about trying to marry Franz-Karl's cousin Frederica to someone in whichever faction won in the Isles. That would still have been a useless waste of time unless they talked to Frederica first, but it came within shouting distance of being a proper thing for the Falkenburg Privy Council to talk about. They were discussing completely impossible ways to intervene, or to take advantage of the situation at no cost to the Privy Purse. Franz-Karl knew from listening to his Papa and uncle Helm-Friedrich and reading various chronicles that there was always a cost, and if you did not see it in the beginning, it was probably going to turn out to be higher than you could afford.

He finally reached the limit of his ability keep still. Franz-Karl scrambled down from his chair and straightened his coat.

His Royal Grace acting Archduke Uncle Helm-Friedrich raised an eyebrow and said, "Grand Duke Franz-Karl?"

Franz-Karl bowed, though not quite as far as kinship and courtesy might have recommended. "Your Royal Grace, I was summoned here as a Notary and Heir to the Duchy of Traventi to bear witness during a discussion of a Traventine Marriage Contract. Since there is no such discussion in progress, nor any apparent prospect of one, I will withdraw to the anteroom and send for my schoolbooks. Kindly send for me when the discussion returns to the Traventine part of the agenda." He bowed to his Mama and again to his Royal Grace, then turned and walked out of the room, with Fritzel following at his shoulder. He did not stomp: stomping when you were seven and not unusually large for your age was just pitiful.

His aide commented in Elderic, "Your Honor did not say anything about false pretenses."

"Not explicitly. It does not matter: in the Duchy a Notary summoned to bear witness would be paid the usual fee for the time, regardless of what happened during that time." He stopped walking and turned and looked up at Fritzel, smiling. Sort of smiling. "Fritzel? Exactly how many hours have we spent in that Council Chamber since I was first summoned to these stupid meetings?"

## CHAPTER XIV: Notarial Diligence

### *Wherein the Falkenburg Council Learns the Foundations of Traventine Government*

When they were called back into the Council Chamber only a few hours later, Fritzel handed a paper to one of the aides of His Royal Grace acting Archduke Uncle Helm-Friedrich. Royalty never handed papers to people with their own hands, or received them with their own hands either. The aide set the paper on the table in front of His Royal Grace, who glanced at it then looked away. Then his head snapped back and he stared at the paper. Finally he looked at Franz-Karl, who was standing quietly in front of his chair: it was not yet an appropriate moment to scramble up into it.

"Your Grace Grand Duke Franz-Karl?"

Franz-Karl said quietly, "My proper style in my capacity as Notary is Your Honor. And that is the only capacity in which my presence at a meeting of the Privy Council of the Falkenburg Domains has any color of legality."

"Of course, Your Honor, my apologies." His Royal Grace gestured toward the paper. "May I ask what this is?"

"One of the two great foundations of Traventine law and government is the rule that Notaries and other citizens must receive compensation for any official activities involving our Manifest heritage, such as Bindings and bearing Witness and the use of Gifts. Otherwise it counts as attempted enslavement, which if proved is a capital crime within Traventi and a cause for war outside it. That paper is an accounting for my time in these Privy Council sessions since I was first summoned to them, with the usual fees assessed at a rate based on today's exchange rate at the bank of Mistella's Karnburg office." He paused, then added, "Your Royal Grace will note that I have charged double for times when the Marriage Contract was not, in fact, being discussed. I will consider negotiating the fee for the wasted time."

His Royal Grace acting Archduke Uncle Helm-Friedrich looked at Franz-Karl for a long moment, then said, "Of course, Your Honor. The fees will be paid from the Special Budget. Will payment to your account at the bank of Mistella's office by the end of the day be satisfactory?"

Franz-Karl bowed. "Of course." He scrambled up into his chair. This was going better than he had hoped: he had seen that the Northern Lords hated to spend the Special Budget on anything. At all. Ever. He was not sure what they thought those funds were for.

His Royal Highness the Prince-Elector of Bremerhaven asked in a snide tone, "I suppose you plan to demand compensation for your Mother as well?"

Franz-Karl looked at the Noble until he squirmed and looked away. He could feel his own hair pulling out of its hair-tie, as usual. "The Reverend Childe Silvia, being necessarily a Notary in her own right, stands outside the limits of my responsibility. If I were serving in an advisory capacity, I would suggest that time spent on a matter where she is a direct party does not require compensation, unlike time spent witnessing other matters."

A Northern Lord pounced. "You do not consider yourself a party to the Marriage Contract?"

Franz-Karl looked at the man – he was a Count and at least three Barons and had a mustache that looked like a dead caterpillar– for a long moment. Franz-Karl finally said, "The Marriage Contract of Silvia of the line of Armorius, Childe of Traventi and Grand Duke Leon-Alexander von Falkenburg was signed and Witnessed more than ten years ago. I have existed with the boundaries of the Living World for less than eight years, counted from the instant of conception. As a matter of law and logic, no person can be a party nor a witness to an event that occurred before they were present in the world." A thought struck him and he grinned and turned to his uncle. "Your Royal Grace, given the ... sloppiness... of the proceedings in this forum, I should remind you that the presence of a Notary, compensated or otherwise, carries no implied promise of confidentiality. Confidentiality requires an explicit contract. My observations on this morning's gossip are already on their way to their Holinesses in Glastonbury and to Her Royal Grace the Grand Duchess Frederica."

"Your Honor wrote to the Isles? And to Frederica?" His Royal Grace acting Archduke Uncle Helm-Friedrich repeated slowly. Frederica was his oldest unmarried daughter and reminded many of people of her Aunt Queen Gertrude at the same age. Most of them did not mean that as a compliment. Aunt Queen Gertrude was considered unfeminine because she had been a better regent than most men, and was generally considered unbiddable, which was supposed to be a bad thing in a woman.

Franz-Karl answered cheerfully, "I thought it would be polite to ask Grand Duchess Cousin Frederica whether she would like to be Queen of whichever Isle it is after the current disturbances are quieter... A public discussion that did not involve her seemed... unwise."

His Royal Grace looked thoughtful, then slightly appalled. "Very likely. At the very least, after a discussion without warning her, I would need to arrange for that place at the University she has mentioned."

The Northern Electors and several of their adherents looked honestly revolted at the thought of a female being allowed entry into a University in any kind of scholarly capacity. The Prince-Elector of Bremerhaven began to lift one hand as though preparing for a formal oration.

Justice von Trebice had the expression of someone who suspected that he would regret his next words, but he said quickly. "Your Honor Franz-Karl, may I ask... what is the second great foundation of Traventine law and government?"

Franz-Karl answered blandly, "Do not gratuitously annoy anyone that might turn you into a newt." He could feel his hair pulling the rest of the way out of its hair-tie.

Someone had a coughing fit. Franz-Karl did not look around to see who it was, but it sounded like Fritzel. There were few people with such deep voices in the world, much less the room.

The Justice asked weakly, "Is that a real possibility?"

Franz-Karl was annoyed enough to answer in detail, repeating text from a journal Reverend Count Adrasteia had written with her own hand. "Reverend Count Adrasteia of the South Valley of Traventi has taught me that there are four observed consequences of attempts to turn people into newts –"

Franz-Karl raised fingers as he counted them off. He did not use the rude finger as the first one, though he was tempted. "The annoying person becomes a man-sized newt which dies within the hour." Second finger: "The person becomes many newt-sized newts, which scatter." Third finger: "The person becomes a single newt-sized newt and a pile of... leftovers." Fourth finger: "Or a person-sized pile of leftovers is created with no sign of the presence of a newt." Franz-Karl's hair had all abandoned its ribbon by this point, so the ribbon fell down his back. He continued, "Her Reverence notes that all four options result in an irrevocable removal of the annoying person and an edifying spectacle for any onlookers, so she judges them equally effective for... strategic purposes."

The Justice looked about to speak, but Franz-Karl took a deep breath, held out one hand, and continued, "In the commentaries, Chief Justice Laurentina of Traventi considers that in recent centuries the phrase 'turn someone into a newt' is used as a customary place-holder for any unspecified but unpleasant use of Gifts or Bindings that might be considered." He lowered the one hand and held up the other. "It has been suggested that at some time there was a more successful – or at least, less deadly – transformation of a person into a newt – possibly by one of the Greater Manifest – and heavy Elderkin have been trying to match that feat ever since. But I am aware of no evidence to support that suggestion." He lowered his hands.

"My compliments to your tutor," His Royal Grace said dryly.

Franz-Karl looked at him directly, "The Falkenburgs have provided me with no tutor in Grammar, Logic or Rhetoric, despite their promises in the Marriage Contract... to which we might usefully turn our attention. Unless there are other matters of surpassing urgency at the moment?"

Someone at the far end of the table muttered something that sounded like "... having a tutor might slow him down a bit..." From a quirk of his lips, Franz-Karl suspected that his Royal Grace his Uncle did not disagree.

"Will Your Honor provide a promise of future confidence?" His Royal Grace asked. His tone was confident.

He looked shocked when Franz-Karl answered flatly, "No."

Franz-Karl continued, "Should a Notary speaking for Traventi give the servants of the Falkenburgs another promise for them to mutilate and their masters to ignore? The publicly forsworn have no basis to ask for exchanges of promises, Your Royal Grace." Franz-Karl slid down from his chair again and stood straight. "I am Franz-Karl of the lines of Falkenburg, Armorius, Leonstein and Capradaventi, Heir in the Line of Succession of the Duchy of Traventi, and a Binder and fully sworn Notary of Traventi. Speak plain truth in my presence, or hold your tongues, or send me away: from this room, or this Palace, or this City, or this Domain, as it may please you. What is your wish?"

By the end of that speech, Franz-Karl's hair was not just entirely out of the ribbon that had held it at the nape of his neck, it was making crackling noises. And it felt like it was moving. He thought it was probably a good thing for him that the sparks from his Mama's hair never seemed to set her clothes on fire. A looming presence at his back told him that Fritzel was also on his feet.

No one at the table moved for a moment. Even idiots who ignored most of their Grannies' stories did not want to hear the word 'wish' spoken by an Elderkin Binder, especially not in the tone Franz-Karl had used. Traventi had spent generations and centuries teaching their neighbors that demanding wishes was demanding disaster, and accepting an offered 'wish' rather than a 'Favor' was almost equally imprudent.

Franz-Karl bowed to His Royal Grace the acting Archduke with crystalline formality, turned and bowed to his Mother with familial warmth to emphasize the difference, then turned and walked out of the Council Chamber. Fritzel followed.

# CHAPTER XV: Pantries and Dinner

## *Wherein the Pantries are Notarized*

When they reached the great staircases, Franz-Karl leaned hard on his 'don't notice me' Gift, and they went up the stairs instead of down. There were exclamations from people in the corridor as the two Elderkin vanished from the path that people expected them to take, but no one followed them, and at least the effort made Franz-Karl's hair stop crackling. They took the first opportunity to move out of the public corridor and into the servants' stairs.

Fritzel leaned against the door. Franz-Karl sank down to sit on the floor, breathing hard. The two of them looked at each other, and Franz-Karl's aide began laughing softly. "Did you see the looks on their faces, just at the last?" he asked in Elderic.

Franz-Karl rolled his eyes. "If I had looked too hard at any of those oath-breakers, there would have been a heap of newt giblets on one of those chairs. Four ways of people turning into newts is near enough to four repetitions to be useful or dangerous, as you care to view it, and there's a reason the Reverend Count mentioned the easiest outcome last."

Fritzel looked startled. "Mmm. Sneaky, that," he said approvingly. "That hair thing was fair impressive even without newt-giblets. D'ye know which line it's from?"

"The moving thing is not in the chronicles, not that I have seen, so it might come through Armorius, which has the fewest records. The sparks are from Capradaventi, or at least, some line that comes to us through Her Grace the Duke my Grandmother: I've seen sparks drip out of the end of her Grace's braid."

"I remember that sight. Fair sets a man's liver sideways, that. Make's being around Her Reverend Grace Childe Silvia a bit uneasy as well."

Franz-Karl sighed, "Mama's hair never sparked until after my Papa's death when people were being stupid. And now with the Council being stupid all of the time there are lots of sparks."

Fritzel braced his hands on the two sides of the narrow passage, and stretched. The stones of the Palace did not groan or shift, which Franz-Karl thought was fairly impressive. "Where now for us, Your Honor?"

Franz-Karl sighed, and considered their few options. "Pantries? Someone should be doing at least one useful thing about preparing for what's coming..."

"And the Servants have been openhanded about their side of the bargain," Fritzel agreed. "I suppose we start in the kitchens again?" He moved away from the door they had come through and began to walk down the dim, narrow staircase beside it.

They did not need to enter the kitchens, which were busy with preparations for the evening meal. The pock-marked man met them as they reached the kitchen door. He introduced himself as Vendal, and asked whether Franz-Karl needed to be fasting to do what he had planned. When Franz-Karl said that he did not, Vendal led them to a side nook where he served Franz-Karl and Fritzel all of the signs of hospitality, and shared them, wordlessly, before the three of them continued toward the pantries and storage rooms.

In each of the first two rooms they visited, Franz-Karl found a few jars of preserves or bales of other supplies that he thought were slightly questionable. They sat unsteadily in the world, like liars. When Vendal checked certain marks on the jars and packages, he said that they were older stock that had been hidden behind newer, and should have been used long before. He set them aside to be fed to pigs and chickens, marking them with colored wax so there would be no mistake.

When they entered the third room, Franz-Karl stopped. Then he walked directly to one long shelf and rearranged the jars on it into groups. It was easy to do: some of the things on the shelf were clearly jars of food to his eyes. Some were less real, resting unhappily in the world, as if someone had sculpted things to look like jars, or perhaps fashioned them as empty stage props. Two were so false that the world would have been happier to have them as bas reliefs or pictures in frescoes than as solid objects with depth and heft, and their colors were vile besides. He avoided touching those two, moving the other jars around them instead.

When he had finished arranging the jars, Franz-Karl turned to Vendal and said, "I believe that all of these --" he waved his hand, "are good food and excellently well preserved. These --" he indicated the middle group, "might do well mixed into the manure heaps for the Palace gardens."

"But not for the pigs and chickens?" Vendal asked.

"I regret I am no master in these matters," Franz-Karl said, "but they strike me as chancy for creature of flesh and blood to eat. Better to let the soil have its way with them."

"And perhaps not the soil of the kitchen gardens," Vendal decided, placing more marks upon them. "And these last two?"

"If you have an outbuilding with a population of unusually stupid rats or other vermin, you may see if they will try this bait... Otherwise? Perhaps burn them, taking care not to breathe the smoke, or empty them into a strong channel of the river, tossing the jars in after. Those two are so very distant from being safe food, I would not be too brave with them."

"We had a pig die after eating preserves a cook doubted, that came from here," Vendal said. "Two jars to the rivers is far better than mistrusting the the whole storeroom, or killing more livestock. Is it permitted ask how your Honor knows which are unsafe?"

"Partly, it's that I have a Binding – a curse – on me to not recognize impure food as food." Franz-Karl gestured vaguely up and around and Vendal nodded. The servants in the Palace kitchens were naturally aware of the Traventine meal requirements, and the uncooperative attitudes of some of the officials who were formal authorities in the Palace. Franz-Karl continued. "And there is also a rare Gift known in the Duchy... not vanishing rare, but rare enough that the Dyers and Distillers Guild pays stiff bonuses to get apprentices that have it. Reverend Count Great Aunt Adrasteia thinks that the curse and the Gift are ... 'usefully entangled' were her words. When I am older, if there have been no untoward occurrences, she will offer a milder version of the Binding to a few of those apprentices to see what comes of it. Until then? With no disrespect intended toward the servants here under his Excellency's roof, I think being very difficult to poison is not a bad thing."

"Your Honor!" Vendal seemed shocked.

Franz-Karl looked up at him and said plainly, "I have not forgotten that they tried to feed us food that was ritually impure at my own father's funeral feast. Would you trust them to stop at ritually impure?" The Old Palace servants had their own word for ritually impure, which he had overheard a few times, so that was the one he had used instead of the Allemanic phrase that meant much the same. Vendal eyed him thoughtfully as they walked toward the next storeroom.

They found varying degrees of corruption of the supplies in the rest of the storerooms – Vendal had keys to all of them and Fritzel helped him move things aside so that they could reach odd corners, so they were very thorough – but none of the other corruption they discovered was as bad as those two jars. When they finished the storerooms under the main Palace, they continued with the ones in the East Palace. There was no hidden connection from the East Palace to the other buildings, so they had to cross an open courtyard to reach it. But no one was looking for Franz-Karl and Fritzel in that direction, so it was easy to keep them unnoticed.

There were many storerooms. The buildings inside the Palace Wall housed dozens of people and fed many more every day, and the Palace and City had survived more than one siege in past decades and centuries. Stores were depleted after the winter, and the shelves would become more empty before the summer harvests refilled them, but the Palace was not a place that depended on constant deliveries of supplies from the countryside. The Palace could last a while on the contents of its storerooms, provided the people had water and firewood. Franz-Karl was oddly comforted by knowing that.

It was getting very late when they finished the East Palace storerooms, so they agreed to leave the West Palace, where the Traventine Residence was, for the next convenient occasion. Vendal returned to the meal preparations in the main Palace and Franz-Karl and Fritzel returned to the Traventine Residence by way of the deep tunnel and the servants' stairs.

They entered the Residence using the servants' door near the nursery: the one that made noise. Tam, Franz-Karl's valet met them and made Franz-Karl and Fritzel change their clothes immediately: the servants passages were as clean as the public parts of the Palace, but some of the storerooms were less well tended. Tam assured them that they were not fit to be seen in polite company in their present state. Franz-Karl, of course, was still wearing the color-of-sorrow of deep mourning, but the clothes Tam brought out for Fritzel, while not his best Court clothes, were possibly his most elegant suit.

Franz-Karl's Mama was not surprised when he and Fritzel appeared from the rear of the residence because of the noisy door. His Royal Grace the acting Archduke Uncle Helm-Friedrich, who was sitting with her, seemed extremely surprised. Franz-Karl had an angry suspicion that His Royal Grace had ordered the Residence searched for them, which violated diplomatic and Palace protocols and bent a few sections of the Marriage Contract. And besides that, the search would not have worked even if they had been in his Mama's home, unless Franz-Karl let it.

Fritzel, behind him, murmured in Elderic, "Your Honor seems to be in a right mood."

Franz-Karl stopped walking, closed his eyes, took a few deep breaths and waited for the crackling in his hair and the feeling of being observed to subside. "Better?"

"Yes, Your Honor."

The guest cup and platter of morsels made from the ritual ingredients rested on a small table beside His Royal Grace, so he was at least formally a guest of Franz-Karl's Mama. But Franz-Karl decided that he was not in the mood to be cooperative unless His Royal Grace had arrived with a twelve point plan, in writing, for setting the Contract to rights. He had never been formally welcomed as guest or kinsman after his return from Traventi the previous fall – not by anyone except his Mama and her attendants – and he did not share the guest cup nor plate with his uncle now. His odd status gave him freedom it would be foolish to give up.

Franz-Karl walked around to the front of his Mama's chair, greeted and bowed to her, kissed her hand, and took his own seat without directly facing toward the acting Archduke, his Uncle. The broad pupils of his Elderkin eyes gave him a better view than His Royal Grace might expect: he could see his Uncle Helm-Friedrich fidget without seeming to look at him.

His Mama smiled at him, and past him, and said, "Tiarna Boukolyos" with a nod, so Fritzel sat down as well. The attendants that had accompanied his Royal Grace the acting Archduke remained standing by the walls.

Attendants and ladies in waiting lived in a broad border area where sometimes they counted as 'fellow nobles' and sometimes they were ignored. Sometimes the difference was political. Sometimes it depended on how unbalanced the numbers at an Allemanic dinner table were likely to be: the entire household sat together at a Traventine table, so balancing numbers was not a consideration in the Residence.

Childe Silvia asked Franz-Karl, "Did you have a pleasant afternoon, my dear?"

Franz-Karl thought for a moment They were using family titles, not formal ones. "I had a reassuring afternoon, Mama. The Palace seems better stocked than we had hoped, even now, with the winter recently past." He saw the acting Archduke wince.

"That is indeed reassuring, Brother." Philip-Augustus bowed and kissed their Mama's hand and bowed to His Royal Grace before he took a seat that was placed between Franz-Karl and His Royal Grace and carefully somewhat behind the direct line between them. "Word has come from Damian at Greenoak Square that they are generally well stocked and laying in stores to replenish a few things where the supply seemed lean. Did you survey the entire Palace complex?"

One of the Elderkin footmen offered a tray of watered wine in six of the best glasses to Franz-Karl, then to His Royal Grace, Philip-Augustus, Fritzel and her Honor the Childe Silvia, setting the extra glass with the Saint's serving aside.

Franz-Karl sipped his drink. "We only visited the main Palace and the East Palace today, since our start was delayed by useless chatter. We'll do the West Palace when next our guide is available... and possibly visit some of the more useful outbuildings as well."

"Could you summon me when you are ready to do the West Palace, here?" Philip-Augustus asked, "I think that I should join you for that part."

"Of course. Fritzel will send someone when we are ready to begin."

His Royal Grace acting Archduke Uncle Helm-Friedrich shifted in his seat.

Franz-Karl's Mama glanced at him, then looked at Franz-Karl. "Your Honor Franz-Karl, my brother-in-law is here to join the Traventine embassy's evening meal, if you have no objection."

Franz-Karl turned to his left – his dominant side: the chairs had been carefully arranged – to look at His Royal Grace. "Of course not, Mama. I hope you are well this evening, Uncle Helm-Friedrich," he said politely, with a slight kinsman's bow. He wondered just how rude those barbarians in the Privy Council had been to his Mama after he left, for her to omit all of the acting Archduke's titles. Or perhaps there had been a particularly annoying search.

Uncle Helm-Friedrich looked... flummoxed, might be the right word. Franz-Karl wondered how long it had been since his uncle dealt with protocol as just a person, not acting Archduke on top of all his own titles – none of which were titles in Traventine places unless Childe Silvia chose to treat them as courtesy titles.

When the meal was announced Childe Silvia offered her arm to her guest to go into the dining room. Franz-Karl offered his arm to his brother – who was not yet a full Notary despite being older – and followed them.

Fritzel and Itron Gwenlian came last, walking together with no one holding anyone's arm. Franz-Karl had not figured out how the aides decided which side to walk on and whether or not to hold arms. Either there were some subtle rules, or they wanted to confuse the non-Elderkin Palace attendants, or both.

Sophie-Alexa and Nurse Rosa were already seated at the table when the senior members of the household arrived. Sophie-Alexa was too big to be easily carried in to dinner, and small enough that things got complicated when she joined the procession of larger people..

Uncle Helm-Friedrich seemed very confused by the arrangement of the dining room. As a concession to Allemanic custom, there was a 'higher' table and a 'lower' table, but the people seated included the servants as well as the family and guests: even the footmen who served the food sat down to eat their own meals once they had offered the platters and tureens of food to everyone else. At this meal the high table was the family, guests, aides, Nurse Rosa and Philip-Augustus's tutor, with the odd chair left as the Saint's place, where the other signs of Hospitality were arranged around the unlit candle. The lower table was Roland the majordomo, Franz-Karl's valet Tam, the other four Traventine men-servants, and four Palace servants who looked profoundly uncomfortable when they noticed the acting Archduke. There were two more 'lower' tables pushed against the wall and not laid out: they had not been needed very often since the death of Leon-Alexander, Franz-Karl's Papa. The only grown women in the room were Franz-Karl's Mama, Itron Gwenlian, Nurse Rosa, and a Palace parlor maid at the lower table.

When Uncle Helm-Friedrich had finished the main part of his meal, he complimented the food, adding in a carefully polite, curious tone, "I see that your cooks do not dine with you?"

"The kitchen is two floors down and also serves others who dwell in this part of the Palace," Childe Silvia explained gently. "The cooks are welcome, but complain that joining us would be too disruptive of their labors."

"Of course." He ate few more bites. "I will confess, despite the complaints about the failure to observe the requirements of the Marriage Contract, I had not realized quite how devoid of women servants this household is..."

Franz-Karl said, helpfully, "In Traventi I had a tiring-woman in my household, not a valet, but I could not ask a respectable Elderkin lady to come to a place where women are treated so barbarously. So now I have Tam."

His Uncle winced.

Philip-Augustus added, "Of course, properly speaking, Itron Gwenlian should not count as one of the five ladies in waiting to be maintained by the Falkenburgs according to the Marriage Contract: she is Her Honor Childe Silvia's aide, as Tiarna Boukolyos is His Honor Franz-Karl's. They are both maintained by Traventine Ducal funds, not the Falkenburg estates and treasuries, not even the Wolfsberg ones that are supposed to be mine and should be supporting part of this household. "

"Furthermore," Franz-Karl offered, "Itron Gwenlian is not a respectable lady suitable for the position of lady in waiting: I was told in Traventi that she is properly termed a 'loathly hag', despite being quite nice to look at."

Philip-Augustus eyed his mother's aide with sudden interest. "She doesn't seem likely to devour someone's heart."

Franz-Karl nodded. "Well, none of the old stories say the heart has to be eaten raw," he pointed out. "I am sure that if Itron Gwenlian has ever had occasion to devour someone's heart, it was properly roasted, and stuffed with onions and mushrooms and breadcrumbs and flavorings." He himself was quite fond of onion and mushroom stuffing.

"And very likely served with a nice cream sauce," his brother agreed. "That seems much more like our Itron Gwenlian."

Their mother was clearly struggling to keep a straight face. Itron Gwenlian did not try: she smiled at them, showing more teeth than she usually did in a smile... more teeth and sharper than a human would possess. Uncle Helm-Friedrich made a sort of strangled sound. The parlormaid at the other table stifled a giggle.

Franz-Karl said seriously, "When I was preparing to return here from Traventi, some of the Ducal Councilors discussed the problem of sending respectable ladies in waiting to a place as savage and uncivilized in their treatment of women as Karnburg and the Falkenburg domains have shown themselves to be – not during a proper session, you understand: this was after dinner and a few glasses of wine. There were names mentioned that I do not know, but the expectation seemed to be that the standard of civility of the Falkenburg court would increase -- one way or another-- if any of those ladies mentioned came to dwell here. But I remember someone said that another of Gwenlian's close kin should not be sent here, because two in one small place tends to get... messy."

"It's true, we need our space," Gwenlian agreed cheerfully. "and these apartments are a bit cramped. But I can certainly recommend some names and Lineages that would suit, if it comes to it that Her Grace the Duke is willing to declare this place open for a Hunt."

"Might teach some of those Northerners some manners," Fritzel said thoughtfully. "Or else reduce their numbers... there do seem to be more of them skittering around the Palace every time you turn around."

Uncle Helm-Friedrich smiled thinly and fidgeted with his glass, and answered with something that would have made sense if the people spoken to were joking.

Franz-Karl hoped that was politeness. There were limits to what what you could ask people to put up with so that others could avoid a war. As one of the people putting up with things he had never volunteered to put up with, Franz-Karl was about reaching his limits, and could hardly blame others who had been in the Palace longer for reaching theirs. That made it even more worrying that Itron Gwenlian was talking openly about a Hunt. Talking about Hunts was not jokes: talking about Hunts was warnings.

Fritzel talking about the Northerners was even scarier: he had not been in Karnburg very long. But His Royal Grace acting Archduke Uncle Helm-Friedrich might not realize that.

It might have helped if the Privy Council had even pretended to be polite or diligent about their contracted responsibilities.

The next day, Franz-Karl was not summoned to the Eastlands Privy Council, but his Mama received a very polite invitation. She took Itron Gwenlian with her, and one of the footmen, since she had no ladies' maids to fetch and carry.

Childe Silvia returned from the Privy Council session before the midday meal and after the Council turned their attention to other matters. The footman carried two letters and a small sheaf of signed and sealed documents. One letter was from the acting Archduke and His Excellency and the chief Minister in charge of dealings with foreign countries and addressed to the Duke and Council of Traventi. It invited them to send 'such ladies as they deemed appropriate' to Karnburg once the borders were open again, to fulfill the requirements of for Childe Silvia's household as specified in the Marriage Contract.

The other letter was from Her Excellency as Mistress of the Household, countersigned by His Royal Grace acting Archduke Uncle Helm-Friedrich. The household letter directed that the Traventine Residence and Embassy should have specific Palace servants, agreed to by the Embassy, permanently assigned to serve it, and permanent cooks as well. The number of servants mentioned was twice as many as Franz-Karl had seen in their rooms since before his father's death.

When Franz-Karl heard of the letter about the servants, he thought that it sounded likely to improve the state of things involving the Marriage Contract if it came into effect. But he did not expect that they would actually ever see the additional servants in the Residence. Her Excellency was the Mistress of the Household for ritual purposes. But there was an official in the Palace hierarchy reporting to the Noble Chamberlain, or one of the Noble chamberlains – a member of the Northern faction – who called himself the Master of the Household and it too frequently seemed that Her Excellency's instructions did not reach his attention. There were a lot of grownups in the Palace who acted as if they were Binders who could shape the world by signing or not signing a piece of paper, and the Master of the Palace was one of them. The Master of the Household had not countersigned the letter about the servants.

The sheaf of documents was a bit more hopeful. Two of their Father's smaller baronies and some other minor properties – including that haunted tower on the northeast border – were confirmed as holdings of Philip-Augustus, with Justice von Trebice as trustee. This was not as good as confirmation of the County of Wolfsberg would have been – the Prince-Elector of Bremerhaven had still deflected that one, according to Itron Gwenlian – but this was more progress than they had seen in months and provided some real benefits. The confirmations gave Philip-Augustus some real titles, not just courtesy titles, which improved his mood. And the income from the estates, and promised assistance from the Justice's office, should aid in untangling some of the Residence accounts that had gotten horribly snarled in the months since Leon-Alexander's death.

Franz-Karl thought that perhaps His Royal Grace acting Archduke Uncle Helm-Friedrich had been almost worried enough by the conversation at dinner the evening before.

# INTERLUDE VI: Conference

## *Wherein Some Treasures Are to Be Hidden*

For the first time in many weeks the Margraff-Elector of Ansbach had not inserted himself into the meeting of the Falkenburg Eastlands Privy Council. Neither his hands nor his back were fit for ordinary use or ordinary clothing. That evening, the Prince-Elector of Bremerhaven and some others among the Select joined him in a public room of his estate that was far from the chambers that served as the White Hall.

The Margraff-Elector was as irritable as might be expected in one who was healing, but still stiff, and unable to move without pain. His mood was not improved when the Prince-Elector of Bremerhaven admitted that the Traventine False Heir of Prince Leon-Alexander had been confirmed as owner of some of the Prince's Holdings. Voices were raised in a way that would be disgraceful in the White Hall, so it was just as well that they were meeting elsewhere.

"What? Why did you not prevent it?" The Margraff-Elector leaned forward as if to spring out of his seat, but caught his breath with a hiss and sank back.

"Our usual methods for diverting the discussion expect two of us of the highest rank: tossing a ball with no one to catch it does not progress very far."

"There are others of the Echelon in the council."

"Not of our rank. Not in the Privy Council of the Falkenburg Eastlands. And certainly not while the Changeling Brat's spell remains in full force. Have you read the Council rules?"

"Of course not!"

"People who are neither Eastlanders nor formally appointed members of the Council – like us – cannot speak unless invited by the acting Archduke, and then only on the topic he chooses ... As it happens, his Royal Grace's chosen topic was not whether the beast-born False Heir should be confirmed as holding Falkenburg lands and titles formerly held by Leon-Alexander. The topic was which holdings should be confirmed immediately."

The Margraff-Elector scoffed. "And you could find no way to delay the matter! Not even by remaining silent?"

His colleague shrugged. "Remaining silent when asked a direct question by the acting Archduke is not impossible, but it is cursed difficult. And as I am not formally a member of the council, they could ignore my voice and vote. The best I could manage was to keep them away from the holdings whose funds have been diverted most thoroughly... that may need some attention: the acting Archduke mentioned auditors."

"That is not the worst problem," said a lesser member of the Echelon attached to the treasury. "We have made good progress diverting the Empire's wealth from the unworthy, but it does not take auditors to notice that some of our coffers are unexpectedly full. Since that fool Moes was demoted, we cannot safely move the diverted coinage out through the Palace Gates to where it can be put to better use. Not in the amounts we are gathering. The new guards ask questions."

Another attempt to rise ended in another hiss. "I thought we had replaced that fool Moes after his deserved demotion from captain to corporal."

The General of the Army of the Empire said patiently, "The officer's position has been filled, of course, but not by a member of the Echelon. Our people are thin on the ground in this part of the Empire and anyone we moved into Moes position would leave a gap elsewhere.

Not that it would matter much: His Excellency announced publicly that guarding the Palace Gates was beneath the dignity of the Army of the Empire and ordered our men returned to our camps in the suburbs, so our regiments are not officially shamed. But His Excellency's private opinion of the purported arrest of his daughter-in-law and grandchildren was... more memorable and extremely emphatic. I'm not sure who will be manning the Palace Gates for the next season or two, but it will not be anyone under my command."

"That bad?" the Prince-Elector said. "Perhaps something can be adjusted..."

"Would you prefer to have me and my regiments patrolling the border with the Sultanate? Or camped within easy reach of the city, as we are now?"

The man from the Treasury ticked items off on his fingers. "We cannot move the coinage through the gates without hearing questions we are not ready to answer. We cannot return disbursed funds to their original beneficiaries without raising worse questions: the sums are too large and the diversions are too longstanding. There is no place in the treasury storerooms to store coins with unmarked destinations or false destinations without raising questions: there are safeguards against looting and embezzlement. So what shall we do with this wealth that has fallen to our guardianship?"

"Can we remove the excess coinage from the treasury stores to some less visible spot within the Palace? At least until we find a way to get it past the gates?" The General was very high among the Select, but spent little time in the Palace.

The Master of the Household scoffed. "And expect to find it waiting for us when we return for it? Karnburger and other Eastlands servants won't keep silent about finding unexpected treasure, and the idolatrous followers of the Grove are likely to pile it on His Excellency's chamber floor. "

"Pity that lot were not cleaned out with the rest when the royal hallows in the north were purged." The Treasurer's tone was bitter.

"A bit late to complain about that..." the Prince-Elector said. "Or perhaps, too soon."

The Margraff-Elector picked up a small book that was lying on the table beside him. His companions politely ignored his fumbling attempts to turn the pages until he found the entries he was looking for, fortunately on facing pages. He considered them for a few moments. "I have a... reliable... source for keys to some treasury chests. Keys that no one else will hold. And my people know a storeroom below the main Palace, full of old furniture, where nothing has moved so much as a finger's width in years. A few locked chests in a corner should go unnoticed. Will that serve our purpose?"

The treasury official's agreement was slow in coming and grudging when it arrived, but he finally said, "Provided the move is done quickly and the chests do not linger in the basement, it may be safe enough."

The discussion continued far too long but arrived at no better suggestions, except that to save bulk, where possible, the silver coins in the hoard should be exchanged for gold.

When the others had left, the Margraff-Elector summoned Coenraad and Fourteen, the blades-man and slave – officially couriers – who performed his less reputable errands within the Palace. He gave them strict, detailed instructions, and a beast-born-made talisman out of one of his locked cupboards, hung on a cord tight around Coenraad's neck, to ensure that the instructions were followed and no gold or silver stuck to Coenraad's fingers.

# CHAPTER XVI: Offices and More Pantries

## *Wherein a Button is Traded for Keys, Leading to Surprises*

It was arranged that Philip-Augustus would meet his new guardian in the main Palace early in the morning after the holdings were confirmed. He took Roland the majordomo with him because Roland knew about some of the affairs of his father's estates. Leon-Alexander's secretary Ernst would have been a better choice, but the Palace authorities had removed him from the Traventine household almost before the Prince's corpse-candles went dark, and it had been months since Ernst was seen in the Palace.

Franz-Karl accompanied them because he also knew a bit about the estates, and he had suspicions about the state of the accounts, and no one was likely to stop him, especially with Fritzel at his shoulder – assuming, of course, that he allowed people to notice the two of them. He was wearing the prayer beads: he had generally worn them whenever he visited the main Palace since the incident in the library. Because he was remembering the library, he slipped the button he had acquired into one of his pockets.

Unlike the East and West Palace buildings, where most of the rooms were grouped into Residences, most of the main Palace was official spaces. There was a central residential area for Their Excellencies in the upper floors, and rarely-used residential areas at each end intended for use only by the most exalted of guests. The rest of the space was filled by ballrooms and dining rooms, Audience chambers and Council chambers, and a warren of small rooms where many of the tasks took place that were needed for the operation of the Palace, and the Archduchy of the Eastlands, and the Imperial Domains of the Falkenburgs.

Some of the business of the King of the Allemans, sometimes referred to as the Emperor of the Remorans, took place in the Palace as well, even though the Kingdom's official capital was in Koenigsberg. The Colleges of the Diet held their formal sessions in Koenigsberg and the coronation regalia were stored there, and many of the past Kings were buried there. Proclamations and laws for the Kingdom were issued from Koenigsberg even if His Excellency signed them in Karnburg. But many of the clerks who handled the Kingdom's taxes and spent them on things like supplies for the Army of the Empire – which answered to the Diet – worked in or near the Palace in Karnburg.

Franz-Karl thought that life would be much pleasanter if people like the Electors – who were doubly members of the Diet, after all – would go to live in Koenigsberg instead of in Karnburg. But as long as his Excellency stayed in Karnburg, that was not likely to happen, and if His Excellency left Karnburg, he would probably take Childe Silvia and her children with him, and the Electors would follow along.

The party from the Traventine Residence arrived at the door of the main Palace a little early because Philip-Augustus was too excited to eat much breakfast and Franz-Karl and Fritzel had grabbed some rolls to finish as they walked. Fritzel handed a roll to Roland, who ate it quickly as they walked through the Palace grounds.

They did not need to wait long. The bells for the appointed hour were still ringing when Justice von Trebice arrived, trailed by a pair of clerks with their arms full of pens and ink and papers and ledgers. The Justice bowed to Philip-Augustus and Franz-Karl and nodded politely to Roland and Fritzel, and used a sweeping gesture of one arm to direct the whole group toward the office they needed to visit.

They quickly learned that the Justice was very good at being politely sarcastic. He was also very good at explaining to Philip-Augustus what he should be seeing in the various documents and journals and ledgers, but was not. Philip-Augustus was soon leaning over the work table, eagerly following a dry pen that was being used as a pointer, while the clerk who belonged to the office became more and more flustered, and Roland took notes in a set of wax tablets and a growing pile of scraps of paper.

There was not really enough space in the office for seven additional people – especially when one of them was Fritzel – so Franz-Karl and Fritzel drifted out into the corridor and leaned against the doorposts, where they could hear what went on without jogging anyone's elbow. If the accounts had been in order, Franz-Karl would have found them interesting to compare with the accounts that he had seen in Traventi, but in their current state they were just confusing and annoying.

From their position in the corridor, Franz-Karl and Fritzel were also able to hear an unpleasantly familiar voice coming from another office farther along the corridor. Franz-Karl suggested to the World that he and Fritzel were not noticeable before he looked in that direction, and was glad he had taken the precaution: the large man with the misshapen jaw was standing in a doorway looking into one of the other offices, where the familiar voice of his partner was once more discussing blades.

The two Elderkin drifted nearer. Near enough to hear the discussion turn to some matter involving keys before it ended. They stepped aside into an office whose clerk was elsewhere while the big man and his nasty partner walked past, then moved on into the office where the discussion had happened. Franz-Karl went all the way in. Fritzel moved to one side once he had entered, avoiding the place the large man had been standing.

A man with graying, mousy brown hair was seated at the work table with his elbows on the table and his face in his hands. The buttons on his cuffs were clearly visible. Franz-Karl pulled a matching button out of one of his inner pockets and set it on the table with a firm click. The man dropped his hands and looked toward the sound, his eyes widening.

Franz-Karl said politely, "Blessed morning. I hope that your family are well?" before the man's face had quite decided what expression it should show at finding two Elderkin suddenly in his office.

Now the expression was purely mystified. "They are all very well, your lordship. Heaven be thanked."

"I am very glad to hear it, since they are outside the scope of my protection."

The man's expression got confused again, but eventually settled on understanding. "Ah." He picked up the button and looked at it, then nodded sharply once. "Your lordship is of the blood of the Falkenburgs." There was not enough doubt in the words for it to be a question.

"I am the younger son of Leon-Alexander von Falkenburg, Franz-Karl." His bow was a little more elaborate than the minimum required, but not enough to be sarcastic or insulting.

The man picked up two key rings that were laying on the table and removed one key from each, placing the loose keys on the table where the button had been moments earlier. "My name is Dusek Urban. And I have been strictly ordered to ensure that all of the keys in these sets not in the personal possession of a Falkenburg should be handed over to a messenger who will arrive shortly. I... I suspect it might be a good thing if one key of each set is in fact held by a Falkenburg." He lifted his fingers off the keys.

Franz-Karl picked up the keys. He looked at their complex wards for a long moment, turning them so that the light and shadows moved across them, and weighed them in his hand. Then he put them away in the inner pocket that had held the button. "I believe that you are correct. I have been taught a little about counteracting the grimoire those fools keep trying to use." He could not help grinning. "They are doing this particular Binding wrong. Again: they are using a very poor translation. But that is no reason for us to correct them."

Dusek Urban winced at the mention of the grimoire, but smiled at them, then stood and performed a proper, formal bow. Franz-Karl and Fritzel both returned the bow, then left the office and walked back toward Philip-Augustus and the others.

"D'ye suppose we'll find the locks for those keys, Your Honor?" Fritzel asked in Elderic.

Franz-Karl shrugged. "I'm a Notary of Traventi and it seems this Palace is brim-full of broken contracts and hedge-wizards, and Heaven and the Saints alone know what all else. There is likely no such thing as an honest coincidence anywhere within a hundred miles from this spot. I just hope the things behind those locks are not too horrible when we find them. The keys themselves are not too bad, but they carry a sort of reflection of something false and slimy."

It took nearly the entire morning for Justice von Trebice to reach a conclusion about Philip-Augustus's holdings. He did not say what that conclusion was, exactly, but the Justice's clerks looked triumphant and at least three of the Palace clerks looked ready to die of sheer mortification. Franz-Karl carefully memorized some of the Justice's more cutting comments and dearly hoped he would someday have the opportunity to use them in a courtroom or council session.

As the group left the offices, Justice von Trebice accepted an invitation from Philip-Augustus to dine at the Traventine Residence, but he asked to delay the meal for a day or two because he had another layer of treasury clerks to chastise, and that was work that should be done promptly. He handed several key-rings to Philip-Augustus and directed one of his clerks to carry a pile of documents and ledgers to the Traventine Residence: fetching and carrying were beneath Roland's dignity as majordomo.

Philip-Augustus laughed and agreed to the delay. He seemed more cheerful than he had been in months. Justice von Trebice had treated him as a client, not a child, and that mattered. He spent part of the afternoon carefully arranging the ledgers and papers the Justice provided in the room that had been their father's study.

Franz-Karl started to lock the keys and prayer beads away, but paused, and returned the beads to his wrist and the keys to his pocket. Better to have them and not need them than vice versa, and the need might be sudden and unexpected.

The next morning after breakfast, Vendal the Rathvin, arrived at the dining room servants' door with a pair of burly looking Old Palace Servants. He and Franz-Karl and Philip-Augustus and Fritzel went through all of the storerooms in the West Palace and some that were in various outbuildings. The other servants did much of the lifting and carrying and moving things aside that was needed, while Fritzel served as formal escort for the two young lords, but on a few occasions the tall Elderkin used his extra height and strength to reach some of the items they wished to examine.

They found more bad food in the West Palace than elsewhere – there were even five more jars for the river – but Vendal frowned at the markings on the worst jars and bundles. He said that some of them had been moved to the West Palace from their proper places, and that he would have them replaced with good supplies and find out who was playing games with the inventories.

His tone suggested that the people found playing games would not be amused.

When they paused for a mid-day meal in an annex of one of the kitchens, they all scrubbed their hands carefully with some of the harsh soap from the laundries. No one wanted to risk swallowing some spatter of the stuff they had been handling, nor any of the dust, and table forks were for Noble dining rooms, not servant dining halls.

Philip-Augustus was impressed when Franz-Karl sorted the supplies. He knew about the 'don't notice us' trick, of course, but the boys had been using that since Franz-Karl could walk, so it was not special. Seeing when food was spoiled or poisoned when other people could not seemed much more like a proper Elderkin Gift. Hunting for dangers and secrets below the ground was as good as being in an adventure story.

When they were finished searching, Vendal and his companions returned to the main Palace through the deep tunnels, while the three Elderkin used the servants' stairs to return to the Traventine Residence.

They had not quite finished changing out of the clothes they had worn in the storerooms when one of Vendal's men appeared at the servants' door nearest the sleeping chambers. He carried a message from Vendal politely but urgently asking for additional advice from Franz-Karl. All three hastily finished dressing, and when Franz-Karl and Fritzel followed the messenger down into the deep tunnels, Philip-Augustus went with them.

They went all the way along the tunnel, past the lamp and the well, to the panel that opened into the main Palace storeroom. When they went through the door-panel, they found Vendal and the other four Rathvins looking at something in the corner of the room nearest to where the panel opened. A few other men and women with the look of the Old Palace Servants were gathered nearer to the door out into the Palace corridor.

There were two small chests, heavily bound with iron straps and showing complicated keyholes, sitting on the floor in the corner of the room. As he walked nearer Franz-Karl could feel something huge paying attention to what they were doing in that shadowy room. The shadows were misbehaving a little, in patterns that matched the same grimoire he had faced before.

"Your Honor, are those trapped?" Vendal asked.

"I think that they are supposed to be... But not if you have one of the proper keys." Franz-Karl took the two keys out of his pocket, but he did not try them immediately. He squatted beside the chests and looked at them and at the keys for a long moment, watching shadows move even though the light did not, then shrugged. "Not much of a trap even without the right keys, but it is safer with them..."

He exchanged the keys between his left and right hands – the shadows on the keys fit the shadows on the chests better that way – and unlocked both of the chests, then stepped back quickly. He had felt a sort of twanggg through the metal of each key as it turned, but no one else seemed to hear anything. Philip-Augustus even complained that nothing had happened.

When Vendal opened the lids of the chests, they found that the chests were stuffed full of small, filled drawstring bags made of thin leather. Some of them had treasury marks showing they held, or had once held, certain large sums in silver. A few others had no marks but scuff marks on the leather.

The unmarked bags were all full of gold when the Rathvins checked them.

Franz-Karl remembered tax days in Traventi, and some Council discussions. "Well, that's foolish," he said.

"Foolish?" Philip-Augustus said.

"Name three honest merchants who sell anything you would need entire sacks of gold to buy." Franz-Karl shrugged. "Name three craftsmen that would even be able to make change if you paid for their wares in gold. With this much gold? Someone is planning to build or buy something huge, like estates or buildings, or decorate an entire cathedral. Or else they plan to buy armies, maybe... but mercenaries prefer chests full of silver so that they can pay their men." He kept well back while he looked at the chests a little longer, thinking, then looked up. "Vendal, can your people provide two shovel-fulls of stable-sweepings?"

"Of course!" Vendal waved a hand and one of the waiting Servants went out the public door of the storeroom into the corridor. The pock-marked Rathvin was not the only grownup in the room that chuckled.

"Oh, good!" Philip-Augustus said eagerly, "You need to make the glamour last until they hand it over to someone. Like in the story." He poked at Franz-Karl's arm.

Franz-Karl moved away, staying at a careful distance from the chests. When Philip-Augustus tried to followed him, he somehow found Fritzel in his way. Franz-Karl was glad to not be poked at: he was trying to remember things from a handful of different stories and some lessons in Traventi, and think of how they might fit together with the safe-keeping Binding from the grimoire. Bindings with Keys were tricky, even after the lessons he had received from Finn Locker in Traventi, and fairy gold was worse.

By the time the Servant returned with a bucket from the stables, Franz-Karl thought that he was ready.

The bags of coins – ten bags of silver and two bags of gold – were removed from the left hand chest and carried to the far side of the room, and the metal-bound box was refilled with stuff from the bucket. Franz-Karl did not bother to speak loudly while he tried to create the Binding: he was not talking to the people in the room. He was not even talking to the chest and its contents – not really. He was fairly certain that he was talking to the listening presence, and most of the important words were not Allemanic or Remoran or even proper modern Elderic: fashioning trash into fairy-gold was an old, old trick. He was not really surprised when things shifted after the third repetition: the oldest Bindings went by threes.

Franz-Karl sank back on the heels of his boots. "Does that look right?"

Vendal peered at the chest's contents without approaching too near, then walked across the room to look at the sacks that had been removed from the chest. "Even the scuffs on the bags look the same, Your Honor."

Franz-Karl closed the chest and turned its key, and reset the protective Binding using better Remoran than the writer of the grimoire had ever written.

Then he moved two steps to the right and did it all again. He wobbled when he tried to stand up afterward, but Fritzel steadied him, and the Rathvins gave him some bread and cheese and sweet, watered wine.

"How long will it hold?" the oldest Rathvin asked.

"Until after each chest is opened and the contents are moved a bit."

Philip-Augustus huffed, "That isn't what I told you to do!"

He reached a hand toward Franz-Karl, but Fritzel caught his wrist, gently, and suggested in Elderic, "Your Lordship is a Binder yourself, and older than His Honor, but I didn't see you offer to set the Binding..."

Philip-Augustus leaned away from Franz-Karl but asked in Allemanic, that the Servants would understand, "What shall we do with all this treasure?"

"Perhaps the one that accepts the eggs could guard it?" Fritzel suggested, and at least two of the Rathvins approved, but Vendal looked worried.

Franz-Karl felt tired, but he knew what Reverend Count Adrasteia would recommend. While she taught him the codes and special inks she had talked about the foolishness of people trying to be too secret and not secret enough, all at the same time. "This is treasure found unattended in a Falkenburg Palace, so it must be Falkenburg treasure. Use as much as is needful to fill the pantries and storerooms, now and during what is coming." He looked around at the rathvins. "Don't hide the rest all in one place," he said. "Don't let any one person know where all of it is hidden. Make sure more than one person not always in each other's company knows where each hiding place is. Lost treasure is no use to anyone."

"Ah." Vendal made a pile of the treasure from one chest: both bags of gold and and all ten of silver, and pushed it toward the three Elderkin. "Will you need help carrying these?"

Fritzel snorted and let his voice drop into its natural deep range. "Hardly." He gathered up the bags of coins and escorted the two boys back through the tunnels to their Residence.

The next day Fritzel left the Palace on one of his regular visits to Greenoak Square. When he returned, he showed the boys a receipt from the Karnburg branch of the Bank of Mistella for the deposit of the bags of gold and half of the bags of silver into an account in the names of the Wolfsberg-Falkenburgs, with the boys and their mother and Fritzel all listed as authorities. The other bags of silver they stored in the Residence, hidden and protected by bindings, in case of need. The receipt went into the locked and hidden and protected document case that stayed under Fritzel's bed when it was not open.

Franz-Karl and his Mama were not summoned to any Privy Council meetings for a few days, but the rain poured out of the sky so that no one was inclined to leave the Residence. Occasionally messages arrived for Philip-Augustus from Justice von Trebice.

On the second evening Philip-Augustus was summoned to Court to swear fealty for the estates he held as a vassal of His Excellency: that was the baronies and their associated estates. The haunted tower was not included in the oath-taking for some reason that made very little sense when Justice von Trebice tried to explain it, even though the income from the tower estate was now a major support of the Traventine Residence.

Childe Silvia was summoned to Court to witness the oath-taking, since Philip-Augustus was her son, and the Wedding Contract was involved. Franz-Karl was not summoned to Court, since he was not properly present in the Palace and also not counted as old enough to attend such ceremonies.

When Childe Silvia and Philip-Augustus returned to the Residence, Philip-Augustus was wearing some jewelry that that did not belong with mourning clothes, so he took it off and set it aside for the next months. Childe Silvia's hair had stopped dripping sparks, and did not begin again until her next conversation with a Palace official.

## CHAPTER XVII: The First Letter

## *Wherein the Bad News Begins to Arrive*

A few days after Philip-Augustus was confirmed as lord of the first few estates, Roland, the majordomo of the Traventine Residence, awakened Childe Silvia just after dawn. Franz-Karl was already awake, and left the nursery to see what was happening. There was a letter addressed to both Heirs of Traventi lying on a table that had been empty at midnight when Roland went to bed: a letter whose Elderkin-green wax seal displayed the shape of a winged sphinx.

When Franz-Karl's Mama picked the letter up, it fell open, but one side of the seal remained attached to the paper. She read it silently, then handed it to Franz-Karl...

The letter was not enciphered in the normal fashion, but the writing quivered on the page, as though the letters wanted to hide themselves in other shapes. Franz-Karl wondered what it would look like to anyone other than the addressees. It said in Elderic:

From Antonia Adrasteia to Armoria Silvia and Falx Franciscocarolus, Heirs of the Succession of the Dukes of Traventi, Greetings.

I am presently in quarantine in a mountain hermitage called the Singer's Well, so to relieve my boredom I have devised a way to send you this news. It is not a method that can be used often. To reply, place a letter sealed with a Notary's signet where this one was found, tonight at midnight. One single seal for pages from both of you would be best.

Some days ago I heard that merchants from Mistella of the Plains had arrived at the House on the Rock a few days earlier. I had sent messages and money to Mistella before the snows to make certain purchases, so I journeyed to the House on the Rock to learn whether my purchases had arrived.

Arriving at the House on the Rock, I greeted Her Grace the Duke, who at that time seemed in fine health.

When I went to the household where the merchants were guests, I observed that some of them were ill in varying degrees. One showed some signs of a rash with an unfamiliar pattern. Some servants of the household who had attended them seemed to be shaping toward feverish.

When asked, the merchants said that they had buried some of their company along the road. Travel is chancy this early in the year, and an occasional death by misadventure, while sad, is not unknown. Deaths, plural, in a company where the survivors were ill, was not likely mere misadventure. I delayed briefly to inquire about the course of their illnesses, which did not match the patterns in the known lists of the pestilences. They also reported rumors of pestilence in the coastal cities and the eastern shores of the Mothersea, but no certainty of sickness in Mistella herself when they set out.

I returned to Her Grace and warned her to declare Greater Plague Law at once, speaking from a distance in case some contagion had attached itself to my person while she was as yet untouched.

I chose the messages carried by the pigeons that were sent to you, and to Greenoak Square, and to certain others.

Then I removed myself to this place of retreat, which is unused during the cold seasons but left well stocked with firewood and preserved foods. It is built around a spring of good water that has not failed in my memory.

I have contrived to acquire pigeons with homes at the House on the Rock and Valens' Market and at Leopard's Watch, but there are none that have their homes here, which is inconvenient: I can send messages in the usual fashion, but receiving replies and reports is complicated. Our people with allies in Mistella and along the road between have been asked to send pigeons south, if they have them, asking for word of this new pestilence.

By Heaven's Grace I arrived at the House on the Rock on the eve of the Cathedral Market, and there had been neither a Cathedral nor a Greater Market since the merchants crossed our borders. It is possible the Passes and Bridges were closed, and the Plague Flags went up, in time to spare many of our people Over the Water from the hazard. But there was an active dispute in the Courts of Justice involving people from Over the Water that finished on the day that I arrived at the House on the Rock, so hope cannot be certainty.

We know that the new sickness was loose in the House on the Rock and likely reached much of the Home Quarter.

There are reports that three people were approaching the South Valley along the Raenos Road and stopped when the flags went up. They are ill and are being tended, cautiously, but no illness has been reported in the South Valley itself as yet. I myself am not sick, but remain in quarantine. I have not lasted these many centuries by being careless.

There has been a report that the sickness reached one household at the very edge of the North Valley, likely before the flags went up, but if it has progressed farther, that news has not reached me here in the south.

From the little I have learned of this menace as yet, it may be as quick or quicker to seize its victims as measles, but slower to release them. It is furtive: any outward signs like pustules or a rash – if they come at all, reports are mixed – come very late. How deadly it is, and whether it has the useful habit of attacking each victim only once, it is too early to judge.

Look to your own safety and the welfare of your households as well as you may.

May Heaven and all the Saints hold you in their keeping.

When Franz-Karl set down the letter, it folded itself back up and resealed itself.

"To whom do we give which warnings?" he asked in Elderic, as he walked to the shelf where pens and ink and stores of paper were kept, along with wax for the seals. If his Mama wrote the messages herself, they would be read differently than if the Childe of Traventi signed messages written by a scribe. The chancery hand that Franz-Karl had learned in Traventi was clear and readable, but  different enough from the styles used by Karnburg scribes to look foreign. That would be useful now: foreign text carrying the seal of a foreign embassy would be difficult to ignore.

His Mama pushed a few limp tendrils of her hair away from her eyes. There were no sparks forming. "We report the count of days, the reports of the merchants, and the known habits of the pestilence... people will need that news for what planning can be done." She counted on her fingers. "Who do you count senior among the Falkenburgs and in the city?"

"Of those within a day's journey from the Palace? His Excellency, the acting Archduke, Aunt Queen Gertrude, Prince Otto, Professor-Baron Walther von Falkenburg, the Rathvins – or perhaps just Vendal, Justice von Trebice, someone at the Cathedral, and two or three of the less useless general officers of various military units. Also Damian at Greenoak Square, of course. So, ten or eleven messages, depending on which generals you prefer."

"A useful list, but His Excellency your Grandfather would disagree about the Professor-Baron," she warned.

"His Excellency my Grandfather can order the University to pay attention to him, being King and Archduke and Emperor, and neither a woman nor a child nor – officially – Elderkin," Franz-Karl answered, in Elderic, in a deliberately bland, reasonable tone. He would not have spoken so plainly in Remoran, and absolutely not in Allemanic, not even here in the relative privacy of their own apartments. The Falkenburg line officially acknowledged no Manifest ancestry.

He continued with a shrug, "The Professor-Baron will know which of his colleagues at the University might make the best use of the warning. Or at least not ignore it entirely."

Franz-Karl wrote a draft in Remoran in his best chancery writing style and showed it to his Mama. She suggested some small changes to the wording and handed it back, and he began to make the formal copies, each with the correct salutation for the specific person addressed. "Does writing diplomatic dispatches in Remoran count as lessons?" he asked hopefully as he handed over the message for his Excellency for her to sign and seal.

"I suppose that it will have to." She smiled tiredly. "Whether or not the authorities announce this formally, you and I will likely be back in that council chamber again today, with little time for your proper lessons." She signed the message for His Excellency and placed wax seals on both the document itself, to attest to its truth, and the wrapper in which it was placed, to protect it from prying eyes.

There was so little news to give that the messages were short: it did not take long to write all of them and hand them over for the messengers to deliver. They finished just a little too late to return to their beds before it was time for breakfast and to prepare for the day's Privy Council meeting.

In the end, the recipients of the messages included just two generals: the Marshall of the Falkenburg Imperial Forces and a General in charge of the defenses of Karnburg, but not the leader of the Imperial Army of the Allemanic Kingdom.

They included a message to Arch-Hierophants Ambrose and Diotima at the Cathedral more to avoid giving offense than because the cathedral might be useful. Diotima was a practical person, but despite what the laws of the Ecclesialist church said about equality of authority in the Sanctuaries, she was likely to be ignored in the Allemanic territory of Karnburg because she was a woman. Ambrose was... Ambrose, and he did not like Elderkin. Franz-Karl's Mama just sighed and shook her head.

Franz-Karl hoped someone who received the messages would take proper precautions, but he suspected that if the city's safety depended on the lords who attended Falkenburg Privy Council meetings, they were all doomed. The Councilors seemed to think that investing Philip-Augustus with some of his inheritance should be balanced by back-sliding in other areas of the Contract.

He spent the entire Council meeting that day drawing newts. Some of the newts were on fire.

# CHAPTER XVIII: The Arrival

## *Wherein Karnburg Receives an Unwanted Guest*

The new sickness arrived in the city through the markets. It was more likely that it came through the ones that sold goods arriving on the river barges than the markets frequented by local farmers. But it spread so subtly that by the time it was unmistakably present, His Royal Highness Prince Otto said that there was no way to tell where it had first arrived: there were hints of it in half of the districts of the city, once people looked, as well as many of the suburbs outside the walls and some of the farming villages still farther from the city's heart.

The sickness arrived in the Palace shortly afterward through the servants, who visited the markets to purchase things that were needful for life, and brought home the sickness along with their purchases. A day would come when someone who worked at the same task every day – or every market day – no longer appeared. Many servants who did appear seemed less than well: weakened or feverish or both, red-eyed, coughing, sneezing, eventually with faces blotched by rashes.

There was really no avoiding it: the servants' quarters were crowded, and servants worked everywhere in the Palace. But very few of the people who considered themselves important in the city or the Palace admitted that there was a problem, here in Karnburg in the Domains of the Falkenburgs, though they spoke to Childe Silvia with shows of extravagant sympathy about the reports of a pestilence in the Sovereign Duchy of Traventi.

The Privy Council continued to meet, and continued to do little useful about the Marriage Contract. Of course, they said – except the Northerners, who openly wanted no more Elderkin in the Palace at all, and would be glad to be rid of the ones already there – of course Elderkin ladies from Traventi would be sent for once the borders opened again: so the councilors counted that particular matter as addressed and no longer needing discussion. For the other matters under discussion – not under dispute, of course: none of the Allemanic Lords acknowledged that there were disputes– agreements about what to do changed from one meeting to the next so that little was accomplished. But they wanted the Heirs of Traventi to observe how very busily they were working at dealing with the matter of the Marriage Contract, so both Childe Silvia and her heir Franz-Karl were required to attend the sessions.

Franz-Karl presented the Council with a letter directing that his fees as a Notary should be delivered to an account in his name at the Bank of Mistella. He was thinking about things to do with the money that would annoy the Councilors, but most of the things he could think of would require trustees in Karnburg, where being a Notary did not count for much: it was getting to be a lot of money. He had consulted more than one tome of Natural Philosophy and determined that pictures of striped newts should have lengthwise stripes, which was more useful than anything achieved by the Privy Council itself.

Even some of the areas of the Palace that were favored by the Chamberlain and the so-called Master of the Household began to show signs of neglect as the healthy servants were spread thinner to fill the gaps left by the sickness that was not happening.

One morning about a week after Reverend Count Adrasteia's letter arrived, Prince Otto was allowed to address the Privy Council. He had been put off three or four times, but their Excellencies were holding formal audiences that afternoon, and complaints about discourtesy from Her Excellency's brother would spoil the tone of the affair, so the Councilors grudgingly let him in to speak.

They began by asking him questions about road repairs, but they asked them politely. His Royal Highness Prince Otto had arrived before the Privy Council dressed for the Imperial audiences with magnificent formality, since there would not be time later to leave the Palace, change his clothes, and return in time to meet with Their Excellencies. The Privy Councilors were vastly underdressed by comparison, and phrased their questions with careful awareness that they were speaking to royalty and to His Excellency's brother-in-law. He answered their questions extremely thoroughly, and managed to mention at the end, as an afterthought, that commerce in the city was sparse even for the season, there had been some surprising deaths, and more house fires than usual in the poorer districts.

Franz-Karl remembered Reverend Count Great Aunt Adrasteia's warning about fire. He wondered whether pestilences brought fires, but did not know who to ask.

Franz-Karl and Philip-Augustus and their Mama had all received individual notes instructing them to attend their Excellencies' audience. Two Privy Councilors who were not summoned to the audience delayed Franz-Karl and his Mama after the Privy Council meeting so that they needed to dress in a rush. Franz-Karl was tempted to not change: it was all just color-of-sorrow anyway.

Franz-Karl's room had been swept and dusted for the first time in several days. He found two signed and sealed documents on his pillow: one was a slightly scuffed and crumpled copy of Her Excellency's letter about assignments of the Palace servants; the other was signed by Dusek Urban and seemed to be a copy of a section of the Palace accounts, listing some shops and merchants, and what wares they supplied, which were a rather odd mix. He had no time to think about what to do with these unexpected gifts – Tam was still trying to tug his hair into some semblance of order while the Traventine party were beginning to walk toward the door of their suite – so he stuffed them into various pockets in the long skirts of his coat.

Once they reached the reception hall that would be used for the audiences, they were announced by the Master of Protocol's announcer, who managed to mangle all of their titles. Philip-Augustus looked very annoyed: his titles – the ones that had seniority at a Court event like this one – were all purely Allemanic and derived from Falkenburg inheritances, so there was no excuse for anyone at the Allemanic and Falkenburg Court to get them wrong. Franz-Karl and his Mama just ignored the butchered titles, which were not as bad as some of the formulas produced during the Privy Council sessions. The previous announcer had been famous for getting titles and protocol correct in languages he did not even know – a skill that somehow had rarely extended to Traventine titles – but he had not been at his post for several days.

Once announced and in the room, the nobles and officials drifted in slow eddies around the audience chamber waiting for Their Excellencies to arrive. Prince Otto was one of the most magnificent: besides his royal rank and imperial kinship, Karnburg was an important and prosperous river port – even with its commerce temporarily muted – and an Imperial capital besides, and he was its governing Lord. There were a few others who tried to match him, and many others who wished they could try.

By contrast, Philip-Augustus, Court Grand Duke and Count of Wolfsberg, was plainly dressed in black, in Allemanic mourning for his father who was less than a year dead. Silvia, Graefinwitwe of Wolfsberg and Childe of Traventi, was wearing the dull color-of-sorrow of Traventine mourning, as was Franz-Karl. Their attendants, Fritzel and Itron Gwenlian, were quietly dressed out of respect for the household's grief, but not in color-of-sorrow. The party stood out in the sparkling throng more than if they had been too laden with jewels to move.

Franz-Karl had his doubts about one Graefin from a district known for its silver mines: if she fell over, they might need a crane to get her back up... though Fritzel could probably manage it, if the need arose.

There were only two chairs in the room: the chairs of state that their Excellencies would occupy. Once they were seated and everyone bowed to them, no one would move without being instructed to. But it was considered rude to plant yourself in a spot with a convenient view and wait for their Excellencies to arrive. The movements of the nobles and officials in the crowd was a bit like a very slow game of musical chairs as everyone tried to achieve a good vantage point without making enemies they could not afford.

Philip-Augustus was a terror at musical chairs. Despite wandering, and politely greeting various people, when Their Excellencies arrived, he grasped Franz-Karl's sleeve with one hand and their Mama's hand with the other. He tugged them two steps to the side and one step forward, and elbowed a minor Baron, and suddenly the boys were in the front row around the open space that faced the chairs of state, with their Mama behind them looking at their Excellencies over the boys' heads.

Their Excellencies finished the official part of the gathering – there were some awards and titles and military ranks that needed to come from His Excellency's own hand, not by way of an acting Archduke – and invited the nobles and officials to mingle. They did so, watching carefully to see whether any of their rivals gained the attention of His Excellency. Philip-Augustus and his Mama stayed in the fringes of the group around His Excellency.

Her Excellency received less attention from the gathering nobles and officials, except from family. By traditional protocol she should have presided with her husband, but Northerners, especially the Reformist faction, were very strongly against women doing anything important or in public, and their attitudes had seeped into the habits of the Palace, partly because they left their wives and daughters elsewhere, so the ladies were greatly outnumbered in the room.

Franz-Karl drifted closer to Her Excellency's chair, and bowed. He did not need much of a Gift to be unnoticed in a room full of a number of ladies in enormous skirts and a much larger number of tall gentlemen in dramatic, full-skirted coats, whose attention was largely elsewhere. He remembered the letter in the deep pocket of his own coat, and pulled it out.

"What do you have there, Your Honor?" Her Excellency asked with a smile.

Franz-Karl handed her the letter and pulled out his signet from where it usually hung on its ribbon inside his clothes, bowing again. "Your Excellency, speaking as a Notary of Traventi, may I ask, Did Your Excellency write this letter?"

Her Excellency's eyes widened slightly when she saw the signet, and then she looked annoyed as she saw the state of the parchment. "I did write it," she said quietly. "And signed it with my own hand, including this copy of it."

"Would Your Excellency like to have it Witnessed by a Notary?"

She looked at him for a moment, then decided, "Do you know, Your Honor, I believe that I would like that letter witnessed by a Notary. Is there anything you will need?"

"Candle-wax would be sufficient, but proper sealing-wax would be better... and a pen and ink to sign with as witness would make it look more official."

"But not make the Witnessing more effective?" Her Royal Highness Aunt Queen Gertrude was standing beside her Excellency's chair.

"Maestro Petros said: Words or wax, Witnessing is Witnessing for a full Notary." Franz-Karl answered absently, watching Vendal arrive almost immediately with a tray bearing pen, ink, wax, and a flame to melt the wax. He wondered how long it had been since the senior servant had actually worked as a footman: his livery looked a little tight.

He Witnessed the letter and Vendal left with the tray before most people in the crowded room noticed that anything was happening.

He offered the letter to her Excellency, but she waved him off. "Kindly give that to Her Honor Childe Silvia, as evidence and for safe-keeping."

"Of course, Your Excellency." Franz-Karl bowed and tucked the letter back into his coat. He added, "Now that it is witnessed, destroying it will just ... lock it away from meddling?... We destroy witnessed things for safety, sometimes. Or for secrecy."

"Do you know who that was, carrying the tray?" Her Royal Highness Aunt Queen Gertrude seemed amused.

"I know a name, Your Highness." Franz-Karl answered carefully, "And I have some suspicions about how the letter arrived in my hand."

His Serene Highness the Prince-Elector of Bremerhaven came toward Her Excellency's chair, and when Her Royal Highness Aunt Queen Gertrude turned to face and greet him, her skirts just happened to obscure Franz-Karl. The noble did not so much speak with the ladies as declaim at them, seeming to expect the widowed Queen to succumb to his manly... something: charms were nowhere on offer. After he turned abruptly, without a bow, and walked away, Franz-Karl said thoughtfully, "I expected him to be slimier, somehow, when speaking privately, but that was worse than a council session. Do you suppose they think rudeness is evidence of virtue?"

"Politeness to females is beneath the dignity of Northern nobles," his Aunt replied dryly in Remoran.

"At least 'human' females stand slightly above livestock on their Ladder of Virtue, unlike Elderkin..." Franz-Karl answered in the same language. "You should hear the way Pristinists talk to my Mama and Itron Gwenlian when no one who outranks them is present."

"Dear Heaven," Her Excellency said. "I can't imagine anything much worse than that... insolence."

Franz-Karl rejoined his Mama and brother shortly before His Excellency signaled the end of the audience gathering by standing up. Everyone in the room bowed, including Her Excellency, who had stood up a moment after her husband.

As Their Excellencies moved toward the door, the Margraff-Elector of Ansbach stepped into their path with an elaborate bow and made a speech inviting His Excellency and the Court to a small entertainment at his city mansion the following evening. There was no mention of Her Excellency: the Margraff-Elector, being a Pristinist, might entertain some high-ranking females, more or less under duress, but he would certainly not publicly announce that he was going to do it.

His Excellency made a speech in response that could equally well be either an acceptance or a demurral. Everyone knew that there were rituals required when the King of the Allemans left the Palace that were a huge nuisance, so it was not likely that His Excellency would actually attend a gathering elsewhere in the city, but by not declining he gave partial status as a Royal and Imperial event to the party. People could act as if they expected that he would be there, or might be there, and dress accordingly.

Franz-Karl did not waste time wondering what the small entertainment would be. Everyone also knew that the inhabitants of the Traventine Residence would not attend entertainments outside their own walls, even in His Excellency's company, being still formally in deep morning. There was a very short list of gatherings that they might or should properly attend, and a small entertainment at the home of a Margraff-Elector was nowhere on that list. There was no need to mention that the Traventines, who were Elderkin while the Margraff-Elector was Pristinist, would neither be willing nor invited to cross his threshold.

Franz-Karl thought that when they finished the mourning period his Mama should host a 'small entertainment' that his Excellency could attend, since it would be within the Palace walls. The Northerners would face a choice between giving proper guesting oaths at the Threshold of the Residence, or missing the party and conversations.

When they had returned home to their own apartments, Franz-Karl gave his Mama the Witnessed copy of Her Excellency's letter.

Philip-Augustus eyed the parchment and its seal warily. "Do you think it will make a difference?" His accent was still 'foreign' when speaking Elderic, but he was reasonably fluent.

"Vendal of the Faithful Ones thought it would."

"The Faithful Ones?" their Mama asked.

"What Papa called 'the Old Palace Servants'. Vendal is important among them, and he guided our survey of the cellars and storerooms. I think... We are not the only ones with problems because there are so many Northerners employed by the Chamberlain's offices." He took out the other paper he had received. "I have also received this, but I do not know what to do with it."

Childe Silvia read the list with satisfaction, then handed it to Itron Gwenlian. "We know what to do with it," she said, smiling slightly.

# CHAPTER XIX: The Sickness Spreads

## *Wherein Too Many Sick People Need Tending*

On the day after the Margraff-Elector's entertainment, the expected meeting of the Falkenburg Privy Council was delayed. At noon, the meeting was officially canceled for the day: it was reported that several of the Margraff-Elector's noble guests had taken to their beds with fever, including a few on the formal list of members of the Privy Council.

Suddenly, people in the Palace were speaking openly about the possibility that there might be an outbreak of some sickness in the city and Palace.

On the following day, the Privy Council meeting was canceled again. His Royal Highness Prince Otto visited the Traventine Residence before leaving the Palace after consulting with His Excellency and His Royal Grace acting Archduke Uncle Helm-Friedrich. Mindful of the traditional prohibition against thanking Elderkin, His Royal Highness said that the warning from Traventi about the new sickness had been very helpful. He also told Her Honor Childe Silvia and her sons that two of the nobles that had been guests at the Margraff-Elector's house had died, and two others had lost family members to the sickness. He finished, "... and there's no telling how long any of them were sick."

"Very likely at least fourteen days," Franz-Karl said slowly. He had been reading Chronicles.

"Your Honor?" Prince Otto always addressed him properly.

"The Reverend Count Adrasteia wrote that it seems to develop like measles, but a bit slower. The chronicles say: measles runs ten days or two weeks to visible signs, with four days of severe fever, and death during the fevered time comes more often late than early."

"Do the chronicles say how many will die?" Prince Otto asked wearily.

"From something new? There is no way to tell until the sickness runs out of new victims to afflict, and then runs its course in those it has afflicted." The Chronicles were both clear and discouraging about that.

Within two more days, more than half of the people in the Palace who had not yet shown undeniable signs of sickness were red-eyed and coughing and some were beginning to be feverish.

Inside the Traventine Residence, Meister Seidl, the scholar who was tutoring Philip-Augustus did not arrive at his appointed time. Roland and most of the other Elderkin men-servants lasted another day before they were clearly affected, along with Nurse Rosa. Fritzel still showed no sign of the sickness, like Franz-Karl himself, but Franz-Karl's valet, Tam, was the last of the Elderkin men taken ill.

Some people working for the Master of the Household came and took Nurse Rosa away to be cared for with other women in the Palace. They said that it was not decent for her to stay and be tended in a household where all of the servants were men. And sick. Franz-Karl saw no fibs on their faces, but that said nothing about what their masters might be planning.

Itron Gwenlian was only mildly sarcastic about being ignored. She was busy tending the sick men-servants, and so far she was untouched by fever. And then, toward sunset, Philip-Augustus and Sophie-Alexa and Childe Silvia all went down with fever together, after showing few other warning signs of the illness.

When the evening meal was late, Fritzel and Franz-Karl went out the servants' door and down to the kitchen and brought some food back up the stairs. The few cooks and workers in the kitchen looked unhappy, but relieved to see them: they were all busy doing other people's jobs besides their own. Clothilde, the chief cook for evenings, apologized repeatedly for the disruption of service.

It took several trips for the two of them to bring enough food for twelve people, even with most of them sick and not very hungry, and by the last trip, the cooks were asking about the sick people.

Franz-Karl was glad they had the barrels of water in Juliana's room. Water needed to be brought up to keep refilling them, but that would be a burden dealt with between other tasks, rather than as a matter of urgency when the fevered called for water and there was none.

There was a long discussion – which went strange because people were feverish and not thinking clearly – about whether Holy Fire should be fetched from the kitchen to the hearth in Juliana's room, or whether they should bring Holy Fire from the lamp in the Household shrine. Franz-Karl was too young to be an initiate, so he was shut out of the room where the discussion took place, and he did not officially know where Fritzel brought the fire from. Itron Gwenlian shut the door while she said the blessings that made the hearth a Hearth. When she opened the door again, they built up the fire and set a kettle of water heating.

"Princes don't get taught cooking," Franz-Karl commented, watching the glowing coals. "Nor are royal seven-year-olds set to tending fires, either."

"I've cooked griddle cakes at harvest," Fritzel said. "And tended fires more than once."

Itron Gwenlian patted Franz-Karl's shoulder, added some herbs to a bowl of hot water, and took it away to the sickrooms.

That night was horrible. Sophie-Alexa's head hurt, and she cried in a scratchy voice for Rosa and for her Mama. Philip-Augustus spent half the night muttering phrases that did not make sense. Childe Silvia slept motionless and limp, which was more worrying than feverish restlessness would have been. And it became clear that six sick men was more than they could manage without more aid than the Palace authorities seemed willing or able to provide. But they did not trust the safety of Elderkin in other areas within the Palace, outside their own consecrated Thresholds.

Before dawn, they wrapped up the two sickest servants, and Fritzel and Roland – who was coughing and sneezing but did not yet have much of a fever – managed to get them out of the Palace gates and through the streets to the townhouse at Greenoak Square. Franz-Karl went as far as the West Gate to help the guards there not notice the people going out. When Fritzel and Roland returned, they brought back a small keg of salt, and dried sausages and some good Traventine cheeses to add to the stores in Juliana's room. They also brought some other things that might be needful for the rites of Hospitality, and mostly worrying news of their people at the townhouse.

Franz-Karl could not decide whether he wished that Roland had stayed at the Greenoak Square house. The majordomo would have been better tended there, and made one less to care for in the Residence, but he had lived in the Residence as long as Itron Gwenlian and Franz-Karl's Mama, longer than anyone else in the household. They might need his authority as well as his knowledge: some people in the Palace ignored that Fritzel was properly a grown man, and almost everyone in the Palace ignored women and children and footmen.

Once the two men returned, they moved Roland's bed into the room with the two remaining footmen, before he collapsed into it. They moved Franz-Karl's valet, Tam, in there as well. It made the room very crowded, but it was more convenient to tend the sick men all together.

They moved Philip-Augustus from his own lonely bedroom and put him into Franz-Karl's proper bed in the Nursery – across from Sophie-Alexa – and made up a pallet on the floor for Franz-Karl using the mattress from Nurse Rosa's bed. Franz-Karl was too small to be much use tending sick grownups, but he could give his brother and little sister drinks of water, and Gwenlian's herbal stuff, and help them with chamberpots... and listen for them in the night when Gwenlian was tending the sick grownups and Fritzel was carrying water and supplies up the servants' stairs and slop-buckets down them.

That next night was a little easier than the ones preceding it.

The next day Itron Gwenlian took to her bed with fever and a patchy rash. She was so very annoyed that Franz-Karl thought that the sickness was brave to attack her.

Only Franz-Karl and Fritzel remained unaffected by what the Palace servants were now calling the Great Sickness. Two boys, and one of them small, were not really enough hands to tend so many sick people, not with aid from the Palace servants being scant and unpredictable, so that they must do the servants' work too.

There were buckets of water and bundles of wood and pots and baskets of food to be hauled up flights of stairs, buckets of ashes and food scraps and the slops from the chamberpots to be hauled down them. Franz-Karl was not undersized for seven, but he was not large for his age either, so most of the heavy work fell to Fritzel. Even within the Residence, Franz-Karl could not safely carry a full pitcher very far, or several plates on a tray, so he did a great deal of scurrying around with smaller burdens. He often needed two or three trips for errands that a grownup could manage in one.

They never knew how long the new letter lay on the table waiting to be noticed. It was after noon before Franz-Karl read it. He had paused in that room to eat a few bites of something and sit in a chair, which he had not time to do since their early breakfast.

The letter read:

From Antonia Adrasteia, writing from Leopard's Watch, to Armoria Silvia and Falx Franciscocarolus, Heirs of the Succession of the Dukes of Traventi, Greetings.

There has been no news of anyone sickening after three full market-weeks away from the company of the sick, either in Traventi or in the lands to the south where the sickness arrived first. It seems a hasty pestilence. Therefore, I have returned home to collect and sift the news that has arrived in these past weeks, after setting the pestilence a maze it is not likely to pass.

I continue to avoid close company: there is still no sickness in the South Valley, and I would not wish to be the one who carried it here if we have misjudged the matter.

The lands south of the mountains report by pigeon that the affliction sometimes lingers, and lingers long, but there is no case reported, yet, of a recovered victim falling ill again with full fever, so it may resemble measles or smallpox in that much, that it strikes its victims but once, however stubbornly.

The sickness is said to be less deadly than smallpox, but it is too soon to judge whether that is fact or hope. The Blessed Serpentilla at Terme fears that the count of outright deaths and the lingering sufferers between them will match or surpass the dead of a strong smallpox outbreak.

Valens reports there were two deaths at the edge of the North Valley, and a handful of people sick, but no new sickness this market-week, so the Plague Laws are holding there, as here in the south.

The sickness is said to lie heavy on the Home Quarter, and unevenly as yet Over the Water.

According to rare pigeons Her Grace the Duke has been very ill, but is past the fever, and her illness does not seem to be the lingering sort. We may hope to hear that she is well in a week or so.

Severin's pigeons come every third day, each carrying a message entirely obscene, by which I judge that he is himself well or has recovered, but his people at the Dance are so sorely afflicted he has neither time nor attention to write further.

Look to your own safety and the welfare of your households as well as you may.

May Heaven and all the Saints hold you in their keeping.

When Franz-Karl read the letter to his Mama, he was not sure she heard him, but on the following day her fever began to subside a little. She did not speak much, except to ask after Philip-Augustus and Sophie-Alexa, but when she did speak, her words were sensible. She was able to eat a little more than she had during the worst of the fever, so Franz-Karl hoped that her strength might begin to return.

One of the footmen, a man called Marius, had a fever that suddenly increased very quickly, until he convulsed and died. Fritzel went out of the apartments to talk to the guard at the door of the West Palace – there was only one guard now – and did not like what he heard, or the guard's attitude, so before they sewed Marius into a clean sheet they cut off his hair to put in memorial tokens in the Household shrine. Fritzel, who was old enough to be an Initiate, looked up the prayers of a short-form funeral and said them before they closed the final clumsy seam and they set what had been Marius outside the Household's Threshold. They did not have a proper carved corpse-candle to give him, but they set up a plain candle in the Shrine beside the tokens to light his way.

The other footman and Tam seemed to be improving, and the others that were sick did not seem to be getting worse.

# CHAPTER XX: Another Letter

## *Wherein Worse News Arrives*

It was a shock to find the third letter waiting on the table only three days after the second, and a worse shock to read the direction on its wrapper: Armoria Silvia, Duke of Traventi and Childe Falx Franciscocarolus, Heir of the Succession of the Dukes of Traventi.

This message was short and terrible.

From Antonia Adrasteia, writing from Leopard's Watch, to Armoria Silvia, Duke of Traventi and Falx Franciscocarolus, Heir of the Succession of the Dukes of Traventi, Greetings.

I must sadly inform you that word has come from the House on the Rock that Her Grace the Duke Adriana has died.

It is imperative that Duke Silvia should immediately write, sign and seal at least two copies of her accession oath, each to be witnessed by a fully sworn Notary. Send one copy in reply to this letter, at midnight as before. Deliver the other to the hands of Archduke Friedrich-Augustus himself, and to no other hands.

I am very sorry to send such ill news. I will send more information about the death of the Duke and the present state of the Duchy when I have them.

May Heaven and the Saints Bless Adriana and Guide her to the Halls of Judgment.

May Heaven and all the Saints hold you both and all of your households in their keeping.

When he had read the letter, Franz-Karl took it to his Mama in her sickbed. She read it and turned even paler than the days of fever and worry had left her. She got out of bed and wrapped a blanket around herself and stumbled to the Nursery to look at her children that she had not seen since they all got sick. Sophie-Alexa opened her eyes and almost smiled at her mother, and reached for Franz-Karl's hand, but Philip-Augustus did not awaken. Then his Mama left Franz-Karl to watch his brother and sister and went into the room that held their Household Shrine, and closed the door.

Franz-Karl called loudly for Fritzel and told him the news without leaving his sister's side. Even as sick as she was, Sophie-Alexa was holding his hand so tight it almost hurt.

Fritzel bowed his head and signed himself and said "May Heaven and the Saints Bless Duke Adriana and Guide her to the Halls of Judgment. What do you need me to do, Your Honor?"

"Mama needs to write her accession oath, and we don't have the archives or the law libraries or anything to do it with. There is a full text of an accession oath from about five hundred years ago in one of the volumes of Elderic chronicles. That's not much to use as a pattern, but it will be better than to try to work with nothing at all: at least it should stop us from leaving out anything really important that the Allemanic Councils could jump on. Top shelf in Mama's study... third or fourth volume from the left, I think... then we will need pens and the good ink and ... parchment probably, not paper... and sealing wax. After it is written, you and I will need to deliver it to His Excellency's hands."

"I think I know the book your Honor means... and if not, I'll find the right one," Fritzel said.

Franz-Karl was shaking, but not really from cold. Fritzel wrapped a big old shawl they used as an extra blanket around Franz-Karl, and squeezed Franz-Karl's shoulder, and went out of the room.

While he sat waiting, watching his sister breathe and listening to his brother, Franz-Karl said the prayers for the dead in a whisper, adding his grandmother's name to his father's name that he had been saying for nearly a year, and Marius the dead footman, too. When he finished, he said a set of prayers for the nameless dead, both those he did not know at all and those he knew but whose deaths had not yet been reported to him. He was sure that there were too many of both kinds.

When Fritzel returned with the book and writing materials, he also brought his own best clothes for attending funerals, and started getting Franz-Karl's out of the clothes chest where they were stored.

Franz-Karl eased his hand out of Sophie-Alexa's grasp and wiggled the fingers to unkink them and get the blood flowing. He set the book of chronicles on the small table where he did his lessons and paged through it until he found the account he had remembered.

The oath was not long: there were only nine short paragraphs between the part that said, "Witnessed here by Heaven and the World and All the Saints and All the Watchful Dead" and the part that said, "All this I swear by my Life and Soul and Hope of the Halls of Judgment."

The oath stated very clearly that the new Duke would make no decree affecting the people of the Duchy under duress, would answer to no one but the Council and Populace of the Duchy, and would always act to protect the Duchy and its people from external attacks, especially from attempts to enslave them or subordinate them, individually or collectively. There were some bits about promising honest treaties with outsiders and honest judgments between insiders, and honest contracts with everybody, and preserving the ancient treasures of Traventi, and a promise to provide for the Heirs of Succession. And that was all.

If the Great Sickness caused people to die of an apoplexy, as Marius had died, there were a few Allemanic Councilors who were likely to be helped along when they heard the terms of this oath: Franz-Karl had spent enough time sitting in Privy Council meetings to know the names and faces of some of them. He started by writing out a translation of the oath into diplomatic Remoran, for the copy that would go to His Excellency. When that was done and ready for Her Grace the Duke His Mama to use, he created a text for an unsigned reference copy in legal Allemanic like the one he had helped Justice von Trebice create for the Marriage Contract.

When Her Grace the Duke His Mama came out of the Household Shrine, she nodded at the Elderic and Remoran versions of the oath, and almost smiled at the Allemanic reference copy.

"Do you think we should leave out 'and all the watchful dead'?" she asked wearily. "We don't know whether my Mother's corpse-candles are still burning."

Franz-Karl thought about it, and decided it felt wrong to leave out the Dead. He was sure that General Maximianus Rano would not approve. "What if we do the signing in the Household Shrine, so the ancestors and guardians can watch and bear witness?"

So that is what they did. Her Grace Duke Silvia wrote copies of the Elderic and Remoran versions of the oath with her own hand. Then she took them into the Shrine and signed them, and sealed them using her personal signet, since the seal of Traventi was far away in the Duchy.

Franz-Karl stood in the Shrine and signed and sealed those two copies with his own signet and added a notation that he was both a full Notary bearing Witness and the next Heir in Succession.

They put the Elderic copy on the table where the letters came and went, and it vanished immediately, like a bubble popping, along with a note about the death of Marius that they had placed there so that the news might move toward the man's family.

Franz-Karl and Fritzel washed their faces and hands and put on their good funeral clothes, and went out the front door of the Traventine Residence carrying a sealed package holding the Remoran and unsigned Allemanic copies of the oath.

# CHAPTER XXI: The Main Palace

*Wherein Our Hero Confers with Their Excellencies*

The guard at the main door of the West Palace did not want to let them out, and the guard at the main door of the central Palace did not want to let them in, but Fritzel let his voice drop into its thunderous natural range and announced loudly, "Urgent message for his Excellency!" and the guards suddenly remembered that the rule that delaying messages counted as treason was being enforced lately, as often as not. The two Elderkin were allowed into the main building of the Palace, and there were witnesses to their arrival.

One they were past the outer doors, no one saw which way they went. Franz-Karl leaned hard on his Gift for not being noticed, and they moved out of the public areas of the Palace and into the servants' stairs and passages as soon as they reached an entry panel. They were able to reach the servants' passages that served Their Excellencies' least public rooms before they encountered even one guard, who was at the servant's entrance leading to his Excellency's study and the bedroom beyond..

Franz-Karl backed up a little, and they made a small detour, and came out through the servants' door in Her Excellency's dressing room. Fritzel glanced around warily, checked the cold hearth and ran a finger across a bit of the woodwork. "No one has been in here in at least a week... but people sleep here in normal times."

"Tiring-woman and a maid or seamstress," Franz-Karl agreed quietly. There was a partly hemmed garment neatly folded on top of one chest. He saw no signs of the dead being tended in the room, but there were personal possessions next to both small beds. "Taken away like Nurse Rosa, perhaps."

In the next room, Her Excellency was laying in a fine bed ... which probably belonged to her chief attendant in normal times. A pale, tired-looking lady was seated beside her, wringing out a cloth to lay on her forehead. A second lady lay on a pallet on the floor next to the bed, limp with exhaustion, though her color was almost healthy. Both the seated lady and Her Excellency looked toward the door when Franz-Karl and Fritzel came through it, but neither made a fuss.

Her Excellency said softly, "Do not come too near, if you are still healthy. If you wish to speak to His Excellency, you will need to wait a little: there are physicians and officials buzzing around Him like flies at the moment." She coughed weakly. "Is there news?"

It took Franz-Karl what felt like a long time to find words, but his grandmother Her Excellency did not seem to notice, so perhaps not. "We hear nothing from the Palace or about the family," he said finally. "Nor about the city outside the Palace walls. Sometimes we hear the death bells at the cathedral, or the sound of drums, but there is no one to tell us who they are for. My mother and brother and sister are sick, but not dying, we think. But word has come that my Mother is now Her Grace the Duke Silvia of Traventi."

"May Heaven and all the Saints guard Duke Adriana, and guide her to the Halls of Judgment," Her Excellency said, slurring the words a little, as though she had said them too many times. The lady in waiting who was awake said the prayer with her. Her Excellency waved a hand, and the lady began to tell them some of the family news while they waited.

Her Serene Grace Grand Duchess Aunt Erminia and her son and husband had moved to their country estate before the winter. No news had come from them. No news had come from His Excellency's daughters who had married into foreign courts, but that might just be the slowness of travel early in the season. It was barely a full month since the Plague law was declared in Traventi.

Her Royal Highness Aunt Dowager Queen Gertrude and her household had shut themselves in their apartments in the East Palace, and there were strange rumors about what was going on in there. No one really knew anything except that a Lesser Chamberlain who had tried to bully his way in had been knifed a little by one of Queen Gertrude's Szekely Hussars. It was not a wound that was likely to be deadly, or even serious, just a little bloodshed to make a point...

Franz-Karl wondered who, if anyone, was using the servants' doors and stairs in the East Palace.

The oldest son of His Royal Grace acting Archduke Uncle Helm-Friedrich had moved his family to one of their estates outside the city when word of the Sickness first came from Traventi, but it seemed that even then, he had waited too long. They either took the Sickness with them or met it on the road. Most of the people on the estate and in the adjoining village were rumored to be sick or dying. And then there had been a fire in the main house on the estate. Helm-Friedrich's elder son and grandson were not among the survivors. His Royal Grace's daughter-in-law had already died bearing her youngest child at Midwinter, so His Royal Grace Uncle Helm-Friedrich brought his remaining daughter and granddaughters back to the city and Palace.

Uncle Helm-Friedrich's wife Denise Amalie was deathly ill of the Sickness. His younger son was a priest who had no children because he had mumps when he was almost grown up. He took care of sick people in the first wave of illness in the city, then he got sick himself. For a few days, he was reported to be doing very well, but then the people tending him sent word that he had died unexpectedly.

Franz-Karl swallowed hard, rubbed a fist across his eyes, and said the longer prayer for the dead very quietly. He had liked Karl-Friedrich, Helm-Friedrich's grandson, who had been near Sophie-Alexa's age, and Karl-Friedrich's father had been a kind, cheerful man who liked children. He had only met his priestly cousin a few times, but remembered a polite, cheerful young man who had not talked down to him.

He was also a little frightened to hear of so many Falkenburg men dying unexpectedly. A few weeks ago his own family had been a minor side-branch of the Falkenburgs, but now his brother Philip-Augustus would be Helm-Friedrich's heir unless their uncle married again and had more sons. That was unfair to the girls, who would have been heirs themselves in Traventi, but even those Allemans who weren't completely stupid about women inheriting property got silly about titles and primogeniture. He felt a bit worried: people were going to be paying more attention to his family, and the attention was not likely to be more friendly than in the past.

So many deaths called 'unexpected'. Franz-Karl wondered suddenly whether the Sickness had helpers with thumbs. There were too many shadows in the world to judge which were dangerous. But perhaps he was too used to watching for human enemies.

Her Excellency had fallen asleep, and the lady was silent, but there were still noises from the room next door. Franz-Karl sat quietly while Fritzel moved around the room, shoveling ashes out of the fireplace and building up the fire with fresh wood, and taking care of various other tasks where it was helpful to be strong, and healthy, and only partly exhausted. He would have been able to do more if their Excellencies' rooms had a convenient store of water and firewood like the one in Juliana's room in the Traventine Residence, but he did what he could.

When the bustle in His Excellency's room finally faded – not without a final echoing slam of the corridor door, which was a rude thing to do in a sickroom – Franz-Karl was dozing, and Fritzel was fidgeting because he had run out of anything useful to set his hands to. Franz-Karl woke up with a start and took the papers for the accession oath out of his pocket and held them up with the seal on the wrapper showing. Fritzel opened the connecting door gently and followed when Franz-Karl walked through.

His Excellency, like his wife, had been left with only two attendants, but both of them were awake. His Excellency's chief secretary, standing beside the bed holding a document in the sunlight from a window, was red-eyed and thin and pale in a blotchy sort of way that might hint at an oncoming or outgoing rash, or just too much worry and too little sleep. Helmund the valet was standing at a table mixing something with water and powders and odd-shaped glassware.

His Excellency blinked toward them through his spectacles with reddened, swollen eyes, and seemed to recognize the sealed documents before the people who carried them. The aide stepped toward them and held out his hand.

Franz-Karl hugged the parchments to his chest. "I am instructed that these are to go to the hand of his Excellency and no other," he said loudly.

The secretary bowed, signed himself, and stepped aside, "Of course, Your Honor."

His Excellency and the valet signed themselves too – urgent news from Traventi, or even just from Franz-Karl's Mama as the Traventine ambassador, was unlikely to be good – but his Excellency began to smile like a sunrise after too many days of rain: watery and uncertain, but brilliant. "Franz-Karl! Come here to me, dear boy."

Franz-Karl walked closer and handed over the sealed package of parchments, bowing politely.

The secretary had to help His Excellency open the sealed package, and he read the unsigned Allemanic copy while His Excellency read the real, signed one written in Remoran, blinking through his spectacles. Franz-Karl's Mama did not write in the clear Notarial style Franz-Karl had learned in Traventi, but her writing was clear enough.

His Excellency signed himself again, saying, "May Heaven and all the Saints guard Duke Adriana, and guide her to the Halls of Judgment."

There was a tap on the outer door. It opened immediately and His Royal Grace acting Archduke Uncle Helm-Friedrich came in alone. When he saw who was in the room, he stopped, closed the door firmly behind him, and cursed the Gods. That was shocking: even Fritzel made a sort of protesting cough, and his swearing sometimes included suggesting various rude acts by some of the more robust Saints.

Franz-Karl had read old stories that said some person or other 'cursed the Gods', but he had not thought it was something that people actually did. Not even people who were not Elderkin and did not need to be as careful about the words they spoke into the world. The acting Archduke cursed all the gods generally, then singled a few out for special attention, using names that Franz-Karl, as a non-Initiate, was not even supposed to know until he was older. That was even more shocking and quite impressive. Finally, his Uncle paused, took a breath, and asked, simply, "Who is dead now?"

"Her late Grace my Grandmother Adriana di Capradaventi, Duke of Traventi," Franz-Karl answered.

His Royal Grace signed himself and said, "May Heaven and all the Saints guard Duke Adriana, and guide her to the Halls of Judgment." He walked to a chair and sat in it as if the strings in his legs had been cut. For just a moment he looked almost as old as His Excellency, his father, who was nearer seventy than forty-five. The valet brought him a cup of water, which seemed to help a little.

Franz-Karl offered, "I liked Karl-Friedrich, and his Papa was nice. May Heaven and all the Saints guard all of our kin, and guide them to the Halls of Judgment." His Royal Grace did not smile, but for a moment the lines of his face were softer and he looked a little less sad, though no less tired.

His Excellency and His Royal Grace both signed the official copy of the accession oath so that no one could claim that it was anything but official. Franz-Karl tried not to be annoyed: when a document had been signed and witnessed by Elderkin Notaries, questioning it was not insulting, it was just useless. Once Bound, the ... matter ... of the document was carved into the structure of the Living World. He did not say anything: interrupting grownups who were trying to do the right thing – unless they were actually doing a wrong thing – just made a mess.

His Excellency wrote a note to Her Grace the Duke Silvia acknowledging her oath of accession. His Royal Grace countersigned that one too, which seemed more likely to be useful. They wrote and signed a few copies of the note of acknowledgment: a copy for Duke Silvia, copies for His Excellency and His Royal Grace, a copy for the Chancellor's records. Franz-Karl Witnessed and signed all of the copies, and had Fritzel sign them, too, so additional copies were made for him and Fritzel to keep, in case questions arose when His Excellency and His Royal Grace were indisposed.

Franz-Karl and Fritzel did not leave the main Palace by way of any of the official entrances. His Royal Grace acting Archduke Uncle Helm-Friedrich offered to escort them home to be absolutely sure that they had no problems with 'ill-trained, hastily recruited guards', but Franz-Karl thought that his Uncle needed to rest more than he needed to climb up and down staircases and deal with people being stupid. He also thought that it was not the newest guards that were likely to be the trouble... but he was fairly certain His Royal Grace knew that too.

They went all the way down the servants' stairs to the deep tunnel and across through the chamber with the pool and lamp. Fritzel fill a couple of buckets of the good water to take up into the West Palace with them – there was no sense in wasting a trip up the stairs – then paused and looked back toward the main Palace for a moment.

Franz-Karl thought Fritzel was worrying about Her Excellency and her ladies, since water was one thing he had not been able to help them with. But when Fritzel held still and the water in the buckets stopped sloshing, Franz-Karl could hear mixed up distant sounds that might be footsteps. They stayed in the chamber, where there was room to move, but moved into a niche that was shaded from the lamp's light by a fold of the rock.

The noise was Vendal, carrying a torch and a bucket, and two other men with the look of Old Palace Servants, carrying buckets. Vendal raised his torch and peered toward their niche. Franz-Karl moved his head so that his Elderkin eyes would reflect the light: his eyes did not shine green like a cat nor red like a dog – unlike some Elderkin. His shiny eyes reflected a pale greenish gold.

Vendal settled his torch in a notch in the rock that was shaped for holding up torches. He took some eggs out of his bucket and arranged them carefully on a flat stone beside the holy pool. Then he walked toward the niche where the Elderkin stood, holding his empty hands out with his fingers spread. "Your Honor?" he called quietly. Loud noises made strange echoes in the tunnels.

Franz-Karl and Fritzel stepped out of their niche, bringing their filled buckets.

Vendal smiled a little, more with his eyes than his mouth. "You did not wear those clothes to fetch water..."

"Her Grace my Mother is now Duke of Traventi," it still sounded strange to Franz-Karl, but at the same time he was tired of saying it.

All three Servants signed themselves and said, "May Heaven and all the Saints guard Duke Adriana, and guide her to the Halls of Judgment."

Elderkin did not speak thanks, so Franz-Karl bowed.

Fritzel asked quietly, "Is there a way to ensure their Excellencies and their attendants have plenty of water?"

Vendal made a face. "That is not a thing that should need to be asked. But the Chamberlain's people have been meddling, and keeping out the city-born servants, and us... Some of our people that were struck early by the sickness are beginning to regain their strength, so we will be spread less thin and can push harder to do our duty. We will see to it." He sighed and rubbed his eyes. "Your household?"

"No word from Greenoak Square, and little word from Traventi – until this. We two have not been struck by the Sickness yet. The rest, upstairs –" Franz-Karl waved toward the tunnel leading toward the West Palace, "everyone else is sick, but maybe not getting sicker? Some may be recovering?"

Vendal rubbed a thumb across a cluster of pock-marks on his left cheek. "Even smallpox misses a few in its passage. I will pray that the gods continue to protect the two of you." He shrugged his shoulders in a stretch to ease some tightness. "There was a market this morning at the Farmers' Gate, and our people managed to buy a few things for the Palace kitchens, though the choice was thin and prices very high. The gate torches at Greenoak Square still burn, and there was smoke from their kitchen fires, early today."

"So someone is likely well enough to cook breakfast? That is good news to hear." Franz-Karl paused, then suggested carefully, "From the little news we got of Her Royal Highness Aunt Queen Gertrude, she might be a useful ally for you against the Chamberlain's people."

Vendal actually chuckled. "When stocking for a siege, the Elderkin gather supplies, the Szekelys gather armed men. Both are handy at need," he said mysteriously. "I will see that the Great Lady hears your news. Perhaps she will send you word."

"That might be helpful."

When they arrived back at the Traventine Residence, Franz-Karl was relieved to find that none of their patients seemed to have gotten much worse during their absence. None of them seemed any better, either, but compared to the emptiness and sickness in the main Palace, and all of the bad news there, the Residence seemed crowded and almost lively. Fritzel poured the buckets of good water into the barrels in Juliana's room, then went back down into the tunnels for more.

Franz-Karl rearranged the tokens in the Household Shrine, moving the ones for people who had died out of the section for tokens of living people. He tried to make the section for the dead look balanced and cared for, but could not really reach high enough to do it well. The lower part of the display was crowded while the upper part stayed sparse.

He wondered how many of the tokens for people in Traventi were sitting in the wrong section.

# INTERLUDE VII: The City and the Echelon

## *Wherein Sickness Floods the Streets*

Some kinds of pestilence can be escaped by luck. The Great Sickness was not one of them. Its spread in and around the city of Karnburg was as inexorable as flood waters: it seemed that everyone in its path got wet.

Some kinds of pestilence can be escaped by avoiding the company of those known to be ill. The Great Sickness was not one of those, either. One wit – before he died – said that the Great Sickness was spread by rumors: if you heard that someone you knew had taken to their bed, you soon would be taking to your own. It was already too late to take precautions by the time the news arrived.

The very young often died. The very old often died. Those who were clearly weak for other reasons often died, except when it was the strong who died instead. Some of those who did not die outright, lingered without recovering. Even those who grew stronger after the fever broke took far longer to recover strength and skill than others did to fall sick past caring for themselves. So the sick in Karnburg tended the sick, and the dying buried the dead.

Outside the city walls, the cemeteries filled quickly, and new charnel pits were opened on land cleared during the siege that had not yet been built on. Inside the city walls, Noble bodies filled the crypts below the mortuary chapels of churches that had them, while poorer folk were hauled outside the walls to the suburban cemeteries and charnel pits. As the living became fewer and weaker, a few charnel pits that had been used during the siege were reopened within the walls to spare some journeys to the suburbs.

It was not clear how many were dead, either within the Walls or outside them. With so many sick, small households joined together to share the work of hauling firewood and water, tending the fires, tending the sick, and feeding both the sick and those who tended them. Cold hearths and empty rooms might mean the tenants were dead... or merely elsewhere. Larger households previously full of servants and staff turned inward. The military camps in the suburbs were no safer than the neighboring villages.

Before the Great Sickness arrived, the Pristinists in Karnburg were spread thin, and their plans were brittle: confident faith in the will of Heaven did not encourage planning for contingencies. Before the Sickness, one officer's demotion had disrupted complex financial plans, and a few days of indisposition for the Margraff-Elector had shaken the Pristinists' careful hold on the Falkenburg Privy Council that had been building since before the Siege.

Once the Sickness arrived, there were too many changes, both among the positions held at Court by members of the Echelon and among the officials that they were dealing with from day to day. But the Great Sickness could not be ignored as evidence of the will of Heaven. Achieving Heaven's Goals became more pressing than the need for caution, despite their losses. Rather than set aside tasks they had been assigned the men of the Echelon – sometimes men whose wits were clouded by fever – took shortcuts and risks they would otherwise have avoided.

At Midwinter, with Pristinist regiments camped near the city, the gathered Echelon had numbered nearly two hundred, and included two of the nine Electors of the King of the Allemans. When the Reawakening approached, the Karnburg Echelon was reduced to forty-three men, and some, like Heinrich Bauer at the bottom of the Echelon would never be assigned tasks that required dignity and authority. A few of the missing were military officers now posted elsewhere, but not enough, and there was no assurance that those officers still lived, or would still live in a month's time.

The Prince-Elector of Bremerhaven had fallen ill after the Margraff-Elector's party. Now there was a new Prince-Elector of Bremerhaven, far away in the Bremerhaven Palace in the North, and he knew little of the Imperial Court, and nothing of the Karnburg Echelon's plans and stratagems.

Preacher Weiss was dead. Teacher Bauer had been preserved thus far by the care of his father, Heinrich, but it was not yet clear whether he would heal or linger or die.

The title of General of the Army of the Empire was no longer held by a Pristinist, or even a Harfneran or other Reformist. The position had passed to an Ecclesialist Colonel born in the Eastlands, who had been touched only lightly by the Sickness, and recovered quickly. Other positions in the various Armies also began to pass to Eastlands Ecclesialists, who had the virtue of being nearby and were subjects of His Excellency as Allemanic King as well as in his role as Archduke of the Eastlands. The sectarian mix among the common soldiers had not yet changed much: the regiments were hollowing out, but not yet recruiting to refill their ranks. There were few men healthy enough to be recruited who were not busy tending the sick and burying the dead.

For a few weeks the working hierarchy of officials in the Palace was never the same two days running, as men became sick, or died, or recovered and returned to higher positions than they had left. Replacements were necessarily local people – thus very rarely Pristinist – so the members of the Echelon who held or achieved positions of authority worked hard to ensure that replacements from the local community were interim appointments, not permanent ones.

Beyond the Echelon, Pristinist losses were worse than in many other communities within the city. The Pristinists shunned their neighbors, so received little aid from them. And a generation of Teachers and Preachers had expounded writings that were held to denigrate squandering wealth on the unworthy. The Sickness lingered in servants and slaves whose bony features advertised their masters' thrifty virtue, and killed them if they returned to their tasks too soon. And then, as the servants in Pristinist households vanished and the women's quarters emptied, there were few left to tend their masters, whether stricken or healthy.

Unlike the Prince-Elector of Bremerhaven and several others among the Select, Margraff-Elector Horst-Konrad von Neumark of Ansbach had not fallen ill directly after his party. It was another week before the Sickness forced him to bed with fevers, and breathlessness, and aches in his joints that gave him terrible dreams of the Purgation, and pain in his hands that gave him dreams of beast-born demons.

By the time the Sickness receded, leaving him as lean as a slave, half of Horst-Konrad's usual retinue were dead and the rest remained unfit to be seen in public. Three quarters of his house servants and city agents were missing or known dead.

The one good piece of news the Margraff-Elector received as he recovered was the word out of Traventi: the old bitch who was claimed to rule the beast-born was now dead. And the new one was within his reach.

# CHAPTER XXII: The New Duke

## *Wherein Palace Officials Attempt a Theft*

It was late in the day after the accession oath was written before the Royal and Imperial authorities, slowed by the Sickness, took official notice of the new status of Her Grace Duke Silvia of Traventi, Franz-Karl's Mama. When the authorities arrived they did it in force: both the Chamberlain and the Chancellor of the Allemanic Kingdom arrived at the door of the Traventine Residence, accompanied by the Falkenburg Steward and the Chancellor of the Falkenburg Eastlands, and an assortment of underlings of all four of the senior officials. One of the lesser underlings did the actual knocking on the door... or pounding.

When the Residence door was opened to the delegation, Roland was waiting to greet them formally He was pale and very shaky and leaned on a stick with one hand and on the Guesting table, unobtrusively, with the other hand. On the Guesting table were all the things needed for the Traventine rites of Hospitality: cups and small plates for the hosts and guests, and an unlit candle, and closed carafes of water and wine, and covered trays of the morsels of food – made with the ingredients needed for the ritual of welcome – that would be shared with properly sworn and welcomed guests. If the guests were expected, or trusted, the candle would already be lit, some of the cups would already be full of watered wine, and at least one of the trays would be uncovered and waiting for its contents to be shared. These guests were neither expected nor trusted.

Franz-Karl's Mama was sitting in a chair of state in the middle of the entry hall of the suite, well within her Household but near enough to the Threshold of the Residence to speak the Host's side of the oaths of Hospitality. She was dressed in plain color-of-sorrow garments, as she had been since her husband died, but her signet, on the ribbon around her neck, was hanging outside her clothes, not hidden within them.

Franz-Karl, being a fully sworn Notary and a sworn Guest and Kin of the Household, was standing by the door that led from the entry hall into the more private sections of the suite, bearing Witness. Fritzel was standing squarely in that doorway, which he filled quite impressively, as a barrier. Franz-Karl was glad to have him there. Some of the delegation's attendants looked to be selected for their size, not their wits.

The two Allemanic officials and their followers pushed past Roland and stood waiting while the Falkenburg officials exchanged shortened versions of the oaths of Hospitality with Roland and Her Grace Duke Silvia. The Allemanic Chancellor literally tapped his foot with annoyance, as if it was his place and not Her Grace the Duke's to choose the pace of the meeting. Franz-Karl thought from the man's expression that the Eastlands' Chancellor had noticed that he was granted safe passage rather than full Guest rights, and knew enough to be worried by that.

The Allemanic Chancellor did not wait to be invited to speak by the monarch he faced. He did not really wait for the final exchange of the Guesting Rite to finish, and his Eastlands counterpart frowned at him for talking over the final courtesies. Franz-Karl snapped the fingers of both hands three times without moving them from his sides, and felt a comforting awareness of being observed, as when a sleeping dog opens its eyes and lifts its head to consider an intruder: if he needed to do something, he would not need four repetitions to begin it.

The Allemanic Chancellor spoke as if he, himself, was the whole government, or both governments, not just the fancy messenger from His Excellency to an allied Sovereign that protocol said he was. "We have heard," he said, and it was the wrong 'we', "that the Duchy of Traventi has come to a widow of the Falkenburgs, so we are here to provide the terms for the subordination of its district government within His

Excellency's territories. Being such a small place, the former Sovereign Duchy will naturally look to one of His Excellency's minor vassals, not directly to His Excellency himself."

Franz-Karl had spent enough time sitting in Privy Council meetings discussing the Marriage Contract to know that last demand was contrary to the Marriage Contract. It was also contrary to Falkenburg custom as much as it was to Traventine law: Philip-Augustus as Count Wolfsberg was a direct vassal of the Archduke, and even if his mother's holdings could be joined to the Eastlands – which the Marriage Contract and the laws of Traventi said they could not – the joining at the most distant, would be through Wolfsberg. But the Wolfsberg inheritance had been a mess for nearly a year, so the Chancellor probably thought that if he could get the false claim accepted while everything was disrupted by the Sickness, he could make it stick through still more foot-dragging.

Her Grace Duke Silvia, Franz-Karl's Mama looked up at the tall man looming over her chair and answered calmly, "I have sworn and signed and sealed my oath of accession, and my late husband's kinsmen Friedrich-Augustus and Helm-Friedrich have accepted it in accordance to the Contract sworn by all of us at the time of my marriage: sworn by our lives and souls and hopes of Judgment. My oath contains no mention of vassalage, or of subordination of the Duchy to either or both of the Allemanic Kingdom or the Falkenburg Domains." She held out her copy of the note from his Excellency and His Royal Grace the acting Archduke.

The Allemanic Chamberlain snatched the paper and without opening or reading it, held it toward a candle on the table beside her. "And what if this oath cannot be found?"

The Chancellor somehow was looking at Her Grace with a neutral expression, but had his back mostly turned to his fellow official. He flickered wildly in Franz-Karl's vision, as he tried to lie to himself and pretend that nothing was happening.

The Falkenburg Steward grabbed the Allemanic Chamberlain's arm and pulled it back from flame, while the Falkenburg Chancellor said, "Hey!" and started to draw his court sword.

Franz-Karl said loudly, trying to sound bored, "Even odds I can summon His Excellency's note intact from the fire: that's my seal as Notary and Witness you'll see on it if you bother to look. Slightly lower odds that I could summon it fully into the chambers of a traitorous heart, but I would be glad to try if you desire it." He took a step away from the doorway, toward Her Grace's chair. "But there is surely no need for such dramatics: there are plenty of copies of that note from the Lords of the Falkenburgs to her Grace of Traventi, and I have not heard that His Excellency or His Royal Grace are too indisposed to acknowledge the work of their own hands. The various copies of the accession oath are also safely stored, naturally."

The Allemanic Chamberlain wavered where he stood, turned pale, and unfolded the note with shaking hands. When he recognized the signatures on it, he turned even paler: trying to destroy an order by His Excellency was outright rebellion. So was trying to break a treaty with an allied monarch of course, but some of the factions did not agree that Traventi was properly its own realm that counted as an ally.

The Chamberlain did not resist when the Falkenburg Steward plucked the paper out of his grasp, and read aloud His Excellency's welcome to an allied, independent monarch, before returning it, respectfully, to Her Grace of Traventi. He protested feebly when the Falkenburg officials, assisted by some of the Allemanic underlings as well as their own, took his court sword from him and bound his hands behind him. He tried to catch the eye of the Allemanic Chancellor, but that gentleman's back was still turned toward him, and the Chancellor was remaining carefully silent to avoid being entangled in his subordinate's downfall as much as possible.

The party turned to leave in some confusion. There were too many witnesses and too many factions present for mention of the blunder to be buried, so there would be a hearing, at least, if not a full trial. Though when that would be was anyone's guess, with His Excellency and His Royal Grace the acting Archduke both afflicted by the Sickness. The Falkenburg Chancellor explained to Her Grace Duke Silvia that the latest report was that His Royal Grace was past the fever and regaining his strength, while His Excellency was still feverish, besides being much affected by his wife's imminent death.

Franz-Karl blinked back tears. He had not thought Her Excellency his Grandmother was as sick as that when he spoke with her the evening before.

He was glad the Allemanic Chamberlain at the least would lose his position for trying to make His Excellency and His Royal Grace into liars and being mean to Franz-Karl's Mama. The Chamberlain might lose his family's estates and titles, if His Excellency or His Royal Grace decided that was warranted. The Chamberlain might even lose his life... but he should have thought of that before he tried to conquer a free realm with nothing but lies: battlefields were not the only places people could die, and Traventi was too small to put much trust in battlefields. Words were Elderkin weapons: there were proverbs about it.

Two of the former Chamberlain's underlings were gazing at him with the speculative eyes of scavengers expecting a feast, two others gazed at Franz-Karl and his Mama with open loathing.

As they filed through the door Franz-Karl called to the Falkenburg Steward, who was walking near the back of the group, "My Lord von Regensburg?"

The man looked toward him. Franz-Karl continued, "If the Allemanic Chamberlain really takes precedence for ordering affairs within a Falkenburg Palace in a Falkenburg city, could you at least try to arrange for his replacement to be more competent? The service and supplies that were his responsibility to supply have been unworthy of His Excellency's dignity of late..."

The man looked startled, then annoyed as he looked around at the slightly shabby room, but he bowed politely. "Most certainly... uh..."

"Your Honor," Roland prompted.

The man blushed, and bowed again. "Most certainly, Your Honor. I am quite sure that things will improve quite promptly."

Fritzel suggested wearily, "A good start would be to have some living people working in the West Palace laundries, and the fires there re-lit." Laundry was one task the Residence could not manage for itself at all.

The Falkenburg Steward looked even more annoyed. He bowed yet again, and hurried after his companions.

When the outer door closed behind the interlopers, Roland collapsed onto a stool and Franz-Karl hurried to pour him a glass of the guesting wine and urge him to eat some of the remaining guest morsels. There was no sense wasting some of the best food they had at hand in the Residence when it could help to rebuild the ailing man's strength.

While the others helped Duke Silvia back to her bed, Franz-Karl wrote a short letter to Reverend Count Adrasteia and placed on the table where the messages came and went.

They needed to let their people at Greenoak Square as well as in Traventi know what was going on. It was stupid to need to use pigeons to send messages to their own townhouse, which was only a few blocks from the Palace and inside Karnburg's walls, but with Sickness in the streets, and the guards at the Palace Gates so often uncooperative about letting Elderkin in and out at the best of times, using pigeons was the best choice. Sometimes it felt like Greenoak Square was as far away as the House on the Rock. Or the Moon.

The pigeon book had numbers for lots of common business and diplomatic messages – 14 was famously 'remit funds immediately' in every bank and diplomatic book north of the Mothersea, and was also the point value of a winning hand in one popular card game, so no one bothered trying to use anything else. Unfortunately, even Traventi's extensive diplomatic codes did not include a number for 'the chamberlain just tried to steal a country', so Franz-Karl and Fritzel pieced together a message and copied the strings of numbers onto the small slips of paper that would go into the capsules for the birds to carry.

When Franz-Karl took a small detour to visit their horses in the part of the Palace stables assigned to the Traventine Residence, he found that they had been taken away, along with all their food and their gear: bridles and saddles and harnesses and even the water buckets. He hurried up the steep stair to their dovecote, and began to cry. The thieves had not taken away the pigeons, or even turned them loose so that they could fly away to their distant homes without carrying any messages with them. All of the clever birds were lying tumbled, dead, on the floor of the dovecote with their necks recently wrung. None of them would fly back to their homes in Greenoak Square or Traventi or other distant places far away from this horrible Palace.

He looked around, and even in adjoining dovecotes and other residence's sections of the stables, but could not find anything to put them in that he could manage: there were too many dead birds and he was too small. Finally, he put one of the birds that had been nicest inside his coat, and went back into the West Palace building and down to the kitchens.

The kitchen at the north end of the building directly below the Residence had been busy yesterday. Now it was cold and empty – as empty as the laundry had been for the past week – but the middle kitchen below the great staircase had people busily at work. No wonder the food they received was now cold. It must take forever to get all the way up to the Residence from here, when the stewards bothered to bring it.

Franz-Karl stomped up to the most senior looking cook he saw. Her face was thinner, and older, but he recognized Clothilde, who should have been bossing people around in the north kitchen near the Residence. A few of the lesser cooks that she was bossing now looked familiar, but not enough of them. He took a deep breath, and went up to her, and demanded, "Clothilde, what goes in pigeon soup besides pigeons?"

Clothilde look startled, but clearly knew who he was. She smiled at him – Franz-Karl was a little surprised that the stern cook knew how to smile. "Why do you want to know about pigeon soup, Your Honor?"

He took the dead pigeon out of his coat and showed it to her. "All of our birds have been murdered. I shall count ..." He choked. "I shall count their meat as the flesh of sacrifice – like martyrs – so they can be Messengers one last time. What goes in pigeon soup besides pigeons?" It was hard to talk, especially in Allemanic: his throat was all tight and scratchy, and thinking about the dead birds was making him cry again.

The chief cook frowned, then looked around. She sent a scullion to collect the rest of the dead birds and bring them to the Traventine Residence. Then she put some onions and roots and salt and a flask of this and a jar of that in a basket, and took Franz-Karl by the hand, just as if he was her own child, and brought him back to his home by way of the servants' stairs. He had time to think while they walked: he did not even need to watch where they were going, with Clothilde leading the way.

When they arrived at the Residence and Franz-Karl told the grownups about the stables and dovecote, Fritzel looked angry and so did Roland. Franz-Karl's Mama just looked very sad and very tired. Itron Gwenlian was asleep, and they did not awaken her with the news: the most useful thing she could do was rest and heal. Philip-Augustus and Sophie-Alexa were not asleep, but they did not tell them the news, either. Franz-Karl's valet, Tam, was awake, and announced that he was well enough to sit up in a chair and pluck pigeons. Tam had been one of the last people in the residence to get sick, but the fever had broken and the rash had faded, so the valet's claimed recovery seemed true enough that Franz-Karl and Tam both believed it.

Franz-Karl wrote in a note that all of their birds were murdered and would not be carrying messages anywhere in the Living World ever again, and sealed it, and put it on the table where the letters from Reverend Count Great Aunt Adrasteia had appeared.

It was not enough.

He sat on his bed holding Harvest Prince, his toy horse, and remembered from an old story that the Allemanic Kingdom had special rules about stolen horses – and special rules for sacrificing them too. The Falkenburg Eastlands had different special rules. There were old court cases that said falsely saying someone was a horse-thief was as bad as saying he was a rapist or murderer, so they were strict rules.

He looked up the special forms for announcing a horse-theft in a book in his Mama's study. She had all sorts of law books, not just Traventine ones.

There was not a pattern for a combined horse theft announcement, so Franz-Karl wrote one of each: Allemanic and Eastlands, both with the names and ages and descriptions of all of their horses that were missing, and a list of the missing gear, too. He wrote them on parchment so the pages would need to be cut, not torn or easily burned, and used ink that would stain deeply, not just sit on top of the leathery material where it could be rubbed off. Then he and Fritzel took both announcements and a hammer and some big nails, and went into the main Palace and nailed the announcements to the big double doors of the room that was used for His Excellency's audiences. The nails went all of the way through, so the Palace officials would probably need to replace the doors... Franz-Karl thought about that, and told Fritzel to bend down the points of the nails that were sticking out of the backs of the doors. Some of them gouged the backs of the doors.

The wording Franz-Karl used for the announcements did not point at anyone in particular as the thieves. It just said that horses and property of guests of His Excellency had been stolen. Nailing the announcements up where they put them said that the guilt would rest on the Allemanic King and Eastlands Archduke unless they named and punished the person who was actually guilty. That might not be modern law, but it was in old stories that everyone knew.

They had brought the announcements to the main Palace through the deep tunnel, but they went home after nailing them up by walking across the Palace grounds in the sunshine.

"Might waken a nest of hornets with that," Fritzel remarked, closing his eyes and raising his face toward the sunshine.

Franz-Karl scoffed, "Do you think they were sleeping 'til now?" He paused to look at one of the garden's prized beds of exotic plants, which was looking a bit scruffy and overgrown due to lack of attention from too few remaining gardeners.

"If that's manioc, I think we want no part of it," Fritzel warned. "I've read that herbal, too!"

"Certainly not," Franz-Karl answered almost cheerfully. It felt good to be out walking in the sunshine, not hurrying between sickrooms or tunneling under the earth like a mole. "Manioc won't grow here: the soil's wrong for it and the weather's worse. And I expect processing manioc is like picking wild mushrooms: you need to learn from someone with experience to do it anything like safely. But half of these beds are supposed to be edible, and too many people have been speaking of food being scarce and expensive... I think when the pigeon soup is all eaten, we may need to plan a harvest, even though it is really too early in the season. There may be some roots left that have overwintered in the ground."

# CHAPTER XXIII: The Fourth Letter

*Wherein the Duke Receives News of the Duchy*

When Franz-Karl brought the Cook Clothilde to the Residence with the dead pigeons, there was some arguing in rapidly-spoken Elderic before they let the Cook into Juliana's room, but Roland and Itron Gwenlian agreed to it in the end. Clothilde looked sad when she saw their preparations, but she only said nice things. She even said that she wished some of her assistant cooks made griddle cakes as well as Fritzel, and it looked to Franz-Karl like she was speaking the truth: her shape was solidly planted in the world and there were no marks of fibs crawling on her. The Cook prepared the onions and things in the bottom of the pot, so that the soup would taste good when they added the pigeons and water, and before she returned to her kitchen she told Fritzel some cooking tricks that he should use to make the soup even better. Shortly after she returned to her kitchen, a messenger arrived at the Residence through the servants' door carrying a container of flour ground to a fineness that was especially good for griddle cakes.

Both Fritzel and Itron Gwenlian knew the prayers that went with sacrificing pigeons, so their pigeon soup could be prepared with full respect and all the proper rites. Gwenlian had taken part in the discussion without leaving her bed, and fretted at not being the one tending the soup in their kitchen, but at least she was getting well enough to fret.

Franz-Karl hoped that the soup would help all of the sick people in the Residence get better. Fresh meat was supposed to be healing, and the meat of sacrifice was supposed to be as good as medicine, even when it was a sort of sideways sacrifice like this one had been. Given the season there had not been much fresh meat in the meals that they were occasionally sent from the Palace kitchens, and when it came it was often served in ways that were – at least – ritually impure, so that none of the Traventine Elderkin should eat it. The rules were relaxed in times of sickness, but Franz-Karl with his odd vision was not the only one who frequently found the dishes that arrived from the kitchens too suspicious-looking to be comfortably edible.

That evening, after they had eaten, they found that Franz-Karl's notes about the Chamberlain and the dead birds had been replaced by a letter to Duke Silvia and Childe Franz-Karl of Traventi.

It read:

From Antonia Adrasteia, writing from Leopard's Watch, to Armoria Silvia, Duke of Traventi and Childe Falx Franciscocarolus, Heir of the Succession of the Dukes of Traventi, Greetings.

I had previously told you that Her Late Grace the Duke Adriana was recovering from the Great Sickness. That was fully true, but it is reported that it was also true that she did not keep to her bed to regain her strength when the fever had broken and the other signs of the Sickness were fading, being exceedingly eager to tend to the House on the Rock and its people.

It was not directly the Sickness that killed her. On the last day of her life, she suffered an attack of vertigo or weakness on the stairs in the Tower for Watching the Stars, missed her footing, landed very badly, and died almost instantly. There were witnesses above and below: the stairs were sound, and no hand came near her until after she was dead.

The transformed effigy of Her Late Grace now rests in the crypt with her ancestors beneath the Shrine of Saints

Clement and Sophia. Only one of the Hierophants was able to officiate, I am not sure which.

I have ordered the late crops planted in the South Valley and Valens has done the same in the North. If the Sickness in the Home Quarter and Over the Water has interrupted the work of farming, our people yet will not hunger too completely in the coming winter. The added crops seem to be prospering.

It is too soon to say that the Sickness never returns to a person that has once recovered, but we have heard no news of it doing so, neither in Traventi nor in the lands south of the mountains. There are reports of other ailments afflicting those too weakened to resist them, but the Sickness itself is not seen to return.

I believe that if we hold to the Plague Laws for a few more market-weeks, we will find when an accounting is made that we are now today already in the last wave of the Sickness in Traventi: the sparks of the Sickness fell into a handful of straw on bare rock, and now the straw is burnt and it is starved of fuel.

What we think we see is this: Of the people that the Sickness was able to reach, out of twenty, two were passed by, four have died or will die of the Sickness itself, another will die, like her Late Grace, because of the Sickness but not directly, two will linger, healing very slowly if at all, and the rest who encountered the Sickness were sickened but will recover. We think that fully half of the people of Traventi have not been touched by the sickness at all, those being mostly in the North and South Valleys and the thinly settled parts of the main Valley. The herds in the main valley moved to the summer pastures a full market-week early in hopes that the people who traveled with them would be spared, and that was largely successful.

The Plague Laws still block a clear accounting of who has died, but we believe most of the deaths were in or near the House on the Rock and the Dance. Messages from Severin are no longer entirely swearing, but little of the news from the center of Over the Water is comforting.

However, there is at last a little news from the Bull's Leap. Aldo the Herdmaster and several of his workers are among those the Sickness passed by entirely, so they were able to tend the sick, and deaths in that district were fewer than in some other places. The old priests Henk and Lavinia journey to the Halls, and the Baron-Notary's daughter now tends the Crossing shrine alone, at least while the Plague Laws remain in force. Imelda's hoped-for child will not join the living this year, and some of the smaller households at the Bull's Leap also mourn. The Baron-Notary and his wife and children and daughter-in-law are all recovering well from the Sickness.

There is also one piece of strange rumor from the Bull's Leap that I am seeking to verify. You will recall that there was a man who behaved badly at the wrestling at the Feast of Saints Clement and Sophia last summer and was sent to the Bull's Leap to learn better manners. It is said that when the Sickness came, there were some that blamed him for desecrating the Rite and Festival, so that not only is he removed from the Living World, instead of receiving the usual funeral rites to guide his soul toward the Halls of Judgment his remains have been Consigned to the Elements to leave him as demon-bait on the Paths beyond the Walls of the World.

The House on the Rock stands, and many of its people live: which ones, it is too soon to say. I do not much trust the rumors that have come south thus far.

Send me your questions and commands and I will try to fulfill them.

May Heaven and all the Saints hold you both, and all of us, in their keeping.

Franz-Karl took the letter to his Mama when he had read it, then sat down with paper and ink to compose his part of a response. He wrote more about the Chamberlain, and the horses, and more details about the pigeons, including the soup. He told his Mama what he was writing, so that she did not need to write about the same things.

On a separate paper he wrote a recommendation that his grown-up cousin Andrea, who was a sworn Notary and eligible for the Line of Succession, should be added to the line of succession as soon as the Plague Laws were lifted and a way could be devised to hold the election safely, so that there would be no gap where the various Chancellors could try to insert their own candidate. He named her as interim heir for the family estates, too, and for all of Her late Grace His Grandmother's personal things. There was a customary procedure for designating a temporary heir if you were not likely to have an heir of your own line for some reason, and being seven years old would count as a good reason. He showed that paper to the Duke his Mama as soon as it was written. She told him to sign and seal it, and then she signed and sealed it as Duke and Witness. As soon as they both signed, Andrea was his official Heir within Traventi until he was grown, and she was proposed for the Succession. The Succession was controlled by the Council and the People of Traventi, not by the Duke or existing Heirs, so that was more complicated, but at least the family estates would have someone to look after them. After some thought Franz-Karl added a list of his other cousins, so that if Andrea was dead, the people in Traventi could go down the list until they reached the name of a person who was alive.

Her Grace the Duke's letter was almost all questions about things in Traventi. Many of them were about things Franz-Karl would never have thought to ask about. Some of the questions used Elderic words Franz-Karl had never seen or heard before, so he could not have asked them at all.

Once she had signed and sealed her own letter, Franz-Karl's Mama fell asleep again very suddenly. Getting up to talk to the Chancellors and Chamberlain and Steward had tired her out so much that she had spent very little time awake since they left. He would need to wait to ask her about her questions.

Franz-Karl was always hungry and tired after doing some serious Witnessing, or other Notary work or Bindings, so it could not be good for a sick person to do very much of it, but he did not know what else they could do. The Palace authorities had rules against Binders living in the Palace, so there really was not anyone but Franz-Karl and his Mama who could officially do some of the things that needed to be done. Philip-Augustus was a Binder, sort of, though not yet a Notary, but he was even sicker than their Mama.

The other patients seemed to be doing better, even Roland who had also gotten out of his bed much too soon to deal with the officials. Roland and Tam had sat up in chairs to eat the pigeon soup before returning to their sick-beds, but none of the rest of the sick people had done so. Sophie-Alexa, eating in bed, had asked for a second bowl of the soup, which Franz-Karl thought was a hopeful thing. Philip-Augustus barely finished his first bowl. George, their remaining footman, ate about a bowl and a half of the soup, and spoke hopefully of sitting in a chair the next day.

# CHAPTER XXIV: The Embassy

## *Wherein Hospitality Becomes Complicated*

The next day, some people – Karnburg folk, not Old Palace Servants -- came to take away the dirty linens and bring clean ones. They brought less than they took, but things had been piling up and there were fewer people in the Residence than there had been not long ago, so that was not a problem. They brought enough, for now. Most of the beds in the Residence were not being used, so they could wait for more sheets.

One of the servants told Fritzel privately that the other Residences near theirs within the West Palace were all empty of people at the moment, and might be worth raiding for sheets and towels if the Traventines ran short of them. He said that the servants' doors were not locked so that the rooms could be tended.

Franz-Karl thought that if the other Residences were all empty, it made it slightly less nasty that the kitchen at their end of the West Palace was cold, but it would have been polite of someone to notify them, and better arrangement should have been made to support their meals. Properly speaking, it was required by the rules of Hospitality to make sure those under your roof were well fed, whether they were willing guests or unwilling hostages or whatever weird in-between thing Franz-

Karl was. It could not all be excused by messages getting lost because people were sick and thought someone else was taking care of things. The Laws of Hospitality did not allow much in the way of excuses at all. And even though Eastlanders did not care about Hospitality as much as Traventines, they still said that Hospitality was important. At least the Ecclesialists did. They should try acting like they really believed it.

Franz-Karl remembered the dim attics where the servants' quarters were, and hoped that someone was taking good care of the cooks and servants who were too sick to work.

That afternoon at sunset, with the wind from the east, they heard the cathedral bells ringing for a female death. There were a lot of bells in the pattern, so they had to be either for Her Excellency, Franz-Karl's Grandmother, or the female Arch-Hierophant, Diotima, who was a very nice, kind person, so it was bad either way. But Franz-Karl was sadly certain that it must be his Grandmother whose death was being reported. He wondered whether he should try to attend the funeral, but since he was too young to be an Initiate, he could not go by himself without a grown member of the family, and his Mama was too sick to go.

He suddenly hoped his other Grandfather, the Admiral, was being careful, far away across the great Ocean. But from everything anyone had ever said about the Admiral of Traventi, being careful was not likely. Maybe Corentin Armorius was at least neither sick, nor dead, unlike Franz-Karl's other three grandparents.

The bells had barely signaled the beginning of the funeral rites of the Mistress of the Palace Household when the Northerner official who called himself the Master of the Household came knocking on the door of the Traventine Residence with a mixed group of middle-ranked officials from both the Allemanic and Falkenburg hierarchies within the Palace.

Franz-Karl stayed in the Nursery with his brother and sister. Philip-Augustus was awake and restless, and Sophie-Alexa had started crying when she heard the bells . She became frantic when Franz-Karl tried to leave to bear Witness to the intruders' audience with Her Grace, and he did not know what to do.

It turned out that he did not need to go to the meeting: the meeting came to them. An entire procession came through the doors of the Nursery, and it was quite crowded by the time people stopped coming in. Fritzel was doing a good job of supporting Her Grace the

Duke while making it look like she was standing and walking almost entirely on her own, not being carried. Roland and Itron Gwenlian leaned on walking sticks that had carved patterns on them that the Palace folk would find mysterious and possibly threatening, and propped themselves against the walls or tall pieces of furniture as soon as they could after they entered the room. Tam walked unaided and gave little sign of weakness: the valet did not even lean against anything.

And behind the Elderkin came the gaggle of Palace officials and their flunkies. Just trying to look at them all gave Franz-Karl a pain behind his eyebrows. Some of them were honest and solidly planted within the Living World – even some of the Allemanic officials. Some of them were so false they looked like they might fall out of the Living World at any moment. And some were just sort of flickery around the edges. If there was a way to know whether the flickery ones were just sometimes fibbers, or whether they were fibbing in the present moment, no one had taught it to Franz-Karl. He should probably ask the Reverend Count Great Aunt Adrasteia the next time they exchanged letters. But it was too late for that now.

One of the officials near the front of the group was the assistant Chamberlain, Baron Philemon von und zu Ostwald: Franz-Karl had learned to dislike him during the preparations for his Father's funeral the previous year. It was only fair: von und zu Ostwald had disliked him first, just for being Elderkin, and he was always rude to the children of the Traventine Residence. When Franz-Karl bowed and addressed him politely as Assistant Chamberlain, he puffed up and announced that he was the new Master of Protocol for the Palace. That was not good: the old Master of Protocol had been awful and mean, but von und zu Ostwald was probably going to try to be worse.

Tam opened two small chests and began to fill them with nightclothes and undergarments and a few regular garments for Philip-Augustus and Sophie-Alexa. Franz-Karl got a dreadful feeling that he knew what was happening.

Her Grace the Duke his Mother said in a voice like Death, "The Palace has decided that the sick children of Leon-Alexander should be moved to a Hall in the main Palace where Physicians are tending the sick. I disagree with this decision, but I cannot claim that we have enough healthy people in this Residence to properly tend our sick." Her voice started to shake, so she paused and took a few deep breaths before she continued.

Her expression was... Franz-Karl had no words for it, but he thought he would count the men who put that expression on his Mother's face as his enemies in the Living World and the World Beyond. He had been shocked when the acting Archduke his Uncle cursed the Gods. This was far worse.

The Duke his Mama said, "We would be able to tend our sick if the Palace had upheld its responsibilities and promises to us during these past weeks –" Several of the officials winced, and not just the honest ones: that was confusing. She continued slowly, "Some of ... these persons... have sworn in my presence by their lives and souls and hope of the Halls of Judgment that the sick children of Leon-Alexander will receive the best care available, and every one of these persons will swear it again, here and now."

In Franz-Karl's presence as Notary and Witness, she meant, and with none of them able to claim the oath did not apply to them because they themselves had not spoken the words. That would only leave most of a corrupt Palace that had not sworn, but it was the best the Elderkin could manage with only two sworn Notaries and a sick Binder child. And Philip-Augustus was too sick at the moment to do any useful Binding, so it was really just one very sick grownup Notary and one healthy child Notary.

The Palace officials swore the oath Her Grace the Duke pronounced for them, the full four times prescribed for a spoken contract Witnessed by an Elderkin Notary. Some of them were very unhappy about the repetitions, but Her Grace was very patient about waiting for them when they stumbled or lagged, so somewhere in the third repetition they stopped struggling. The fourth repetition almost went smoothly.

Tam beckoned to Franz-Karl. Together they changed Philip-Augustus out of his sweat-stained nightclothes and into clean linens and respectable outer garments in the deep black of full Allemanic mourning. Then they did the same for Sophie-Alexa, who wept and clung to them. Franz-Karl wept too, but he gently untangled her fingers from his sleeve.

Some of the lower-ranked men in the official party gently wrapped the two sick children in blankets to carry them away. They made a sort of stretcher to carry Philip-Augustus, who was getting too big to be carried by one person unless it was Fritzel. Franz-Karl was relieved to see that the man who carried Sophie-Alexa seemed to know how to carry a very small girl. Government officials must have children of their own to take care of. Perhaps the man had a daughter.

When the officials had taken the children away and the public doors of the Traventine Residence and Embassy were closed behind them, Tam found George, who had been recovering, lying crumpled and dead beside his bed in the room the two men were sharing with Roland. He had not died of Sickness.

No one said, "This is what Karnburg Palace oaths are worth," out loud, but Franz-Karl was sure that he was not the only one thinking it. Her Grace the Duke collapsed in a faint, and Fritzel carried her back to her bed as easily as if she was Sophie-Alexa.

When Fritzel returned, he lifted George back onto his bed and straightened his limbs. "No marks of violence."

Tam was sitting on the next bed. The valet shrugged, then suddenly lay back as if sitting up was too much work. "There are not many Elderkin who can breathe through a feather pillow."

They tended George as they had tended Marius, cutting his hair for memorial tokens and giving him an abbreviated funeral because they did not trust their 'Hosts' to give him the proper rites for his soul's safety. Then Fritzel set the shrouded corpse outside the Residence and notified the guard at the main door of the West Palace. Franz-Karl wrote another note to Count Adrasteia talking about... everything.

They locked the public doors of the Residence, and even latched the servants' doors, so that they could be private for a little while. Roland, well-wrapped against the chance that he might take a chill, sat to watch Her Grace the Duke Franz-Karl's Mama, while the others all gathered in Juliana's room, where their consecrated Hearth was. There was plenty of room for everyone now: it was only Fritzel and Tam and Gwenlian that needed places to sit, besides Franz-Karl. Gwenlian was as swathed in shawls and wraps as Roland.

"I don't know why they did not ask to take me as well, but I'm glad of it. That argument already stretched my Mama past her strength." Franz-Karl said. "I was not... hiding..."

"Her Grace was careful to always speak of Leon-Alexander's sick children," Fritzel observed.

Tam was sitting in a chair, peeling foreign roots. "There's more than one way to go unnoticed," the valet said. "Look at the nursery through Lowlander eyes – two fair children sleeping in beds with rich garments in mourning black laid out for them, and one browner child sleeping on a pallet, doing a servant's work and wearing plain clothes in his Lady's color."

"They took me for a servant?"

"The colors of your skin and hair are as near to mine or Gwenlian's as they are to your Ma's... and your shape doesn't much favor your brother and sister, though you have their features, largely."

"And I was not near Her Grace my Mama when they looked at me, and her face is thinner since the Sickness took hold, even thinner than mine." Franz-Karl thought it almost made sense. "But the new Master of Protocol knows me: he was part of the big argument about whether I should wear black or color-of-sorrow at my Father's funeral..."

Gwenlian said, "And then they sent you away, and the official records after your return are a tangled mess."

"Everything after my return was a tangled mess." When Franz-Karl thought about that mess, he felt annoyed, instead of sad and worried about the latest messiness. But more than anything else, he felt tired. "von und zu Ostwald has seen me in the North Gallery since then."

"In attendance on your brother and sister?" Fritzel suggested.

"Perhaps." Franz-Karl felt even more tired. "I suppose I will need to remind a few people that Franz-Karl the Notary, in the Line of Succession for Traventi is also Franz-Karl von Falkenburg in the Line of Succession for the Archduchy of the Eastlands and the Domains of the Falkenburgs. There's only Philip-Augustus and me, now, after His Royal Grace Uncle Helm-Friedrich."

Franz-Karl checked his Mama once in a while, in case she needed something that Roland could not manage, but he spent most of the afternoon in Juliana's room with Tam and Gwenlian, making sure there was nothing that they needed and were too sick to manage for themselves. It was warm, because of the Hearth, and it was the place in the Residence that was most theirs. The emptiness of the Nursery was more than he could bear even in daylight, and he was not looking forward to the coming night.

Fritzel spent the afternoon moving beds and bedding, and storage chests, so that Tam and Roland would not be sleeping in the room where Marius and George had died. They had no shortage of empty rooms for the attendants to sleep in.

They changed the mattress on Franz-Karl's bed that Philip-Augustus had been using, and made it up with clean linens and blankets. There were other rooms that he could have used, and the Nursery was a terrible place now that it was empty, but all of his things were there. Taking them away felt like saying that Sophie-Alexa would not return.

They finished the last of the pigeon soup at their evening meal. It would not have been enough, even stretched with griddle cakes and some sausages from their supplies, but Her Grace Franz-Karl's Mama only ate some bread soaked in a little of the broth and drank a little watered wine. She had eaten with a good appetite that morning, but could not bear sausages or more of the soup in the evening after the day's trouble and sadness.

Gwenlian went to sit with Her Grace while Roland came out to Juliana's room to rest and eat his meal. He sighed when he finished. "It has been good to have fresh meat in our bowls. The meat of sacrifice is good for the health."

Franz-Karl considered. "Our dovecote was not the only one inside the Palace walls that held birds that were not His Excellency's. It seems unfair that ours should be the only one empty," he said slowly.

Fritzel stopped frowning and stretched, popping things in his shoulders. "Proper, planned sacrifices should happen in the Shrine, and fetching the birds back living will want a raid after midnight... Do any of those Northern weasels keep pigeons within the Palace walls?"

"The lands of the Northern Lords are even farther away than Traventi," Franz-Karl said. He had often visited the various stables and dovecotes with his Papa. It seemed like a long time ago, but it was barely a year. "They use a lot of pigeons, whether the Lords are living in Karnburg and sending orders to people there, or living in their own domains and sending orders to their agents here. After all, they don't have an ancient and mighty Sorceress getting bored and devising clever ways to send messages. Some of the Northern pigeons live here in the Palace at his Excellency's expense... but not mixed with His Excellency's birds, any more than ours were. Not even the birds the councils use to send messages north." He sipped from his cup of watered wine. "We should probably avoid all the dovecotes attached to the main Palace as a courtesy to His Excellency and His Royal Grace. And avoid the East Palace one used by Her Royal Highness Aunt Queen Gertrude, if we can figure out which one it is."

"Sleep until midnight and then stir about a bit?" Fritzel suggested.

Roland sent Fritzel to open a particular chest among the several Roland owned, and bring back what he found there. The things Fritzel brought back were a pair of fine new Elderkin boots for himself, and a similar pair for Franz-Karl.

"It will take powerfully soft ground for those to leave a mark that even our own people could follow," Roland remarked casually. "Dogs might do better, I fear, but not much better."

Franz-Karl and Fritzel both bowed respectfully. Elderkin did not speak thanks, and Elderkin Cobblers, especially, were never to be thanked or paid, but no one with half a wit rejected shoes of Elderkin make.

Franz-Karl's boots fit him perfectly, of course. Aside from being made by an Elderkin Cobbler, they were made by the same Cobbler who had made and tended all of his boots his whole life, except for the few months he spent in Traventi. The Cobblers in Traventi had been impressed by his boots, and said "Of course" when he said the workmanship was Roland's.

Franz-Karl did not sleep well, even though Tam had tucked his wooden horse into the bed beside him. He kept waking to listen for his brother's coughing or his sister's crying: she had a tendency toward bad dreams even before she got sick. And of course, whenever he woke, they were not there. It was a relief when it was time to get up for their outing.

When they rose from their beds and prepared to 'stir about', Fritzel and Franz-Karl did not dress any differently than usual, except that they were wearing their fine new boots. They were residents of the Palace, and could not officially be questioned for walking around in it, even at night, provided they were not doing something clearly odd such as openly carrying live pigeons or dressing and behaving furtively.

They both carried various useful items in their pockets, but there would be blood on the tiles well before any situation reached the point of searches of their persons. Franz-Karl was both a foreign crown prince and a Falkenburg princeling, when he cared to press the matter. And Fritzel was... large... and not entirely human in shape or voice. Besides all that, problems rarely progressed very far within the Palace unless there was some Noble or senior official poking his nose in and making a fuss, which was very unlikely at any time after midnight. Nobles and senior officials liked to sleep. The guards at the gates were sometimes a different matter, but Franz-Karl and Fritzel were used to moving where they pleased within the Palace walls.

The dovecotes nearest the central Palace served the His Excellency and the Falkenburgs, so they began their exploration by going past them to the outbuildings that served the East Palace.

The first place they tried had a cheerful Szekely Hussar camped at the entrance with a bedroll and some supplies. The man had eaten at the Traventine table a few times and was a fair linguist: Franz-Karl was nearly certain that his name was Bartak. He handed Franz-Karl a thick letter from his Aunt, Dowager Queen Gertrude of the Szekelys, and gave them advice on which dovecote belonging to the 'pig-bothering Northerners' could be raided most usefully. He insisted on sharing a drink of something served in very small glasses – and even then, Franz-Karl's serving was just a taste at the bottom of his glass, for Hospitality's sake. Fritzel eyed the flask with respect after drinking his much larger serving. Their Host seemed much more relaxed once the two Elderkin had shared a drink with him.

"What is this made from?" Franz-Karl asked. He was fairly certain no grapes had been anywhere near it.

"Palinka? Cherries... sometimes other things, but this is cherries." The man shrugged. "I think the Captain has a cousin with a cherry orchard and a still. The company gets a keg most years." Hands sketched an impressively large keg.

They wished their Host well and continued toward the dovecote that he had recommended.

There were a lot of pigeons there. They did not take all of them: there were far too many to carry while they were living, and they had no good way to preserve or store the extra meat once they got them back to the Residence... better to leave most of them as living birds: if there was food available, the best way to store meat was as living creatures, and the Elderkin did not need to worry about feeding these birds. That was someone else's job and expense.

They did not try to take all of the birds that went to a particular destination: they did not know where any of the birds thought their homes were. They took a dozen of the fattest and a handful of others that felt right or necessary to Franz-Karl and stashed them in the deep pockets in the skirts of their coats.

Then they strolled back to the West Palace, where they handed the pigeons over to Roland and Tam, and returned to their beds.

Franz-Karl slept soundly until mid-morning, without waking to listen for anything. Perhaps it was the drop of palinka.

# CHAPTER XXV: Letter from the Queen

## *Wherein News Arrives of Karnburg and Elsewhere Outside the Palace*

When he looked at it in the morning light, Franz-Karl discovered that the letter from her Royal Highness Aunt Queen Gertrude was addressed to him, not to Her Grace the Duke His Mama. But he waited until he was in her room, taking a turn at watching her, before he opened it.

It was actually several documents, including an inventory list of the other documents, all inside a single wrapper.

It was... almost strange. After the long days spent surrounded by the walls of the Traventine Residence, or moving through the corridors and tunnels of the Palace's buildings, reading the package of documents was like opening a window and letting in a fresh breeze bearing scents from the outside world.

There was news of the city of Karnburg outside the Palace walls, and news of the rest of the Falkenburg Eastlands. There was news from the other Falkenburg Domains, and from the parts of the Allemanic Kingdom that were not Falkenburg Domains except by answering to a King who happened to be a Falkenburg. There was news from all of the places where the sisters and aunts and great aunts and assorted female cousins of Aunt Queen Gertrude had gone to be Queens and Duchesses and Countesses. And there were rumors about the places around them and in between them, so very few of the lands that lay north of the Mothersea or gathered around its shores were not mentioned.

Franz-Karl had to get out three books of maps and two chronicles that listed rulers and treaties to figure out where all the places mentioned were.

Franz-Karl was used to thinking about his connections to Traventi, which was small and isolated, and almost frighteningly far away: weeks by mule train or riverboat. Suddenly he was connected to... well... everywhere. His cousin Andrea, who now held the interim position after him in the Line of Succession of the Duke of Traventi, was his mother's mother's sister's daughter's daughter, and there were many of those Queens and Duchesses and Countesses – and their children – who were closer kin than that.

He had always thought that Allemanic habit of ignoring and suppressing the females lines of inheritance was stupid. Every time he learned more about it, it seemed even more stupid than the last time.

He also strongly suspected that the wrong child of His Excellency was trying to run the Falkenburg Empire. If Aunt Queen Gertrude could gather all of this news without having any kind of official position, imagine what she could do with even a small part of the authority that was attached to her younger brother Helm-Friedrich.

Late that morning some of the Palace Physicians finally arrived to attend Her Grace the Duke of Traventi, Franz-Karl's Mama. Franz-Karl did not leave the room because they asked him to: they thought he was a servant and were quite willing to have him fetch and carry. But being in the room with them made him dizzy and gave him a terrible headache. The quirk in his vision that made liars not fit their spaces in the World accepted most of them as honest men – as men in the Palace went – except for two that were terrible. The other strangeness in his vision, the one that warned him against food that was unhealthful or served improperly was doing very strange things around the medicines the physicians carried.

The food rules were different for sick people. Franz-Karl hoped that the flickering weirdness he was seeing was because he was not sick, so things that might be needful for his Mama would be wrong for him.

One of the terrible physicians was attended by a Bound and enslaved Elderkin – not a Traventine, of course, one from somewhere else – who followed him like a whipped and silenced dog. Franz-Karl could hardly see through the pulsing wrongness of the Bindings to tell whether the person had been a man or a woman. He was honestly not entirely certain that the person was still alive in there. He objected to that presence within the Residence: Elderkin slaves did not exist in Traventi and the Marriage Contract guaranteed that they would not be allowed across the Threshold of the Traventine Residence and Embassy. He was so angry he could hardly manage to call Fritzel and Roland.

While Roland and Fritzel and the Physician argued – rather loudly – Franz-Karl quietly suggested to the Living World that since Bound Elderkin could not cross the Threshold, therefore an Elderkin who had been brought across the Threshold must not be Bound…

By the time that horrible Physician went away, leading his captive as if on an invisible leash, the Bindings were beginning to show a few gaps, rather like a sheet of paper cast on the fire that was not fully alight but had a few empty burned spots that were expanding as their charred edges moved outward. The gaps got bigger and more numerous when the Physician and his companion crossed the Threshold again on their way out, so Franz-Karl had some hope that the Physician was due for an unpleasant surprise quite soon.

While all of this was going on, the other Physicians had been treating and dosing Her Grace the Duke. When they came out of her sickroom and walked toward the entrance of the Residence, they seemed satisfied and hopeful. They said that she would soon join those who had recovered from the Sickness.

Franz-Karl was hopeful after listening to them, but when he went into his Mama's room to sit with her for a while, he thought at first that she seemed even quieter and paler than before the Physicians arrived. When he touched her hand, she felt neither hot nor cold, as if her long fever had finally broken, so it seemed the Physicians had done that much good. Perhaps the quietness was because she was finally resting.

Eating the meat of sacrifice at midday seemed to help her, even though it was just fresh pigeon soup. It was good that they had that much: most of the food sent up from the kitchens that day was neither encouraging, nor appetizing, though the bread remained edible and very good.

The Palace received the best grain and flour, but it was more than that. Franz-Karl thought that no one dared to disrespect the consecrated Ovens to make bad bread, not in a place that was full of Ecclesialist Initiates. And with too few people in the kitchens doing too much work, no one had time to find ways to spoil the bread once it was made. He thought Clothilde might cook them if they tried: she was scary when people were being stupid in the kitchens, even important people like Philip-Augustus.

Fritzel said that people who arranged Palace banquets ignored the proper bread-sharing rites at meals and served separate little loaves to people. Some of them probably thought it was an insult to give the Traventines proper large loaves instead of the little ones.

After their meal, Franz-Karl and Fritzel consulted the best herbals in their library and prepared to raid the gardens, while Roland, as majordomo tended the Threshold and Itron Gwenlian attended her Grace.

That left Tam to go to the kitchens for a discussion with the cooks and the stewards of the pantries about the state of their food. Franz-Karl's valet went out through the front entrance of the Residence, since they had decided to treat this as official household business. He never returned that day, and the Cooks and Stewards swore – honestly, to Franz-Karl's eyes – that he had never reached them.

Franz-Karl could generally tell when he was being lied to, but that only worked if a person – or sometimes a document – was in front of him to lie to him. If someone with guilty knowledge avoided him entirely, there was no way for him to know. There might be tricks that grownups Notaries knew, but he was seven, and the officials running the Palace had made sure that he had no grownup Notaries to teach him but his Mama, who was busy with other matters even before the Sickness came, and had never been trained as a Justice or Advocate.

Losing Tam was worse than Marius dying or George being killed. There had been two people who were part of Franz-Karl's own personal household, not his Mama's household or the Residence as a whole, and now one was taken. Tam had taken care of Franz-Karl and his clothes and things every day since the preceding summer. Tam had volunteered to come out of Traventi where there were fewer mean people. And now the valet was just ... gone... completely gone except for one lock of stuff that was not quite hair in the living-people side of the Household Shrine.

If Tam was dead, the valet's soul would wander lost in the World Beyond without at least a partial funeral. If the valet was not entirely dead, any kind of funeral might be deadly.

Franz-Karl remembered the Physician's Bound slave, and shuddered. He rifled through Tam's things and found a hairbrush that had not been tended carefully, what with the Sickness and everyone doing three people's jobs. He used the few stray hairs from it to anchor a formal written and sealed declaration reminding the Living World that Tam was an Elderkin of Traventi and could not be Bound contrary to his own will. Franz-Karl had never seen a declaration like that mentioned in any of the histories and chronicles, not even in any of the old tales, but he thought it would do no harm, and might do some good. He sealed it with some of his own hairs under the wax along with Tam's, and added a drop of his own blood to the signature. When the Binding was as complete as he could make it, he set it in the Household Shrine, in the same cupboard as his Mama's accession oath.

Then Franz-Karl asked Fritzel and Itron Gwenlian and Roland if they knew any other tricks that might give Tam a stronger anchor and lifeline. They looked at each other over his head and said, no, not that he could use before he was an Initiate, and he could see in their eyes that they believed that Tam was probably dead.

If Franz-Karl was honest with himself, as a Notary had to be, he did not really believe that he would ever see Tam again this side of the Halls of Judgment. He also believed, very firmly, that whoever had harmed his attendant would regret it both within the Living World and in the World Beyond.

# INTERLUDE VIII: Stratagems

## *Wherein The Echelon Changes*

The Margraff-Elector rose from his sickbed before his physicians advised it. He answered their warnings by saying that news of losses among the Echelon in Karnburg, and especially among the Select, could not be ignored. The influence of his nearest rival in the Echelon was gone from Karnburg. The entire Echelon was shrinking toward the size of the list of the Select a year earlier. And men would be taking actions outside their proper authority if affairs were not set in order and a proper hierarchy reestablished under proper authority. His authority.

Horst-Konrad's first destination when he left his bedchamber was his study. He began by sending messages to find out what was left of both the official Pristinist community and the less official agents they had employed. His secretaries were dead or still sick, but that was less trouble than it might have been: unlike some men of rank, he customarily wrote instructions to the lesser authorities in the Pristinist community himself, and always wrote the instructions for his private agents. As one of the highest among the Select he was not unfamiliar with his colleagues' projects, though naturally some agents who served his rivals had been kept secret. If any were left master-less that desired employment, they would eventually seek out the Echelon.

The Pristinists were surrounded by enemies. A handful of Select in an Echelon of forty in a Pristinist community of hundreds could not complete the all of intentions of an Echelon four times the size in a community of thousands, but it was not safe to let the various ploys simply unravel. Too much might be revealed to the wrong people. It would be best if various projects could be set aside neatly in ways that would not draw attention.

Once he had taken steps to pick up the reins of the Pristinists in Karnburg, Horst-Konrad von Neumark summoned his new House-master, Heinrich – who had been a mere footman a few days earlier – to learn the true state of his own household. Heinrich arrived armed with a sheaf of notes about the state of the house, the contents of the storerooms, and the humans and livestock who resided within its walls.

The remaining member of the household of Preacher Weiss was a clerk called Cardel, a scrawny fellow with an unimpressive voice whose face now showed the fading blotches of the Sickness. But he was alive, and held a minor certificate from a Pristinist School, so Horst-Konrad sent a message that he should to prepare his texts for the next gathering in the White Hall. The writings insisted that the Echelon should not be allowed to fragment during times of trouble.

Heinrich mentioned that the women's quarters of the house were empty, but the House-master – whoever he was – always mentioned that. One of the responsibilities of the House-master was to maintain the household on behalf of his lord as a place of order and virtue, and a household devoid of women did not fit the patterns of proper household order described by Pristinus de Millau and his followers. In the time of the Siege, the highborn women living in Karnburg had been sent 'home' to the Ansbach estates in the North, and their female slaves and serf-born attendants had gone with them. The apartments had remained empty in the years since then, which was not entirely respectable. At best – in a house as strict as the Margraff-Elector's – it smacked too much of Ecclesialist monasticism. At worst – under a less rigorous lord – order and virtue were perhaps not terms that might readily apply to such a household.

Horst-Konrad frowned. "The main purpose and value of the women's quarters lies in the production of sons for the House of

Neumark. I have lived as a younger son and remember the ... disputes ... about allocations of family property among my father and his brothers. I have two living sons, well reported, and see no need to invite more such disputes."

Heinrich looked unhappy, but he bowed deeply and turned to the next page of his report about the household.

Supplies were adequate for the next while, given the reduced population of the house. Finding hands to perform the work of the household was a greater problem.

Nearly three quarters of the household slaves were dead, and nearly two thirds of the indentured and serf-born. Among the respectable men in the household, more than half survived, but they were mostly the younger men: assistants, not their masters. The chief cook was gone, and the stable-master, and the secretaries and clerks who saw to the principality affairs of the Margravate of Ansbach.

"And the kennels?" Horst-Konrad prompted after the House-master paused.

Heinrich looked down and shuffled his papers, but he finally said, "The Margraff-Elector will need to find yet another kennel-master. But the kennels are not empty. Your Eminence has only lost half of the beast-born locked in their solitary cells. The agent known as Coenraad and the slave called Fourteen made sure the wretched things were fed. No one else was willing to go near the kennels and their accursed residents after the kennel-master died."

The Margraff-Elector set down the account book he was holding and looked directly at his House-master. "Coenraad and Fourteen? Are those two Sick?"

"Yes, your Eminence."

"See that they are well-tended. If they survive, I shall consider making them my new special clerk and kennel-master."

The House-master shuddered visibly, but did not look away from Horst-Konrad's gaze. He took a deep breath, then said quietly, "If your Eminence thinks that is advisable."

"It will need some careful thought, true. But, now is a time for caution, but not too much caution." The Margraff-Elector tapped the desk top with the fingertips of one gloved hand. "The big slave will very likely do well enough as kennel-master – strength is good in a kennel-master and lack of fear is even better, and sometimes diligent is better than clever. And with so few left in the kennels he'll not be too busy for other tasks." He added the designation to the list he had been writing, then looked back at the House-master. "The blades-man, Coenraad, is clever, though not as clever as he thinks he is, and he at least pretends to be unafraid of the talismans. The man claims to be a follower of Pristinus, but if he has a hair's-weight of loyalty to anything but gold and blood, I have not seen it. He will need to be carefully enrolled and Bound to our service before he lays eyes on any of the Books of Secrets."

Heinrich said, "Your Eminence," in a careful tone that was neither agreement nor protest.

"Find me someone better if you can. If you don't, and the Sickness takes Coenraad, the clerk's tasks will be your responsibility along with the rest."

The House-master shuddered again, but his departure when he was dismissed was only a little more hasty than was strictly proper.

Other than the special problems of the Preacher and the kennels, the Margraff-Elector was able to restaff the household quickly. As news arrived about deaths and survivals in various households among the Select and the rest of the Echelon, Horst-Konrad and Heinrich decided which among the surviving master-less dependents would be most useful, and summoned them. Respectable men and minor Nobles – members of the Echelon who had lost their patrons – received offers of positions that were slightly more polite, but not very.

As the Margraff-Elector was turning his attention to the women's quarters of his late rivals, news the Great Sickness and deaths arrived from Ansbach that clarified matters usefully. The Heir of the von Neumarks still lived, but the younger boy and many others did not.

A few lesser nobles who had served Bremerhaven or the General of the Imperial Army seemed unhappy about the Margraff-Elector's handling of their women's quarters. But the questioners, much like some of the Falkenburgs, turned out not to survive the Great Sickness after all, so that was no great problem, though the Margraff-Elector's appropriation of the ladies did cause some – very quiet – gossip among the higher end of the Echelon. Within the von Ansbach household in Karnburg there were no complaints: highborn ladies in the women's quarters meant that there would be maid-servants and female slaves there as well, which was considered an improvement by the lesser men who served the household.

The General's chief wife had died of the Sickness, he had no daughters at home, and his sons were in the North. By tradition the other ladies under the General's protection should have passed, with their doweries, to his heirs – who were a month's travel away even if the roads had been clear and the countryside was free of pestilence – or else returned to their birth families, assuming the Sickness had spared them. Given the current turbulent times, and the fact that the chief wife's dower goods were properly sent North, none of the other ladies or their families complained too loudly at finding themselves entangled with one of the six Prince-Electors of the Allemans.

The new Prince-Elector of Bremerhaven was inclined to protest the arrangements made for his predecessor's household – before he ran out of pigeons – but he was very far away from Karnburg. And the Bremerhaven vassals and advocates and servants that would have supported his claim were largely either very far away from Karnburg, or dead. And Friedrich -Augustus, Elected King of the Allemans and Claimed Emperor of the Remorans was sick, and mourning his own heirs. And the Great Sickness had reached the North...

The surviving residents of the Bremerhaven women's quarters in Karnburg who arrived in Ansbach's... guardianship... included three not very minor ladies with extremely impressive doweries in treasure and land, a marriageable Bremerhaven daughter, and the late Prince-Elector of Bremerhaven's very pregnant chief widow. The possibilities for future Bremerhaven embarrassment were vast and varied, depending on the survival and gender of the unborn infant. The inheritance of the Prince-Elector's title was not in question but many other matters were.

Besides the ladies and possible future child, and possibly even more useful, the Bremerhaven women's quarters also held two enslaved eunuchs who had been gelded as infants because they were Bremerhaven bastards by slave mothers. They were not legally the new Prince-Elector's nephews, but everyone who mattered knew that they were his nephews... and now those who mattered would know that the Prince-Elector's nephews were slaves in Horst-Konrad's household. It was a situation that would mean nothing officially, and everything socially, especially in the strict hierarchy of the Echelons where women were properly ignored.

With the top of the Echelon well sorted, the rest of the Pristinist community could shake itself and reshuffle. When things settled a bit, there were no women or children lacking protectors, nor men of the servile classes lacking masters, and each Echelon household had moved into the most prestigious available residence. The women had no say in where they ended up – and neither did most men who were not considered free and free-born – but that was always the case among the Pristinists.

Actual residence did not much match the city's records of ownership, but people paid city taxes and fees 'on behalf of' the owners of record, and the city records would be updated by 'inheritance' when the legal owners died. By long tradition in Karnburg, sales of buildings were taxed far more heavily than inheritance, so the Pristinists were not the only community who managed their own property transfers. With the spate of recent deaths attributable to the Sickness, the city's records would soon be more accurate than they had been since the end of the Siege.

As the Echelon settled, the Select in Karnburg did not gather in the Inner Hall of the White Hall. Instead, they attended an audience in the reception rooms of the Margraff-Elector's house: the first gathering there since the 'small entertainment' that had been followed by so much sickness and death. The dozen surviving Select were all recovering from the Great Sickness and generally lacked stamina for the long session and Purgation that would accompany a formal Gathering. But in the less formal setting, the discussion went quickly: there was no Prince-Elector of Bremerhaven to council prudence, nor General of the Army of the Empire to speak of practicalities, nor Preacher Weiss to chide unrighteousness. The replacement Preacher, Cardel, was not summoned to the gathering since it was outside his precincts; neither was the younger Bauer, the Teacher.

It did not take the Select long to agree that there was still no need to avoid the deaths of their opponents – or any of the inconvenient unworthy – provided those deaths came in a form that could be assumed to be the fault of the Sickness. Once the dead entered the crypts and charnel pits there would be none to ask how they got there. The one bit of prudence anyone agreed to was that any dead likely to receive formal funerals should show no clear marks of violence.

Similarly, with half the Palace and City dead, and another half sickened, and yet another half set to unaccustomed tasks, the plethora of badly written accounts and spoiled receipts could usefully confuse the movements of coinage and other goods. The Palace gate guards and doorwards were different from day to day and the people passing through were changing from day to day. As long as good Allemans supported one another against questions, and the guards were encouraged to stop foreigners and the unworthy, movement in and out and within the Palace should remain convenient for members of the Echelon, whether or not they properly had business within the Palace.

Before they adjourned, one of the newer members of the Select, Baron Ten Broeck, suggested that it was past time to do something about the pernicious Southern custom of attaching perfectly good lands and other property to childless widows dwelling in households without male masters. The rest of the Select saw no reason to disagree with the suggestion: by Pristinist customs, women held no property: the bride with her dowery passed from her father's possession to her husband's. And a childless widow past the age of bearing had no value. The southern custom of giving a widow a life interest in her dower lands was viewed as scandalous, or outrageous, depending on how many Southern widows the Pristinist families were stuck with after trying to marry wealth.

Ten Broeck's case was notorious among them. A few years after Ten Broeck's father inherited their estates and and title, he had found himself short of funds and demanded money from his widowed sister-in-law, who was still entitled to the income from the prosperous dower lands she had brought to her marriage. She had dared to offer him a loan at very good terms. But, of course, no decent follower of Pristinus de Millau could acknowledge a debt to a woman. Now the new Baron had inherited more debts than income, and a fierce grudge against his uncle's wealthy widow.

Ritter von und zu Ostwald commented that there were many people dying in the city, so it was not unlikely that women, being feeble creatures, would be among them. As long as there were no marks not caused by the Sickness to raise questions, the Baron's problems should resolve themselves.

The Margraff-Elector said nothing during the discussion about the widows: his own widowed aunt was his Excellency's sister, and some comments would not be safely spoken aloud even within the Echelon. But when the others had left, he reviewed a list of the many widows living under Falkenburg protection in the Palace and city, and wrote a carefully worded note hinting at future benefits to the Landgraff who governed the Eastlands province across the Raenos River from Traventi. Landgraff von Steinach went by his family name, not the name of the province, because the province's name was considered unlucky. He was not a Pristinist, but he was a leader of the southern faction that was most strongly opposed to Traventi and the Elderkin.

# CHAPTER XXVI: The Good Neighbors

## *Wherein Some Ladies Are Stolen Away*

Very early in the morning, even before the bells for morning prayers rang, someone pounded on the main door of the Traventine Residence. Fritzel opened the door, with Franz-Karl standing a little behind him.

Dusek Urban was standing at the door in his battered coat with the fancy buttons, though it hung a little loose. He was thinner than he had been not long before, and his face showed the fading blotchiness of recovery from the Sickness. Franz-Karl thought there might be more gray in his hair.

Urban signed himself. "Thank Heaven and all the saints! I feared... ah! I don't know what I feared..."

Franz-Karl recited the Allemanic translation of the general Host oath and prompted the clerk through a version of the guest-and-ally oath, and they brought Urban inside and fed him watered wine and aogreamana morsels by candle-light.

Urban slumped in his chair wearily.

"Should you have left your bed?" From Fritzel it was a friendly question between two men who worked in royal households. It was not a question Franz-Karl could ask a grownup or the Childe of Traventi would ask a Palace clerk.

"I left my bed and returned to my office this morning for the first time, after..." he waved a hand toward the blotches on his face. "I fear someone has been trying to meddle with the keys and seals. No one with proper authority: I... had the master key and master seal safe with me at home, and no one sent to demand them for any needful task. I thought ... I feared... I don't know what I feared. The laundry here was certainly closed without proper authority, though I have found a recent note ordering its reopening. The records for the pantries are a jumbled mess, And there are not even jumbled records of what they did to the North Kitchen: with the Flame dead, we'll have to assume desecration and get people in from the Cathedral in to deconsecrate and reconsecrate the Hearths and Ovens before they can be used again."

"Nah, " Fritzel said. "The north kitchen here was closed clean with the seasonal rites..."

Franz-Karl turned his back to the speakers and walked over to the far wall, and began studying the frescoes. Not being an Initiate was sometimes a nuisance, but since he had not made any oaths or promises to the High Gods, he did not need to worry much about upsetting them. Considering the mess of the Marriage Contract, he hoped that people were keeping their promises to the Gods, though the number of recent deaths suggested that Someone was annoyed. There was always a chance that the people in and around the Palace might surprise him and behave properly.

Fritzel was continuing, "and we've got the Flame and Leaven preserved, so reopening the north Kitchen should need only Initiates and maybe a minor priestess or two." He took a sip of the watered wine used for the welcome rites. "The kitchen I'd worry about is the Central one. When they bother to send us meals, the food lately is Impure past decent use. But I've noticed that we are stricter about the Rites of Hospitality than city folk seem to be."

Franz-Karl returned to face the speakers. "The bread from the middle kitchen is all right – or it was two days ago – so the baking Rites were still being done properly then, with a proper Hearth and Ovens."

Dusek Urban looked even more worried. "Are you sure, Your Honor?"

"I'm a Traventine Notary, and Hospitality is Oaths. I can tell."
That ... was not nearly the entire truth of the matter, but it was not at all
a lie. Franz-Karl did not think that Dusek Urban had time to listen to the
full explanation – some things that were simple in Elderic and among
Elderkin just ... weren't ... when you tried to explain them to Worldfolk.
The full explanation would not likely be a comfort to the clerk in any
case.

As Urban took his leave, he commented that for thoroughness
sake, he should visit Graefinwitwe Wiborada von Steinach and her ladies
before he returned to his desk.

Fritzel stiffened, and set down his wine-glass very carefully.

Franz-Karl felt cold, but he said carefully, "Dusek Urban. We
were told – by a man who believed his own words – that this is the only
inhabited Residence in this end of the West Palace: it was part of the
excuse for closing the North kitchen." Dusek Urban went pale. Franz-
Karl continued, "He also said that the servants' doors are open, in case we
wanted to scavenge linens. It will be quicker to check from that side."

Fritzel left immediately, but Franz-Karl found that the neglected
servants' passages were too dim to be safe for the clerk's human eyes. By
the time he found and lit a candle-lantern, his aide was far ahead of them.

When they had gone down the stairs to the pantries, then up the
flight to what should be the service entrance to the Graefinwitwe's dining
room, they found Fritzel waiting. "Locked. Locked or barred. And the
other door is the same." His voice had dropped to a dangerous rumble
deep in his chest.

Franz-Karl peeked through the keyhole, and worked the door
handle, and thumped a panel with his ear held close. "Not locked: the
latch moves but the door does not. I think it's been nailed or wedged...
something like that... from the other side. Fetch an ax."

"Your Honor. " Servants' stairs did not have banisters, exactly,
but there were narrow moldings people braced burdens against when
they needed a hand free. Fritzel was wide enough to brace against both
moldings and slide down quickly without touching the steps, provided
he was wearing gloves.

There had been a whiff of something through the keyhole:
Franz-Karl called after his friend, "Fetch salt and candles, too..."

"Aye," came the fading answer.

Dusek Urban began muttering something. The words were in one of the Eastern languages Franz-Karl did not know – Slovak, maybe? or something from farther east? nothing like the Magyar his Aunt's Szekely Hussars spoke – but he could hear enough of the intent to know that it was cursing, not the good kind of praying. Very, very thorough cursing. Three repetitions, then a fourth... In front of a Traventine Notary. He would need to ask Count Adrasteia whether Bindings could happen when you did not know the language being spoken, or the full intent of the words...

When the clerk finished, he did not want to ask about what he had been saying, so Franz-Karl looked for another topic. There were no good ones. He asked, "Dusek Urban? Your family?"

The clerk wiped his face with a handkerchief. "Some yet live," he answered, wearily.

"Same," Franz-Karl agreed. What else was there to say?

They sat on the top step of the stairs while they waited. It was not a long wait.

Fritzel returned with candles, salt,the ax, and a full goatskin water-sack looped over his shoulder. He handed the bundle of candles to Franz-Karl and the cask of salt to Dusek Urban to hold while he used the ax on the oaken rails and mullions that framed the panels of the door.

The Residence was quite tidy, once they got in. There was not a spec of food or droplet of water in the place, and the ladies were laid out on the tops of their beds, properly dressed for their funerals.

Except that three of the five ladies were not yet entirely dead.

Franz-Karl set lit candles at the heads and feet of the two dead ladies, to guide them to the Halls of Judgment and protect them from demons along the Road. He hoped that he and Fritzel and Dusek Urban had arrived in time, and nobody nice had their soul eaten yet.

The grownups propped the living ladies up with pillows, then found some cups and filled them with water from Fritzel's water-skin. There were three ladies and three of them – Fritzel and Dusek Urban and Franz-Karl – so they each sat with one of the ladies and they each began to pour tiny sips of water into them. Carefully, so carefully, so as not to drown them by pouring the water wrong. Franz-Karl had too much practice giving water to people who were not drinking properly: it took him a while to figure out that the lady he was helping was not cold, she was just not feverish.

It seemed to Franz-Karl that a long time passed before all three ladies were even swallowing properly. And their breathing was not right. But they were not all equally bad. The youngest one, Henrietta, blinked her eyes open and tried to raise a hand to help steady her cup while Graefinwitwe Wiborada was still horribly limp. The third lady – Franz-Karl was hoping no one would ask him her name and trying to remember whether he had ever heard it – did not open her eyes, but she shifted her head against the pillow and began to sip the water on purpose.

When Graefinwitwe Wiborada seemed to be swallowing and breathing well, Fritzel carefully wrapped her draperies around her so that they would not snag on anything in the tunnels or trip him up on the stairs. Then he picked her up and carried her toward the door they had broken open. He stuck his head into the room where Franz-Karl was giving water to the nameless lady and asked, "Your Honor, do we have all of the crow-cage stuff?"

"Most of it? I think? Itron Gwenlian should know…"

"Crow-cage stuff?" Dusek Urban called from the other room, as Fritzel vanished.

"We have been told by a man with experience that when you rescue someone from a crow cage – or a bare knob of rock they were shipwrecked on without food or water – you cannot just plunk a feast down in front of them. If they try to eat too much before their humors are rebalanced and their innards are gently reminded of their proper tasks, the good food will kill them. Some of the doses for re-balancing the humors after crow-cages are a bit uncommon."

Urban was silent for a moment. "I had an uncle that died two days after the great siege ended… it might have been from that. Unbalanced humors, eh? Well, if what you need can be had in Karnburg, I will get it for you. The Palace buyers have sources that others do not."

While they waited, Dusek Urban moved between Henrietta and the other lady, giving them water when they would take it, while Franz-Karl sometimes helped and sometimes prowled through the Residence.

"Your Honor, may I ask what you are looking for?" Dusek Urban asked when he rejoined him after one of his forays.

"Keys, mostly… keys to open the locks and bolts of the public doors. And the hammer that set the wedges on the servants' doors. They are not here, so the ladies did not do this to themselves: someone locked them in."

"Yes," the clerk agreed sadly. "Is it rude that I hoped Your Honor was too young to understand that?"

Franz-Karl looked at him. "Not rude. Just kind." He shivered: unhallowed dead people so close to the sick people in his own Residence was scary. But the old stories told about ways to make things safer. Doing what he could would feel better than just waiting, now that the living ladies did not need him so frequently.

He picked up the salt cask and a pair of scissors from the Graefinwitwe's sewing basket and went away to the saddest rooms in the Residence. The first part was too easy. He did not need to think about cutting the locks of hair off dead people and preparing the locks of hair to be memorial tokens: his fingers knew what to do after doing it too many times already.

The salt was trickier. According to the stories and Chronicles, the very best fence against both the outraged dead and the servants of the Judges was sacrificial blood poured in a ditch, but a line of salt was nearly as good. And salt did not splash or dry out or get icky. But putting out the salt needed to be done right or it might be worse than useless.

This might be a bad time and place for the salt to be worse than useless: the Judges were not mean, exactly – strict was different than mean – but sometimes they got cranky about people being awful, and let hunters and furies loose to start punishing even before people died. Locking up nice widow ladies and leaving them to parch and starve and die with no funerals to guide them to the Halls of Judgment was as bad as breaking Host and Guest oaths... maybe worse. The Judges were probably going to be very cranky, this next while.

The salt in Lady Roxana's room was almost easy to manage. He was quite sure the Sickness had really killed her, and her bed was narrow and level and not complicated or pushed against a wall on one side. Franz-Karl poured a line of salt as thick as one of his fingers all around her on the coverlet of the bed, starting and finishing at the candle above the top of her head. Then he carefully checked the whole line for gaps or breaks and added pinches of salt to a few places that looked thin. He said a prayer for her, but he was a child, not an Initiate, so the prayers he knew were ... 'saying goodnight to your ancestors' prayers ... not proper funeral prayers. Lady Roxana would need to wait for Fritzel and Dusek Urban to tell her some funeral prayers for her journey.

Lady Margretha's room was much, much worse. Franz-Karl was pretty sure that Elderkin were not supposed to think that places felt spooky – they were supposed to be spooky themselves – but Lady Margretha's room managed to feel spooky anyway, not just sad. The shadows in the room fell strangely and did not quite match the direction of the light. That was never a good thing to see.

The wide, heavy bed frame included four big square pillars that held up a wooden canopy, while the body was nestled among pillows and lumpy bedclothes. Cutting the locks was a little scary: he needed to stand on a footstool and lean way over the bed pillows to reach.

The pillows and lumpy bedclothes meant that a salt ring on top of the bed would not work: the sections of the line of salt would not connect. And he did not think that even Fritzel's long arms would be able to reach across to draw the part of the ring between her body and the wall. Not without touching her. Ick.

When he got down on the floor to look at the supports of the bed frame, Franz-Karl was relieved to find that the supports on the far side were not flush against the wall: there was a narrow gap between the walls and the support pillars. And the bed frame was tall enough that he could squirm underneath it.

He spilled salt into the fold of a piece of paper and used it to draw the salt lines in places he could not quite reach directly. He made the outline of salt around the bed a thick, unbroken line, with extra loops around the bottoms of the support pillars, and then he redrew the line thicker and thicker until he used up all of the salt that was left.

He gave Lady Margretha an extra prayer, one from an old story that was supposed to be 'comforting for the souls of the unjustly dead'. It was long, and in a complicated Remoran verse form, so he sang it – there were at least three tunes that went with that verse form and did not need a choir and soloists – and counted time with his hands and feet to avoid getting lost in the verses. The shadows looked more natural after he finished.

When he finished drawing the salt fences, Franz-Karl found that Fritzel had come and gone while he was busy, taking Henrietta away to their Residence where there was food and medicine and warmth and more water. Dusek Urban was sitting with the final lady, who looked like she was napping. Franz-Karl was coughing a little because it had been dusty under the bed, so Dusek Urban handed him a cup of water and watched carefully while he drank every drop of it, and then gave him another cupful.

While they waited, Franz-Karl finally remembered that this final lady's name was Roderica. Somehow that made him feel a little better about all of this awfulness. He wondered whether the people who blocked the doors knew or cared that her name was Roderica.

When Fritzel returned, Franz-Karl stayed tending Lady Roderica while Fritzel and Dusek Urban went to light more candles and say the funeral prayers for Roxana and Margretha. Then Fritzel picked up Roderica and they all went back to the Traventine Residence.

Going back was very strange. The public door of Graefinwitwe Wiborada's Residence opened into the North Gallery, just like the Traventine Residence Threshold. So the way to move between the Residences in the servants' passages should be to go down some stairs, and then across, then up some stairs. But when they brought Roderica home through the passages, it felt like they were moving upward the whole way, beginning somewhere very deep.

They put the three ladies together in one room that had been empty since before Franz-Karl was born. It was next to Juliana's room, with their consecrated Hearth, so just one person could tend them easily, and they were near the food and water and warmth. But Palace officials who had been in the Residence would not expect to find anyone there, and the door could be locked so that people could not barge in and find out the room was not empty. Franz-Karl left one of the keys hanging on a cord on the inside of the door, so the danger from their enemies could be locked out, but the ladies would never be locked in.

Dusek Urban went away to his office to begin looking for the ingredients on the list that Itron Gwenlian gave him. Franz-Karl wrote a note – signed Franz-Karl von Falkenburg – for Fritzel to leave at the well in the tunnel, warning the Rathvins of the Old Palace Servants to check all of the residences, especially the the ones that they thought were empty.

Franz-Karl wrote another note about finding the ladies and bringing them into the Residence left it on the message table for Count Great Aunt Adrasteia. Carrying people across Thresholds without asking them was probably against all sorts of rules and laws.

## CHAPTER XXVII: Death Bells

### *Wherein Deaths are Reported that the Falkenburgs can Ill Afford*

After all that had happened, it was still only mid-morning. Franz-Karl changed his dusty clothes – there had been spiderwebs under Lady Margretha's bed – and brushed his hair and washed his face and hands before he went to sit with his Mama. He did not tell her about the ladies immediately because she was so quiet. He thought is was better to wait until she was more wakeful.

Just before noon, they heard the death bells ringing for a male death. Roland listened for a moment. "That can't be His Excellency. There would be cannons."

When the officials knocked on the door of the Residence, Franz-Karl's Mama was too weak to leave her bed to greet them. Roland administered the short forms of the welcome rites and let the leader of the party, the Chancellor of the Falkenburg Domains, enter as far as the doorway of her room. Franz-Karl was sitting on a low chair between the bed and a small table that held a basin of water and some cloths for dampening. He removed the cloth from Her Grace the Duke's brow when the Chancellor stood in the doorway and bowed. She turned her head listlessly to look toward the door without raising her head from the pillow.

The Chancellor said, in a quiet but clear voice, "Your Grace, I am very sorry to have to report this, but the bells are ringing to guide Philip-Augustus, son of Leon-Alexander, to the Halls of Judgment, along with Helm-Friedrich, son of Friedrich-Augustus."

Franz-Karl gasped. His Mama's lips moved silently in what was probably Philip-Augustus's name.

The Chancellor said even more quietly, with a helpless gesture of his hands, "Both deaths were very unexpected, despite the Sickness. They seemed to be improving. Then they were... gone." Franz-Karl could not see any fibs.

Her Grace made a horrible sound, then managed, to say "May Heaven protect..." before her voice faded to nothing and her eyes closed.

"I shall send for the physicians," the Chancellor said hastily.

"Have they not done enough harm yet?" Franz-Karl asked angrily, meeting the man's eyes, though the Chancellor tried to look elsewhere. "Will the funerals be at the cathedral?"

The unhappy Chancellor was still trying not to meet Franz-Karl's eyes. He hesitated before answering, "The Palace mortuary chapel. In the ... current state of things... that was judged safer than going out of the Palace Gates."

"So the honored dead of the Falkenburgs will be treated as servants are in better times." The man winced at Franz-Karl's words, or tone, or both.

Franz-Karl turned away for a moment to place another damp cloth on his Mama's forehead, then turned back to the men at the door. "Roland, after you escort this gentleman to the door, please ask Gwenlian to come sit with Her Grace the Duke my Mama for a while, and ask Fritzel to attend me. And tell him to bring scissors." He could feel his hair pulling itself out of its hair-tie.

The Chancellor's eyes widened, but he bowed – a bit hastily – and retreated.

Itron Gwenlian and Fritzel arrived in the room almost together. "Where are you going, your Honor?" Gwenlian asked.

"We are going to fetch the locks of my late brother's hair for the memorial tokens for Her Grace my Mama, and me, and Sophie-Alexa," he said, speaking very precisely in Elderic. He rubbed a fist across his eyes and continued, "We should probably fetch some locks from His Royal Grace the acting Archduke my Uncle Helm-Friedrich at the same time. I don't trust these Lowlanders to manage a proper funeral after the way they have bungled everything else beneath the Unconquered Sun. They never yet gave us the funeral tokens for Her Excellency my late Grandmother: the markers in the Household Shrine are still the ones she gave us living." He was trying to stay too angry to cry: he was not sure he would be able to stop.

Franz-Karl did not bother to change into better clothes. Or worse clothes. They would all be color-of-sorrow, regardless, and have too many buttons. And most of them did not quite fit right.

Franz-Karl was Childe of Traventi and a prince of the direct line of Falkenburg. He and Fritzel did not use the deep passages like servants, but walked out of the door of the Traventine Residence and along the North Gallery and down the stairs and then out of the West Palace and across the Palace grounds to the main building of the Palace.

The chapel was attached to the main Palace, but the structure was older, and the worn stone did not match the grandeur of the newer construction. It was a better match for the stone of the old tower that held the Menagerie. The proper entrance on the east side of the chapel could only be reached from inside the Palace, so they entered the main Palace building. One of the guards seemed ready to say something, but he looked past and above Franz-Karl at Fritzel, and changed his mind about whatever he was about to say, and stepped aside.

When they reached the room where the priests and some other people were preparing the bodies, one of the men not wearing priests' robes was arguing that Philip-August's body should be kept off to one side, away from Helm-Friedrich. The Priests offered to send to the Cardinal-Arch-hierophant's office for instructions, and the other man stepped back. But his fists were clenched.

Franz-Karl asked very politely for some locks of his brother's hair for the Household shrine in the Traventine Residence. He did not expect a simple request to work, but he did not want anyone to be able to say later that he had not tried the simple way before turning to other methods.

The priests who were preparing the bodies and the chapel looked sadly at him, and offered their condolences properly, and one said that he would go fetch some scissors.

Before Franz-Karl could say that he had brought scissors, the priest was stopped by the three men not in priests' robes who were standing around getting in the way of the people preparing things. One of them even grabbed the priest's arm.

The one who had wanted Philip-Augustus left to the side said, "We are the Chamberlain's men, here as an honor guard for the late acting Archduke. We will allow no such corrupt interruption." One of the priests winced.

The speaker's accent was very Northern, which was not a great surprise. The Northern Reformists – especially the Pristinists, but most of the others as well – had stopped keeping their own Household Shrines a few generations ago. Franz-Karl thought the Northern Ancestors and Guardians must be getting very annoyed at being neglected after all this time, but he was not going to let them make him neglect his own Shrines and Ancestors and Guardians. It was very strange to think that Philip-Augustus was an ancestor now. It was less strange to think it about Uncle Helm-Friedrich, but he really would prefer that the acting Archduke was alive to glare at these mean, stupid people and give them some orders.

Thinking about what his Uncle would do, Franz-Karl eyed the man who had spoken and asked coldly, "Which Chancellor?"

"*The* Chancellor."

Franz-Karl rolled his eyes. "I am a Falkenburg, and Philip-Augustus son of Leon-Alexander is a Falkenburg, and Helm-Friedrich son of Friedrich-Augustus is a Falkenburg, and this Falkenburg Chapel stands in a Falkenburg Palace on Falkenburg land in a Falkenburg province. If you are not from the Chancellor of the Falkenburg Domains, you have no business here and less than no authority."

The priests looked surprised, and sort of thoughtful. One of the three intruders looked thoughtful and another looked worried.

The spokesman made a wordless snarl and reached toward Franz-Karl's shoulder, but Fritzel grabbed his shoulder and looked at him. Fritzel made sure he was facing into the light so his cow-eyes were clearly visible. People always seemed to be surprised that the large dark eyes of cows had wide pupils, just like goats and sheep, so sometimes it was useful to remind them. Fritzel's nearly white-less eyes did not look human at all in bright light. The man flinched away and Franz-Karl slid out of reach.

Franz-Karl was so angry that he suggested, out loud – in Allemanic that everyone would understand – that the Living World might find it convenient for those three men with no business there to slowly, over the next few weeks, lose every hair on them except their eyelashes, and it would itch, terribly, both during the losing and after. It was not a proper Binding that was signed and sealed, or marked by ritual repetitions. But the Living World was sometimes moody. Even if it did not work as a Binding he was looking at three men who would very likely worry at every slight itch for the next while.

He had expected them to say 'No'. He had not expected them to be so nasty about it, in the funeral chapel itself, while talking to a relative of the dead people, and bossing the priests around. He stepped toward the Chancellor's men, looking each of them in the eyes, so that they backed away and left room for the priests to do their work.

Franz-Karl stood watching the preparations for a little while. He asked himself what mean things the people who wanted to be awful might do. He thought that the mean people might cut the hair off and burn it while he was away, just to prevent the 'barbaric' rites that they disliked. So he set a Binding so that no one but he himself or Fritzel could cut off or shave or do anything to Philip-Augustus's hair. This one was a real Binding with the full ceremonies for spoken contracts, and he pressed his signet into some soft wax from one of the candles, besides.

He put the same Binding on his late Grace the acting Archduke his Uncle Helm-Friedrich, just to be thorough. It felt a little rude, but then he remembered that he was the last Eastlands Falkenburg in the male line: he was Helm-Friedrich's last heir, along with all the others he was heir of, and needed to take care of him.

Franz-Karl stopped the Priestess, when she left the chapel on some errand, and found out the time the ceremony would start. Then he and Fritzel went home to change into their best color of sorrow clothes that they wore for funerals, and to get some small cloths to wrap the locks of hair in.

Franz-Karl's suit was getting tight and short and would need to be let out, or remade soon, even though he had been working and was not eating enough so it was not as tight as it should have been. It would not work for Gwenlian to take in one of Philip-Augustus's suits that he would not need any more: Philip-Augustus had worn black mourning clothes, not color-of-sorrow. Before the Sickness came, Franz-Karl had been looking forward to wearing regular colors again, but he was going to be wearing color-of-sorrow for a long time now: until a year after the last funeral... there were so many dead relatives, just counting the ones he knew about. A year after the last funeral was going to be a long time.

Franz-Karl swallowed hard. He could not cry yet. Once he started he would not stop, and there were things that needed doing, and no one else left to do them.

They returned to the chapel just before the ceremony was supposed to start. There were a few military officers and officials there for Uncle Helm-Friedrich, and Her Royal Highness Aunt Queen Gertrude, Dowager Queen of the Szekelys, who was Helm-Friedrich's full sister and Philip-Augustus' aunt, was there with her companion, Lady Lenke. Franz-Karl and Fritzel were the only ones there mostly for Philip-Augustus.

Franz-Karl went over to stand by his Aunt Queen Gertrude. It seemed they were the only members of the family that were alive and not too sick to attend this funeral. She and her companion were both thinner than Franz-Karl remembered, and they were sort of blotchy where the rash from the Sickness was still fading. Even with her face blotchy, Lady Lenke was still prettier than almost anyone else in the Palace.

The Arch-Hierophants arrived from the Cathedral, with some assistants and special musicians. They all put on special funeral robes and the musicians tuned up and began to play.

Some of the Chancellor's people were standing along the side walls of the chapel, including the man Franz-Karl had argued with earlier. But he whispered a very, very strong Binding so that the Living World would make it hard for them to interrupt the ceremony for anything short of an earthquake or a fire breaking out.

There was a disturbance outside the chapel, and all the music stopped. People turned their heads and twisted their bodies to look toward the main doors, where the noise was happening. The doors opened and a group of haggard servants staggered in carrying a wooden armchair that had wooden poles pushed through it so that more people could share the job of lifting. They carried the chair over to the group of mourners and set it down. When the servants stepped back, Franz-Karl saw that Her Serene Grace Great Aunt Sophia-Augusta was sitting in the chair, wearing black and wrapped in layers of shawls. He bowed to her very respectfully: there was no time for a more elaborate greeting, since the choirmaster was raising his baton again.

Before the music could start again, Her Serene Grace Great Aunt Sophia-Augusta announced quietly, but in a firm voice, "With my dear sister-in-law Aurelia lost to us, I am taking the position of Mistress of the Household and Guardian of the Household Shrine for my brother Friedrich-Augustus, of the Line of Falkenburg, until such time as he may choose to remarry."

The priests and priestesses all bowed deeper to Her Serene Grace, who was now in charge if Falkenburg funerals. Except Serene Grace was wrong now: as Mistress of His Excellency's Household she should be called Her Excellency Great Aunt Sophia-Augusta. Franz-Karl thought that the female Arch-Hierophant from the Cathedral looked relieved. Several of the male officials looked variously upset and annoyed: the face of the latest man who called himself Master of the Household turned purple.

Franz-Karl hoped that Her Excellency had guards who were strong, and sneaky, both. People were murdering nice widow ladies in the Palace of Karnburg.

When the priests and choir started singing the very first hymn, Franz-Karl and Fritzel walked forward in time to the slow music. They bowed to the priests, and bowed to Philip-Augustus. Then Fritzel turned back the cloth at Philip-Augustus's head and lifted Franz-Karl up so that he could reach into the open coffin that the cloth had covered. Franz-Karl used the special scissors from the Household Shrine to cut off enough locks of hair for everyone he could think of. He still needed fewer locks than they had needed at his Papa's funeral. Half of the people in Karnburg who had received locks of his Papa's hair were dead, and Her Grace the Duke his late Grandmother was dead, and there was no Uncle Helm-Friedrich to send the locks to the others who lived in foreign places.

After Franz-Karl was finished attending to Philip-Augustus, Fritzel put him down and put the cloth back, and they bowed to everyone again. Then they marched formally over to his Uncle the late acting Archduke Helm-Friedrich and did it all again. His Grace the late acting Archduke Helm-Friedrich had been about half bald and wore the rest of his hair quite short under a fancy wig, so his locks of hair were small. But at least the remaining family would have them for whatever memorials they chose to keep.

With Fritzel following him, Franz-Karl walked back toward his Aunt Queen Gertrude and Her Excellency Great Aunt Sophia-Augusta, still in time with the music: three of the soloists were improvising so there would be no gap in the rite, which was very kind of them. Her Royal Highness Aunt Queen Gertrude bowed to him and held out both hands in an accepting gesture. He bowed in return and gave her a lock of her brother's hair and a lock from Philip-Augustus.

Her Excellency Great Aunt Sophia-Augusta wrapped one hand around the other fist and bowed over her joined hands. He bowed deeply and gave her the locks for herself and the ones for His Excellency. Then he bowed again and returned to his original place beside Her Royal Highness. He tucked all of the rest of the locks of hair inside the pockets of his coat and waistcoat and waited to do the other parts of the beginning funeral rite that a non-Initiate could perform.

Franz-Karl had never attended the two later services in a full state funeral rite before, because people had thought he was too young for the ones at midnight and dawn, and there was not much someone who was not an Initiate could do during those rites. Franz-Karl and Fritzel were going to attend all three services of the funeral rites for Philip-Augustus and Uncle Helm-Friedrich anyway, because Franz-Karl did not trust the chancellor's 'honor guards' not to do something stupid and mean, or at least try to. Fritzel was an Initiate, so the priests would let him into places where Franz-Karl could not yet go. But first they needed to finish the first rites.

Everything went well during the first service except that there were so few of the family in the chapel. Her Royal Highness Aunt Queen Gertrude poured the wine for the Blood Trench because Franz-Karl was not an Initiate, and Her Excellency could not stand steadily, and no other relatives were there to do it. Fritzel could possibly have done it for Philip-Augustus, but not for Uncle Helm-Friedrich, while Her Royal Highness Aunt Queen Gertrude could do it for both, even though Arch-hierophant Ambrose frowned at her.

And then outer rites were done and the bodies and their lit corpse-candles were carried down into the crypt, where non-initiates could not go. Fritzel went to the inner rites, along with Her Royal

Highness Aunt Queen Gertrude and her companion and most of the officers and officials.

Her Excellency Great Aunt Sophia-Augusta stayed sitting in her chair in the chapel of preparation, so Franz-Karl went to stand beside her, and followed along when her servants carried her out into the vestibule. Considering what had happened in the vestibule at his Father's funeral, he thought that near Her Excellency might be the safest place to be. The Hussar Captain who served Her Royal Highness Aunt Queen Gertrude, came to stand near them, which made it even better.

The servants took Her Excellency away when the Initiates returned from the crypt. She warned Franz-Karl and Aunt Queen Gertrude that she would not be returning: she was not well enough yet to attend the other two services.

Her Royal Highness Aunt Queen Gertrude and Lady Lenke said that Fritzel would not be the only Initiate at the two later services: they would attend them as well. That meant that the Captain and some of his Hussars would also be in the chapel while the Initiates were in the crypt. Franz-Karl felt something relax in his shoulders.

People were not eating proper funeral suppers between the services during the Sickness: finding people to do the preparations was tricky, and people had finally decided to be twitchy about gathering together. But for His Excellency's Heir, and the Heir's own most recent heir, they managed to arrange something. Franz-Karl, expected that they would play stupid games with the food they served him, as usual at Palace banquets. But he was next of kin and heir to both of the dead, so he decided that he should attend to make sure the wrong Chancellor's men did not do something stupid and even more disrespectful than just stupid games with the food. He left Roland and Itron Gwenlian to tend his mother and the three ladies as best they could and went with Fritzel to the banquet hall.

His Excellency was still too weak to attend, so Franz-Karl ended up formally presiding because he was the senior male Falkenburg available: he was the only male Falkenburg in the Palace besides His Excellency now. So he said some of the blessings, with Her new Excellency counting as formal hostess and saying the rest, which did not please some of the officials who had bothered to attend. Having Her Royal Highness Aunt Queen Gertrude as hostess would have pleased some people even less, even though she was the sister of one of the dead people and the aunt of the other.

The food served was ... adequate ... It made Franz-Karl a little less annoyed at what the kitchens were sending to the Traventine Residence lately. The food they were receiving from the official kitchens was only a little worse than the food for the banquet. There was not much food, either, just small portions of the important kinds of foods, so the very uncomfortable dinner did not last as long as it might have in more prosperous times. And no one tried to play open games with the Hospitality rules when they served things to Franz-Karl: it was all honest food.

He wondered if the Falkenburg Steward had claimed his proper jurisdiction. Or possibly the destruction of the former Chamberlain was recent enough that people were still wary. It was not likely that people were just being nice. He had lived in the Palace too long to believe that.

After the meal, the new Allemanic Chamberlain approached Franz-Karl to offer formal condolences. His expression was almost sad, but there was a smirk behind it. He ended his formal speech with "... and they say your brother was raving at the end. It is all very sad."

"Raving?" Franz-Karl was startled: his brother had been awake, and seemed improving, when they had taken him away.

"Something about three roads... and impressing a frog. Or so the attendants report." The smirk was not nearly as far in the background.

"Three?... OH!" Franz-Karl was so pleased he smiled, which was not really the right thing to do at a funeral dinner. "That wasn't raving. That was a warning."

"A... warning." The Chamberlain shuffled his feet, as if he wished protocol would let him back away.

Franz-Karl looked up at the man. "There are three kinds of death curses," he said seriously. And quite loudly. People in the Palace seemed to need reminding. "Death curses that kill someone; death curses that awaken when an Elderkin dies untimely – for purposes of vengeance and such – and curses that gain their force from a stream of death, much as a mill gains its force from a stream of water or wind. There was a sorcerer known as the Frog – Maximianus Rano – who famously combined the second and third forms of death curse to produce a Curse that is still annoying people more than a thousand years later. But his death curse is not usually counted as the deadly kind that kills people outright. I expect my brother was trying to warn his minders that he had combined all three in his own death curse: there are certainly enough people dying within the Palace walls and in the city around us to lend it a mighty force."

The Chamberlain's eyes were wide. He had started to sweat.

Franz-Karl shook his head sadly. "Philip-Augustus was not yet a fully sworn Notary, so his aim may have been a bit erratic, but he was often a solid Binder... a little blood-thirsty, but solid. But of course, he was receiving the very best of care, being His Excellency's grandson, so I am sure there will be nothing in his death to awaken a death curse."

Franz-Karl bowed, very slightly, and turned away. He wanted to wait elsewhere, away from the officials, especially that Chamberlain, until it was time to return to the funeral chapel at midnight for the next part of the funeral rites. He knew the same stories Philip-Augustus knew. If Philip-Augustus had talked about death curses to the people taking care of him, he did not believe that he was receiving the best possible care. Philip-Augustus thought they were going to kill him.

If Franz-Karl had to look at these people until midnight, he was going to do something rude. Or worse. After all, there were two kinds of death curses that did not require his own death.

The only people at the midnight service other than the priests and musicians were the the two family parties: Franz-Karl's and Her Royal Highness's. Fortunately, after a short section at the beginning when the Initiates visited the crypt, most of that service was sung in the public chapel. The family parts were mostly just keeping the dead people company and bearing witness. And as a Notary, Franz-Karl was very good at Witnessing.

Franz-Karl and Fritzel went back to the Residence and slept for a while between the midnight service and the dawn one, leaving the priests and choristers chanting in shifts in the chapel.

In the morning, after the candles were out and the final farewell was sung, and they were sure that everything had been done properly – the Initiates, including Fritzel, made a final visit to the crypt just as the candles were ending – Franz-Karl returned to the Traventine Residence. He went into Her Grace his Mama's bedroom, and gave her a lock of Philip-Augustus's hair, and one from Uncle Helm-Friedrich, who had been her friend. Itron Gwenlian helped him put one lock of hair from each of the dead people into the frames of their images in the Household shrine. He put the rest of the locks of hair safely in the waiting-cupboard in their Household Shrine. He even turned the key in the waiting-cupboard door and gave it to Gwenlian to keep safe, until he could send the tokens to the right people.

He was not entirely sure how all of that could be arranged, without the acting Archduke to manage things and send out messengers. But most of the people outside the Palace who needed to receive tokens for Philip-Augustus and Uncle Helm-Friedrich were the families of Falkenburg women who had gone away to be Queens and Grand Duchesses in foreign lands, like Her Royal Highness Aunt Queen Gertrude. Her Serene Grace Great Aunt Sophia-Augusta, who was now Her Excellency, had been a Margraffin when she was younger. Her Excellency and Her Royal Highness would probably know who needed to receive things so grownups would not start wars because of being insulted, and they might know how to arrange for reliable couriers.

# CHAPTER XXVIII: His Excellency

## *Wherein Our Hero Visits His Grandfather*

Franz-Karl slept most of the morning: he was so tired that he did not even awaken to listen for Sophie-Alexa as he had some previous nights. He visited Graefinwitwe Wiborada and Lady Henrietta and Lady Roderica very briefly after he ate his late breakfast: it was still too soon to give them large meals, but they were drinking broth, and water mixed with medicines and a little honey, and eating tiny bits of bread soaked in the broth. And they were awake, and chatting with each other sometimes.

There was a little parcel of documents from Traventi waiting for Franz-Karl on the message table. The cover sheet of the package was a note that was – absolutely – the traditional speech about 'now that you have brought that puppy home, you need to plan to take care of it'... except it was about the three ladies they had brought into the Residence. Reverend Count Great Aunt Adrasteia thought the situation was funny for some reason. Franz-Karl did not understand why rescuing some ladies and carrying them into the Residence without any oaths at the Threshold was funny, but amused was much better than angry or horrified.

The packet contained a document and several lists. According to a notation in tiny writing in the top margin, the document was a copy of

Saint Jerome's Letter about People Stolen Away by Elderkin. Franz-Karl had seen official lists of Saint Jerome's many letters, and none of them had mentioned a letter about people stolen away by Elderkin, so this was something the great Archive in Traventi possessed and other collections did not. He was not surprised that the letter began 'To Antonia Adrasteia, greetings.'

There was a list of laws and treaties and pontifical decrees about legal aspects of consecrated Thresholds and of people being stolen away by Elderkin. It had a note at the bottom saying that if the Palace libraries were unable to produce copies, the Archive in Traventi could supply them.

There was a list of rules for people who had crossed a Threshold not by their own choice and without exchanging vows. They were not properly in the house so it was not false to tell someone who came seeking them that the stolen people were not there, even if you were looking at them. But they were not elsewhere, so they could not be found and taken away without your permission. It was sort of the opposite of the way that Franz-Karl could be present in parts of the Palace that did not have proper Thresholds.

Some of the rules in the lists made sense: like what to do if the house caught fire so that the stolen people were saved without 'revealing' them to their enemies or possible rescuers. Some rules were just strange, like stolen people not wearing clothes with visible buttons and buttonholes. And some rules were complicated because you couldn't just push the people back across the Threshold and wave goodbye if you wanted to un-steal them, and people from outside the Threshold could not just reach across and grab them and pull them out: that was what a lot of the laws and treaties were about.

One of the papers was a list of 'considerations' for Elderkin who freely crossed places that should be Thresholds without exchanging oaths, as Franz-Karl had been doing for months. Most of those were things that seemed sensible: things that he was already doing. But there were a few things mentioned that he was going to remember for when he needed to be exceedingly annoying.

He spent the afternoon in his Mama's room. The physicians had come again while Franz-Karl was asleep, but Her Grace Duke Silvia seemed to be fading rather than improving. She seemed less sad with one of her children near at hand. He held her hand when she was awake and read about 'people stolen away by Elderkin' while she was asleep.

Or when she was not awake, at least. His Mama was quiet and worryingly limp most of the time, but sometimes she said things when her eyes were closed. Her voice was usually too quiet to understand, but sometimes Franz-Karl recognized the names of people she was talking to. His Father. His grandmothers. His brother. Even his uncle. It was always people who were dead. He also recognized lines from the Great Hymn – the tune more than the words – which was almost more worrying than talking to dead people.

Saint Jerome's letter gave Franz-Karl something to keep his mind busy during the quiet times. It was not about rules.

Part of the letter talked about the nature of Boundaries and Thresholds… and it was not talking about things inside the Living World – at least not entirely. It did not mention any names that Franz-Karl did not officially know, but Arch-Hierophant Ambrose would probably think it said things too plainly. Some of the things the Saint wrote echoed strangely when Franz-Karl thought about them.

Another part of it was about laws within the Living World, but not just the laws that people made. It talked about the rules about being free, or imprisoned, or enslaved – in places other than Traventi – or stolen away, and how those were all four different things. It was like reading a very complicated logic puzzle, until he recognized a few phrases from the Remoran version of the Marriage Contract.

The second time he read the letter, Franz-Karl thought that the complications in the letter were because the Saint was trying to use Remoran to talk about something that really needed Elderic. And he was almost certain that someone preparing the Marriage Contract had been thinking about Saint Jerome's letter: it was not just phrases that were mirrored between them. Perhaps that was part of what Reverend Count Adrasteia thought was funny: part of the Contract was talking about shapes of freedom, and the rest was not.

Then Franz-Karl's Mama awakened and he became busy with other things for a while.

During their evening meal in Juliana's room, Franz-Karl told Itron Gwenlian and Roland that his Mama was talking to dead people. He did not say anything about the Great Hymn. The rules for the uninitiated talking about the Hymn were complicated, especially for the part his Mama had been reciting, but mostly he did not want to talk about something so scary. Talking to dead people was enough to worry about.

Itron Gwenlian and Roland each closed their eyes and bowed their heads and signed themselves. Everyone knew that when sick people talked to the dead more than the living, it meant that they were more than halfway into the next world. When Fritzel came out of the sickroom to eat his own meal while Itron Gwenlian tried to help her Grace the Duke to eat the bread and soup and cheese that they had prepared for her meal, he was looking sad and very worried.

Franz-Karl had plenty of time to think, sitting quietly beside his Mama all afternoon. One of the things he thought about was that he was worried about His Excellency His Grandfather, who had not come to the funeral of his own Heir. Besides that, he was now His Excellency's last heir in the direct line, so it was probably his duty to see his Grandfather for himself. People at the funeral had spoken as if His Excellency was improving, or at least not getting worse, but they had said similar things about his brother and uncle only a few days ago. And Her Excellency His Grandmother before that. And now their bodies were all lying in the crypts, and their souls were traveling on the paths to the Halls of Judgment.

A few hours after their evening meal, when the main Palace should be quiet, Franz-Karl told Fritzel filled to fill his pockets with silver from their hiding places, in case of need, and they went down to the deep tunnel and across to the main Palace building.

The guards in the servants' stairs were as sparse as they had been when they came to report the death of Her Grace the Duke Adriana. This was convenient for Franz-Karl and Fritzel, but possibly also for others who disliked His Excellency, so Franz-Karl was much more worried than relieved. He was glad that they had brought the silver.

Franz-Karl changed direction and went looking for Old Palace Servants, or even Karnburg-born servants. He found very few of either group in the more prestigious areas of the main Palace: the servants he saw there came from elsewhere, and many seemed not very good at their jobs. He found a few local people and Old Palace Servants in the sculleries and laundries and workrooms. And eventually he found Vendal.

"Are your people getting as scarce as Falkenburgs?" Franz-Karl asked worriedly, after greeting him.

"Not quite, Your Honor," Vendal answered with a slight bow. "Her Excellency is moving over from the East Palace this evening. She will not share His Excellency Her Brother's apartments the way a wife would, so things are a bit disrupted at the moment while her new apartments are being settled and arranged."

Franz-Karl looked up at him as seriously as he could manage. "I did not like the way the Master of the Household was looking at her during the funeral of my brother and uncle," he said. "I think he would be happy if there was another unexpected death that would let him sling you and your people out of the Palace without any higher authority to prevent it. He might find either of their Excellency's deaths very convenient, and I think you might find them very inconvenient."

Vendal's eyes widened. "That is not a problem we will ignore," he said firmly.

Franz-Karl eyed him for a moment. "Did you receive my note about the empty residences?"

Vendal bowed deeper. "One Residence in the East Palace with wedged doors, and ladies dead of the Sickness, that we had thought were recovering. A few others are in need of very careful tending. Shall we reseal the broken door in the West Palace?"

"I suppose so. Graefinwitwe von Steinach and her surviving ladies will be residing with us for this next while. But they are properly stolen away and should not be mentioned outside our Thresholds."

Vendal smiled in a way that managed to be both satisfied and scary: the pock marks did not help. He bowed even more deeply. "As your Honor commands, Lord von Falkenburg."

According to the Rites of Hospitality, Franz-Karl was not actually fully present in the Palace, which could be useful, but meant that he needed to be careful not to claim authority there. He tried to remember to give advice, not orders. How long that would last, now that he was Heir Presumptive in the Line of Succession to the Falkenburg Domains – or at least the Eastlands -- as well as Childe of Traventi? That remained to be seen.

The Old Palace Servants were rarely mentioned in the histories and chronicles that Franz-Karl had seen. There were some strange hints in the Chronicles, and some things his Papa had said, but he did not know with certainty whether they had any formal purpose beyond being people whose families had lived and served in the various Imperial Palaces longer than any of the dynasties that had held Great Karl's throne and crown. They were much, much older than even the Falkenburgs, who had lasted about a dozen generations so far.

He turned back toward the prestigious areas of the upper floors, with Fritzel following.

"D'ye think he'll take the hint about Her Excellency?" Fritzel asked.

Franz-Karl stopped and looked up at him. "We've done what we can. I can't do the job of every grownup in this Palace." Then he turned and started walking again.

Fritzel said, very quietly in Elderic, "I expect I can get us out to Greenoak Square, or back home to the House on the Rock if that seems needful, when the time comes."

"I'm sure that you can, if that seems to be our best path."

"Just... don't go out from the Residence into the greater Palace without me, this next while."

Franz-Karl turned to look up at his friend, and aide. "I will not. Not willingly." This would all be so much worse without Fritzel looking after him.

When they reached His Excellency's apartments, they approached through the servants' stair. Fritzel stayed back, where there was a niche that would keep him shadowed and out of the way of anyone in a hurry.

There was only a single guard at the main servants' door of the Imperial suite, which was open so that a servant carrying a huge pile of used linens could come out. Franz-Karl slipped under and in while the pile of linen was in the way and the guard and servant were both distracted. He still needed to be careful not to look at their eyes for the Gift to work, but grownups tended to look above his head, so that was not very difficult.

There was an attendant in the front room, but he was slumped in a chair with his head on the table beside him, snoring and drooling, with a candle beside him that was nearly burned down to nothing. The only light in the bed chamber itself was was a small candle in the corner behind a screen, but the night vision that came with Elderkin eyes meant that was not a problem for Franz-Karl. He moved closer to the bed and stood looking.

After a few moments, the eyes of his Excellency Franz-Karl's grandfather opened. He did not sit up or lift his head from the pillow, but turned his head to look toward Franz-Karl. "Are you... a ghost?"

"No, your Excellency my Grandfather. I'm just me. The Allemanic Chamberlain said you were getting better, but he lies a lot, so I came to see."

His Excellency spoke very slowly and with long pauses between the words, but he did not seem short of breath. "He does... lie. I... think... I am... not... getting... better, but... perhaps... I have... stopped... getting... worse."

There was a noise from the doorway. Franz-Karl stepped behind a drapery, pressing back against the wall so that he would not make a lump.

An attendant bustled in through the public door. The man jerked the bedclothes straight quite roughly, fluffed the pillows that were propping up the Emperor in a way that was gentler to the pillows than to the patient, and tidied the small bedside table by moving everything useful out of the the sick man's reach. All the while, he talked, in a syrupy sort of baby talk that would have made Franz-Karl angry when he was three. He ignored the few questions that his Excellency Franz-Karl's grandfather tried to ask.

After the man bustled out again, Franz-Karl came out from behind the curtain and moved the table closer to the bed. He filled the water glass from the pitcher and set it on the side of the table nearest the bed, beside a pile of clean handkerchiefs.

"Have... you... been... sick?"

"No. The Physicians say I probably would have been by now, if I was going to be. I am not sure that I trust them..."

"I... thank... Heaven's mercy... Elderkin?"

Franz-Karl shrugged. "There are lots of dead people and sick people in the Duchy." He did not want to think about that, so he continued quickly, "The doctors say Her Grace my Mama is recovering. My sister Sophie-Alexa is supposed to be recovering but they won't let me see her, so I don't know whether to believe them – a few days ago they said Philip-Augustus was recovering... Did they tell you about Philip-Augustus?" He waved a hand vaguely.

"Yes... may... the Halls... of Judgment... grant... healing.. and quick... rebirth."

Franz-Karl signed himself and bowed his head a moment before continuing. "Her Royal Highness Aunt Queen Gertrude was at the funeral with her companion. Her Excellency Great Aunt Sophia-Augusta was there, but not walking, and announced that she is your new Mistress of the Household and will preside in your Household Shrine."

"Correct."

Franz-Karl took a deep breath. "I think, with Philip-Augustus gone, I am now your heir as well as Mama's." He considered, and added, "At least for the Eastlands."

"I am... honored."

A clock chimed in the distance.

His Excellency made a "Tsk" sound. "The guard... will change... soon... Go... carefully. Thank you... for visiting... dear heart."

Franz-Karl looked at the old man and wondered if there was something else he could do to keep them both alive, this next while. "You should not thank Elderkin. But it would be helpful if Your Excellency would stay alive for a while."

"Heh... I ... will ... try..."

Franz-Karl could not think of anything else to say, so he bowed and slipped out of His Excellency's room – he was still worried by the lack of guards, though it did make things easier – and back into the servants' stair to rejoin Fritzel.

When they reached the ground floor of the Palace, instead of continuing down into the deeper tunnels, Franz-Karl brought them out into the public areas of the Palace and then into the area behind the Great Staircase that led up toward the Throne Room and Reception Rooms and Banquet Rooms on the floor above. Dusek Urban's office was not far away, but farther from the main entrance and grand staircase.

The area nearest the Staircase was not all just offices and rooms for clerks. Some of the rooms had soldiers in them, at least during the daytime. Franz-Karl's Papa had said that the rooms behind the staircase were where honor guards for formal occasions kept their duty rosters and special gear, and gathered to get themselves organized, and that officers making reports to the privy councils used the rooms as offices. There was more than one room for the soldiers because there were different military units that were in charge of different events – or sometimes just took turns – and they all had officers that needed to report. There were Falkenburg Regiments and Eastlands Regiments – which got their pay and orders differently – and Regiments belonging to the Kingdom of the Allemans. There was at least one regiment that mostly watched over Prince Otto and the city of Karnburg, but had a detachment inside the Palace for some reason.

There were at least two Independent Regiments that had been in Karnburg since the great siege before Franz-Karl was born, and were still being paid, but no one seemed to know who they belonged to. Franz-Karl's Papa and Uncle Helm-Friedrich had joked about them one evening... because, of course, they were mercenaries answering to their employers, not to any of the Councils, and who they belonged to was His Excellency and the Falkenburgs.

Franz-Karl was looking for Independent officers, but he would settle for any officer not attached to the Kingdom of the Allemans, because the Northerners were part of the Kingdom but outside the Falkenburg Domains. He had valid claims to status as a Falkenburg, but the Allemans were complicated, even aside from what many of the Northerners thought about Elderkin.

He found an officer writing a report or roster who looked more honest than usual for the Palace. He was too high in rank to wear a uniform, but his features and style of dress were both wrong for the Northern provinces. More Southern, than anything: farther south than the Eastlands.

Franz-Karl left Fritzel standing by the door and walked over to stand in front of the officer's work table. He waited until the officer was moving his pen toward the inkwell before leaning away from his Gift of not being noticed. He asked, "Who do you serve, Colonel?"

The officer dropped his pen – which was why Franz-Karl had waited until just before it was dipped into the inkwell. The man saluted, seriously, not mockingly, and said, "We serve the Archduke of the Eastlands, Your Honor."

It was probably a good sign that he was addressed properly. "I am Franz-Karl, son of Leon-Alexander, son of His Excellency, Friedrich-Augustus. A little while ago I entered His Excellency's bedroom without being challenged. It is true that I am Elderkin and sometimes hard to notice, but I saw nothing to suggest that a drunken Kufic porter with two left feet singing at the top of his lungs would have had any greater difficulty." That complaint was a quote from a story, but it was true. "If there are soldiers serving the Archduke they don't seem to be very busy about it."

The man stood up, went to the door, called someone out of the next office, then gave some quick orders. He turned back to Franz-Karl and bowed formally. "I am Ottavio di Pazzi. Soldiers moving near his Excellency without orders can lead to some very pointed questions."

Even Franz-Karl had heard of di Pazzi: Philip-Augustus had talked about him a lot. He had done something important at the end of the siege. And he was famous for staying bought, even under extreme provocation.

Staying bought. It would be nice if the Privy Council stayed bought, but the River Daonas was likely to catch fire first.

"Colonel? Are the wages for you and your men all paid up according to your contract?"

"Not entirely, Your Honor, but in the current state of things we have no complaints." A hand waved to indicate the surrounding Palace... or perhaps the surrounding world.

"How much are you owed?"

The number was much smaller than Franz-Karl expected. No wonder di Pazzi was not worried yet.

"And for next month?"

That number was higher, but Franz-Karl had handled more silver than that not very long ago. Fritzel had more silver than that in his pockets. He said to Fritzel in Elderic, "I think we want to pay through the end of next month and give an escrow letter against the gold in the Bank of Mistella for the rest of the year."

"Aye." Fritzel eyed the officer for a long moment, then nodded and began taking small bags of silver coins out of his pockets and piling them onto a side table.

Franz-Karl turned back to Colonel di Pazzi, taking out his signet. "How should your orders be worded, Colonel?"

di Pazzi did not dictate the orders. He offered a few suggestions and explained the benefits and possible problems of each. The document Franz-Karl prepared included parts of two of the suggestions, and by the time it was written and signed and sealed, Fritzel had counted out enough of the sacks of silver that they had replaced with fairy gold to pay for a mercenary regiment for more than a month.

"You'll want to count this," Fritzel said cheerfully in diplomatic Remoran. "These purses came to us sealed. If there is a shortfall, we'll make it up, of course."

The Colonel's eyes widened as the pile of small sacks of silver thudded onto his work table. "Your Honor?"

"Payment from the Falkenburgs for your contract up to now, and for the coming month. You should expect to take orders from His Excellency, me, or Her Royal Highness Aunt Queen Gertrude... and if things are moving fast, Her Excellency my Great Aunt Sophia-Augusta. I will write you a Notarized contract saying that."

"Of course, Your Honor."

"And I will also give you a paper with a claim against funds held in escrow at the Bank of Mistella to cover the rest of the year."

Colonel di Pazzi looked down at Franz-Karl. He was not as tall as Fritzel, but it was still a long way down. "Escrow, Your Honor?"

"I am a Notary of Traventi. I was training to be an advocate before the Duke my Grandmother died. I have learned a little about taxes and accounts."

"Ah. Of course."

They wrote and signed and sealed all of the papers, with copies for both sides of the agreements and extra copies to be filed in various places... including the Bank of Mistella... and then Franz-Karl took his leave of the Colonel.

Franz-Karl turned and walked away, and pulled his Gift around himself and Fritzel when he was halfway to the door of the room. He heard the officer gasp.

# CHAPTER XXIX: More Death

## *Wherein the Daughters of Traventi Pass Beyond*

The next morning, a little after breakfast time, there was a knock on the public door of the Traventine Residence. When Roland opened the door, he found the new Master of the Household – it was now von und zu Ostwald – standing in the outer landing with several servants including one who had a sort of knob on the end of a pole for knocking with. There were no higher ranked officials: no Chancellor or Steward or Chamberlain. Just the man who called himself Master of the Household even though a formal, consecrated Household properly had a Mistress.

Von und zu Ostwald thrust himself across the Threshold of the Residence, followed by his companions, without waiting for any polite formalities, not even the sketchy ones observed in Northern households.

Franz-Karl had been sitting holding his Mama's hand, but when he heard rough fumbling at the door, he moved so that her bedside table would be between him and the doorway. He did not let go of her hand: it had tightened around his, just a little, when he started to move. He did not duck down behind the table – not yet – but when he did it would break any intruders' sight-lines, and they would not be able to find him thereafter. If it came to it, he would fit under this bed as he had fit under

Lady Margretha's. He had decided that he would not let them take him away from his Mama.

He wondered what was happening, to bring people from outside to the Residence. There were no bells ringing to signal an important death, and the intruders were not behaving like a formal delegation in any case. He was even more confused when the Master of the Household entered the room: the man was just barely of high enough rank to speak to Her Grace the Duke directly if she had been well. With Her Grace the Duke so ill, the Master of the Household should really be dealing with Itron Gwenlian, or even Roland.

He was certainly not dressed with the formality appropriate to someone about to have an audience with a reigning monarch, and his companions were worse. They were just... sloppy, and scruffy. The 'Master' himself, besides various jewels displaying his family's arms and referring to his rank, was wearing a fancy chain that he claimed was a symbol of his authority... Franz-Karl did not remember anyone at all wearing it in the Palace even a year earlier, before his Papa died.

All of that wrongness had not stopped von und zu Ostwald from bursting into the sickroom and it did not stop him from strutting toward Her Grace's bed. His companions came into the room but stayed huddled in a cluster just inside the door. A few of them had the wits to be uneasy, and tried to keep their companions between themselves and the Elderkin.

Franz-Karl whispered a formula to summon the attention of the Living World. He recited it three and a half times, since his oaths as a Notary required four repetitions for a valid Binding, and he wanted to be ready. Anyone who lifted a hand to strike his Mama would regret it. While he was sitting with her he had figured out at least three things he could do that would probably not be blocked by either the Child Blessings or the oaths he had taken when he became a Notary. There were also two others that were possible but might not work until he was older and the Child Blessings unraveled a bit more.

Newts were not yet an option, even if he was being tricky.

For all her illness and his own self-importance, the Master of the Household did not dare to look the Elderkin monarch in the eyes at all. Von und zu Ostwald glanced at Duke Silvia quickly, then addressed the headboard of her bed, even though she had managed to sit up a little to face him. "We regret to inform you that the Elderkin child known as

Sophie has succumbed to the Sickness. Her body has been disposed of safely to prevent the spread of contagion." The man's tone was not regretful. His tone was smug.

Franz-Karl's Mama's scream before she fainted was not loud, but it cracked every window pane in the apartments that constituted the Traventine Residence and set plaster dust puffing out of joints in  the walls and ceiling. Franz-Karl learned later that there was not an intact window in the north end of the West Palace and people felt the shock as a sort of thump throughout the Palace and in half the city beyond its walls.

Franz-Karl himself very briefly had – not a vision so much as a flicker of knowledge – of every weak spot for a hundred feet in every direction in everything, living or otherwise, including the Master of the Household's liver, and the heart of one of his servants and spine of another. And all of the terrible things that were preparing to fail within the form of Her Grace, Silvia, Duke of Traventi, like cracks in a thin piece of glass that would shatter to splinters if you blew on it. The knowledge faded immediately and he had no idea what to do with it while he had it, but he did not forget having it.

He would not forget, either, that Master of the Household von und zu Ostwald, puffed up in the insignia and jewels of his own titles, had robbed his little sister of her own proper titles as decreed by his Excellency, and refused to speak or acknowledge the titles of their Mama, and even tried to rob Sophie-Alexa of half of her name. And beyond all that, not letting Sophie-Alexa have a proper funeral was completely evil, and mean. Wandering in the wild border lands between the Worlds without a guide or a path to follow would be too scary for her. She was just little.

Fritzel and Roland hurried into the room and stood between the bed and the Master of the Household. The Elderkin servants were careful not to touch von und zu Ostwald – Fritzel was gripping his right wrist behind him so tightly that the knuckles of his left had were white – but Fritzel loomed at him and Roland glared at him with vertically slit pupils like those of a cat or a snake, and they both... leaned.

The Master of the Household turned pale and backed away, holding up his hands as if to fend them off. He set a foot wrong and stumbled, then turned and stumbled again before he caught himself and hurried away. His minions hurried after him.

Franz-Karl could hear that Itron Gwenlian called something after the intruders in Elderic as she shut the outer door of the Residence behind them, but he did not quite catch the words. Most of his attention was on his Mama, who was lying limp on the bed as if asleep or unconscious, except that the grip of her hand on his was stronger than he remembered since the Sickness came. She tugged, just a little, and he climbed up onto the bed beside her and cuddled against her, and began to cry. He wondered if it hurt, to be all cracked inside like that, but did not ask: Elderkin could not speak falsely, so almost as soon as they learned to ask questions, they learned there were questions that it was better not to ask.

When he had cried himself out, Franz-Karl got out of the bed. He washed his hands and his face, which was sticky with tears and snot. Then he lit candles in the Household Shrine and set them beside a doll that held some of Sophie-Alexa's hair that had been cut at her first birthday. And he and Fritzel went out to acquire some pigeons to sacrifice for the sake of his sister's soul, and his Mama, even though it was daylight.

They walked openly across the Palace grounds through the spring rain to the East Palace, and went in the main entrance – Fritzel offered to tie one of the guards there into a bow-knot when he tried to block them – and went up the Great Stairs and knocked on the door of the Residence of the Dowager Queen of the Szekelys. They were welcomed formally in the Elderkin style with all of the markers of hospitality: fire and water and wine and the four kinds of food. It seemed very strange to Franz-Karl to be speaking the guest side of the oaths of peace in diplomatic Remoran. In Traventi the words had always been Elderic, and he had not been greeted formally when he returned to the Palace by anyone outside his Mother's household.

"Do you bring news?" Her Highness asked, when they were seated beside a small fireplace, finishing the wine of greeting.

Franz-Karl tried to speak, but could not. He just started crying again. Lady Lenke passed him a handkerchief, and a lozenge for his throat.

Fritzel answered for him. He said quietly in Remoran, "They have told Her Grace that Sophie-Alexa is dead, but not returned her body, nor named a time for funeral rites. It takes a deal of blood for a funeral without a corpse, and pigeons don't hold much," he shrugged, "it seemed best not to delay."

Her Highness went away and returned with two of the carved candles used as corpse-candles at proper funerals, and a small doll with a long thin braid of graying hair looped through its clothes. She laid a finger on the doll and said, "A remembrance of Her Excellency your Grandmother," then touched the candles. "For Sophie-Alexa."

"You should –" Franz-Karl choked. "You should save one for Mama."

"We have hers set aside," Her Royal Highness Aunt Queen Gertrude assured him. "It may not be long until they are needed?"

Franz-Karl shook his head and started crying again. Lady Lenke handed him another handkerchief and used her own.

Her Royal Highness bowed her head and signed herself. "I shall warn Otto and Walther to be ready."

"Are they still alive?" It took Franz-Karl three tries to ask the question.

"It may have helped that they both live outside this accursed Palace," Lady Lenke said.

"Well, if it wasn't accursed before, it certainly is now," Fritzel said, "even if they put the Little Lady outside it." He mostly sounded tired, but there was angry underneath it. A lot of angry.

Her Royal Highness rubbed her eyebrows with a thumb and forefinger. "I shall warn Otto and Walther about that, too... we warned them to reconsecrate the Hearths and Ovens after the Great Siege, but I don't know how much was done..."

"We have a Hearth in the Traventine Residence," Franz-Karl told her.

Fritzel added, "No Oven, though, unless you count the bit of iron I use for griddle cakes."

Her Highness looked thoughtful, and seemed to count something on her fingers. "I shall remember that."

The Szekely Hussars did not help Franz-Karl and Fritzel gather the pigeons, of course. That would have broken laws and Palace rules and possibly a couple of treaties. But the guards in that part of the Palace grounds were from a western Allemanic regiment that had a grudge against the Szekely Hussars, and by an amazing coincidence, some of the Hussars had business nearby. The guards disliked the Hussars so much that most of them followed the Hussars around, watching them carefully and saying rude things in their hearing, instead of remaining at their posts.

Franz-Karl and Fritzel emptied the dovecote that held pigeons used by the Margraff-Elector of Ansbach, who was the Master of the Household's patron. It seemed appropriate, and it was still thinly populated after their previous raid.

It was not really a proper funeral, though having proper corpse-candles helped greatly. Itron Gwenlian was able to arrange things in the Household Shrine so that they nearly fit the shapes the prayers expected. They used Sophie-Alexa's favorite doll, Mina, to hold the few memorial tokens they had available. Her Grace Franz-Karl's Mama was too weak to get out of bed, even for the funeral, but she cut off a lock of her own hair to be her presence in the Shrine.

Fritzel knew the forms of the prayers for a service for the dead when there were no remains available, which were not quite the same as the shortened funerals they had used previously. Franz-Karl wondered why his aide knew those forms, but that was not a question for the present circumstances. Possibly not for the present year...

It was not really a proper funeral supper, either, though it was better than just plain pigeon soup and bread. Franz-Karl opened a treasure box that had been a gift from Argens the Spice merchant in Traventi, so his sister's memorial dinner was enriched by the most precious flavors from all parts of the world. But it was a hard dinner to prepare, both from knowing the reason, and from remembering Tam plucking pigeons a few days earlier.

Eating the meal was easier. They did that in Her Grace's room, so that she would be present for that much, and so that she would not be alone while she ate the meat of sacrifice for her daughter's memorial. They used up the last bottle they had outside the wine-cellars of the good wine that Franz-Karl's Papa had kept to serve to guests.

Afterward, Itron Gwenlian sat with Her Grace, while Franz-Karl and Fritzel went out again into the greater Palace. There were serious guards from di Pazzi's regiment at the doors and around His Excellency in the main Palace, and His Excellency was sitting up in bed and able to speak entire phrases without pausing, which Franz-Karl thought – hoped – might both be good signs. His Excellency's real valet, Helmund, was back from being sick, which was a good sign also, and meant that His

Excellency would have someone taking proper care of him at least part of each day.

As Franz-Karl had suspected, no one had told their Grandfather about Sophie-Alexa's death. The old man wept, and Franz-Karl thought that if His Excellency had been stronger he would have been angry.

When they returned to the Residence, and Franz-Karl went to his Mama's room to bid her goodnight, she did not speak at first, but caught his hand and tugged him up onto the bed beside her. He cuddled against her, and dozed, but wakened immediately at the sound of her voice.

The fourth to the last thing that Franz-Karl's mother said to him was, "Beware the plots of the factions of the Kingdom of the Allemans, and especially those that would call it the Remoran Empire instead of its proper name. Do not trust the Pristinists: their cult teaches that they have no need to speak honest words to Elderkin, so their falsehoods may not seem to be lies..." She stroked his hair with the hand he was not holding, and seemed to sleep again for a while.

The third to the last thing she said was, "I believe that your sister would have lived if she had received proper care and food. The same for Her Excellency your Grandmother, since I have touched her hair. I am less certain about your brother and cousins and uncle. May any hands rot that are stained with their blood and lives." She shifted a little, and Franz-Karl helped her move in the bed before she slept again.

Duke Silvia of Traventi woke again in the dark hours, before the light of the Unconquered Sun returned to the city, and stroked Franz-Karl's hair for a little while before speaking. The second to the last thing that his Mama ever said to him was, "My death curse upon the lot of them. May their schemes tangle and turn to bite them, their fortunes fall through their hands like sand, and their crimes be revealed and punished in this world and the next." She continued for a little after that, saying terrible things and using names that Franz-Karl had only heard when his Uncle Helm-Friedrich cursed the Gods, and some other names that even Helm-Friedrich had not spoken. His Mama, Her Grace Silvia, Duke of Traventi, Binder and fully sworn Notary, was not cursing the Gods, and her words would be carved into the walls of the World. When she fell silent again, Franz-Karl was pursued by terrible dreams when he tried to rest as well.

The windows of the room, with their cracked panes, faced west, not east. Itron Gwenlian had left them uncovered by the draperies, so Franz-Karl, drifting at the edge of sleep, eventually noticed that the sky outside was beginning to lighten. It was not yet sunrise, when his Mama stirred again, but the mullions were dark silhouettes against the brightening sky beyond them. The very last thing that Franz-Karl's Mama said to him was, "All my love and final blessings to you Franz-Karl, my child. Please forgive me, that I have not the strength to stay with you. May you find joy beyond these shadows."

She tugged gently at the hand holding hers until he moved so that she could kiss his forehead. He kissed her cheek and hugged her neck and stayed cuddled against her until the end of her breathing, and a little after.

Then he went to summon the others to tend to her.

# INTERLUDE IX: News from the Palace and City

## *Wherein the White Hall Revives the Echelon and Receives News*

The diminished Pristinist Echelon came together in the White Hall in Karnburg for a full Gathering including a Purgation. It was more celebration of the Echelon's continuation than a memorial service for those lost. Most of the Purgation was planned to be the lesser sort that was used when no great threat of corruption was suspected, so the lists of questions would be short and carefully chosen, with the full forty-eight question reserved for cases of aspirants to join the Echelon, or where the questioners and witnesses found cause for doubt in a man's answers. It was hoped that none of those still recuperating would be overstrained by the ordeal, but there was no intention to skimp.

The Beginning of the Purgation was Heinrich Bauer, as usual, and his replies were counted as ten and two: most of the men who would have insisted on the full forty-eight questions for him had been taken by the Great Sickness.

The first candidate had a letter of introduction from the Echelon in his previous home, and his answers were five and one – no one joined the Echelon without passing under the Rod. His rank in the Echelon was set above the midpoint but below the Select, until his actions gave cause for a change.

The second candidate answered the first question by refusing to give a name at all, accepted a blow from the Rod, and then answered forty-eight questions of increasing doctrinal complexity posed by the Teacher and the acting Preacher, the clerk Cardel. At the end of the questions, Cardel greeted the candidate as Preacher Groen, welcomed him to the lectern, and returned to his own original place in the Echelon: Cardel's answers in the Purgation were four and naught. Teacher Bauer's answers were counted as ten and naught.

The third candidate was the Margraff-Elector's agent Coenraad, who had previously been considered beneath the Echelon, despite being apparently free. He was accepted into the Echelon because the Teacher and the Preacher found no basis to exclude him in the rules, but there were few members of the Echelon who welcomed him. Coenraad's numbers were forty-eight and seventeen. Five of the seventeen failures were statements that the questions were not his to answer, and the other twelve were repeated refusals to provide a family or lineage name, or a town or district of origin. At the next Purgation involving them both, he would be questioned even before Heinrich Bauer, who at least had a known origin, even though it was an appalling one.

Only two of the existing members of the Echelon were required to give more than twelve answers: one collapsed at thirty and ten and could not be roused; the other lasted to forty-eight and twenty, and that was as much as could be said for him. The count of forty-six men in the Echelon after the day's gathering might drop back to forty-four or forty-five sooner rather than later.

After the Purgation finished – the Margraff-Elector's numbers were eight and naught – there were readings by Teacher Bauer. The new Preacher Groen demonstrated that his skills as a Preacher exceeded his already impressive knowledge of doctrine.

After the official agenda was complete, the unconscious man was taken away. A few others from the lower end of the Echelon also left the White Hall, and a few from the middle who had duties elsewhere. The rest of the Echelon remained in the White Hall to discuss the situation in the city and Palace of Karnburg.

Coenraad did not bother to wait until Bauer spoke. He began the Conversation as Lowest Man with a warning that Ottavio di Pazzi had somehow received written orders to guard the Residences and Doors of the main Palace building.

"What concern is that of ours?"a voice from the middle of the Echelon asked. "They are just one watch..."

"Two. He's divided his men to cover the morning and evening watches, when the doors and passages are busiest. Midday and the night watch are still clear, for the moment. If the Echelon is planning to move anything in or out of the Palace, we had better do it soon: by all accounts Louis de Castres is up and out of his sickbed, out in the camps. If the deCastres troops start standing alternate watches with di Pazzi's? Anyone without a formal appointment within the Palace might as well stay home."

The official from the Treasury held a different position now than he had a week ago, like all the rest of the Echelon. "Well, then, those two locked boxes we have stored within the Palace will need to be moved elsewhere. It should have been done before now, but..." He shrugged.

The Margraff-Elector remained silent during the discussion of how and where to move the lockboxes, merely assuring the assembly that the keys were safe in his possession, and were not the only protections the boxes had. Two men who had been angling to be guardians of the chests changed their minds when they heard that.

Despite providing the warning, Coenraad was not included in the planning or given a task in the plans, nor was any other man below the middle of the Echelon.

As the discussion moved up the Echelon, much of the news and many of the rumors were found satisfactory by the gathering. Officials and noble members of the Ecclesialist factions – and those like the Harfnerans that were falsely described as Reformist – had been removed from the government and the realm, one way and another, and even the corrupt tree of the Falkenburg line had been well pruned. Wealth and authority were flowing in convenient directions. The purification of the nations seemed likely to continue, though it was slowing now after the recent surge of changes.

The stain of the beast-born in the city was known to be diminished: more than half of the known kenneled beast-born were known dead, and most holders of Bound but un-kenneled beast-born had prudently slaughtered their stock when they themselves became ill.

It was known as a matter of doctrine that master-less beast-born would be a disaster ravaging the city and countryside, and few such disasters were being reported, so it was confidently assumed that beast-born left un-Bound by the Sickness had been safely Bound by new masters or dragged back into whatever accursed realms had vomited out their accursed ancestors. One of the exceptions to the lack of disasters was a physician who served the Palace: assisting healing was the Second Lawful Occasion for using beast-born, but that did not mean that it was any more safe than other uses: there were at least seven different pleasantly horrifying rumors about how the physician had died.

No one in the Echelon could name the Master of the beast-born in Traventi, not even the Teacher and Preacher, nor the other Select: they only knew that he must exist and that he was weeks away by any available mode of travel. That would provide opportunities during the sickness of the purported Duke Silvia, but there were dangers as well as the bitch's leash slipped. The cracked windows in the Palace were a reminder of that. The discussion of how to take advantage of that slippage was ... wide ranging.

Ritter von und zu Ostwald doubted that the bitch Silvia would be a problem much longer. Some of the Echelon looked forward to her death, hoping that dealing a purported child heir and a regency council would provide even more opportunities for advantage. Those who had been touched by the Changeling Brat's curse at the Privy Council session were less hopeful.

The Margraff-Elector mentioned that he intended to add the Changeling Brat to his own kennels. Ritter von und zu Ostwald, whose power within the Palace was steadily increasing, assured the head of the Echelon confidently that the brat would be delivered to his hand.

After the meeting, the Margraff-Elector prepared pigeon-capsules intended for nearly a dozen destinations in the North, his own estates and the Palace at Bremerhaven not least among them. When he received reports that the pigeon-keepers of the Northern dovecotes in the Palace were dead or still sick, and the birds were gone, possibly fled, he was forced to change his plans. A few birds from the small dovecote at his Karnburg estate were sent north with the most urgent messages, which included instructions for replacement birds for the various destinations to be south by barge and mule train.

# CHAPTER XXX: His Grace the Duke

## *Wherein Our Hero becomes the Protector of the Elderkin*

Franz-Karl walked from his Mama's room to Juliana's room where they had made their Hearth and stopped just inside the door. Itron Gwenlian looked up from where she was stirring something in a bowl. "Come closer to the fire, Your Honor. There's a chill in the air, this early."

"Are there rules about approaching the Hearth or the Household Shrine after being with the dead?" No one bothered to tell small children these things: they expected that there would be grownups taking care of things.

Itron Gwenlian signed herself. She brought a handful of something over to where he was standing. "Close your eyes." He did, trying to stand motionless, but flinching a little. She continued gently, "Ah, easy, Your Grace. 'Tis salt, merely. Just no need to sting your eyes with it."

Franz-Karl flinched worse at that: 'your grace' was a style for the Duke, not the heir. Being called 'your grace' made it real... Realer.

Gwenlian patted his shoulder, then she tossed a bit of the salt in his face and sprinkled more of it all over him. Then she put some clean water from one of the barrels into a basin and told him to wash his face and hands with a bit of soap. When that was done she sat him in a chair by the fire with a small bowl of porridge sweetened with a bit of honey from their small stock. "Fill your belly, Your Grace. Then we'll plan."

While Franz-Karl ate, she went to wake Fritzel and Roland.

Fritzel arrived first because he had a bull's pelt not human hair and this was not one of the rare weeks when he needed a shave. His good clothes were hanging, not so much loose as wrong: he was gaunt from weeks of constant work and worry and rations that were a little short for such a large young man, but that had not stopped his bones from growing. He filled a bowl with as much as they could spare for him before their next visit to the pantries while leaving some for the ladies, and began to eat.

When Roland and Itron Gwenlian arrived, Franz-Karl asked, "Can we dress my ... her Late Grace... in something that will stop them noticing that her hair has already been cut off?"

The others exchanged glances and Roland muttered something that Franz-Karl was not supposed to hear, so he did not.

Itron Gwenlian thought for a moment. "Aye. That's easy enough to manage."

"Should I notify the guards?" Fritzel asked between spoonfuls of porridge.

"Not them... and not until my oath of accession is written and sealed and sent where it belongs," Franz-Karl said. "The Allemanic officials wanted to steal the Duchy from Her late Grace the Duke my Mama, so I'm sure they will try to take from me if we do not arrange defenses to prevent them." He set aside his empty bowl. "It should not take very long. The books we used for Mama's oath have not been put back, and I have her oath for an example. While I tend that task, think about how to safely bring papers to Greenoak Square and to the Cathedral." He took a deep breath and let it out. "Without vanishing on whatever path Tam took, if ... if it can be avoided."

While the others ate, Franz-Karl opened the books, which still had bookmarks in the places he needed, and fetched the copy of his Mama's accession oath from the locked cupboard in the Shrine, and gathered pens and parchment and paper and ink and wax for the seals. He also fetched a wax tablet with a stylus to try ideas on. His oaths as a Notary specified that the Living World should ignore anything that was written in wax, not ink, and not make it a Binding, so it was safe to scratch things in wax while he was thinking about them. Most things.

He decided that he would need to change a few things compared to the example of his Mother's oath, but not many. There was one paragraph with a slippery Elderic verb form where he wrote what he thought it meant, not what the words used in his mothers' oath said. The Remoran version had been kind of uncomfortable there, trying to match the Elderic.

There was a paragraph where his Mother, a grown woman with living children, had mentioned herself and the heirs of her body: Franz-Karl changed it to speak of himself and his proper Elderkin heirs ... which was currently his cousin Andrea, back in the Duchy, but he did not write that: the imperial authorities would likely not think to look for a female heir and reminding them about her would be foolish.

There were two paragraphs that he combined into one to remove a place where the Privy Council might think they could wedge their way in. It was clear in the Elderic that would not work, but he wanted the Remoran and Allemanic translations to be just as clear.

In the end Franz-Karl's oath was a little longer than his Mama's: there were only eight paragraphs instead of nine between the part that said, "Witnessed here by Heaven and the World and All the Saints and All the Watchful Dead" and the part that said, "All this I swear by my Life and Soul and Hope of the Halls of Judgment," but he had used more words ... plainer words ... unmistakable words ... to say things the things that needed to be said.

He wrote two copies of the oath in Elderic in his best script, marked 'one of four' and 'two of four' in tiny letters down below where the signatures and seals would be. Then he made two copies in Remoran that were marked 'three of four' and 'four of four'. He added a Court Allemanic translation as a courtesy, that was not numbered and would not be signed nor sealed.

Everyone knew – even the Northerners knew and hated it – that a verbal contract repeated four time was Binding when Elderkin were involved. Franz-Karl did not know whether having four official copies made a written contract even stronger, but he suspected that the Allemanic and Falkenburg officials would be willing to believe that it did. Especially the stupid ones who thought Elderkin were hiding in their cupboards to drag them away and eat them or something.

He sat looking at the pile of parchments for a few minutes. Something was missing... Finally he remembered an old quip that something was as foolish as sending a single pigeon when there were hawks in the sky. He wrote a second full set of numbered copies, and made several extra copies on parchment of 'two of four' and an extra copy on paper – not parchment – of 'four of four'.

He called Fritzel and Roland and Itron Gwenlian into the Household Shrine. They watched as he signed all of the various numbered copies, and sealed them with his signet. And then they signed as witnesses. Traventine law did not usually expect witnesses for something signed by a Notary, but the Reverend Count Great Aunt Adrasteia had wanted a witness for the oath of Her Grace Silvia Duke of Traventi, so it was better to have witnesses for this.

One copy of 'one of four' went into the locked cupboard to keep Duke Silvia His Mama's oath company. One copy of 'three of four' was set aside for a while.

Roland took the paper copy of 'four of four' and one of the parchment copies and set out for the Cathedral. The parchment copy would be added to the Cathedral archives – in return for a signed and sworn receipt. The paper copy was to burn on the Incense Altar, to put it safely into the keeping of the Gods.

They wrapped up two packages of documents for Fritzel to take to Greenoak Square. One package was a full set of the numbered copies for Damian – or whoever the Sickness had left in charge of the place – to store safely in the strongroom. The other package contained all but one of the remaining copies marked 'two of four', which were to be sent toward Traventi by fast couriers following different paths. Franz-Karl also sent a note saying that if Greenoak Square had any remaining pigeons whose homes were in Traventi, a few – but not all – of the birds should be sent with news of Her Grace the Duke's death and Franz-Karl's accession.

Franz-Karl placed the final copy marked 'two of four' on the table where communications with Reverend Count Great Aunt Adrasteia sometimes came and went. Perhaps she would try to send them a letter and notice that one was waiting for her, or perhaps a pigeon would reach Traventi, so that she would know to look. Or perhaps the first message to reach Traventi would be carried by a courier on horseback and take a long time to get there. They could only try their best.

Once the men were off on their errands, Franz-Karl bathed as best he could in the water they had available and dressed in fresh linens from the skin out. He put on his best trousers – the ones that fit best this week, not the ones made from the best cloth – and a waistcoat and coat for wearing at home, and set out his best coat and waistcoat, ready for when he needed them.

While he waited for Fritzel and Roland to return, Franz-Karl sat in the Household shrine, thinking and worrying. Things were falling apart too fast.

He remembered something from one of the books that everyone except Adrasteia thought was too old for him. He set three tall, narrow pieces of paper next to each other, and wrote out the words of his Mama's death curse across all of them. He had not forgotten any of the words. He thought he would probably never forget any of the words.

He did not use capitals or punctuation, and he separated the words with spaces instead of joining them with dots in the usual way when writing Elderic. He wanted to put as many gaps as possible in the sentences of the curse and break it into tiny, little pieces. He was very careful that no sentence or important phrase, however short, fell completely on a single strip of paper, so some of the spaces were huge.

When he was done, he sat and shuddered for a few minutes, then wrapped the pages in a cover sheet, sealed it closed very thoroughly, and placed it on the table beside the oath copy 'two of four'.

He went to Juliana's room and Itron Gwenlian fed him a morsel of bread and salt and meat and cheese, and a sip of some watered wine that had been heated over the consecrated fire. When he had stopped shaking, he went back to the Shrine and wrote out a second copy of the curse, trying to use different breaks at the edges of the pages. He wrapped and sealed those pages, and stored them in a different locked cupboard in the Shrine than the oaths were in, or memorial tokens, or anything else that was good.

He came out of the Shrine planning to ask Itron Gwenlian for another sip and morsel, but it was put out of his head by two important things.

The first important thing was that Roland was back from the Cathedral, with his errand accomplished. He had not known how worried he was that Roland might be lost on the errand until the worry ended and he could hug Roland around the waist.

The second important thing was that the table where the letters came and went had nothing on it but a small folded piece of paper bearing the Reverend Count's seal. Copy 'two of four' of his oath and the text of Duke Silvia's death curse had gone away. Unsealed and unfolded, the new message read simply "From Antonia Adrasteia in haste to Franciscocarolus Duke of Traventi. Well done. Do your best and your best shall be enough. More soon. May Heaven and the Saints protect her. And you."

Franz-Karl heaved a great sigh of relief, and suddenly felt very tired. At least Traventi knew that there was a new Duke stuck here in Karnburg, and could take precautions. He sat in the armchair that his Mama had used as a chair of state when the officials visited, watching the door.

He was awakened when Fritzel came in through the main entrance of the Residence. Franz-Karl straightened himself in the chair and his tall attendant took a knee to bring their heads nearer the same level. "All done, Your Grace... And there's a small bit of good news on this sad day: Tam is not yet dead, and likely to live."

Franz-Karl felt so dizzy for a moment that he was glad that he was sitting down. "What happened?" he finally managed.

Fritzel shrugged. "Late yesterday evening a peddler called Lame Henning found Tam lying in an alley near one of the charnel pits they're using for the poor who die of the Sickness. Being a decent sort, he took Tam around to Greenoak Square instead of chucking him back in the pit. Tam hasn't wakened yet, to tell the story, but the Healers are hopeful. The knife wound in the back missed the kidney – Tam's kidneys being a mite oddly placed to Worldfolk eyes – and the damage to the lung is already healing."

"That is very good news," Franz-Karl agreed. "We should arrange to something nice for Lame Henning, when we have a moment to spare." Fritzel helped him get out of the chair, which was really much too large for him. "And more good news is that my oath is recorded at the Cathedral, and Traventi knows that there is a new Duke... or Reverend Count Adrasteia does, at any rate." He sighed. "Now I suppose we should both dress for an audience with his Excellency. We still have the copy 'three of four' to deliver, and Her Grace the Duke my Mama's funeral to arrange."

Roland said, "If Your Grace leaves this building by the east entrance, you will likely find a number of Hussars idling about the grounds in ... useful... locations between here and the main Palace."

"That's helpful... and I expect there should be Colonel di Pazzi and some of his men in the main Palace, once we get that far."

Leaving Roland and Itron Gwenlian to tend the Residence, and the ladies, and the remains of Her late Grace the Duke Silvia, Franz-Karl left the Residence, accompanied by Fritzel, who was carrying the final copy of 'three of four' of the oath in its sealed wrapper. As Roland had predicted, their route from the West Palace to the main Palace building was observed at various points by an assortment of loitering Hussars. They were met at the main Palace door by Colonel Ottavio di Pazzi and three of his men, and escorted very politely to His Excellency's apartments.

It felt a bit strange to be climbing the main Staircase instead of taking the servants' routes. It felt especially strange to be doing it without his Mama.

Franz-Karl took the document from Fritzel, leaving him near the outer door. The Colonel and his men stayed there as well. The outer room was half full of important people, with their various aides and secretaries left standing around the edges.

His Excellency was in his bedroom and in bed, but he was fully dressed and sitting on top of the covers, propped up by a pile of pillows. There were several ornately dressed men standing around trying to politely pretend they were not really arguing in the presence of their lord: they were just discussing things rather loudly. They were government people, mostly, not palace people: the Allemanic Chamberlain was there but not the Master of the Palace. The Allemanic Chancellor was kind of looming at people even though he was shorter than a lot of them, and the Falkenburg Steward was looming back much more effectively, being a tiny fraction taller than di Pazzi and the second tallest man in the suite except Fritzel.

There were generals and ministers of various departments, including a few important-looking people talking about tax collection and the treasury, trailed by squashed-looking clerks carrying arm-loads of papers. The clerks did not stand by the walls.

Prince Otto of Karnburg was there, the brother of her late Excellency Franz-Karl's Grandma, but it was because he was Governor of the City and Province of Karnburg, not because he was family. That was clear from some of the things being said in the loud discussion.

Her Excellency Franz-Karl's Great Aunt Sophia-Augusta was the only woman present. She was sitting in a chair beside her brother's bed with her hands folded on the top of her cane, looking worried, and not saying anything. The chair was one that Franz-Karl had seen in the room before, so she had not been carried into the room. She had walked.

Franz-Karl wound his way between the counselors without being noticed, but made sure that people would notice him once he arrived at the bed. He bowed very slightly to his Excellency, and presented copy 'three of four' of his oath. Several of the people standing nearby made startled noises.

His Excellency unsealed and read the document. "Please accept... my condolences, and those... of the empire. Someone fetch a chair... for His Grace... the Honorable... Sovereign Duke... of the Elderkin... of Traventi."

Her Excellency Great Aunt Sophia-Augusta took out a handkerchief and pressed it to her eyes.

His Excellency held the parchment out at extreme arm's reach and squinted at the signatures of the witnesses. Franz-Karl wondered where the stupid night attendant had put his Excellency's spectacles. "Yourself... and three witnesses. All Elderkin with weight for witnessing contracts, I assume."

Franz-Karl had stayed perched at the front of the chair, so that his legs could bend at the knees. He bowed slightly, "Naturally, your Excellency."

"My name is Friedrich-Augustus."

"Sophia-Augusta."

"And I am Franz-Karl." They all bowed to each other again.

His Excellency Franz-Karl's Grandfather held up the parchment again, squinting. "Copy three of four?"

"My own copy and one for the Traventine archives, both in Elderic. Your copy and one for the Cathedral archives, both in Remoran."

"Ah. " The emperor handed his copy to one of his secretaries. "When is the funeral?"

"I assume preparations should be complete at sunset."

"We shall attend."

There was a lot of murmuring, but only the Allemanic Chancellor actually tried to protest. He got as far as "Your Excellency should not..." before His Excellency Franz-Karl's Grandpa lifted a hand to stop him.

His Excellency looked around. "A fellow monarch... has died under my roof. I must attend... or be shamed... before the nations." All the counselors bowed slightly – the kind that was a head-nod that started at the hips – but some still looked grumpy. His Excellency continued, "The rites... for a monarch... should be ... performed... in the ... cathedral... by both of the Arch-hierophants."

He let them argue him to a compromise where the funeral chapel in the Palace would be used, since it would require less travel for His Excellency, but both the Arch-Hierophants and the good choir – or what the Sickness had left of it – would come from the cathedral to the Palace to perform the rites, and the cathedral bells would be tolled for the late Duke of the Elderkin. There would be no great, public funeral supper, but 'an abundance of food' would be supplied to the Traventine Residence for a private one.

His Excellency finished by apologizing profusely – if haltingly – to Franz-Karl for any apparent lack of respect for the Elderkin of Traventi or their late monarch, finishing, "Surely... we have ... no need ... for crop failures ... or other... additional... disasters... beyond... the ongoing ones." Some of the gathered officials looked startled, others looked worried.

Franz-Karl slipped forward off the chair to stand in front of it. "I am certain that crop failures would be... inappropriate," he said with a bow that from a grownup would keep them guessing whether 'inappropriate' meant 'too little' or 'too much' or 'insufficiently artistic'. When you learned to bow before you learned to walk, bows generally did what you wanted them to, but grownups often ignored children. To be honest, Franz-Karl was almost leaning toward 'insufficiently artistic': the Arch-Hierophant – the male one: Ambrose – had argued very strongly against performing the rites for an Elderkin woman himself, suggesting his colleague would be sufficient. Arch-Hierophant Diotima was a nicer person and much better at singing the responses, but that did not make the suggestion less insulting. Ambrose was definitely on Franz-Karl's private short list of people to be turned into newts, if and when.

His thoughts sort of hiccuped: considering his Mama's death curse, if some of his guesses were right, there were people in this room who were likely to wish crop failures were all that hit them. Even being turned into newts might be preferable in a few cases.

Franz-Karl bowed again, neutrally. "I must see to the preparations of the funeral chapel." The Allemanic Chamberlain tried to accidentally stand in his way, but was very busy looking at the Allemanic Chancellor. Prince Otto came to stand beside Franz-Karl, bowed and walked him to the door, patting Franz-Karl's shoulder before he returned to His Excellency's side.

Fritzel was waiting at the door for Franz-Karl, with Colonel di Pazzi, and he felt some of the tightness in his chest release, and the band of tension across his shoulders relax once he reached his large aide's side.

# CHAPTER XXXI: The Duke's Funeral

## *Wherein There Are Terrors and Wonders*

Shortly after Franz-Karl returned to the Residence, Vendal arrived at the main entrance of the Traventine Residence with a number of other servants. Some of them would transport her Grace's remains to the funeral chapel. The rest, supervised by Vendal himself, would look after the Residence so that all of the usual inhabitants could attend their Duke's funeral.

Roland was so grateful that he asked the servants whether any of them needed shoes. He had expected to stay in the Residence to keep watch instead of attending Duke Silvia's funeral.

Vendal and two of his companions agreed that new shoes would be a great kindness: no one sensible who knew the old stories would turn down shoes offered by an Elderkin cobbler. And not just from the risk of giving offense.

Franz-Karl carefully showed Vendal – and only Vendal – the room where Wiborada and Henrietta and Roderica were recovering their strength. He explained some of the most important rules. Vendal looked thoughtful, but he agreed politely, and did not say anything rude about Elderkin stealing people.

The funeral chapel was ready well before the appointed time. It was freshly cleaned and polished, with the chapel candles in place and ready to be lit and the Blood Trench carefully cleared of debris and dried spills from previous funerals. The late Duke's body in her coffin rested on the bier surrounded by the Blood Trench, and covered by the funeral cloth. Gwenlian placed one carved corpse candle at her head on behalf of the women of the Duchy. It looked very lonely.

They began to light the candles – except the corpse candle, of course – when one of the priests, who was keeping watch, reported that His Excellency was approaching. His Excellency arrived in the funeral chapel in a chair carried by two sturdy servants – well, they were probably the sturdiest available.

Her Excellency Great Aunt Sophia-Augusta leaned on her cane and on the arm of Justice Marek von Trebice. She sat in a chair as soon as she reached the chapel. A young woman and two tiny girls followed her wearing very expensive black mourning clothes in the Allemanic style. They curtsied deeply to Franz-Karl and to the deceased, and placed beautifully carved corpse candles at Her Grace's feet before they went to stand behind Her Excellency. One was unmistakably his uncle Helm-Friedrich's unmarried daughter Frederica and the others must be the granddaughters, but they were so thin and pale and shadowed by the blotchiness left by the Sickness that Franz-Karl hardly recognized them. He was very, very grateful for the corpse candles, since none of his Mama's own female relatives were available to set any out.

Her Highness Queen Aunt Gertrude and her companion Lady Lenke arrived almost immediately after Her Excellency, dressed in black clothes that showed no colors even to Franz-Karl's strange eyes. He wondered how they had managed it. Black cloth always had other colors in it. Her Highness Aunt Queen Gertrude placed a truly magnificent corpse candle at the late Duke's head. Her companion placed a plainer one.

Being a small boy, Franz-Karl had not been taught the details of the symbols carved on the candles, but he was pretty sure that the plainer candle was on behalf of the servants and other non-kin in the Palace.

Franz-Karl did not do anything as ill-mannered as openly counting, but he thought most of the courtiers from his Grandfather's earlier meeting filed into the chapel and stood waiting. Prince Otto was standing beside Her Excellency Great Aunt Sophia-Augusta on the other side from the Justice, leaning heavily on his own stick.

There was another man standing with Prince Otto who looked like family – Falkenburg family: it was something in the nose and jawline – wearing a scholar's robe. That must be Baron-Professor Walther von Falkenburg. Being previously kept out of grownup gatherings because he was small meant that Franz-Karl was going to need to learn who everyone was. Soon. Small children could mix people up. Dukes should not.

There was a final small disturbance at the door. Damian and several other people from Greenoak Square came in. They each bowed or curtsied to Her late Grace, and then to Franz-Karl before they went to stand with Roland and Itron Gwenlian. Two of the women set corpse-candles. Franz-Karl was surprised by how many there were, considering that they must have left people behind to guard the house and look after Tam and anyone else who was still sick. He had been afraid to ask, but it seemed that the Great Sickness had rested lightly on Greenoak Square, at least when compared to the Palace.

The choir arrived in plenty of time. It was nearly the full cathedral choir: men and women and all three castrato soloists and even some boys and girls from the children's choir. They had brought their best funeral robes, and the chapel was full of soft shushing noises while they were shaking out the silks and brocades and putting them on over their street clothes. Each of them bowed deeply to Franz-Karl and to the late Duke on her catafalque before they went to their places. One of the castrati began an ancient requiem while they waited for the actual beginning of the rites, and the high clear tones filled the chapel in a way that was more than a little eerie.

The female Arch-Hierophant, Diotima, came in just after the last of the choristers, but still on time. She curtsied deeply to Franz-Karl, then dropped to one knee and hugged him. She smelled like incense and flowers, which was a relief after days – weeks – of smelling sickness and death. It took her longer to robe than the choristers: her ritual garments had lots of layers and fiddly bits. Three of the female choristers helped her with the robes, and one of the castrati, who was even taller than Fritzel, arranged her headdress.

The male Arch-Hierophant, Ambrose, did not actually arrive late. He would just be late by the time he finished robing, which he was doing very, very slowly. There was no way to move him any higher toward the top of the newt list, unfortunately. The choir started on time regardless, adding lots of ornamental bits to the opening hymns to stall for time.

The Arch-Hierophant finally finished robing and took his place. The choir finished a complicated improvisation involving all 8 soloists – soprano, alto, tenor, baritone, bass, and all three musico soloists.

Fritzel stepped over to the Blood Trench and held up a sealed bottle of the best wine from the Duchy. He sang an old verse-prayer in Elderic entreating the watchful Dead for mercy, snapped the neck of the bottle, and poured the entire contents into the Trench before stepping back. The groove that claimed to be a Blood Trench could barely hold the full bottle.

The wine in the Trench burst into unnatural flames leaping as tall as Fritzel: not red or yellow or even the blue of brandy flames, but a sort of shifting pale green, like the torches at the gate at Greenoak Square. The chapel was completely silent while the flames burned for what seemed like a very long time. No one moved and most people seemed to be holding their breaths as much as they could manage.

The flames had begun to die down and people were beginning to inhale gratefully when the chapel door opened with a loud creak. Those hinges had been oiled regularly for decades and had never creaked in all that time. They had been silent while all of the people now in the chapel entered, opening and closing the door silently many times, but they creaked now.

Everyone turned to look, and a very small girl staggered into the chapel, clad only in a nightgown that was covered in slime and ick. Her movements were sickeningly floppy, like a marionette with all its strings broken but one: it was not the strength or shape of her limbs that kept her nearly upright. Her head dangled and wobbled instead of perching on top of her spine.

The door closed behind her with another creak and a small bang. There was no one visible who could have closed it. Or opened it, for that matter. At least three people fainted and several others made odd sounds. Franz-Karl did not turn to look. He could not stop watching his sister.

The little girl stumbled to the bier where the late Reverend Duke was lying. The flames had faded while she crossed the Trench. She paused beside the bier, swaying. It would have been too high for her to climb onto by herself even when she was alive. She had not reached the age of four, as the Allemans counted age.

Fritzel stepped forward and lifted her up gently to lay her beside the corpse of her mother., straightening the nightgown a little. The small body went hideously limp, as though she had never moved from the place where she had been discarded. The flames went out completely, and the Trench appeared to be empty and polished clean.

Franz-Karl stepped forward. The bier was high enough and he was small enough that he had trouble reaching, so Fritzel lifted him up, too, and held him steady while he cut the locks of Sophie's hair. He had brought the special scissors from the Shrine even though his mother's hair had been cut earlier and he had not expected to need them. The nearest kin bringing scissors was how you did a funeral.

As he worked, Franz-Karl began to sing the Great Hymn, the one his mother had been reciting in those last few days. Things got even quieter in the chapel: nothing else had the same three notes at the beginning. He began with the early part that was almost never repeated in church: the section whose lines his mother had repeated, where the Great Goddess Cursed the World that had taken her child, cursed root and branch, stock and stone and the fact of death within it.

When he reached the kinder part of the hymn that did get used in church, he went back to the beginning instead of reciting it. The lead musico began a descant that wrapped around Franz-Karl's voice without drowning it, despite the vocal power that the choir master had available.

Sophie-Alexa's nightgown smelled like a kitchen midden, not a grave. Franz-Karl thought that even when the funeral prayers were finally said at the mass graves filled by the Sickness, they would not have touched her. He felt nauseated, and not by the smell, but he did not stop the prayer.

He recited the story of the great Curse a third time while he gave locks of hair to their Excellencies his Grandfather and Great Aunt Sophia-Augusta and Her Highness Aunt Queen Gertrude and tucked one inside his own jacket. All seven soloists joined him softly, mostly just singing, without fancy stuff. He lifted the tapestry that covered his mother's still form – Fritzel helped – and placed a lock of the hair under the hands that were crossed on her breast, then let the cloth fall back into place.

As he finished the third repetition of the hymn/curse, Sophie-Alexa's small form collapsed into dust, body and nightgown both together. Franz-Karl handed the rest of the locks of hair to Gwenlian for safekeeping in exchange for an urn and the special raven's wing brush.

He began a fourth repetition of the hymn as he carefully brushed Sophie's remains into the urn. This time he continued into the later section, and the entire choir joined in, singing the part of the hymn about rejoicing that the child of the Great Goddess was found. When he finished the hymn, every particle was in the urn. He wiped the surface of the bier and the feathers of the brush with a white cloth, then tucked it over the dust at the bottom of the urn like a little blanket before closing the urn with its lid. He settled the urn against his mother's side and returned the raven wing brush to Gwenlian.

Fritzel produced a second bottle of wine – one of three that Roland had brought in case they were needed to fill the trench completely. He snapped its neck, and poured it into the empty Blood Trench on the floor. Everyone held their breath. This time, the wine sat there as if nothing odd had ever happened.

Franz-Karl wondered for a strange moment what would have happened if they had followed the oldest custom and bled chickens or rabbits into the trench instead of the wine bottles – there was no room in the poor so-called trench for the blood of any big proper offering like a sheep or goat, much less a horse or a bull.

Franz-Karl rejoined the congregation and bowed to the Arch-Hierophants and choir. "If we may continue?"

Funerals had generally been done for one person at a time before the great Sickness, even for people who died together, but in recent months everyone had become accustomed to shared ceremonies.

Arch-Hierophant Diotima began the rite, since the deceased were a woman and a girl, and she and the choir master automatically made the adjustments needed for two dead people where one had been expected. It changed the poetry a little.

Arch-Hierophant Ambrose stumbled in his first few responses, but it was almost certainly not the number that was troubling him. They were using the Traventine funeral rite instead of the one favored by the Falkenburgs – just as well, since the chapel's crypt was nearly full – but that was not bothering his colleague or the singers. The whites of his eyes were showing more than usual, even for Worldfolk, and he kept glancing toward Franz-Karl.

The funeral went along without further incident until the end of the first rite, when the corpse candles were lit with holy fire from the altar, and the Falkenburg rite called for the dead person to be removed to the crypt but the Traventine rite left them guarded safely within the Blood Trench.

Their Excellencies and the girl cousins and the counselors all left then. A few of them might return for the later rites. The corpse candles now were sometimes narrower and shorter than those used in better times, but they were still supposed to be sized to last past dawn. The candles at this funeral were all full sized, so there was little doubt that they would last.

Since the Sickness had arrived in Karnburg, most people had started leaving the second part of the rite, that was supposed to happen just after midnight, to the priests and choir. Franz-Karl would not do anything so rude to Mama and Sophie-Alexa: he would come back to the chapel at midnight and make sure things were done properly, then return again at dawn for the final part of the funeral.

Franz-Karl and all of his Elderkin household returned to their Residence between the sunset rite and the midnight one. The ones from Greenoak Square had all been sworn to his Mother's service, so the rites needed at the Threshold were brief.

The locks of Sophie-Alexa's hair were put away in the household shrine and they ate a meal together that included the most important parts of a proper funeral feast: bread and wine and salt at the beginning, and fresh meat, and the special number of dishes, including two at the end that included one that was sweet and another that was sour or bitter. The palace kitchens had provided everything that was proper with only a slight delay, and there was enough for everybody. Franz-Karl said the table blessings and guest blessings at the door: he had heard them often enough to know all of the words, but it felt very strange to be the head of their household when he was so far from being a grownup. His brother's funeral dinner had been bad. This was worse.

Despite everything Franz-Karl found he was almost hungry for the first time in many days, and after the midnight rite he slept soundly until nearly sunrise.

Her Excellency Great Aunt Sophia-Augusta was in the chapel when Franz-Karl and his people returned to it in the morning, still leaning on her friend the Justice. "The doctors said that Friedrich-Augustus should not come out again, but he sends his love to you and his regards to them." She bowed toward the bier with its urn and draped corpse.

Her Highness Aunt Queen Gertrude arrived a few minutes later with Lady Lenke. There were also a few other courtiers who had come, and a few Palace servants at the back near the door. Vendal and his companions had traded off with other Old Palace Servants so that they could attend the final rite despite missing the earlier one. One of the other surviving Rathvins – there were only three left of the five Franz-Karl had originally met – was in charge at the Residence.

The chapel windows faced east toward the sunrise, and had colored glass pictures that were just beginning to be visible as the sky behind them lightened. Most of the corpse candles were still burning brightly, but they were reaching the bottoms of their wicks, and the plainest one was beginning to flicker.

The chapel priests arrived, with the palace choir master and a few singers to do the responses. The Arch-Hierophants would not be returning through the streets from the cathedral in the predawn darkness, but the two younger castrato soloists had come, which was kind of them. The Cathedral Choir Master was quite old, and Franz-Karl hoped he was being well taken care of.

The Palace singers were not quite as wonderful as the Cathedral choir, and they were a much smaller group, but they were still very good.

The Chapel Priest hurried over to Franz-Karl and bowed deeply. "Your Grace, I am so very sorry," he said, wringing his hands, "There has been no arrangement made for the tomb for Her late Grace the Duke your Lady Mother. This is most irregular."

"The tomb? We can take care of that afterward. Do you need the tapestry back?"

The Priestess, who had followed her colleague, answered, "No, Your Grace, you are welcome to keep it as your mother's shroud, if you wish. Though I fear it is old and the moths have been at it a bit, at least it is clean. We have needed so many funerals these past months that some of the newer cloths have become... stained."

Franz-Karl walked to the head of the bier. He could not reach, so Fritzel folded the cloth down away from his mother's face and lifted Franz-Karl up to look at her for a few moments. She looked strange with the veil wrapped around her head where her hair had been cut short, but he thought her face looked quiet rather than sad.

The first candle guttered out. The choir master played a note on his pipe, the Priestess chanted the first line of the final farewell, and the singers answered in harmony. The Priest joined in when the second candle began to flicker.

When the second candle died, Franz-Karl's mother's body transformed so that it appeared to be something carved out of pieces of vine-wood fitted together instead of something made of flesh. The cloth covering her was replaced by a sort of lacework of vines. Her Excellency Great Aunt Sophia-Augusta gasped and the Justice said "Heaven protect us." Her Highness Aunt Gertrude and her companion signed themselves and murmured something in Szekely. All of the Elderkin in the chapel took a knee except Franz-Karl, who went to both knees. The Old Palace Servants knelt but the other servants did not.

The Priest turned very pale and sat down on the floor. The Priestess and the singers would have performed the final hymn without him, but Justice von Trebice sang that part: not entirely on key, but he knew all the words and seemed to mean them.

When the last verse of the hymn was finished, the rest of the corpse candles went out all at once. Her Grace Silvia the late Duke of the Elderkin of Traventi crumbled to dust just as her daughter had done the day before. All that was left on the bier was Sophie's urn and a heap of dust and a few small wisps of gold and silver that had been threads in the tapestry, sparkling a little.

Gwenlian brought out the raven wing brush and a plainer urn than Sophie-Alexa's, who was in her mother's intended urn. Her Excellency Great Aunt Sophia-Augusta held the urn while Franz-Karl brushed the dust into it and Fritzel picked up Sophie's urn and held it out of the way.

The wing looked kind of small. Franz-Karl wondered whether it was really a crow's wing playing the role of a raven's wing. It was better than thinking too hard about what he was doing. He wondered whether the crows and ravens had death feuds with the people who made the funeral brushes. Crows were famously cranky about people who hurt their relatives. He did not blame them for that, not even a little bit. And now he was thinking about things again...

He wiped the bier and the brush, and tucked the cloth gently over his mother's dust – the cloth was her favorite shade of green, *not* the color-of-sorrow that she had worn since his father's death – and closed the urn. He bowed to the priests and singers. "Your presence here was very helpful." He hoped they remembered the Elderkin rule about saying 'Thank you' and did not think he was being rude.

Her Excellency Great Aunt Sophia-Augusta knelt down and hugged him so hard he squeaked. "That was very well done." she said in his ear. When she stood up again, the Justice gave the priests and singers a donation on behalf of His Excellency, and Roland gave a donation on behalf of His Grace the Duke of the Elderkin, So that was probably all right.

Her Highness Aunt Gertrude hugged him and then curtsied. When she promised to stand by him, she did not speak quietly. People outside the chapel might not have heard her speak, quite, but they would certainly hear about what she said, from the courtiers that were there, or the servants standing at the back.

Roland and Gwenlian carried the urns back to the Residence because Franz-Karl was too small to do it safely, and Fritzel was busy guarding everybody. Her Excellency Great Aunt Sophia-Augusta with her cane and the Justice came with them, because she had authority over Falkenburg funerals, so they walked slowly. The group from Greenoak Square trailed behind: Franz-Karl thought they might officially be even less present in the Palace than he was himself.

Most servants that saw them pass by bowed, and the men that were wearing hats doffed them. One page ran ahead when he saw them coming, so they arrived at the locked doors of the Elderkin suite to find servants waiting with bottles of wine, bread and cheese and pastries, and things to make tea. The servants who had been locked inside to keep watch had set the tables in the dining room that had been rarely used since the people living in the Residence became so few.

Damian and the group from Greenoak Square did not pass through the doors of the Residence again. They just bowed to Franz-Karl, and said quiet, traditional things in Elderic, and went away.

Once the urns had been placed on the altar of the household shrine, their small group of mourners sat in the dining room to eat an after-funeral breakfast.

Justice von Trebice asked, "If it is not rude to ask... was that ending expected?"

Itron Gwenlian was sitting at the household end of the table. She wobbled her hand in the 'more or less' gesture. "It is presumptuous to expect it, but foolish not to be prepared. It is not very surprising for one who carries a great deal of Blessed heritage to come to their urn without needing a pyre. Very rarely, someone carrying quarter blood of the Blessed or better will remain an effigy of wood or stone: we have heard that her Grace's late mother, her late Grace the Duke Adriana, was one such. But most Elderkin come to be burned or buried in the common fashion."

Fritzel swallowed a bite of cheese. "Sometimes less common than others. When my great-grandmother came to her pyre the flames were very hungry, and some amazing colors." There was a tradition in old stories that talking about less recent dead was safer than discussing those who might still be traveling to the Halls of Judgment, while still acknowledging the presence of death.

"I met that lady once," Roland said, pouring wine and tea for people. "And heard of her often, of course. I'm half surprised she did not turn out to be an effigy made of fireworks."

Fritzel smiled fondly. "She had outlived all of her greatest rivals, by the end. I'm told it mellowed her mood considerably. I can't judge: She was always kind to me."

Franz-Karl was very glad that he had seen his Mama's beautiful effigy form, but he was secretly also glad that she had not stayed that way. The Arch-Hierophants would most likely have claimed her for the Cathedral. Getting her effigy out of the Cathedral crypt in the city, and home to the crypt in the cathedral of Saints Clement and Sophia where she belonged? That would be the kind of project that showed up in the chronicles and stories and usually took several generations, a couple of minor wars and a dynastic marriage to accomplish.

And all that was before you considered that an effigy made a terribly strong anchor for a death curse.

After their official guests left, the Elderkin shared what was left of the feast with Wiborada and the other ladies: just a few mouthfuls each, so they were not left out, but – everyone hoped – not endangered by too much food too soon.

# CHAPTER XXXII: Night Visitor

## *Wherein There is an Outrageous Attack*

The Residence seemed very empty after the funeral guests left. Franz-Karl spent part of of the day reorganizing the Household Shrine, finding the best place to put the urns and moving pictures from the living-family panel of the iconostasis to the panel for the revered dead. He could not find an arrangement he liked, so he kept going back to change things, but finally admitted to himself that there was never going to be a right arrangement that had his father and mother and brother and sister all among the dead, along with so many others. At least his grandmothers had been old. Older.

He started crying again. When he could not stop, Gwenlian gave him a hot drink and put him to bed for a nap. It was still his own small bed in the Nursery, not his mother's bed that belonged to the Duke, because she had been sick and died there. They were planning to replace the mattress and bedding before anyone else used that one. There were purification ceremonies for the room, as well.

The afternoon and evening were as bad as the morning. The whole World was as wrong as the iconostasis, and he had run out of things that needed to be moved around. He took more naps because ... why, not? The ladies were safe and being fed slowly, and Tam was safe and being tended over in the House in Greenoak Square, and everyone else was either recovering or healthy and did not need him, or else they were dead.

Franz-Karl did not sleep soundly that night because he had already slept most of the day. He heard the midnight bell and opened one eye long enough to mumble the new-day's welcome prayer, which he usually did not bother with until he got out of bed in the morning. He felt hot, so squirmed out from under the covers to lie on top in just his nightshirt.

Sometime later, he heard the familiar snap and thump of the Residence's rear servants' entrance, the one that always stuck. He vaguely wondered what bit of cleaning or preparation was planned, but rolled over to try to go back to sleep.

Hands grabbed him, picking him up from his bed by his shoulder and one leg. He grabbed Harvest Prince by one rear leg and yelled: just noise not words. Yelling words when you were startled was dangerous for a Binder or Notary. All the stories and chronicles agreed about that, so children were taught not to yell words.

The person that grabbed him had dark eyes that did not catch the night candle. The Old Palace Servants had left after tidying the dining room. There were no resident servants left to be in the Traventine rooms after midnight, unless they came in through the servants' doors. The ladies were still too weak to pick anyone up. Everyone else left living inside their Residence had Elderkin eyes that would catch the light.

Franz-Karl kicked, hit a soft belly with one foot, too low or too high to be useful. He twisted and flailed, still yelling, got his second leg free, kicked higher. A nose crunched under one heel, the other foot could not quite reach the stubbled throat below it. The angle was wrong or his legs were too short. The intruder shifted his grip, but guessed wrong and shifted the arm waving Harvest Prince closer to his own head. Wooden forelegs struck home.

The full throated scream of an outraged stallion was far too loud for a small indoor space.

A small mountain loomed in the shadows, eyes catching the light, making a rumble like a landslide. Fritzel. There were glimmers of light reflecting from the horns he did not have.

Something crunched in one of the hands that held Franz-Karl, and he was pulled away and set down on his bed. Then Fritzel lifted up the dark-eyed man and shook him, hard, so that the shadow of his head flopped back and forth. Franz-Karl sat up on the bed, and pulled his knees up under his chin and hugged his legs and shivered.

He hoped that his Excellency his Grandfather was not dying. This person seemed too unworried about penalties for an attack under His Excellency's roof. Even an attack on someone who was merely present.

He heard the intruder struggling to get away from Fritzel as he was dragged through the Residence. There were thumps and grunts. Something crashed after being bumped or kicked. Then the main doors of the Residence opened – there were little chimes hanging that were part of the greeting for Guests, put back up now there was officially no one sick inside – there was a scuffling sound as the man was hauled through the North Gallery, and there was a huge, thump-thump thumping crash as the man fell or was thrown down the slippery, polished stone steps of the main staircase of the West Palace.

The main Residence door shut, firmly but without slamming, making the chimes sound again. Fritzel returned. "That pig-botherer landed better than Her late Grace your Grandmother, worse luck."

He picked up Franz-Karl and carried him into his own small room next to the study, where no one would expect to find a Duke. Even wrapped in blankets and huddled against Fritzel's warm strength, it took a long time for Franz-Karl to stop shivering

The walled city of Karnburg was a trap and the Palace was a trap inside a trap... he was sure that they would not willingly let him leave, any more than they had let his Mama leave any time after her marriage. That would not stop an Elderkin with the 'don't notice me' Gift, if Traventi summoned him home, but he did not know what to do about the traps around his people. He could not hide everyone.

After a sleepless while, Franz-Karl thought of something to try that might begin to pry things open a little. Elderkin were famous for making mischief. Well, anyone who expected him to cooperate was going to be in for a shock. Notaries made their own choices: it was part of the oaths.

As soon as it was light enough to read using Elderkin eyes, Franz-Karl went to what had once been his parents' study and started pulling books off the shelves. Three volumes of chronicles. One of the more blood-thirsty collections of old stories – much worse than Lives of the

Notaries. Two different compilations of the Lives of the Notaries. A pile of signed treaties and agreements selected from two different chests. And a book on diplomatic protocols that even Franz-Karl usually found boring.

Fritzel was always good about not jogging Franz-Karl's elbow when he was busy. Now he sat reading Natural Philosophy in a chair by the window. "Let me know if I can help."

By the time Gwenlian called them to breakfast, Franz-Karl had a dozen places marked in the books, and the beginnings of a plan scratched into the five wax-coated tablets of his notebook. He found the treasure box for the spices, and similar boxes he had brought back from Traventi as gifts for his mother and brother and sister, and examined them, and tried to remember. The boxes had special locks with Bindings that only opened to their owners, and one other person chosen by their owner. Finn Locker – the Elderkin who made the special locks – had taught Franz-Karl how that was done and he had done the locks on some of the boxes himself – but that seemed forever ago, and that exact pattern would not quite work: not for doors where people needed to go in and out.

Finn used a particular rare Gift to set the locks, but Bindings were more general: Bindings could do anything Gifts could do if you could figure out how to tell the Living World what you wanted. Just pointing and saying 'make it like that' would never entirely work – Franz-Karl suspected from the stories that the Living World either had trouble seeing inside itself, or did not really understand what it saw – but it might help.

He told Roland to hire a locksmith to change or install locks on all of the entrances to the Elderkin suite, including the servants' entrances, and to add special latches to all of the windows. Unlike the cracked window panes, this was not something to leave to the Palace authorities.

"Even if we hire more of our own servants and bring in a few of our people from Greenoak Square, we can't live in this Palace without letting the Palace servants come in and out," Gwenlian said in Elderic.

"When I handed his Excellency my Grandfather his copy of my oath, he greeted me as a fellow monarch and a guest – not a proper Guest, but still, a guest –" There were at least five words for 'guest' in Elderic as it was spoken in Traventi. "– and there were many important people among those present to witness it. Either we can choose which Palace servants and officials can come in, or they have to admit that I am a prisoner and hostage, which sets free a whole herd of cats they won't want to deal with, even if they have less sense than Heaven gave an earthworm in the rain. I am Duke of Traventi, but I am also His Excellency's last remaining heir through descent in the male line, which matters to the Allemans: the rest of his descendants are all daughters and their children." He was talking too fast. He took a deep breath and tried to slow down. "Besides, the locks and keys are going to be partly misdirection, and partly anchors for our real defenses."

Roland said flatly, "They don't teach the Gates of Air to small children that still have most of their baby teeth. Not even Recognized Heirs."

Franz-Karl turned one hand palm up. "They don't need to. I am a fully sworn Notary and Duke of the Elderkin, and I have had the Hiding Gift fully Manifest since before I went to the Duchy last year. And I don't lack invention."

"Manifest Gifts are a fine thing in one so young," Roland sounded surprised and impressed, which was oddly comforting. Franz-Karl had always half-suspected that the Elderkin attendants were just humoring him when they did not seem to notice him. "And Bindings can do many things. Of course, Your Grace. Is there anything else?"

He sighed. "I have a beginning of a plan, but to make it work I shall need to keep something closer to proper state for a visiting monarch. That will mean we need our own housemaids and footmen, and guards, and someone in the stable, as well as our choice among the Palace servants who come in to us. Try to find people with Elderkin eyes, or who have relatives that have them. That should help the Bindings recognize them." He had a thought. "Try to avoid hiring people from other Residences within the Palace. It will be too hard to judge their loyalties. I don't think the Old Palace Servants will change their employment, or those who serve Her Royal Highness, but we should ask their advice. Or perhaps some of the Old Palace Servants can make us their special concern while still belonging to the Palace."

"And if the Palace officials refuse to notice that you are a monarch?" Itron Gwenlian sounded very tired.

"Oh, Well, as to that," Franz-Karl closed his eyes for a moment, then opened them and smiled. "The good folk of Karnburg have a Duke of the Elderkin dwelling among them. I do not think that they will fail to notice."

Fritzel smiled back at him, but Roland and Gwenlian looked worried. There was a reason the Duchy's ancient neighbors had proverbs about smiling Elderkin Dukes, and Franz-Karl had been reading some very fierce books.

"It may be that I will I need to give them a little kick, to make sure that they notice..." Franz-Karl continued, "But I am not only Duke of the Elderkin. His Excellency my Grandfather is Archduke of the Eastlands and Overlord of the other Falkenburg lands by right of birth, and King of the Allemans by right of Election, and holds various other titles in other ways. But he does not rule the city of Remora, nor receive tribute from it, nor have those who do rule it granted him any courtesy title. Some of his Excellency's ancestors were properly crowned as Emperor of Remora by the Pontiffs at the Holy See. But the last time that happened was more than a century ago, before the Sectarian Wars got really bloody. And in any case, the Duchy of the Elderkin of Traventi stopped paying taxes to Remora more than a thousand years before the first Falkenburg was elected King and crowned Emperor. We do not recognize that the Remoran Empire is a real thing in these modern times." He fetched pen and ink and parchment, wax and seal, and made it an official Binding decree that the Duchy of Traventi did not consider the Remoran Empire a real thing unless its heads were crowned by their Holinesses in Remora, and would neither speak its name on formal occasions nor treat with any entity falsely purporting to be it. He put a copy of the decree on the table where the letters came and went, and set another copy aside to take to His Excellency when they felt the time was right.

"That will get up a few people's noses." Roland sounded very satisfied.

"Does this break any treaties?" Fritzel asked. He just sounded curious, not worried.

"No important ones that I could find. That book on protocols needs an index. Most treaties say things like 'Kingdom of the Allemans *and* the Remoran Empire'. And for signatures the person usually matters, not the title, except for identification. Titles change holders, even without the Great Sickness... there are some oddities in the Marriage

Contract where some Allemanic nobles signed only their titles, not their names... but that should not matter for this."

He returned to poking at the lock Bindings. He was getting rather good at picking ordinary locks – especially after he took one or two apart and reassembled them. The Binding he was trying to create kept coming close, then failing, like a lock-pick that suddenly went skidding off in some bizarre, impossible direction..

Fritzel was not quite a Binder himself, but he came from a whole family full of Binders, and he had seen more of people doing useful things with Bindings than Franz-Karl ever had. It was helpful to grow up in a place where the authorities had not banned Binders that were not Bound themselves. He was able to offer some useful advice – and not flinch very often – while Franz-Karl spent the day poking at the treasure boxes and door locks and staring at walls and doors and windows without actually seeing their outsides.

They barricaded the servants' doors that night.

Franz-Karl did not sleep in the Nursery, though they left the little night-lamp burning there as usual. For nearly a year before their father's death – before Philip-Augustus supposedly inherited the rank and status of Count of Wolfsberg – Franz-Karl had shared a room with his brother instead of sleeping on the other side of the Nursery from his sister. Now that the Nursery had become a dreadful place, and Sophie-Alexa would not be returning, he returned to the other room, which had the added benefit of being farther from either of the servants' doors than the nursery was. He did not even need to sleep in what had been his brother's bed: they simply rescued his own former bed from under a pile of the possessions of Philip-Augustus.

The next day three of the Elderkin from Greenoak Square came to join the Traventine Residence in the Palace. Two of them were young-looking Elderkin men named Finbar and Lorcan: young enough to pass for Worldfolk... when they were fully clothed, anyway, and provided you ignored their eyes. The blonder one had green cats' eyes, and the darker one had amber goats' eyes, and neither of the two had whites to their eyes worth mentioning, and their eyes were a bit too far apart, besides, compared to most Worldfolk. They were not as large as Fritzel – hardly anyone was as large as Fritzel, even among Elderkin – but they were definitely what people had in mind when they talked about 'sturdy footmen'. If the Great Sickness had afflicted them, they were well recovered now.

Fritzel showed Finbar and Lorcan all of the entrances to the Residence, and the well in the deep tunnel, and the place they got wood to replenish the store in Juliana's room.

The third newcomer was an Elderkin woman, Neasa, who seemed very old. She had a round face that was as wrinkly and cheerful as an apple doll and and wrinkly hands, and that was all of her that was visible. Her clothes looked ancient, too. They were wrapped and flowing rather than tailored and form-fitting, like something in an old painting: one of the rare ones where the painted people had clothes on. The cuffs on her sleeves reached to the bases of her thumbs, and she wore a wimple and a tall, complicated headdress. Her eyebrows were not feathery, and her eyes were not feline, so Franz-Karl thought she probably had horns or something under there. She gathered with Itron Gwenlian and the three rescued ladies, and planned things.

Franz-Karl went into his new/old room, laid down on his bed and spent most of the rest of the day asleep. He did not even awaken for the midday meal. Working with Gifts and Bindings was tiring, especially after a night of broken sleep.

The Residence was a little less echo-y now that there were ten people, instead of just seven, moving around in a set of rooms intended for a handful of family and any number of attendants and servants. Though of course, the three ladies were not moving much yet.

When they all sat down to eat the evening meal together in proper Traventine style, Franz-Karl looked around at them, and looked at the room, which had gone a bit wavery to his sight, and asked almost cheerfully, in Elderic, "So... how large of a Manifest Demon could the seven of us handle, do you think?"

Lorcan inhaled some of what he was eating and started coughing. Neasa smiled at Franz-Karl approvingly. "Not the very largest ones – not until Your Grace reaches his majority and the Child Blessings wear away entirely. The middling ones may remain a bit tricky for the next few years only."

Roland looked confused. "Your Grace?"

Franz-Karl waved a hand at the table. "We should use the larger table next time. The walls of the World are not as nearly as stretched as when I sat too near Her Grace my late Grandmother and Reverend

Count Great Aunt Adrasteia both at once, but I think we are pressing them a bit, here." There were people claiming to run the Palace who would be furious if they understood what that implied... but decrees barring heavy Elderkin only worked if you knew how to recognize those that carried large amounts of Manifest heritage, and Franz-Karl did not plan to give them any pointers.

Gwenlian smiled thinly, not showing her teeth. "With Heaven's grace, we'll have some Worldfolk added to the Household soon, besides the ladies, so that we will be spread thinner. But I'll set the larger table next time, regardless."

Broken Oaths & Boundaries

# CHAPTER XXXIII: Locks and Scales

## *Wherein Some Matters Are Closed and Others Are Opened*

The next day Roland brought Franz-Karl a senior apprentice locksmith whose master had died of the Sickness. Being a Notary who knew when he was being lied to was very handy sometimes: Franz-Karl could reject any candidate who did not look truthful enough to rest firmly in their place in the World.

Rutger was honest, and willing to become a member of the household as well as helping them fix their locks immediately. He swore the oaths of a new household member and ally, not Guest oaths. Franz-Karl thought that was a wonderful, useful thing: once he got the locks working as he wanted and gossip spread about Rutger's history, Worldfolk who failed to get into the Residence would think, 'Oh, they changed the locks again. Curse that locksmith-footman' before they ever considered that Bindings might be involved.

Rutger was a native of Karnburg, a small young man with a wiry build that needed feeding up and blue human eyes with a very faint hint of Elderkin strangeness. He was not frightened at the idea of the Bindings Franz-Karl was trying to create. He asked lots of sensible questions about the project and made some excellent suggestions about adding anchors into the ornamentation of the various locks and latches. He also made a quite passable footman once Neasa and Itron Gwenlian provided him with a properly tailored set of livery.

By the end of the day, they showed Rutger both the door of Household Shrine and what was inside the door to Juliana's room. He signed himself when they said the Hearth was consecrated, and said the proper Ecclesialist greeting for a Hearth, but in Karnburger Allemanic. Franz-Karl had never heard the Allemanic version before: only the Elderic and Remoran versions.

"My Granny had a proper Heath when I was small, Your Grace, before the Siege," Rutger explained. "And my Ma has always mourned its loss. I'm well glad to have fallen among old-fashioned, Gods-fearing folk."

They told him about the ladies, and Rutger looked angry when he heard how they had been locked in. He muttered something about a sin against locks, and promised to make extra keys for the ladies to carry, so that they need not fear being locked in ever again.

While the locks were being worked on and the keys were being changed, Franz-Karl sat in the study with a wax tablet and several books, adjusting his plans to take advantage of the anchors Rutger was providing. He wrote bits of formulas on the wax and quickly smooshed the wax smooth again when he decided they were wrong to use. He smooshed them even more quickly when he decided they were right. There were things that would be more useful if they were not left written down where unexpected people might see them. After a while, he finally had a text for the Bindings that seemed likely to work.

After dinner the household gathered in the main room of the suite. They included all seven Elderkin and Rutger, and the three ladies. There were also Gerta, a new housemaid to help Itron Gwenlian and Neasa look after the clothes and linens, and a very young man named Udo – even younger than Fritzel and nearly as large – who would be a combination stable-boy and pigeon-keeper, sleeping in the Residence but working in the stables and dovecote. Franz-Karl's Ducal household was already much larger than it had been when he first became Duke.

Franz-Karl wrote a note to himself to consider adding some ... subtle... defenses for the pigeons and horses in the stable block, once they got some again that lived inside the Palace walls. For the moment, living things that lacked speech were being tended at Greenoak Square, out of easy reach of malice.

They set all of the new keys out on a cloth on the table, and Franz-Karl said the Binding formulas he had chosen four times, binding locks to keys, and keys to each other, and keys to people in several different ways. One of the trickier bindings would only allow someone from outside the household to use a key they had received directly from a household member – Franz-Karl was not sure he had got that one entirely right, but it was worth trying.

Not letting illicit copies of keys work was a very old trick, and one he was more sure of: there were three versions of that Binding reported but not described in different old stories, besides the one Finn Locker had taught him. He had also added a Binding he hoped would make their keys – especially any forged copies made from their keys – very bitey when they were used by someone who was not supposed to have one.

They gave keys to some of the Old Palace Servants that they trusted to do things like cleaning, and delivering laundry and firewood. After thinking about it, and discussing the plan with Fritzel and Itron Gwenlian and Roland, Franz-Karl gave Vendal a key to the front entrance of the Residence in addition to Vendal's copies of the ones for both servants' doors: the example of the ladies being locked in and aid locked out had left them all wary.

The next day there was a scratching and banging at the servants' door near the dining room very early in the morning. Also a strange sizzling snap sound, somewhat later, followed by a sort of yelp. But the door and its lock did not move.

They removed the barricades from in front of the servant's doors, since it seemed the new locks were working as they had hoped.

After the midday meal, one of the Old Palace Servants who came to take away the ashes from the fireplaces notified them that His Excellency was holding audiences that afternoon. They had not been summoned, but Franz-Karl was neither a Guest nor a member of the Court.

He and Fritzel dressed in the clothes they wore for official visits to His Excellency. They took Lorcan with them to carry the declaration about the Holy Remoran Empire on a tray and make the point that as the Sovereign Duke and a Tiarna of Traventi they were far too important to do anything as useful as carry a document across the Palace grounds. This was not like the accession oath, which needed to be handed from monarch to monarch partly because of some wording in the Marriage Contract.

They found His Excellency Friedrich-Augustus, King of the Allemans, Archduke of the Eastlands and Patriarch of the Falkenburg Domains, High Priest of the Grove, and so forth and so on, sitting in his bedroom and admitting only a few people at a time from the outer waiting room. But His Excellency was dressed formally and sitting in a chair, which was good. He held out his arms and gave Franz-Karl a good hug, which was better.

One of His Excellency's footmen took the document from the tray Lorcan carried and presented it to one of His Excellency's secretaries.

"Is this a matter of importance, Your Grace?" His Excellency asked.

Franz-Karl flicked a hand. "Merely a small clarification of terms... as faithful adherents of their Holinesses in Remora, the Council and People of Traventi must regretfully decline to acknowledge any claims to the title of Remoran Emperor when no coronation has taken place in more than a century."

Two of the of the three nobles in the room swelled up like frogs preparing to croak. It was very gratifying. One of them was Horst-Konrad von Neumark, the Margraff-Elector of Ansbach, but it was the other noble who said "What?" in a voice that rose to a squeak. His features and dress looked Northern, but Franz-Karl did not recognize him. He wondered whether the Prince-Elector of Bremerhaven had not yet recovered from the Sickness: it was so rare to see the Margraff-Elector without his usual yoke-mate. He made a mental note to find a good source of Palace gossip.

His Excellency was not upset. He chuckled a little – without coughing – and waved down the noble who had spoken, then asked Franz-Karl in a sympathetic tone, "Notary oaths chafing a bit, are they?"

Franz-Karl answered, "Well... partly."

"No problems with the other titles: King and Archduke and such?"

"Of course not!" Franz-Karl was honestly surprised at the suggestion. "I have never heard of any legal or ceremonial irregularities in those positions."

"I am overjoyed to hear it," His Excellency said. "Well, I suppose it is better to use titles the Traventines respect instead of boasting of being heirs of people they famously defeated in battle. In documents involving Traventi We will henceforth restrict Ourselves to titles with solid historical provenance."

The Nobles still looked unhappy. Franz-Karl thought he could see the moment when the Margraff-Elector decided His Excellency's comment had not been official enough to matter.

When Franz-Karl returned to the outer room, he looked around for the Steward of the Falkenburg Domains. He started to walk toward him, but remembered himself – a Sovereign Duke outranked a Steward – and beckoned to the Steward to approach him.

The man stopped a polite distance from Franz-Karl and bowed. "Good day, Your Grace."

"Blessed day," Franz-Karl said, as if he was translating from Elderic to Allemanic. "We have acquired several people to fill some of the gaps in my household. I assume the Palace servants and kitchens and suppliers should be informed."

The man bowed again. "Of course, Your Grace. I shall have someone make the arrangements." He glanced around, probably looking for one of his subordinates to pass the task to.

Most High Nobles were even less likely to say 'thank you' than Elderkin, and generally with less reason. Franz-Karl nodded. "That would be helpful."

The Falkenburg Steward had looked back at Franz-Karl and begun to ask, "Will Your Grace be – " when the Allemanic Chamberlain strutted up to them and demanded, using highly insubordinate language to know what was being discussed. This was bold, and vastly improper, since he was a subordinate of the Chancellor of the Allemanic Kingdom, not in the line of authority of the Falkenburg Steward, who outranked him, and certainly not in any line of authority that included Franz-Karl.

Franz-Karl sighed and answered extremely patiently, as though he was speaking to someone dim of wit or hard of hearing or both. "I am Franz-Karl of the lines of Falkenburg and Armorius and Leonstein and Capradaventi, Sovereign Duke of Traventi, greeted as a fellow monarch by his Excellency, and also the landed heir of certain territories within the Domains of the Falkenburgs. I was discussing a small matter with the

Steward of the Falkenburg Domains. If you chance to see the Falkenburg Chamberlain, you might usefully commend us to his attention."

Franz-Karl pointedly turned back to the Steward, who bowed and repeated his question about His Grace's plans for the staffing of the Traventine Residence. Franz-Karl was watching the Allemanic Chamberlain with the edge of his broad Elderkin vision: he certainly was not going to turn his back on the man entirely.

The Chamberlain remained standing beside them, seething at being instructed to perform a task suited to a messenger boy. He opened and closed his mouth without forming coherent words, and his face had turned an unbecoming sort of mottled purple. Franz-Karl wondered whether the Chamberlain was one of those who had developed a rash while afflicted with the Great Sickness: the pattern had the look of a remembered rash. Finally he turned with what could only be called a flounce and walked away.

Franz-Karl let him get a few steps away before calling him back. "Martin." No title. No name of estate or family. Just the name, and complete certainty that the man would answer. He kept his voice gentle, but he was thinking about turning the Chamberlain into something squishy and embarrassing and amusing: those kinds of thoughts leaked into your voice. And your eyes. And the way you stood, unless you were being careful to hide them. Franz-Karl was not trying to stand in a way that would hide his thoughts. Not at all. He cocked his head slightly and waited again.

The Chamberlain finally turned back toward him and said, "Yes, your Grace."

"I have informed my attendants that the next time thy... minion... Philemon seeks to lay insubordinate hands upon my person, Fritzel is to tear his arm all the way off, and beat him over the head with it while he bleeds out. Hast thou heard me?"

Fritzel shifted his weight only slightly and blew out his breath through his nose. It was too soft to be considered a snort – even the twitchiest ox or bullock would not take it as a challenge – but it was unusual enough in that place that those standing nearby looked at the huge Elderkin, then others turned to follow their gaze. Soon everyone in the room was looking at Fritzel and Franz-Karl, and the Chamberlain. The so-called Master of the Palace, Philemon von und zu Ostwald, standing not far away, made a little sound in his throat, somewhat muffled by his bruised face and broken nose.

The Chamberlain's mouth had dropped open again. He closed it and managed a "Yes, your Grace" that was actually prompt, but immediately turned away again.

Franz-Karl let him take only one step this time. "Martin."

The Chamberlain's flinch was clearly visible to everyone nearby. He turned back, and bowed properly this time. "Yes, your Grace?"

"The Duchy of the Elderkin of Traventi will of course decline to pay for repairing the damage done by any blood spray."

"Yes, Your Grace." With an immediate bow, and he waited for Franz-Karl, higher in rank, to turn away. Then he breathed a sigh of relief... too soon.

"Martin." This voice was baritone – though strikingly similar to Franz-Karl's – and very familiar to everyone in the room.

Franz-Karl turned to face where His Excellency stood in the doorway of his bedroom, leaning on a secretary and a walking stick. Franz-Karl, di Armorius and von Falkenburg, Sovereign Duke of Traventi, bowed slightly to his grandfather. Everyone else in the room took a knee, except Fritzel – who was no vassal or subject of Friedrich-Augustus – and Ritter von und zu Ostwald, who apparently could not move that far. The Chamberlain of the Kingdom of the Allemans was now deathly pale instead of mottled purple.

His Excellency said, "Your Grace, as a Traventine Notary, Bound to truth, did this man Ostwald lay hands upon you?" No 'zu'... not even a 'von'...

Franz-Karl remembered Ostwald referring to his sister as just Sophie, without her titles or the rest of her name.

Franz-Karl spoke clearly and did his best to match His Excellency's accent and rhythm. "During the night after the funeral of Her Grace the Duke my late Mother, a man entered the Traventine Residence and attempted to pull me from my bed. Tiarna Boukolyos tossed him down the main staircase of the West Palace. I did not see his face, but Philemon Ostwald shows injuries from a fall down a staircase ... well, except the nose: I kicked my opponent in the face as he tried to lift me up, and felt the nose crunch."

"And those marks on his face, like tiny horseshoes?" His Excellency needed spectacles for reading and close work, but his distance vision was still excellent.

"I have a wooden horse I won at the Saints' Day festival. Harvest Prince was in reach as I lay in my bed." Franz-Karl did not think it was necessary to mention that Harvest Prince did not wear horseshoes: his wooden legs ended in smooth stubs. The wooden horse did not have a voice either, but that had not kept him silent during the scuffle.

The Allemanic Chamberlain said, "No Bindings, Your Grace?" He did not quite manage to resist returning to the habit of sneering. He turned even paler by the time he had finished the words: hearing the tone of his own words might have wakened him to sense too late.

"My purpose was to fight one man not level the Palace," Franz-Karl answered in a tone he made cheerful. He cocked his head, considering, without moving his eyes away from his Excellency. "There are some people that I like who live here... and some of the art is quite nice." And the Child Blessings would limit what he could do for a few years yet, but there was no need to mention that in a roomful of enemies and bystanders.

His Excellency said dryly, "That was very considerate of Your Sovereign Grace of Traventi. Colonel di Pazzi... " The officer Franz-Karl had paid to look after the main Palace bowed elaborately. "Take Ostwald into custody on charges of treason."

"Hardly treason, Your Excellency," the Margraff-Elector of Ansbach protested.

His Excellency looked at the Northern noble for a long moment. He snapped, "My vassal laid hands on my heir. Under my roof," then turned away, giving orders to various officials as he recognized them among those gathered in the room. Ostwald had two days to produce witnesses that could swear honestly in the presence of a Traventine Notary that he had been elsewhere when Franz-Karl was attacked. Unless he could prove his innocence, he would be executed as a traitor and his family would be stripped of any titles or property they held in fealty to His Excellency in any of his various capacities. Martin, who had been chamberlain of the Allemanic kingdom – Martin winced – was immediately demoted to only holding whatever authority Ostwald had recently held.

When the Allemanic Kingdom's Chancellor suggested that his Excellency was being a bit hasty, he was asked whether he had an ambition to serve as a Chamberlain, and warned to be more careful about those he recommended for positions in the Palace hierarchy.

There was a final decree: that the Chamberlain of the Falkenburg Domains would be in charge of the Palace alone in the absence of a trusted Allemanic Chamberlain, until one could be found and appointed, and approved by His Excellency personally.

The Margraff-Elector seemed about to say something again, but he changed his mind when His Excellency glared at him.

Franz-Karl was glad to watch while Ostwald was taken away. It was good to see his name broken as he had broken Sophie-Alexa's. It was encouraging to know that a man who had afflicted his family since his father's death – if not longer – would no longer be making trouble in the Palace. And he would sleep better when he could do it knowing that the hands that had attacked him in his own bed were no longer in the world.

The World had lost too many good people lately. It could stand to lose a few nasty ones.

Broken Oaths & Boundaries

# INTERLUDE X: Upheavals

## *Wherein the Echelon Continues to Change*

When the news from Court reached the White Hall, Preacher Groen insisted on a full Purgation of every member of the Echelon who had been present at His Excellency's audience.

Ostwald, of course, was no longer among their number, though no one would begin to scavenge his household until his time for seeking witnesses in his defense had ended. No one expected him to produce any witnesses, not witnesses that could face a Traventine Notary. But the men making plans about his family and properties would not move until after his execution.

The former Chamberlain came shockingly close to failing the Purgation entirely: the count of his questions was forty-eight and thirty-seven, and he had to be carried home on a stretcher. Despite his wealth, and noble title, and position at Court, if he survived to return to the White Hall he would no longer be counted among the Select.

The task of moving the locked boxes of treasure out of the Palace had become urgent: with the Echelon's influence within the imperial household suddenly greatly diminished and di Pazzi's regiment augmenting the door guards, free movement to and from the Palace could no longer be relied on.

Until the treasure was rescued, other plans, like the redistribution of what had been dower lands and a hoped-for tightening of certain rules around the borders of Traventi, would be delayed.

# CHAPTER XXXIV: The Living and the Dead

## *Wherein Our Hero Converses with His Kin and Others*

During the afternoon of the day between His Excellency's audience and the time set for Ostwald's execution, the new Master of the Household, formerly the Allemanic Chamberlain, tried to enter the front door of the Traventine residence without even knocking. He demanded a set of the Residence keys when he failed.

The door was opened by Roland – backed by the footmen Finbar and Lorcan, and even Rutger – but not opened far enough for any one to enter. "All of those who properly have keys to this Residence have them in their possession," Roland said. He repeated the same sentence, exactly, twice more when the so-called 'Master' repeated his demands, then finally said, "All of those who properly have keys to this Residence have them in their possession... and that was the fourth time of asking," and shut the door firmly in the Master's face.

The Master of the Household returned with a written plan to move Franz-Karl into the main Palace – because he was his Excellency's heir – and permit him only a few attendants –because he was not a grownup. It was signed by the wrong Privy Council and not by His

Excellency, and without either the late acting Archduke or His Excellency, the Council's decrees had no force besides.

Franz-Karl sent out an answer written in Elderic: since the Master's paper had been written in Allemanic he did not bother to use diplomatic Remoran. It said that he refused to leave his Mother's Household shrine: If he had to deconsecrate the one in the Residence, he would move to Greenoak Square, or possibly all the way back to Traventi.

Franz-Karl was spending a lot of time in the Shrine. He did not talk to his Mama's remains. She had said straight out when she was dying that she was planning a serious death curse, and he did not want to draw her attention back to the Living World. If it came to a choice between his Mama staying far away in the Lands of the Blest beyond the Halls of Judgment being happy with his Papa, and his Mama staying near Franz-Karl and turning into a terrible Vengeful Spirit, Franz-Karl thought the choice was not hard. Vengeful Spirits were not happy – Franz-Karl suspected that being a Vengeful Spirit probably hurt – and they were famous for having very bad aim.

He talked to Sophie-Alexa because some of the old stories said you should talk to Elderkin who had died alone and in fear. And because he needed someone to talk to that was not a grownup. He could tell his sister that he was frightened and she would not try to do anything stupid about it. Probably. Elderkin children who had not lost even a single baby tooth usually did not become Vengeful Spirits, but they usually did not become Walking Dead either.

He hoped the people who had been mean to Sophie-Alexa had everything going wrong in their lives that could possibly go wrong. He hoped very much that at least some of the guilty ones had seen her Walk, and were seeing her Walk in their dreams every night. But he did not say that to Sophie-Alexa: he said it to the Living World and only when he was outside the Shrine and the Shrine's door was closed tightly.

He talked to his Papa and Grandmothers, and uncle Helm-Friedrich sometimes, in case they wanted to know what was going on. He occasionally talked to his brother, and minded that Philip-Augustus could not answer less than with most of the others.

The day after Ostwald was reported dead, Franz-Karl received a summons to the Falkenburg Council, where His Highness Prince Otto of Karnburg was now presiding during the continuing infirmity of His

Excellency. They wanted him to sign some papers to 'regularize' relations between Traventi and the Falkenburg Domains. He dressed carefully for the gathering, adding the Ivy and Iron crown he had received at his Recognition to his most formal color-of-sorrow garments: it was not the Ducal coronet, but even some of the Alemannic tales mentioned Ivy and Iron

Duke Franz-Karl of Traventi entered the Falkenburg council room accompanied by Fritzel, Colonel di Pazzi, an honor guard of di Pazzi's men and four Traventine Borderers from Greenoak Square in tunics and cloaks – he had chosen the ones that were most notably inhuman in the details of their eyes and features – including Damian the Centurion. There was no exchange of oaths of peaceful intent or honest dealing at the entrance to the Main Palace or the door to the council room. Di Pazzi and his men stopped just inside the chamber door, and it was not entirely clear who they were protecting from whom.

Franz-Karl did not sit down in any of the chairs at the council table. Standing, he was the Duke of Traventi, but when seated he would just look like a small boy in a large chair.

Standing at the end of the long table opposite His Highness Prince Otto, Franz-Karl listened quietly while the councilors explained – in Allemanic – what they had decided to do about Traventi. At the end, he asked them – in diplomatic Remoran – to translate their 'notes' into the proper language of formal diplomacy.

One of the councilors protested that the translation would take time. Franz-Karl answered, still in Remoran, that the Duke of the Elderkin of Traventi had been summoned to hear a formal proposal by the council, and was prepared to wait until it was produced. He stood waiting with Fritzel and the Borderers at his back.

That was not a quick process, but Franz-Karl stood waiting. When the document had been produced and he had read it, he simply said, still in diplomatic Remoran, "No. I think not." He did not include any titles or styles or polite flourishes.

Prince Otto seemed more amused than surprised.

The rest of council spent a great deal of time assuring each other – and Franz-Karl – that he had no reasonable alternative. Most of them spoke in Allemanic, which he calmly ignored. Finally, one of them repeated the opinion in moderately coherent Remoran.

"I cannot sign the papers this council has prepared," Franz-Karl said firmly, still speaking only Remoran. He thought that they should be relieved that he was addressing them in the language of international affairs and not insisting on Elderic. He was planning to insist on Elderic if they got too annoying. The next step would be insisting that they come to him and being extremely fussy about oaths for anyone crossing his Threshold. He took one step closer to the table.

"I am forbidden by Traventine Law and custom to sign any such agreement before I am an Initiate and reach my majority. And I am reluctant to sign anything proposed by a pack of forsworn traitors and horse-thieves who have invited the curse of Heaven and the Living World upon themselves and those who rely upon their honor. When I am an adult and an Initiate, if you are still alive – and have heirs – you may submit an amended proposal. Until then, the Marriage Contract stands, battered though it may be."

He turned on his heel, and his companions prepared to follow him out of the room.

The newly installed Master of Protocol was present even though not properly part of the Council. He bowed to Prince Otto and received a wave of permission, then spoke hastily. "Your Grace has not yet sworn fealty for your various Wolfsberg holdings..." He had sense enough to try to to use Remoran, but his accent was bad and his grammar suggested he had not looked at a Remoran text since his schoolboy days.

Franz-Karl turned to face him. "The rules for inheritance of properties and titles within the Falkenburg Domains only partly coincide with the rules elsewhere in the Kingdom of the Allemans. Philip-Augustus von Falkenburg died one year and two days after the death of Leon-Alexander von Falkenburg, and none of the required rituals and formulas for the County of Wolfsberg had been completed in the intervening year. Whether that was due to deliberate malice or official incompetence does not matter: the Wolfsberg estate and most of the other major components of what should have been my brother's inheritance have reverted to Leon-Alexander's overlord and no longer exist as such unless His Excellency chooses to reinstate them. A few exceptions – like that haunted tower on the border – pass by blood-right, not fealty, so they require no oaths. This all, of course, constitutes an additional breach of the Marriage Contract."

The official said, "But –" but Franz-Karl continued, and the man could not quite bring himself to interrupt a sovereign Duke standing there wearing a crown and everything.

"There are also, of course, the properties and titles assigned to my Uncle Helm-Friedrich and his family, now extinct in the male line. Those have not lapsed, and I am now heir presumptive for the properties not reserved for doweries. However, as a Notary of Traventi I am barred from swearing an empty oath, as my late brother did for the false promise of the minor Wolfsberg holdings. I will not be swearing anything – to anyone – until there is a pile of attested deeds and completed charters in front of me, all sworn before me in my capacity as Notary. I imagine the pile will be nearly as tall as me." He made a bow that was little more than a nod, turned away, then turned back. "I refer, of course, to my present height: given the rate of progress with the late Leon-Alexander's holdings, I am sure that before the inheritances are sorted out I will be a good deal taller... and possibly a baritone." He looked around and saw several people who looked slightly stunned, but none who seemed prepared to speak.

Franz-Karl and his attendants finally left the room. Di Pazzi and his men joined them as they reached the door.

# INTERLUDE XI: Urgency

## *Wherein The Locked Chests Are to Be Moved*

The highest members of the Echelon went directly from the council chamber to the inner chamber of the White Hall. Preacher Groen and Teacher Bauer had of course not been present at the council session, but they were soon informed of what had happened there.

A report arrived that Colonel Louis de Castres had entered the Palace through the main gate, but he had not been seen near any of the Generals of the various armies.

After a hasty scramble to make plans – it became clear that none of the remaining Select really trusted each other to store the treasure – it was decided that the locked boxes of treasure must be moved that evening, after di Pazzi's men went off duty and before any other units with an excessive attention to the details of their orders could join the guards at the doors and gates of the Palace.

The boxes in their current, locked state would be moved to a storeroom in the home of the highest remaining Pristinist treasury official, at least temporarily. The keys to open them would remain in the possession of the Margraff-Elector of Ansbach.

The men to do the actual moving presented a problem. The chests had been placed in the storeroom before they were filled and locked, so their present weight was uncertain, and there were few Pristinists left who could come and go from the Palace who could plausibly move heavy boxes. It was not a task the Echelon members were willing to trust to slaves or serfs, which might have been the simplest solution. In the end they sent three trusted men, directed by a fourth who was too important to lend a hand for carrying things, with a cart to wait outside the Palace Gate, and rough sacking to swaddle the boxes and obscure their fine locks and sturdy construction.

Three men were barely enough to lift the first lockbox and wrap it, haul it out into the narrow corridor and up the even narrower servants' stair to the ground floor of the Palace. They did not use the entrance the servants used to bring in supplies: that area was too busy in the evening and they were the wrong men to pass through that door. So they lugged their heavy burden to the main entrance of the Palace building, and down the short flight of outer stairs, and along the path to the gate, and out into the street and then a distance – it seemed to grow farther as they walked – to the waiting cart.

They could not leave the first chest unattended, so one of the trusted men remained with the cart, replaced by the carter for the project of moving the second chest. It was fortunate they had the carter: one of the weary men tripped while hauling their burden up the servants' stair and the unburdened man directing things tumbled down the stairs. They managed not to drop the chest, but it wedged itself into the narrow width of the stairwell when the other bearers tried to avoid falling down the stairs after him, chest and all. The carter got the chest un-wedged and the bearers steadied.

When the second chest had joined its partner on the cart, they traveled toward the treasury official's home by an indirect route. Near the midpoint of their journey through the unlit city streets , they passed one of the charnel pits that held the bodies of poor men dead of the pestilence, lit by a few guttering torches instead of the corpse-candles of a proper funeral. They knifed the carter and made sure that he was pushed deep enough in the pit that few would notice him.

The cart and its mule were taken away to a stable near the city's market gate, where they could be disposed of with few questions being asked.

# CHAPTER XXXV: Thresholds

## *Wherein the Season Is Reawakened*

When Franz-Karl, Duke of Traventi, dressed on the morning of the Feast of Reawakening, his new clothes for the feast day fit him exactly. There was nothing a little too short or a little too long or a little too tight or a little too loose. The hems were deep and the seam allowances were wide, to allow for adjustments for expected growth, but in that moment his new coat and waistcoat and breeches just... fit.

The buttons were ivory, saved from the clothes his Mama had worn to his Papa's funeral. The fine wool fabric in color-of-sorrow had come from the yardage of one of her skirts and carried a faint scent of the herbs in her wardrobe.

His valet Tam helped him to dress, and combed his hair before pinning the Crown of Ivy and Iron into place. Tam was still recovering from illness and injury, so worked seated rather than standing, but Franz-Karl was still short enough that Tam working seated was convenient for both of them.

As he walked toward the main entrance of the Residence, he was joined by his aide Fritzel, who was wearing very dark gray. The suit was not black: Fritzel's hair was the black of a bull's pelt, and clearly darker, and the embroidery along his seams and hems and lapels and around his buttons and buttonholes was done in true black thread, and white, and a pale silvery gray.

There were several people waiting in the North Gallery when Franz-Karl and Fritzel walked out though the Residence doorway. One was Damian, leader of the Borderers stationed at the House in Greenoak Square that served as the Traventine embassy. He bowed deeply and offered Franz-Karl a small package sealed with the great seal of Traventi and the seals of the three territorial Counts of Traventi.

When the package was opened, the wrappings vanished , and Franz-Karl was left holding the Traveling Seal of Traventi – the great seal never passed outside the borders – hanging from a complicated chain fashioned from a dark substance that did not break the rules against wearing ornaments and treasure during mourning. The Seal itself was Traventi, and did not count as an ornament: not when the Duke wore it.

The chain had no catch, so Fritzel helped him put on the chain over his head without getting it tangled in the crown of Ivy and Iron. Wearing the Seal was a relief: it provided an option for the next rite that an uninitiated child could otherwise not have managed.

Fritzel took a sheaf of papers from one of his pockets, set aside the ones they had prepared in case the Seal did not arrive from Traventi in time, and handed the others to Franz-Karl.

He turned to face the doorway, which was now flanked by two tall narrow sculptures in the shape that traditionally meant that they were torches. On one side was a flag stand bearing the banner of Traventi: the symbols from the great seal done in black and white and Elderkin green, surrounded by a wide gold fringe of the sort that was used on the banner that indicated his Excellency's presence. On the other side was another flag stand carrying a banner with the arms of the Falkenburgs – with Franz-Karl's personal compass star added – and surrounded by the crimson fringe that indicated a member of the direct line.

Franz-Karl pushed the door wide open, and summoned everyone in the Residence except the three ladies out into the North Gallery, and used the instructions Count Adrasteia had sent, and the Seal, and certain items retrieved from the Household Shrine, to renew the consecration of the Threshold. The tune for the Blessing was very old-fashioned and tricky to sing, but Damian had brought his flute, so Franz-

Karl had something to sing with and did not have to do it all from memory.

When he was done with the reconsecration, the Threshold was no longer Bound to his late parents, whose home this had been, or to His Excellency, whose Palace it was in: the main Threshold of the Traventine Residence was Bound to Duke Franz-Karl and to Traventi. When he finished, the two sculptures of 'torches' began to glow faintly green, which was comforting evidence that he had gotten it right, though everyone else, even the Elderkin from Traventi, seemed surprised. That seemed a little unfair since the ones from Greenoak Square had been living in a place with green-glowing torch sculptures since Franz-Karl woke the Household Shrine there.

Franz-Karl stepped across the Threshold, turned, and accepted Fritzel's renewed oath of service and alliance, updated since Fritzel's original contract had been with Her Grace the late Duke Adriana.

When he was done consecrating the Threshold at the main entrance of the Residence, Franz-Karl performed the Threshold consecration three more times, but he did not set Thresholds at the servants' entrances within the Residence. He opened the door near the nursery – it did not snap and pop, since it had finally been repaired properly after being wrong for as long as Franz-Karl could remember – and went down into the service corridors, and summoned the cooks and others who served the north section of the West Palace out into the common corridors.

Franz-Karl consecrated a Threshold between the north service entrance of the West Palace and the kitchen and laundry and storage rooms that served the north section of the West Palace and the stairs that went up to the servants' quarters in the attics. And then he consecrated a Threshold between the northern service areas and the main entrance of the West Palace. And then finally he went into one particular pantry, accompanied only by Fritzel, and consecrated the Threshold of the secret door that opened into the deeper passages.

Then he formally welcomed the cooks and other servants back into the consecrated space, along with Vendal and a few others. The oaths of alliance for the Old Palace Servants were carefully crafted to not conflict with their bonds to His Excellency. The oaths of Karnburger servants like Clothilde and Marna the baker were similar to those of the Elderkin members of the household.

When Franz-Karl returned to the inside of the main Residence door, he opened the wine and uncovered the trays of aogreamana morsels waiting there. Everyone waiting in the North Gallery who crossed the Threshold to enter the Residence was greeted properly, one at a time, and they each exchanged proper oaths of Host and Guest, or friendship and alliance, or membership in the household. Some of them had their oaths written on slips of paper, so that they would not forget any of the words, but Franz-Karl did all of the variations of his sides of the oaths from memory. After all, he was a Notary

More people had arrived while he was dealing with the servants' entrances, so the ceremonies took a while, but all of the tables in the dining room were arranged for the Reawakening Day Breakfast., and the servers had followed him up from the kitchens and began setting out the food while the oath-taking was happening. Itron Gwenlian and Roland were the first to exchange oaths with Franz-Karl after Fritzel and Tam, so they could manage things in the dining room.

His Excellency had been invited to the breakfast and had invited the Duke, in turn, to his own meals throughout the day, though the old man remained so ill that it was uncertain how long he would last at his own table. Franz-Karl planned to make an appearance at His Excellency's midday meal and hoped that the senior members of his surviving family – other than his Excellency – would share the evening meal in the Residence. He would not leave his Residence to go anywhere but to his Excellency's table: with very rare exceptions for senior kin, a reigning monarch did not go to others, they came to him.

For the breakfast, which Traventines considered the most important meal of the Reawakening Feast because of the Threshold Renewal, the guests at the Residence's table were suitably diverse in the Traventine style. Unlike the Allemanic customs, the cooks and other servants took turns looking after things in the kitchens and sitting in the dining room sharing the holy meal along with the other members of the household.

The residents of the embassy at Greenoak Square also took turns: some attended their Duke's table at breakfast, others would come for the evening meal. Other guests from outside included Dusek Urban and his family – as the Duke of Traventi Franz-Karl now had the scope to openly hold them under his protection – and the people who had found and tended Tam.

Colonel Ottavio di Pazzi and two companions were among the last who arrived at the door of the Residence before it closed for the duration of the meal. Franz-Karl tended to divide people into children, grownups and old people, especially since his visit to Traventi, where his grandmother was old, but Count Great Aunt Adrasteia was not, though she had been in the world for centuries longer. By that reckoning, Ottavio di Pazzi was grownup getting toward old, like the acting Archduke had been. One of the Colonel's companions – a handsome, elegantly dressed man with his empty left sleeve pinned up above the elbow and the shadows of the Sickness still fading from his face – was just a grownup. The third man was much younger – but probably older than Fritzel – and had bright hair of the color humans called red and so many freckles that they had probably hidden the rash when he was sick.

Di Pazzi bowed deeply. "Your Grace... may I offer to your consideration my colleagues, Louis de Castres and Colin McCallum?" He was speaking diplomatic Remoran, not Allemanic.

"Of course," Franz-Karl answered in Remoran, with a nod that was not at all a bow. "You are both welcome to enter here as guests. Colonel de Castres, I have seen your name in the chronicles and heard my father and uncle speak of you." He looked at the youngest soldier. "I fear I do not recognize your name, sir: my brother cared more for soldiers, while I preferred contracts and statecraft. Did the Great Sickness take your commanders?"

"It did, Your Grace," the young officer answered. "I've been holding what's left of the Independent Artillery Company together, but some of the high command seem to think the old contract died with the Captain and that I'm too young to sign a new one."

"As you gentlemen may imagine, I have opinions on what counts as too young for contracts and statecraft." di Pazzi chuckled and the other officers' eyes widened. Franz-Karl continued. "His Excellency needs some officials who occasionally read the chronicles: I know not paying your mercenaries never goes well, and I'm seven. I expect not paying artillery is worse: the councilors should be grateful they haven't been gifted with a cannonball somewhere unpleasant. Bring me your contracts and accounts when the holiday is past, and we shall see what can be arranged."

When they exchanged oaths, di Pazzi used an oath for a contracted ally. Franz-Karl offered the other two officers simple Guest oaths. Colonel de Castres used the guest oath. McCallum took a few deep breaths... and then used the same form as di Pazzi.

As they walked together toward the dining room, Franz-Karl wondered how hungry McCallum's men were getting... and how expensive an artillery company was likely to be. But as things seemed to be going, mercenaries might not be the worst use for the coinage from the chests they had filled with fairy gold.

Before the meal properly began, Franz-Karl – being both the Host and a child of the Household – stood before the company and sang the Great Hymn, the same one that he had repeated at his Mama's funeral. As he had at the funeral, he sang the entire Hymn: both the early, sad and angry part that was usually avoided and the later rejoicing part that was memorialized in the day's festival.

# EPILOGUE: His Excellency

## *Wherein Friedrich-Augustus von Falkenburg is Weary Past All Strength*

His Excellency Friedrich-Augustus, Imperial Lord of the Domains of the Falkenburgs, Archduke of the Eastlands, King of the Allemans, designated but uncrowned Emperor of the Remorans, High Priest of the Groves and holder of many other titles, lay in his bed too weary to move beyond the tiny but impossibly huge effort required for breathing. The weight of illness and grief and failure and dread was too great for sleep or for weeping and made a mockery of the festival just ending.

Since coming of age during the worst excesses of the Sectarian Wars, Friedrich-Augustus had devoted his own strength and wits and the strength and wits and blood of his kin to serve three goals. He had preserved the priestly functions of the Kingship of the Allemans from desecration at the impious hands of the Harfnerans or Pristinists and other Reformists. He had protected his lands and people from a recurrence of the worst excesses of death and destruction that would accompany a renewal of the Sectarian Wars. And he had supported the numbers and prosperity of his own lineage within the Falkenburgs.

A little more than a year earlier, things had seemed very hopeful. The hazard of the Reformists to the royal cult of the Groves seemed to be abating. The provinces and people were secure enough that wrecked and depopulated villages were being rebuilt and fallow fields were being brought back under the plow. And Friedrich-Augustus had fine sons, who had sons of their own – there was even a great grandson in the direct line – and his daughters and granddaughters had made brilliant marriages into foreign courts that should help to preserve the general peace and prosperity of all concerned.

Since then... The Falkenburgs had been gutted by plague and malice until all that remained of the direct male line in the Eastlands was Friedrich-Augustus himself and one small grandson ten years from his majority. And it was clear the thrice-cursed Reformists had renewed designs on both the Crown and the peace.

And the Sickness continued to drain his strength as thoroughly as if it had left some hidden wound constantly threatening to bleed out.

He had poured out what little strength he had regained to shield and shelter his final heir. He would do so again if Heaven granted him some recovery from this weight of affliction. Until then, he was doing what he could: setting his sister – who had more reason than most to loathe and distrust the Reformists – as Mistress of the Palace; and invoking every penalty in law and legend against the disobedient, oath-breaking vassal who had dared lay hands on his last heir.

He thought about setting his fierce and brilliant eldest daughter as a guardian of the child who had come far too early to a foreign sovereignty. He thought Gertrude was fond of Franz-Karl and he was sure that she would enjoy the challenge. He should discuss the matter with her the next time he had the strength for conversation.

He took a deeper breath and the effort left him dizzy.

Friedrich-Augustus remembered, suddenly, the first time he had held Leon-Alexander's younger son, when the boy was three months old and had just received his unexpected name. His daughter Princess Elmeria had pronounced the baby hideous, which was a bit rich given that at a similar point in the proceedings her own son had been a struggling, purple-faced, squalling mess, while Franz-Karl rested calmly in his velvet and lace robes, watching the world with white-less eyes like dark pools. The parti-colored green and russet hair had grown beyond mere wisps and the baby's complexion was no darker than half the highborn at

Court. His features were much like Leon-Alexander's at the same age. So much like Leon-Alexander's.

Leon-Alexander had shrugged and said something in Remoran to the child's Mother about "the Childe of Traventi's incarnate vengeance" that had sounded like a joke at the time. Friedrich-Augustus suddenly hoped that it had not been a joke. Or not entirely a joke, in the Elderkin manner, where every sentence meant three things. He hoped it was not entirely a joke, but carried what the Elderkin called Manifest weight: even graced by Heaven's mercy, those of his family that remained would need every possible advantage to survive the decade until Franz-Karl came of age.

He took a deeper breath that came easier than the last, and did not leave him so dizzy.

There were so few of those that had been at that Naming remaining among the living. So many were dead among his family and others he had trusted.

Finally, the tears came.

The End of Volume II of the Elderkin Chronicles
to be continued in
Elderkin Chronicles Volume III.

# Acknowledgments

Useful information and encouragement have come from the participants of the ScribesAndMakers, WordWeavers and WritersCoffeeClub hashtag discussion groups on Mastodon

Nanette Furman has been reading my writings for decades and served as an alpha and beta reader in addition to reading an amazing number of earlier drafts and fragments. I am profoundly grateful for her help and encouragement.

# Colophon

The image on the cover was created by the author in Krita, and involves no AI based tools.

The title font used is Black Chancery, which has been released into the public domain. The body fonts are EB Garamond and the font in the Superior Magpie logo is Essays1743, which are both covered by the SIL Open Font License (OFL).

No AI was used in the production of this book.

www.ingramcontent.com/pod-product-compliance
Lightning Source LLC
Chambersburg PA
CBHW072309020726
47501CB00002B/454